Praise for Carole Nelson Douglas
and Midnight Louie

"A catastrophically cool crime caper."
—*Publishers Weekly* on *Cat in a Quicksilver Caper*

"Fans of the series will not be disappointed and new readers will delight in the fun."   —*Romantic Times BOOKreviews* (4 ½ stars) on *Cat in a Hot Pink Pursuit*

"This feisty feline detective is fast gaining a reputation of being one of America's top investigators. . . . If either Mike Hammer or Columbo had a cat, it would be Midnight Louie."
—*Cat Fancy* on *Cat in a Neon Nightmare*

"Douglas just keeps getting better at juggling mystery, humor, and romance. . . . Established fans will welcome another intriguing piece of the puzzle."
—*Publishers Weekly* (starred review) on *Cat in a Midnight Choir*

"Never a dull moment."
—*Library Journal* on *Cat in a Leopard Spot*

"If Midnight Louie prowled only the predictable streets of genre fiction, all the murders in his ersatz world would be resolved. But each new installment in this exuberant series compounds the complexity, leaving us between books with mysterious bodies and looming menace."
—*Kirkus Reviews* on *Cat in a Kiwi Con*

D0047032

Cat in a Red Hot Rage

A MIDNIGHT LOUIE MYSTERY

Carole Nelson Douglas

A TOM DOHERTY ASSOCIATES BOOK
NEW YORK

This novel has not been authorized or endorsed by the Red Hat Society.

CAT IN A RED HOT RAGE: A MIDNIGHT LOUIE MYSTERY

A Forge Book
Published by Tom Doherty Associates, LLC
175 Fifth Avenue
New York, NY 10010

www.tor-forge.com

Forge ® is a registered trademark of Tom Doherty Associates, LLC.

ISBN-13: 978-0-7653-5270-5
ISBN-10: 0-7653-5270-2

First Edition: May 2007
First Mass Market Edition: March 2008

Printed in the United States of America

0 9 8 7 6 5 4 3 2 1

For all the women whose zest for life and spirit of
survival and sisterhood never fades at any age,
whether they wear pink ribbons or red hats
or their hearts on their sleeves.

Contents

Previously in Midnight Louie's
Lives and Times . . .   1

Chapter 1: Last Seen Dead   6

Chapter 2: Limp Biscuit   9

Chapter 3: Riders of the Purple Rage   16

Chapter 4: Mr. Know-It-All   18

Chapter 5: Twist and Shout   21

Chapter 6: Louie Among the Sisterhood   34

Chapter 7: Fatal Flair   37

Chapter 8: Honorary Older Women   41

Chapter 9: No Kitting   52

Chapter 10: Mad Hattery   56

Chapter 11: Old Flame-Points   61

Chapter 12: Old Acquaintances   66

Chapter 13: The League of Extraordinary Gentlewomen   71

Chapter 14: Film Noir   78

Chapter 15: No Longer in Service   84

Chapter 16: Electra's Larks   92

Chapter 17: Sob Sister, Soul Brother   102

Chapter 18: Vanishing Powder   107

viii • Contents

Chapter 19: Ding-Dong Daddy 112

Chapter 20: Truth Has Consequences 119

Chapter 21: The Third Degree 123

Chapter 22: Midnight Madness 128

Chapter 23: Diamond Razzle Dazzle 135

Chapter 24: Bad Boy, Bad Boy, Whatcha Gonna Do? 141

Chapter 25: Hot Water and Cool Tequila 145

Chapter 26: Mr. Midnight Sings the Blues 155

Chapter 27: The Scene of the Climb 159

Chapter 28: Debate to the Death 165

Chapter 29: Lark to Lark? 171

Chapter 30: Mad as a Hatter 176

Chapter 31: E-mailed to Death 180

Chapter 32: Ms. Sherlock Strikes a Holmes Run 187

Chapter 33: Big Wheels 189

Chapter 34: Molina Mia! 197

Chapter 35: Hints and Intimations 205

Chapter 36: Loving Dangerously 209

Chapter 37: Electra Lite 216

Chapter 38: A Kick in the Karma 220

Chapter 39: Dangerous Curves 225

Chapter 40: Dead of Night 230

Chapter 41: Transportation 236

Chapter 42: Lost in Space 239

Chapter 43: Love and Hate: He Said, She Said 242

Contents • ix

Chapter 44: Red Hot Mama   251

Chapter 45: Toodle Who?   259

Chapter 46: Sewed Up   264

Chapter 47: Mop-up Operation   267

Chapter 48: Knife Act   272

Chapter 49: Getaway   277

Chapter 50: A Paler Shade of Pink   284

Chapter 51: The Flirting Fontanas   289

Chapter 52: Ms. Apprehension   296

Chapter 53: Drop-Dead Red   302

Chapter 54: The Red Hat Rage Brigade   307

Chapter 55: Red Tide   312

Chapter 56: Crack Cocaine for Cats   318

Chapter 57: The Naked Truth   322

Chapter 58: Dude with Hattitude   330

Chapter 59: Curb Service   333

Chapter 60: A Fool and His Honey   335

Chapter 61: Footnotes   344

Chapter 62: A Dazzling Engagement   353

Chapter 63: Future Perfect   359

Chapter 64: You'll Take Me Home Again, Kathleen   364

Tailpiece: Midnight Louie's Deep Purple Mood   369

Carole Nelson Douglas Foresees a
Rosy Future   371

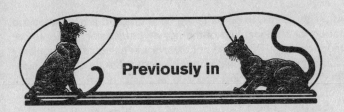

Previously in

Midnight Louie's Lives and Times . . .

Crime, chicanery, and chicks are my beat.

I am a noir kind of guy, inside and out.

I admit it. I am a shameless admirer of the female of the species. Any species. Of course, not all females are dames. Some are little dolls, like my petite roommate, Miss Temple Barr.

The difference between dames and little dolls? Dames can take care of themselves, period. Little dolls can take care of themselves also but they are not averse to letting the male of the species think that they have an occasional role in the Master Plan too.

That is why my Miss Temple and I are perfect roomies. She tolerates my wandering ways. I make myself useful looking after her without letting her know about it. Call me Muscle in

Midnight Black. In our time we have cracked a few cases too tough for the local fuzz of the human persuasion, law enforcement division. That does not always win either of us popularity contests, but we would rather be right there than on the sidelines when something crooked is going down. We share a well-honed sense of justice and long, sharp fingernails.

So when I hear that any major new attraction is coming to Las Vegas, I figure that one way or another my lively little roommate, the petite and toothsome, will be spike heel–high in the planning and execution. She is, after all, a freelance public relations specialist, and Las Vegas is full of public relations of all stripes and legalities. In this case, though, I did not figure just how personally she would be involved in murder with hattitude.

I should introduce myself: Midnight Louie, PI. I am not your usual gumshoe, in that my feet do not wear shoes of any stripe, but shivs. I have certain attributes, such as being short, dark, and handsome . . . really short. That gets me overlooked and underestimated, which is what the savvy operative wants anyway. I am your perfect undercover guy. I also like to hunker down under the covers with my little doll. My adventures would fill a book, and in fact I have several out. My life is one ongoing TV series in which I as hero extract my hapless human friends from fixes of their own making and literally nail crooks.

After the recent dramatic turn of events, most of my human associates are pretty shell-shocked. Not even an ace feline PI may be able to solve their various predicaments in the areas of crime and punishment . . . and PR, as in Personal Relationships.

As a serial killer finder in a multivolume mystery series (not to mention a primo mouthpiece), it behooves me to update my readers old and new on past crimes and present tensions.

None can deny that the Las Vegas crime scene is a pretty busy place, and I have been treading these mean neon streets for nineteen books now. When I call myself an "alphacat," some think I am merely asserting my natural male and feline dominance, but no. I merely reference the fact that since I debuted in *Catnap* and *Pussyfoot*, I then commenced to a title sequence that is as sweet and simple as B to Z.

That is where I began my alphabet, with the B in *Cat on a Blue Monday*. From then on, the color word in the title is in alphabetical order up to the current volume, *Cat in a Red Hot Rage*.

Since I associate with a multifarious and nefarious crew of human beings, and since Las Vegas is littered with guidebooks as well as bodies, I wish to provide a rundown of the local landmarks on my particular map of the world. A cast of characters, so to speak:

To wit, my lovely roommate and high-heel devotee, Miss Nancy Drew on killer spikes, freelance PR ace MISS TEMPLE BARR, who had reunited with her elusive love . . .

. . . the once missing-in-action magician MR. MAX KINSELLA, who has good reason for invisibility. After his cousin SEAN died in a bomb attack during a post–high school jaunt to Ireland, he went into undercover counterterrorism work with his mentor, GANDOLPH THE GREAT, whose unsolved murder while unmasking phony psychics at a Halloween séance is still on the books. . . .

Meanwhile, Mr. Max is sought by another dame, Las Vegas homicide detective LIEUTENANT C. R. MOLINA, mother of teenage MARIAH . . .

. . . and the good friend of Miss Temple's recent good friend, MR. MATT DEVINE, a radio talk-show shrink and former Roman Catholic priest who came to Las Vegas to track down his abusive stepfather, now dead and buried. By whose hand no one is quite sure.

Speaking of unhappy pasts, Miss Lieutenant Carmen Regina Molina is not thrilled that her former flame, MR. RAFI NADIR, the unsuspecting father of Mariah, is in Las Vegas taking on shady muscle jobs after blowing his career at the LAPD . . .

. . . or that Mr. Max Kinsella is aware of Rafi and his past relationship to hers truly.

In the meantime, Mr. Matt drew a stalker, the local lass that young Max and his cousin Sean boyishly competed for in that long-ago Ireland . . .

. . . one MISS KATHLEEN O'CONNOR, deservedly christened by Miss Temple as Kitty the Cutter. Finding Mr. Max impossible to trace, she settled for harassing with tooth and claw the nearest innocent bystander, Mr. Matt Devine . . .

. . . who is still trying to recover from the crush he developed on Miss Temple, his neighbor at the Circle Ritz condominiums, while Mr. Max was missing in action. He did that by not very boldly seeking new women, all of whom were in danger from said Kitty the Cutter.

In fact, on the advice of counsel, i.e., AMBROSIA, Mr. Matt's talk-show producer, and none other than the aforesaid Lieutenant Molina, he had attempted to disarm Miss Kitty's pathological interest in his sexual state by supposedly losing his virginity with a call girl least likely to be the object of K. the Cutter's retaliation. Did he or didn't he? One thing is certain: hours after their iffy assignation at the Goliath Hotel, said call girl turned up deader than an ice-cold deck of Bicycle playing cards. But there are almost forty million potential victims in this old town, if you include the constant come and go of tourists, and everything is up for grabs in Las Vegas 24/7: guilt, innocence, money, power, love, loss, death, and significant others.

All this human sex and violence makes me glad that I have a simpler social life, such as just trying to get along with my unacknowledged daughter . . .

. . . MISS MIDNIGHT LOUISE, who insinuated herself into my cases until I was forced to set up shop with her as Midnight Inc. Investigations, and who has also nosed herself into my long-running duel with . . .

. . . the evil Siamese assassin HYACINTH, first met as the onstage assistant to the mysterious lady magician . . .

. . . SHANGRI-LA, who made off with Miss Temple's semi-engagement ring from Mr. Max during an onstage trick and has been seen since only in sinister glimpses . . .

. . . just like THE SYNTH, an ancient cabal of magicians that may deserve contemporary credit for the ambiguous death of Mr. Max's mentor in magic, Gandolph the Great, not to mention Gandolph's former onstage assistant as well as a professor of magic at the University of Nevada at Las Vegas.

Well, there you have it, the usual human stew, all mixed up

and at odds with one another and within themselves. Obviously, it is up to me to solve all their mysteries and nail a few crooks along the way. Like Las Vegas, the City That Never Sleeps, Midnight Louie, private eye, also has a sobriquet: the Kitty That Never Sleeps.

With this crew, who could?

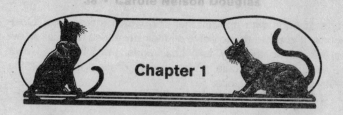

Chapter 1

Last Seen Dead

It is enough to break a guy's heart . . .

. . . if a macho dude like me could ever admit to having one.

I sit, apparently calm and dignified, on the off-white sofa in the living room of what you could call my digs, my crib, my flat . . . okay, "our" condominium unit at Las Vegas's only round five-story 1950s landmark, the Circle Ritz.

The round part you probably get. The Ritz part is a word that was chichi way-back-when in the mid-twentieth century and sounds more like a cracker nowadays. Although that cracker is indeed round.

But crackers can be easily crushed, and that is exactly what my esteemed roommate, Miss Temple Barr, would be if she knew what I knew: that her longtime squeeze, Mr. Max Kinsella, is pretty thoroughly crushed himself these days. In fact, I and my partner in crime solving saw him plunge five stories into a solid black wall thirty-six hours ago at the nightclub called Neon Nightmare. Talk about an apt name.

Miss Midnight Louise is my partner (and a would-be descendant in her own mind if only I would admit to being a deadbeat dad). She suspects that someone sinister had arranged Mr. Max's unscheduled landing, from which he was taken away by ambulance.

Granted that performing bungee-cord acrobatics and illusions over a nightclub floor is a pretty dangerous pastime, but Mr. Max Kinsella had formerly been a top Vegas magic act under the name of The Mystifying Max.

What is so mystifying is why he was performing masked under the moniker of the Phantom Mage at Neon Nightmare. Not even his girlfriend—and mine—Miss Temple Barr, knew about it.

The lady in question ambles into the living room even as I muse about her. She is talking on one of those obnoxious cell phones that I wish had been drowned at invention in an acid bath. As if the world needed more distracted people wandering around forcing everyone to overhear the details of their professional and personal lives.

Overhearing all that stuff is *my* job!

However, it is sometimes handy to eavesdrop on one's nearest and dearest, though in this instance it is more than somewhat heartbreaking.

"Max!" my Miss Temple admonishes the tiny instrument pressed to her ear. "Answer! Pick up the phone. You have got to be home sometime during one of my hundred and one calls. I've got to talk to you. Soon!"

She folds the already mouse-size phone in half and tosses it onto the sofa seat in disgust. Then she spots me and does her Cary Grant imitation: "*Lou*-ie, *Lou*-ie, *Lou*-ie."

I do not know what ancient film that is from, but I never object to being associated with a leading man like Mr. Cary Grant, the twentieth-century equivalent of Mr. George Clooney in the suave department.

Miss Temple picks up the phone and sits beside me, glum as the holiday-hijacking Grinch.

"Louie, what am I to do with a man who won't ever answer the phone, even when I'm going to dump him?"

Well. . . . For the first time in my long career as a primo PI, all-around hip cat, and career-girl companion, I wish I had not taken a vow of silence when it comes to conversing with humans.

I long to offer my Miss Temple some trenchant "Dear Tabby" advice. I wish I at least had the option of warning her that her not-so-beloved-lately was in the hands of the paramedics and the city hospital system, if not the county coroner.

Usually I like knowing what other folks do not: that is a crack PI's job.

Now I just feel as low-down and guilty as any back-alley goldfish-gulper caught raiding the koi pond at the Crystal Phoenix Hotel and Casino.

"I am so glad I have you to talk to when I am upset," she continues, twisting the knife.

Who knew a conscience could be so painful? Not *moi*. I am glad that I do not have a soul, at least, although some on the ailurophile fringe might debate that.

I understand her problem, of course. She has gone forth and consummated her long-simmering attraction to our upstairs neighbor, Mr. Matt Devine, ex-priest now in need of a nice dark confessional, if the church authorities had not scotched these handy dramatic devices of film and story long ago.

I saw that coming from almost a year ago, not that anybody would listen to me. And not that I would want them to. I do not talk to people, and thus save myself from a lot of drivel.

Mr. Max is a swell fellow, but enmeshed in intrigue local and international. Such an agenda does not allow a man to keep the home fires burning as hotly as they should. It is the old story: a romantic triangle turned tragic, only nobody knows it but me.

I will have to see what I can do to change that.

Chapter 2

Limp Biscuit

Temple hiked herself onto one of the two breakfast stools in her tiny black-and-white kitchen. Then she ravaged the upper cupboard for something salty, crunchy, and frustration-reducing.

All she found was a long-opened box of Ritz crackers, half full of soggy imposters of crunch. She tossed the box toward the Albertson's paper bag that served as a temporary trash receptacle.

Okay. She'd finally made the most momentous decision of her life. She'd picked which of two totally wonderful guys she wanted to spend that life with. She took a deep breath. Matt was so sweet. So totally amazing. So hot!

He had been, like, worried about seventeen priestly years of celibacy cramping his style?

Not!

Oh! She was sounding so teenager-y-in-love.

Temple sobered. She'd felt that much in love with Max once, almost three years ago. A year in love here in Las Vegas after instant-everything in Minneapolis. A year of Max gone. Not even a full year of Max back.

Temple went for her refrigerator, hunting something, something . . . crisp and sour. No pickles. Okay. Sweet. What? Was she pregnant? Or just having a change of hormones. Of heart? Or a heart still torn two ways?

A knock on her doorbell put her into cardiac arrest. *On her door!* Not door*bell*, dumbbell! She had to cut herself some slack. After all, she was just a teenager in love.

Matt always knocked.

She opened the door, hungry and anxious and edgy.

And it was all, well, all right.

"I'm not bothering you?" Matt asked in his polite Midwestern way.

She pulled him inside, slammed the door shut, and pushed him up against the entry-hall wall.

"Yes, you are. What are you going to do about it?"

He didn't hesitate, just drew her into a mind-blowing soul kiss and during it turned her into the wall herself, so she was pressed hard against, well, everything.

Several minutes later, they ambled into the living room to admire Midnight Louie on the couch.

"Have you reached him?" Matt asked warily.

Temple knew he didn't mean Midnight Louie. She eyed his ruffled blond hair, his warm brown eyes hotter than black coffee from their make-out session in the hall, his expression of uneasy concern.

He realized their new intimate relationship would never feel entirely real until Temple formally broke it off with Max. Although neither one would say this or even mention Max's name at the moment.

That was Max. Mystique to the end. Temple swallowed a sob.

Matt was there, holding her. "It's all right."

"What's all right?"

"However you feel."

"I feel horrible. I feel like a rat. I've got to reach him. It's not like he didn't know this was coming."

"He knew?" Matt held her away, staring hard into her eyes, seeing the troubled emotions she hadn't wanted him to notice.

"He's Max. Of course he knew."

Matt's lips tightened.

"He gave me permission, for God's sake."

"Permission?"

"His blessing?" Temple added with a sob she had to cup with a hand to her mouth to stop.

For some strange reason, Matt smiled. "Yeah. I kinda got that from him too. I don't think your faith in him was ever misplaced."

"But *he* is! Max is. I can't find him. I can't get him to call me back so I can say, 'Hi. 'Bye.' I need to be up front with him about this. That's all. Let him know. For sure. Nothing about us is a problem, Matt. But I warned you, saying good-bye to someone is hell."

"What about the ring?"

"What about it?"

"Where are you keeping it, since you don't wear it? Yet."

Temple breathed deep. "In my scarf drawer," she said in a small, wee voice.

"Scarf drawer?"

"It's where I keep everything I don't know what to do with safe."

"Temple, that ring is worth, well, way more than it should be."

"I know, Matt. Fred Leighton. I was hoping I could put it openly on my finger soon. Like . . . today. Then it would take a mugger cutting my finger off to get it."

"Temple!" Matt was half laughing, half shaking his head. "Look. Danny built a floor safe into my bedroom redo. I'll just keep it there for the time being. Your scarf drawer doesn't sound terribly secure, unless you also keep boa constrictors in there to fend off burglars."

"You're right. The ring needs to be worn or kept someplace secure. Come into my boudoir and we will unearth it from a pile of lovely but annoyingly unmanageable scarves. French-women really know how to accessorize with those things, but I am about as French as Midnight Louie."

She took his hand to lead him away, thinking maybe it was time her Circle Ritz bedroom had a new sensuous adventure to record.

Matt hesitated at the threshold. Temple knew what he was thinking: this had been Max's and her bedroom for more than a year. The bed was California king-length, for six-foot-four Max, and Matt sure didn't need that.

She stepped close. "It's all right. You know I'm all yours, anytime, anyplace. Ring or no ring."

So they ended up ruffling the zebra-stripe coverlet, both of them the better for it.

"Where's this fabled scarf drawer?" Matt asked finally.

Temple guessed he'd never consummate anything with her in that bed.

"Over here, sir." She got up and opened the top drawer of the small chest against the wall. "Every scarf I was ever given as a gift, and that I wronged with an inept knot, a careless twist, a hopeless loop, lies interred here, along with other odds and ends. It is yours to riffle as you please. As am I." She finished with a curtsy.

Matt grinned at her presentation. "No one can oversell like you."

"Thanks for the professional compliment."

He began sifting through the frothy rainbow of scarves. "This should be good practice for violating your lingerie drawer in future. Aha! The significant clue. A ring box."

He pulled out a plain white box and opened it to reveal something Temple didn't recognize at first. When she did, her cheeks flushed.

"That's not it. That's just a tawdry cubic zirconia ring I bought somewhere."

It was also oddly similar to the Tiffany opal-and-diamond ring Max had given her in New York City Christmas last, when she and he had thought his dangerous past was history and their glowing future was now.

She'd bought this cheap reminder of that lost ring for less than forty dollars in a weak moment, for which she'd been noted recently.

Matt tossed the box on the bed.

"Okay," he said. "More scarves. Am I supposed to deduce something from this mass of scarves?"

He held up two, stretched out. Gave her all sorts of ideas.

"Danny did give your bedroom a four-poster bed," she said.

Danny Dove was Temple's dear friend and a noted Vegas choreographer. Nothing better than a gay choreographer for masterminding a straight guy's bedroom decor.

There was a moment of prolonged silence. Matt had read his *Joy of Sex* book religiously. But at least now he'd forgotten the ersatz opal-diamond ring. Mission accomplished.

He lifted another cheap ring box with a quizzical look.

"Something I picked up somewhere, sometime. Don't ask me what that is."

Matt opened it. Stared. Looked up at her with real worry.

"I do, Temple."

"What?" The wedding vow answer had both startled and encouraged her.

"I know what this is, and it's not good. This is the ring Kathleen O'Connor mailed to me."

"No! What was that about? It's a nasty snaky thing, no wonder it came from that vixen."

"Not a snake." Matt held up the sinuous gold circle between his thumb and forefinger, like a dissection specimen. "It's a dragon, really, swallowing its own tail; an ancient symbol of eternity called the worm Ouroboros."

"Ouroboro-what? Kitty the Cutter sent you a ring? I didn't know about that."

"I didn't want you to. It was another of her sick stalking games. She said I had to wear it or she'd hurt someone near me. So I carried it in my pocket when I was out and left it on my living room side table when I was in. I never put it on my finger. Where did you get it?"

Temple thought. "I don't know. I put everything I don't know what to do with in that drawer."

"Including this?" Matt lifted the gray velvet box containing his . . . her . . . ring.

"Yes, but only for safekeeping. Until I can, you know, reach Max."

"What if you never reach him? Are we on hold until then?"

"No! I just want to do the right thing."

"Temple." Matt came to sit beside her on the bed. "I've spent all my life trying to do exactly the right thing and I've learned that can be paralyzing. Look. I'll take this ring up to my safe for now. But I need you to think about when, and where, you got Kitty the Cutter's ring, the one she made me carry as a sign of her power over me."

"Good Lord! What an awful talisman! How did you lose it?"

"She loved to show that she could come and go in my place as she pleased. It disappeared one day. After . . . Vassar died. That's all. I figured that meant she was finally disappointed in me. It disappeared. Just like she ultimately did."

"Yeah, she *died*. Gee, Matt, I just can't remember where I got that thing right now. But I did get it. It's ended up here. You don't think Kitty—?"

"I hope not, but she is dead now, at least."

"Somehow I came across it, but where or when—?"

Temple pushed her hands into the blond hair at her temples, warding off the headache that was sure to come.

Matt caught and removed her hands. "Take it easy, Goldilocks. You'll never remember something trying that hard. Just let the question bounce around in your brain for a while."

"What brain? I'm a blonde, haven't you noticed?"

"Only temporarily, and I don't mind. I'm a blond too, so dumb blond jokes are personal." He leaned in and kissed her hair. "Besides, I think that's what did it."

"What did what?"

"Your bottle-blonde undercover makeover job. It made you look just different enough to make me think that I might have a chance with a Brave New Temple."

"Oh."

Of course he had to kiss her surprise away. Too bad she wasn't brave, or very new. Just the same old bundle of chutzpah, humor, and hope a single girl had to be nowadays.

Not quite single.

"Matt, I'm sorry to be so neurotic about Max. It's just that I've been worrying about him for so long."

"I wouldn't love you if you didn't. What can I do?"

"Love me when I'm being a ditz."

"Easy."

"Safeguard our ring." She closed her hands over his holding the box. "I'll try to zen my way into remembering Kitty's ugly offering. In fact, take that ugly ring thing up to your safe too. There might be fingerprints on it."

"What good will that do us?" he asked.

"Molina can get it analyzed, if we figure out a good excuse."

"I'm not sure she would—"

"I am. All we have to do is have you ask her."

"I don't have any pull with Molina."

"*Hmmm.* We'll see."

Chapter 3

Riders of the Purple Rage

Matt had only been gone a few minutes when the phone rang.

Temple shook herself out of her meditation session on the sofa and dove for the receiver. It might be Max at last.

So far, she hadn't a clue about when she could have gotten the wormy gold ring Matt was so concerned about. Maybe this was it: the first senior moment, a tendril of looming peri-menopause striking out at her fifteen years too soon. She was only almost thirty-one, God!

"Temple, dear," said a well-known voice. "I'm in such a pickle and I really need your help."

"Electra?" Temple sat up straight, jolted out of her meditations. Trouble would take her mind off a lot of personal issues. "I can run right up to the penthouse."

"Don't, dear. I'm not there."

The landlady of the Circle Ritz was always somewhere about the place. When not in her fifth-floor penthouse digs she was running the Lovers' Knot Wedding Chapel with Drive-by Window—Photo Shoots free—at the side of the condominium-cum-apartment building. Everything here did double duty, including the angst.

"Electra! Where are you? What's going on?"

"I'm at the Crystal Phoenix."

"You have good taste."

"Not really, dear. I have never been guilty of that. But I'm afraid I may be found guilty of something else."

"Guilty? Of what?"

"I volunteered for security for this damn convention, Temple, dear. I thought I had picked up a thing or two from you and Max. Alas, apparently not. They're planning on taking me in."

"In where?"

"To stir, as we say in the security trade. Somewhere downtown, as they always say on TV. Can you come bail me out?"

"Yes! But, Electra, why?"

"They say I knocked off a Pink Lady."

"I've been known to knock back a Pink Lady or two in my day too."

"Not the drink, dear. A live one. Now dead. Please come! This Detective Su is very small, smart, and stern, and my using your name is having no effect whatsoever."

The call ended on that alarming note.

Temple grabbed her cell phone and auto-dialed Max's number one more time, just in case. No answer. "I'm leaving the Circle Ritz and heading for the Crystal Phoenix," she told the messaging function. "You can catch up with me there. Electra's in big trouble."

Maybe that cryptic message would draw Max out of his disappearing act.

She threw the cell phone in her tote bag, pushed her bare feet into the Steve Madden slides under the coffee table, blew Louie a good-bye kiss, and skidded out the door.

Electra? In trouble with the law? Impossible!

Chapter 4

Mr. Know-It-All

Once my frazzled roomie has done her little-doll skidoo, I gaze sadly at the morning paper, which she has neglected to read, given the enthralling appearance of Mr. Matt Devine on her doorstep . . . and in her scarf drawer.

A dude of my age, position, and gravitas is above peeking in on bedroom antics, but I did hear mention of their late archenemy, and therefore mine, Miss Kathleen O'Connor. I could tell Miss Temple exactly when and where she acquired the sinister ring Mr. Matt took away, quite rightly.

It is not that I *could* talk, if I wanted to, though I like to think I can do anything. But it is also against my principles to talk to humans. Besides, that would be spoiling my Miss Temple's fun. She does love a mystery.

So do I.

I am eager to follow her over to the Crystal Phoenix and find out what our beloved landlady is up to.

But first I ponder the newspaper. Those of my ilk are hopelessly drawn to paper products. Maybe it is the heady aroma of fresh ink. Maybe it is because we are smarter than we let on, and can read quite well if we apply ourselves and the seats of our pants to it. Pantaloons, I should say, in our case. We have bibs, we have ruffs, we have pantaloons and feathering. You would think we were cavalier poets.

Maybe it is because we are like those men I've heard talk of, who feel most wanted when they interrupt their women at some absorbing minor task and sweep them away to the bedroom, or the living room carpet.

The French do not worry about these things, but simply say, *"Je ne sais quoi." I know not what.* Those French! Quite the cards.

Me, I worry about the bigger picture.

Sometimes I am the only one who sees it, and that is when I worry most.

I lean forward to regard the small news story below the fold on that morning's front page.

NEON NIGHTMARE MAGICIAN-ACROBAT FALLS TO DEATH, it reads. The "jump" is on page 4. *Ouch!* Most unfortunate terminology in this case. "Terminology." *Ouch!*

Now only I know why Mr. Max Kinsella is not answering his cell phone or his home phone or any phone on earth of late. "Of late." *Ouch!*

I think I have had enough of phones and "jumps" lately myself.

So that emergency ambulance run from the Neon Nightmare was for naught. My poor Miss Temple! Just when she had intended to tell Mr. Max "good-bye," he has gone to the Great Good-bye in the Sky.

My whiskers droop. He died young. I can understand Miss Midnight Louise's fury at the accident. It had looked rigged to me too. Mr. Max was too expert to take a fall without sabotage in the picture. I admit that I will miss my human rival and look-alike.

My Miss Temple will be beside herself when she finds out. For now, I must forsake the trail of Mr. Max's fatal fall and go whither she goeth, to be there when the roof caves in. And it will.

Chapter 5

Twist and Shout

Temple pulled her red Miata into the Crystal Phoenix's entry area to shouts and applause.

She jumped out as the parking valet took it, realizing she was wearing her hot pink Steve Madden slides. Maybe that was what was getting all the twisting of necks and shouting.

"*Amore*," the Italian word for love, was supposed to hit your eye like a "big pizza pie," according to the old song, but Temple was being whomped in the iris by a wave of purple and red clothing.

People clothed in both colors were streaming through the glass doors into the Crystal Phoenix lobby like so many bicolor birds of paradise.

People. Check that: women. Women wearing T-shirts and

feather boas and high heels and wide-brimmed hats, dragging wheeled purple leopard-pattern luggage, wearing red lipstick and purple eye shadow, women of size, women of no size, like her. Wait! Older women. Well, "seasoned" women, as Gail Sheehy had put it so profitably in her latest life-state book.

The lobby was teaming with red and purple. Temple felt positively dowdy in pink. Then she spotted a pink hat here and there amid the flock and felt better.

Until she remembered that a woman in pink had been killed.

She had no idea where Electra might be, so she dialed her landlady's cell phone.

"Yes?"

The voice was brisk, female, and not Electra's.

Temple couldn't have misdialed; Electra's cell phone number was in her directory.

She muttered something about misdialing anyway.

"You were calling Mrs. Lark?"

"Yes."

"Who is this?"

"Who is *this*?"

"The police. Who are you and why are you calling?"

"I'm a friend of Mrs. Lark's and I heard that something had gone wrong at the hotel."

At that moment Temple became aware of a tall pale figure behind her, and turned. It wasn't a ghost, it was a Fontana brother in an expensive Italian ice-cream suit, accompanied by her errant aunt Kit, who had not come home to the Circle Ritz the night before and was looking not the least worse for wear.

Temple's mother's sister, a New York City actress turned romance novelist, had come to stay with Temple for a few days. She had surprised the heck out of Temple by ending up having more than a few dates with the eldest of Vegas's Most Eligible Bachelor frat pack, the nine single Fontana brothers. Their uncle, Macho Mario Fontana, was the last of the mob bosses. The brothers were presumed to be elegant quasi-muscle around town. They owned, among other things, Gangsters' vintage limousine service. The youngest, and number ten, was married and owned this hotel.

Aldo Fontana—tall, dark, and dangerous—took the phone from a frazzled Temple's hand. "This is Crystal Phoenix security," his majestic baritone mentioned, almost threatened in a silky, seductive way. Kit rolled her eyes behind his looming back and pantomimed fanning herself and swooning.

"May I help you?" Aldo held the phone away from his ear so that Temple could hear the raging soprano aria on the other end. Temple guessed who it was; a female seriously disinclined to swooning: Detective Su.

Meanwhile, her aunt Kit, a thirty-year-older petite version of herself, cozied up to her side.

"Sorry I didn't call to announce a change of venue last night, but it was awfully late."

Temple could easily imagine a woman forgetting the time in Aldo's company, and shrugged. "I know a New Yorker like you can take care of yourself, Aunt, and anything that might come up."

"Speaking of that, what's going on? Why are you here apparently being berated by a cell phone?"

"Electra called me at the Circle Ritz. There's a death connected to this convention and the authorities are holding her for questioning. That was one of the detectives in charge of the case."

Meanwhile, Aldo had snapped her cell phone shut and returned it with a flourish.

"The Lalique Suite. The police have set up shop there."

Temple raised an eyebrow. She'd been the hotel's PR person for a year now. The Crystal Suites were pretty fancy for police use.

" 'This convention'?" Kit looked around, as if seeing all the purple and red for the first time, and indeed, she probably was. A swarthy Italian hunk in expensive clothes as pale and soft as creamery butter would be hard to see past.

Temple took her aunt's arm as they followed Aldo to the private elevators. " 'Big Wheel in Las Vegas' convention for the Red Hat Sisterhood," she explained, having gleaned all that from attendees on the way in. "It's for older women with style, joy, and pizzazz. Like you."

"Oh. Except that I'm with Aldo and they're not."

Temple eyed the many women around them who had stopped short, riveted by his tall, smooth passage through them.

"I wouldn't bet on that if you were so foolish as to unhand his arm and let him loose. They'd be on him like an expensive suit."

"But I'm not going to unhand him," Kit said. "I'm sure Aldo can convince the police that Electra Lark is not a crook."

"It's ridiculous," Temple agreed when the three of them were alone in the stainless-steel elevator, wafting upward, "for anyone to think my landlady would kill someone."

Aldo waved his manicured fingers. One would never guess they were rattlesnake-fast to draw a Beretta.

"The police always make snap judgments," he said, suiting gesture to words. "It saves them thinking. I've paged Nicky. He'll put a stop to this police nonsense."

"Nicky?" Kit asked.

Aldo smiled tenderly down at her and even Temple felt the heat. "My youngest brother. He owns the hotel."

"Wow. And what do you own, big boy, besides a Viper and an expensive collection of aged scotch?"

"For one thing, my luscious linguini, a race horse."

Kit was truly shocked, and Temple too. She'd never known what supported the litter of Fontana brothers, excepting Nicky, the white sheep of the family, and some iffy side businesses.

Kit leaned into Temple to whisper an explanation for the pet name. "He thinks I'm really rather . . . supple for my age. All those cheerleader splits didn't hurt."

"Aunt! I don't need to know these things," Temple hissed back. "What's your horse's name?" she asked Aldo to get the discussion onto a higher plane.

"Midnight Louie," he answered. "Black as coal, fast as greased stainless steel, took second in his last race. A real comer on the inside."

"But—"

"I figure your cat has been lucky for you and has at least nineteen lives, from what I've seen. What can it hurt?"

Louie with a thoroughbred namesake! Temple doubted that he cared much about such connections, but she was impressed.

The elevator doors spit them out onto an aubergine-carpeted hallway, deep purple to the common folk. Temple had never seen the Crystal Suites, nor had much needed to. Now she did.

The soft-lit sconces along the silver suede-covered halls were priceless vintage Lalique frosted glass.

The suite itself had huge Lalique door handles of facing phoenixes, commissioned for the hotel.

Another Fontana brother opened it before they could ring the bell, but it was not a usual member of the "frat pack."

"Nicky!" Temple cried, embracing her boss (as near as a free-lancer can have a boss) and biggest client and remembering to add, "It's me, Temple, passing as a blonde."

"Good thing it's you," he said. "Van doesn't like me canoodling with any blondes but her."

Van had just arrived to peek over his shoulder.

"Temple, I see you've come over to the light side," she said, smiling at the blond dye job.

Nicky's wife was an Alfred Hitchcock blonde, smooth, cool, and dignified, like the stars of his best films: Grace Kelly, Kim Novak, Eva Marie Saint, and animal rescuer Tippi Hedron. One of her films, a rare lesser Hitchcock effort named *Marnie*, had featured a young pre-Bond Sean Connery! *Yum.* Temple may be engaged now, but age did not wither nor custom stale the Scottish actor's sex appeal.

Van von Rhine was Nicky's wife and the hotel manager. Where he was all macho charm, like any Fontana brother, she was cool Anglo efficiency and smoldering drive. If they were both on this scene, the situation was serious.

Nicky high-fived Aldo, then the couple settled in to hear Kit introduced, managing not to appear surprised that Aldo's latest squeeze was also Temple's visiting maternal aunt.

"Listen," Nicky said, his low tone pulling everybody con-spiratorially close.

"Van and I got this TV cop show off the main floor. We do have a murder on the premises, and your friend Electra was there for the denouement," he told Temple. "I don't know how even a sharp PR diva like you is gonna keep both the hotel and your friend out of the headlines."

"Electra's my landlady and I doubt she'd kill a gnat. Can I talk to her?"

Van spoke for the first time. "It's a he-she detective team. She spits nails; he slings mashed potatoes. Do love your hair."

"Su and Alch," Temple diagnosed. "I know them. He's tougher than he acts, but she isn't. She's the real deal, a mini-Molina. Lieutenant Molina is my bane on the LVMPD. Born to be bad, particularly to me. Thanks for the vote for the hair color. It's temporary, though."

"Bleach never is, baby," Nicky put in.

"Eventually," Temple said, finished with coiffure matters. "Keep Aldo and Kit on the fringes with your camp. I'll wade in and see if they'll let me talk privately to Electra."

"You a lawyer now?" Aldo asked incredulously.

"No," Kit answered, "but she is a Carlson on the distaff side and we are nothing to mess with. Viking stock, you know."

Aldo blinked at the image of petite, low-rise Kit, or Temple, as Valkyries.

What did he know? Columbus had been preceded to North America by the Vikings. Everyone north of the forty-fifth parallel knew that!

Temple went inside first. The room was expensively pale in decor and furnishings, except for a big bright blob of red and purple in the seating area near the floor-to-ceiling windows.

As she approached, Temple saw the canny detectives had placed Electra facing the windows so her features were in blinding daylight while they were silhouettes to her aging eyes.

Bullies!

But it worked.

Electra was in her sixties, which Temple now regarded with shock and awe after a heart-to-heart with her aunt about what aging women could expect. She was almost thirty-one, unmarried (although with strong prospects), and suddenly very sympathetic to the problems of aging women in a culture that worshiped young and thin and shallow.

She appreciated Electra's free spirit even more after a few heart-to-hearts with her aunt.

She appreciated the landlady's tropical muumuus color-coordinated to the temporary dyes she sprayed onto her halo of springy white hair. The wedding chapel business she ran out of the Circle Ritz. Being game to hop on a motorcycle at her age, wearing a helmet that proclaimed "Speed Queen." Her warm and lively interest in all her tenants, including Matt's emergence from ex-priest to buff boy about town. All were part of the Circle Ritz mystique, and Electra Lark was its resident fairy godmother.

No way would this lady off somebody. Of course, such a conviction would never stand up in court, so Temple would have to see that it never got that far.

As she came even with the silhouettes of Alch and Su, she noticed with astonishment that Electra's hair was all-over purple. An ex-undercover girl in honey-bunnie blond shade number 43 was hardly one to criticize.

"Electra!" Temple said, to let her know she had backup.

The face that turned to her, usually haloed with good cheer and motherly encouragement, suddenly looked pale, aged, drained.

"Temple! Thank God you've come."

"Just what do you think she can do for you?" Su asked.

Su was a tiny Asian-American woman not much older than Temple who managed to convey Green Giant–size competency. Temple supposed that was from being a little woman in a big man's profession.

"Can we talk?" Temple asked the detectives, moving away from the windows.

They followed her out of Electra's hearing range.

"I know this woman," Temple said. "She's not a killer."

"Neither are most of us," Su pointed out, "until something pushes us over the edge."

Morrie Alch, a teddy bear of a homicide detective with nicely polished claws, was staying out of it. Women's business.

"At least you can tell me why Electra's being questioned," Temple said.

"We don't have to tell you anything," Su said, close to a sneer.

It must have chapped Su's chopsticks that her boss, Lieutenant

C. R. Molina, had sent Temple undercover as a teenager at the recent Teen Queen Idol reality TV show set, instead of her.

Competing guys were standard police issue, but dueling gals could be meaner.

"Okay, ladies." Alch puckered his lips judiciously. "Miss Barr might get something we can't out of the . . . suspect. The lieutenant would like that."

"And then," Temple said, "I'd like you to let Electra go about her business."

"Not!" Su.

Alch frowned.

"I bet you couldn't pry her away from this convention," Temple argued. "She's volunteered to set things up. And she wouldn't leave Las Vegas. She runs two local businesses. She has local people like me to look out for her. Simply being found near a dead body would have had me in lockup numerous times."

"Should have," Su said.

"Lighten up, ladies," Alch said. While they were both scowling at him for that method of address, his palms lifted in a peace gesture.

"We have grounds for holding Mrs. Lark," he told Temple, dead serious. "But not enough. I've checked with Molina. She's not ready to bring Mrs. Lark in for questioning on the evidence so far. So, you can take her outta here when you go, or put her back with the other birds of a feather."

Su glared at him with soundless fury, but Alch gave her A Look. He gave Temple another one. "I'm going to let you take her out of here, but that's not an irreversible option. And anything of interest she tells you, you tell us. Right?"

"Absolutely, Detective Alch."

Su snorted.

Molina had okayed Temple's custody of Electra? What was the Iron Maiden of the Las Vegas Metropolitan Police Department up to?

That's what Nicky and Van and Aldo and Kit wanted to know as Temple retreated to their position by the long Italian leather sofa against the wall.

"What's the deal?" Nicky asked in a whisper.

"I get to talk to Electra, and take her out of here if she doesn't do something foolish and confess."

"Great, but why?" Aldo wanted to know. "The cops never back off unless they have to."

"Not enough evidence to hold her," Temple said. "I think. Maybe they're just giving her enough rope."

"We don't want this case dragging on any more than they do," Van said.

Nicky winked at Temple. "She's saying you better solve this one for the cops. Get them out of our hair. Out of her vanilla-smooth French twist." Nicky ran teasing fingers into it, making Van's eyes glare steel-blue. She shook him loose.

Not many people knew "Van" was short for "Vanilla." Temple did.

Van smoothed her hair back into place. "Do whatever you can, Temple, to cool down this situation."

"Right." First, she had to find out from Electra what was really going on.

"I'm lucky I got them to cut you loose," Temple whispered as she settled beside Electra on the cushy leather sofa.

Electra clasped her hand with matronly zest.

"So nice to see you here, dear. Who gave you permission? Was it that nice Detective Alch?" Electra whispered, glancing coyly at the fiftyish detective.

"Yeah. Luckily, Morrie likes to pull Su's chain."

"Morrie. Such a cute name. Do you think he's married?"

"I think he's fifteen years younger than you are, Electra."

"Just right. Boy-toy age for me."

Temple sighed. "Electra, why are they holding you for questioning? Who died here?"

"It's so silly, Temple. You know me. Always eager to help. I volunteered to set things up before the convention—"

"You mean that wave of purple and red in the lobby is just the advance troops?"

"Heavens, yes! We'll soon have five thousand Red Hatters in town, splitting up between the Crystal Phoenix and the Goliath.

We have several hundred here now to help with setup. My Red-Hatted League is one of the local chapters."

"So that's why you're here. And you are being questioned by the police because—?"

"There was this Pink Lady—"

"Not a drink."

"No! Girly cocktails are so passé now. They really knock back those martinis on S*ex in the City*."

"That's *Sex* and *the City* and it's in reruns now, Electra. Not hot. Speaking of hot, just how many Red Hat Sisterhood members live in Vegas?"

"I don't know. The Las Vegas area has more than one hundred chapters with up to forty-some members, and that's who's here setting up."

"Yowie. That alone almost makes five thousand! How did a local PR ace like me miss knowing about all of them?"

"Not everyone is helping with setup. And you're too young to be a Red Hatter, which is age fifty and over, just like AARP. Although you could be a Pink Lady, dear."

"Since they appear to have a short life span, maybe not. And a Pink Lady is—"

"A member-in-waiting to turn the golden age of fifty and be eligible for the Red Hat, kind of like a cardinal in the Roman Catholic Church, don't you know? They never let anybody too young into the full sisterhood; it might upset the applecart."

"Or lead to murder?"

"No, it's just that the Red Hat Sisterhood is one of the few things in life that older ladies can call their very own. Whatever. I was just trying to help out that helpless Pink Lady. She'd fallen facedown, I'd thought. I didn't know she'd been strangled. A lot of us wear scarves and boas to hide the jowls, you know." Electra patted at the scarlet feathers making her face into an island without a telltale neck.

"Okay. Which Pink Lady?"

Electra's voice and expression hardened. Temple was glad Su and Alch were out of earshot. "Just some bimbo, dearie, who maybe wished she was old enough to be a real Red Hat Sister."

"And why is this anonymous 'some bimbo' attached to your movements and motivations?"

"Um, there's an awkward connection the police found out about."

"What awkward connection?"

"The good detectives—"

"There are not good detectives in a case like this, just suspicious and determined and not on your side."

"Whatever. Anyway, I'd been seen earlier at the preregistration desk, showing newbies how to tie their scarves."

"Around their throats to hide awkward wrinkles and sags, I presume."

"Exactly, dear. Hides the turkey wattle and all those nasty sagging horizontal lines. What more could a woman do for her sisters?"

"And?"

"When they found the Pink Lady dead a few hours later, strangled by a scarf, naturally I came to mind."

"Because—?" Electra was being way too evasive.

"I did use her earlier to demonstrate properly tying a scarf to the other ladies."

"Not good, but not damning. So—?"

Electra looked down and wrung her hands. She even wore red and purple rings and some looked like real rubies and amethysts.

"Electra?"

"This convention meant so much to me. I wanted our chapter to shine, Temple. I wanted the Red Hat Sisterhood to have a stellar time in our uniquely glitzy city. I just wanted to help."

"So what was the problem with that particular Pink Lady?"

"She was from Hollywood."

Temple waited.

"Florida."

"So?"

"So was my third husband."

"But that must have been long ago. You've ditched several more husbands since then."

"Oh, yes. We split almost thirty years ago. I'd thoroughly

washed my hands of the cad after I found out he was stepping out on me, and this was back when I still looked like someone who shouldn't be stepped out on."

"You still do," Temple said, putting a firm hand on Electra's nervous ones.

Tears filled Electra's gray eyes. "It was the name tags. So cute. Our chapter designed them. A chorus line of high-kicking red Eiffel Towers on a lavender border. The Eiffel Tower in Paris was originally painted red, you know."

Temple shook her head. She didn't know, and she didn't know what that had to do with anything. Electra probably didn't either at this point.

"Everything was perfect," Electra went on, "was going to be perfect, until *she* came along."

"The name tags. The Pink Lady's name—?"

"Was Lark, just like mine. I hadn't noticed it during the scarf-tying demonstration."

"I had no idea you knew your way around scarves and knots, because I certainly could use tutoring in that knack."

"Call on me anytime, dear, if I'm not in jail."

"And you didn't know you were advising an ex-rival?"

"Honey chile, she'd changed as much as I had. And my attention was on her neck, not her name tag. But when I saw it, after I'd done the scarf demonstration, I knew she was the formerly teenaged bimbo who'd lured Elmore Lark away from me. It wouldn't have mattered, except I'd kept his last name because it turned out to be the only thing I liked about him."

"So . . . Lark met Lark."

"Then she got insulting. Said she'd never have recognized me and I said the same, because, believe me, those husband-stealing teen tootsies who shine at that age lose it faster than Bruce Willis loses hair."

"Apparently you discussed your mutual revelations and revilements in front of God and everybody."

"No. If God had been there, He would have struck her dead for illegal parking with my then-legal husband."

Temple winced. "And within hours, she was really dead."

"I didn't do that. I respect a Red Hat Sisterhood scarf too

much to wring that witch's neck with it. Even with a lesser Pink Lady version. It is a sacred trust."

"So is a marriage," Temple said, who'd had reason to think about that very thing long and hard lately. "You know that. You operate a wedding chapel, after all."

"Yes." Electra sniffled. "That is my expression of optimism in a pessimistic world and time. I may have wanted to wring Oleta's cheating neck, Temple, but I never would have killed her. And that's why I was so surprised to find the fallen woman, excuse the expression, that I tried to help was her. Again."

Electra's purple-mascara-loaded lashes beat hard to drive back the tears.

Temple believed her. Wanting to wring someone's neck was a common urge and almost never acted upon.

But maybe someone who'd had it in for this particular Pink Lady had witnessed Electra's shock and fury and had decided to ride on it. . . .

An opportunist among a . . . brimful . . . a feather . . . a hat pin . . . of innocuous Red Hat Sisterhood ladies.

Or maybe not innocuous. Not all of them.

Chapter 6

Louie Among the Sisterhood

It is not a cakewalk to ease unseen into a suite at the Crystal Phoenix, much harder than fronting on down a yellow brick road out in Las Vegas proper, and there are plenty of yellow brick roads in this town, only they all are covered in green felt.

Thankfully, I know these Crystal Phoenix grounds and buildings well from my stint as an unofficial house detective here. Those room-service carts always hide the tableware and such under a thick white linen cloth. And I was always to the fine linen born.

So today I have gotten the lay of the land and the dramatis personae through a tablecloth, darkly. Thank heaven and Bast for these sharp black ears of mine.

I manage to sneak a peek or two when nobody is looking. Since I am always at ankle level, nobody is looking most of the time.

First of all, I cannot believe that Miss Electra Lark, major dame-o of the Circle Ritz, has sprayed her hair completely purple! It was one thing when she went multicolored. I know a lot of cats with coats like that. But I have never seen a purple cat. And Miss Electra does not even have the excuse of St. Paddy's Day and green. Does she not realize that white-haired ladies tinting their hair blue is a cliché? That purple is just one half step up from that? That Blond is the New Blue for the post-sixty set?

Of course, I also cannot believe that Miss Electra Lark (even if she is a reformed "Mrs.") would off some so-called Pink Lady just for the act of lassoing her man some decades before. If he was so lasso-able, he was lose-able in my estimation.

We all have our issues, and hopefully outgrow them. Like I have forgotten and forgiven Miss Midnight Louise for taking over my primo PI position here at the Phoenix.

Not!

Okay. I am a cool dude. I go where I am needed, I do what I must, and I always keep my whiskers dry.

I know my Miss Temple will not sit still for our beloved landlady being railroaded for murder one, so we both are here for the duration.

I also know that if Miss Electra Lark is not returned soon to the Circle Ritz, someone will have to assume the duties of feeding and watering her reclusive Birman cat, Karma. And that will not be *me!* Every time I am around that mystical feline dame I get the heebie-jeebies. I do not know what the "heebie-jeebies" are (maybe a relative of cooties), but they are not conducive to the hair lying flat along my spine. Unless I wish to be known as the feline Rod Stewart, I will keep myself away from Karma and any hair-raising encounters.

In a way, though, I am glad this has happened. It will keep my Miss Temple's mind off her romantic dilemma. That is the trouble with romance, in my view; it always leads to dilemmas.

I advocate the way cats of my kind do it: wham, bam, thank you, ma'am, and off to one's dudely pursuits until the next free-for-all called "heat" comes along.

Humans are so primitive in certain matters.

Chapter 7

Fatal Flair

Nicky Fontana himself escorted Temple to the scene of the crime after she'd left Electra at the registration desk doing volunteer work.

This was a relatively quiet corner of the ballroom holding dozens of Red Hat Sisterhood shopping booths and ringed by stages featuring products of allied interest.

It was all a girly shopper's paradise, but with racks of clothing and feathers on three sides, the booth in question formed a perfect cul-de-sac for murder, now sheltered from the public gaze by freestanding screens. Inside them, yellow crime scene tape looked like a garish and tacky ribbon garlanding all the flower-shop reds, purples, lavenders, and pinks.

You'd have thought they were filming *C.S.I.: Crime Scene*

Investigation on-site. Worker bees were teeming over the body and its surrounding area. None of them were Attractive Babes Showing Lots of Cleavage on the job. None of them were Nerdy Young Brainy Guys with Possibilities.

They were just average working people, squinting through spectacles, wearing wrinkle-free khakis, and free of nipple-showing T-shirts and blouses. Their salaries were likely lower than hers, and she was a risk-laden freelancer.

Temple compared their ordinariness to their TV alter egos to avoid staring rudely at the corpse. But now she did.

Oleta Lark's face was turned Temple's way. She looked like a fallen department store mannequin lying there. Several were already on display in the ballroom, some of them decked out in unabashedly girly doses of pink and lavender. Oleta's own skin color was still normal, lifelike, but her eyes were open and glassy, sightless, so unnervingly still. Her pink hat had fallen aside to reveal hair so highlighted that any base color was lost in the red-gold-brown blur.

Though the pink hat proclaimed her as under fifty, it wasn't by much. The dead flesh was pasty and slack and her body had a sacklike look that an upright position and animation might have made hard to notice.

The Lolita of yesterday who'd stolen Electra's husband had been history long before someone had wrapped the purple scarf dotted with red flowers around her neck and pulled until dead.

"The detectives okay this?" a CSI woman asked Temple, rising from the floor next to the corpse. She didn't have chiseled features and a hot haircut. In fact, she had a double chin and a couple of not-telegenic zits.

"Detective Alch did," Nicky said, turning on a hundred-watt smile. "I'm Nicky Fontana. This is my hotel, and this is my PR representative, Miss Barr. I want her to be able to give an accurate account of where we're all *not* at on this."

Nicky being modest and genuine was pretty irresistible. He may have been married, but he still had that Fontana brother charisma down pat.

The woman smiled.

"We're just working the scene. Detective Alch will make what he sees fit available to the hotel and the press. If it's okay with him that you gawk for a while, gawk. Even we won't know a thing until the lab processes everything. It ain't as fast as on TV."

"Understood," Nicky murmured.

Temple took that invitation at face value and gawked to take in more detail.

She'd seen a few dead bodies in her time and on her sensitive job of making Las Vegas safe for good news, not bad.

She'd never seen a strangling victim before.

She'd been relieved that Oleta Lark's tongue wasn't extended and black in a pallid post-death face. The scarf wound around her neck did not cut into flaccid flesh like a piece of barbed wire. It looked like an accessory. There was a "Got Milk" ad slash of foam on her bright pink lipstick and her open blue eyes were bloodshot.

Still, if ever a wronged wife had wanted to see a rival brought down, this postmortem image would do it. Temple couldn't have wished anything more demeaning on Kitty the Cutter, and God knew she had her reasons, number one being Max, number two being Matt.

Electra hadn't done this. It would take not only strength but deep, long-simmering hatred to pull tighter and tighter until a body's breath was just a memory. Temple couldn't believe Electra would ever succumb to such a rage.

Temple liked to think no woman could or would do this, and most strangulation murderers were indeed men, something sexual about the process. Often they were sons of smothering mothers. But Temple had learned to know her own gender in all its proud and petty glory, and didn't underestimate the female of the species.

Anyone would have the strength to do this, if determined: man or woman. And, face it; this was a convention of women drawn from all over the country. Grudges recognized no borders. Women were more than their ages, despite social assumptions that cast them as either pursuable young bunnies or uninteresting maternal mama rabbits.

Oleta had started out to be someone's bunny and had ended up a helpless rabbit choked to death. But why?

For what she knew? For what she was?

Or for what she was not?

Chapter 8

Honorary Older Women

"Okay," Temple told Electra when they were safely back in the bosom of the Red Hat Sisterhood thronging the hotel's main floor. "You haven't been arrested. Yet. Su would love to; Alch is Mr. Wait-and-See. I need to be on the scene."

"But here you are! And you work for the hotel."

"No. I need better credentials. A reason to be able to enter all the convention event rooms. And," she added, spotting Kit's hand waving above the milling hats as her aunt spied them and darted forward, "it wouldn't hurt to have Aunt Kit on our side."

"Easy," Electra said. "We get you both registered for the convention. We could say she's a Red Hat hottie from Manhattan. I've been handling registration among some other things. That's it! We have the Sinsinatti Reds chapter. Why not the Ragin' Red

Manhattan Hatties? And you? You're such a baby. You have to be a Pink Hat."

"So *think Pink*."

Electra cupped her double chin in her hand and thought. She straightened, grinning. "I know! You solve crimes, right?"

"Sometimes."

"The Hot Pink Panthers chapter!"

"Seems to me a lot of the Red Hat Sisterhood chapter names use the word 'hot.' Is there a hidden statement in that?"

"Hat. Hot. They're so close. I guess we think women who wear hats *are* hot."

Kit joined them. "Make mine pink."

"That's cheating," Temple said.

"What's cheating?" a passing Red Hat woman stopped to ask with the speed of an ice skater turning on the toe of a blade.

All three were struck dumb with guilt.

"It's great to see new members enlisting at the convention," she went on. "Are you from Las Vegas?"

"I'm from Las Vegas," Electra said quickly. "The Red-Hatted League chapter."

"I'm a Vegasite too," Temple admitted.

"Manhattan," Kit said.

"Wonderful! I'm Jeanne Johnson."

The name struck Temple as familiar. Maybe because it was a good Nordic Minnesota name and Jeanne Johnson had that natural blond, semiathletic look about her. Like she could ski down an Alp on tennis racquets if she had to, enjoying the below-zero windchill. In other words, one cheerfully determined woman.

Then Temple got it, encouraged by Electra's elbow digging into her side. She'd seen the name in the Red Hat Sisterhood program book she'd been studying.

"Oh! You're the founder."

Jeanne released a six-hundred-watt grin.

"My official title is 'Her Royal Hatness.' Who would have believed that we supposedly over-the-hill dames can all don tiaras and be queens of our own inclusive kingdom? Who would have believed in a few short years we'd be a national phenomenon with hundreds of thousands of members? It's all based on a poem, you know. Not many organizations are."

"A poem," Kit asked. "That's pretty amazing. Something from Shakespeare's *Winter's Tale*?"

"No, it's by Jenny Joseph, about a woman musing that when she's older she'll indulge herself by wearing purple, and a red hat that doesn't go with it by conventional standards."

"Free spirit," Kit summed up.

"Exactly. Women of a certain age often find themselves with empty nests, or divorced or widowed, with no intense job commitments and falling faces and fannies. The Red Hat Sisterhood encourages them to band together. Sure, we have crazy, mixed-up fun, but we have a thirst for moving in new directions and mutual support too. And even spreading good cheer among the less fortunate than we."

"I can't wait until I'm a full Red Hatter," Temple said, catching Red Hat fever.

Her Royal Hatness assumed a sober expression. "We'd love to have you then, but don't wish your youth away. Too many women do. Now, what can I do for you? You looked at a loss standing here."

So Temple explained the difficulty straight out.

"Oh." Jeanne's natural buoyancy flattened. "That killing was awful. The hotel was wonderful about sparing the poor woman public display, and the police have been cooperative too."

"That's important in Las Vegas," Temple said.

"That's why they and the hotel want Temple keeping an eye on things," Electra said proudly. "She's got a knack for spotting killers."

"Only I don't want any killers spotting me," Temple said, "so we were trying to figure out how I could go undercover as a member. You hide a leaf in a forest, and here you'd hide your presence in a hat."

"I'd certainly like this matter settled as soon as possible," Jeanne said. "I'm Queen. I'll name you an honorary member, Temple."

"And my aunt too? I could use a partner."

"And Miss—"

"Carlson," Kit said.

"Ah. And Miss Carlson too." She ushered them to one of the registration stations and whispered her instructions to the wearer of the red hat there.

"This would be wonderful," Jeanne Johnson said as she turned back to them, "if a woman and an honorary Red Hat Sisterhood member found whoever killed Oleta Lark."

She glanced at Electra's name tag with sudden concern. "A relative?"

"Once removed." By a murderer.

"No wonder you want your crime-solving friends present and accounted for, Electra! Carry on, Hatters, and do us proud."

The royal audience ended with Jeanne Johnson grinning as she produced two enameled pink-hat brooches with the Red Hat Sisterhood logo. She dropped them into Kit's and Temple's purple canvas convention bags filled with informational sheets, convention programs, and favors from bars of soap to decks of playing cards.

"Good luck on your serious quest, but remember to *have fun!*"

"That's an order everyone would like to take," Temple commented, but Kit looked a bit chagrined.

As they left Electra at the registration desk with her Red Hat friends, Kit caught Temple's elbow in a death grip to steer her out of hearing range.

"Aldo must never hear of this," she said, pulling Temple aside from the crowded registration lines. "That I'm really qualified to be a Red Hat."

"Yes. I mean, no! Never. But he knows that you're my aunt. I don't buy the dumb hunk thing. Can't he do simple arithmetic?"

"Aldo is an emperor of enterprise. He just thinks *you*'re as old as you look, sixteen, and that I was your mother's youngest, hippest, most not-Midwestern sister."

"This whole Red Hat Sisterhood movement wants women to be proud of their lives and ages and futures."

"Right. Meanwhile, I got myself listed in Actors Equity as ten years younger ages ago and I'm not going to lose that edge now. Not even for you, niece, would I go undercover as an over-fifty. You or your landlady, the old darling."

"You and Electra are probably about the same age, Kit, although you don't look it."

Kit sighed her deep relief. "There is some advantage in short stature and a slight frame. You are going to inherit it, dear niece, so honor my position now because someday you'll be here."

"I hope so, because you're a pretty cool lady. If you want to think Aldo digs you for the age on your Actors' Equity card, fine."

Temple was a legitimate Pink Lady, but not the youngest. She spied a few twenty-something daughters accompanying their mothers. For her trouble, she'd scored a truly darling name tag: a hot pink miniature straw hat with feathers framing her name on the front: Temple.

Kit's shorter name fit her miniature pink hat much better, but she was cheating. In every respect.

"So we are both Pink Ladies," Kit noted, "for the record. Lord, every time I hear that phrase I could use a drink. How do we do this undercover sleuth stuff?"

"We're registered, but first we must find the proper hats to disguise us and announce our status."

Luckily, the convention store, called the Hatorium Emporium, was mostly set up. Temple and Kit trolled the aisles, trying on hats and giggling like five-year-olds until both had suitable chapeaux, wide-brimmed for purposes of disguise.

"Short women aren't supposed to wear wide-brimmed hats," Temple told Kit.

"Pink Hat women don't worry about silly fashion rules."

"Is mine too . . . bridesmaid-y?"

Kit stepped back to assess. The hat was pink with a lavender touch, both colors permitted the under-fifty Pink Lady member. Temple had figured she might actually wear the hot pink straw hat later, after removing the pale pink cloud of marabou feathers and cluster of silk lavender flowers around the crown.

"It's utterly charming, Temple," Kit said. "You look like an angel. And I'd say it was more bridal than 'bridesmaid-y.' "

Temple felt her cheeks pink to match the marabou. She hadn't announced her marital potential to anyone yet.

"Well, yours is a showstopper," Temple told Kit in turn.

The front of Kit's wide-brimmed pink straw was a huge, rhinestone-dotted organdy bow anchored with pink satin roses and wisps of ostrich feathers.

"The hat! The hat," Kit intoned in a Broadway musical style as she spun to display the back. "The hat is nothing ratty. The hat! The hat! Is that which makes us all look batty!"

"Batty is beautiful," Temple interrupted. "Golly, I'm glad I'm still a temporary blond. Pink would do nothing for my natural red hair color, and vice versa."

"Speaking of blond and unnatural," Kit said, stopping in midstep. "What or who is that?"

"Oh, Lord. I hope it's not another of Electra's husband's ex-wives. That would be too much of a coincidence to bear."

"The whole entourage is too much to bear," Kit murmured, pulling Temple aside so the oncoming parade could pass.

It was led by a woman on hot-pink stilettos, crowned by a hot pink hat with a brim so wide it would suffice to shade an elephant. Even so, it barely shaded the cleavage on her Pamela Anderson–size enhanced Hollywood breasts. The woman was pulled along by two tiny pink-dyed Chihuahuas on rhinestone-studded leashes.

She was trailed by an assistant attired in pink checks who toted two pink canvas pet carriers and was followed by a large brass luggage trolley that had been mugged by a pink polka-dot matched set of baggage.

Temple let her jaw drop in horror.

Kit eyed her sagely. "You know her."

"To my everlasting regret. Surely a former actress like you has heard of Savannah Ashleigh."

Kit pulled her red-framed reading glasses off her nose to stare at the entourage in naked disbelief.

"She makes Pamela Anderson look like Oscar material. And all that pink. She's no more under fifty than I am! Oh!" Kit cupped her mouth and looked around, but no Fontana brothers were lurking to overhear her confession.

"That woman," Temple said, "has made this town headquarters for the rotten actress retirement home. She's the one who wanted to slice the balls off Midnight Louie."

"No! Well, those pink Chihuahuas looked pretty neutered."

"I've got to find out what Savannah Ashleigh is doing here. Could you amble over and grill her, Auntie? She kinda really hates me since I took her to *People's Court* and won."

"This will be like grilling an unzipped banana," Kit promised. "I'll smash her."

She skittered over on her low-heeled slides to stand in the registration line behind the lady in question.

Not that Savannah was content to wait in line. Oh, no. Apparently Temple hadn't needed an undercover agent aunt. Savannah was broadcasting live from the Crystal Phoenix lobby.

"I do not do lines, unless they're waiting for my autographs. I am the celebrity emcee of this shebang and should have a prestige suite waiting for me, and mine." She beamed upon the yappy pink Chihuahuas. "Taco! Belle! Hush, babies."

Taco and Bell? Temple thought, cattily. Are we angling to be a fast-food commercial huckster as well as an over-the-hill Paris Hilton wannabe?

Kit came skittering back. "What a bad name that woman gives airhead starlets. You heard, I presume. Her voice has the projection quality of a buzz saw."

Since both Kit and Temple had been blessed with arresting, slightly raspy voices to counterbalance their petite size, that was saying something.

"Hey, Kit. I just realized that I'm a dumb blonde now, just like Savannah. At least she might not recognize me."

A shriek erupted at the front desk area. Savannah was prettily perched atop her hot pink luggage trolley as if she'd seen a mouse.

Actually, Temple saw, she'd just glimpsed Midnight Louie sniffing around the pink canvas pet carriers, which must contain Savannah's Persian cats, Yvette and Solange. The Crystal Phoenix was a favorite hangout of his.

"That cat is a criminal!" Savannah shrieked. "Arrest him. He wants to rape my babies."

Bellmen came running over, but Louie had dashed under the cart. He wasn't there when the bellmen went on their knees to look (and possibly to look up Savannah's miniskirt). He'd pulled a disappearing act under everybody's noses. That made Temple think of Max. She began patting down her tote bag for the lump of her cell phone.

Meanwhile, Savannah opened the fancy pet carriers with maternal panic. Out pussyfooted the shaded golden Persian, Solange, wearing a red hat with purple flowers, and the shaded silver Persian, Yvette, with a red marabou boa around her neck and edging her purple cape and a red pillbox hat tied to her silver-platinum head.

Camera lights sparked as Red Hat Sisterhood ladies circled around, taking dozens of photos of Savannah and her red hat cats and pink-dyed pooches, who also wore pink hats, one a fedora (must be the boy, Taco) and one a beret (the putative girl, Bell). Or Belle, rather. Bell*whether*? Temple stood unmoving, dazed by the possibilities.

But never underestimate an alley cat born and bred. Into the sea of red and purple dashed a flash of solid black. When it disappeared, Taco was whimpering and sitting on his tail, hatless as well as hairless.

Temple let her mouth drop open.

"Who was that masked cat?" Kit asked.

"All I can say is that Louie was forced to wear a flamingo-pink fedora in a cat food commercial when we were in New York last Christmas. I think Taco's semi-sombrero is dog meat."

"What a nuthouse. No wonder the second Mrs. Lark was killed with no one caught red-handed at the scene. With everybody wearing a red or pink hat, who's to say who did what to whom? It's like costuming; if it works, nobody can see past it."

"You're absolutely right, Kit. It's even possible the wrong victim died."

"Now that's a thought. That would clear Electra lickety-split."

"Nothing about crime solving is lickety-split."

Even as they spoke a wave of cool neutral colors washed

into the tide of red and purple. Nicky's brothers, calming and charming the troubled waters.

Emilio bent and came up holding Taco and Belle, while Armando captured Yvette and Solange. Julio escorted Savannah to the elevators, color-coordinated pets in tow. Giuseppe and the second youngest, Ralph, were doing duty as community photographers. Their impeccable Italian tailored suit coats hung with a half-dozen instant cameras as they obligingly photographed groups of Red Hat ladies posing naughtily for the camera, knees cocked and hands on generous hips. In Italy, women of substance were considered sexy, so Red Hat lady and Fontana brother had met their match.

"Ridiculous," Kit sniffed, no doubt worrying about Aldo amid all these happy hussies. "Women my age and older preening like fading chorus girls in front of the entire world."

A solo Fontana brother waltzed up to Temple; no lavish, wide-brimmed hat could fool a fine Italian eye. Besides, he'd inadvertently spent some recent time around her, so she recognized him immediately.

"Our difficult guest," Aldo told her, "is assured that Midnight Louise will no longer trouble her purse pooches. Any ideas how I can indeed ensure that?"

"Of course!" Temple said. "The Crystal Phoenix is Midnight *Louise's* beat now, not Louie's. Funny, even I took that black speedball for Louie. He was framed!"

Mixing up the two black cats also underlined Kit's point that everybody in the Red Hat Sisterhood was inadvertently in disguise.

Aldo had other things on his mind than cats and hats.

"Where, my lovely Miss Temple, is your delightful aunt? I seem to have lost her in this parade of feminine fripperies. Never have I seen so many bright, and large, hats."

Kit, hidden by her huge pink brim, turned sheepishly to lift her face and also admit her membership in the silly sisterhood.

"*Bellissima!* Is this you under that charming chapeau? Such a blazing pink is certainly your color."

"Hot pink," Temple corrected him.

Aldo's dark eyes grew mock-rebuking. "I did not wish to

compromise your adorable relative's reputation in a public place, but it is indeed a very . . . hot . . . pink." On the last word he touched his forefinger to Kit's lips.

Well, Temple thought, she'd swoon right there and too-dignified-to-preen Kit was blushing the same color as her hat. It was nice to know the older woman was still capable of blushing, although a dreadful facial flush called rosacea was another thing Kit had mentioned the aging belle had to fight.

"Go and have a Pink Lady with Aldo, Kit, in the Crystal Bar. I'll snoop around here and head back to the Circle Ritz once I can pry Electra from her volunteer post."

Actually, Kit looked terribly smart in her hat as she ambled away. She didn't walk off "into the sunset" with Aldo, because, thanks to the hat, she *was* the sunset.

Temple spared a couple minutes to take in the scene.

It looked as if the giant blown-glass blossoms from the huge Chihuly chandelier at the Bellagio had drifted down to cover every female head in sight.

If the advance guard of six hundred Red Hat Sisterhood members could command such a presence in a Las Vegas hotel lobby, then the incoming five thousand should really take over the old town. The press was sure to giggle at this overblown convention of aging women refusing to be invisible, but Temple felt a sinister chill.

It reminded her of the Father Brown mysteries (which she'd quietly started reading a year or so ago in honor of meeting an ex-Catholic priest). Luckily, the modest, often-overlooked British priest-detective (no Red Hat candidate in any context, he) bore not the slightest resemblance to a certain modern American ex-priest, Matt. Her Matt. That thought felt so right.

But the Father Brown stories were philosophical, even metaphysical and often metaphorical. She remembered one about "where would you hide a leaf?" The answer was "in a forest," only, in the story, the leaf was a murdered body and the forest was a battlefield.

The Crystal Phoenix was a different kind of battlefield now, against aging, not death itself. But the issues and motives could be as desperate. Every woman attending the convention had lived long enough to have a story, to be the heroine or villain of one. Maybe it was all jovial girly celebration, but loss and heartbreak had to be lurking in the background.

And Temple was one who didn't believe that murder had a gender, despite all the dead lovelies on the crime-show autopsy tables.

Women could kill as well as die, and she knew her bubbly landlady had firmly landed in the unpleasant police category labeled "under suspicion."

Chapter 9

No Kitting

I have decided to take a small detour from the lobby, since my natural territorial urges have caused a stir.

No dog crosses Midnight Louie's path unpunished, even if it is the size of an English muffin and dyed pink.

My step is firm and my heart is high, for I have seen the Ashleigh sisters all togged out in felt and feathers and buttons and bows and know that I can pursue both this case *and* my personal interests.

Right now these interests are invested in the Delightful Solange, she of the honey-blond hair. Since her sister, formerly the Divine Yvette, now busted down—in my book—to the Supine Yvette, snubbed me for being common and possibly having an alley cat for an ancestor and a daughter, I have reconsidered my preference for the shaded silver over the shaded golden Persian.

Solange is sweet and affable where Yvette is sour and demanding.

I will always choose sweet over sour.

I am making my way to my former office, the canna lily stand by the koi pond, when a bolt of cold black lightning knocks me over near the hotel service entrance.

Bolt lightning may be cold, but this particular edition is hot, and bothered.

"Traitor!" it says, hissing and spitting and thoroughly dampening my impeccable shirtfront. "Lazy, self-serving, koi-sucking, no-good, overweight layabout, poor excuse for a partner, tail-chasing son of a—"

This is getting serious and I raise my dukes. Also my mitts. And my tail.

"Nobody disses my esteemed dam, Ma Barker."

"I was about to say 'lazy, self-serving, koi-sucking, no-good son of an overweight layabout' at Lake Mead."

I let my guard down. "When did you hear about my old man, Three O'clock Louie?"

"When I had a little heart-to-heart with your old lady, Ma Barker."

I sit down and restore an eyebrow to its usual pasted-down suave state. "Louise, Louise, Louise. You have got to do something about that hot temper of yours."

"*I* am hot? When you're easing on through to take over my spot at the rear of the Crystal Phoenix? I am the house muscle here now."

"Your spot was my spot once. I am merely taking the opportunity to survey my old stomping grounds."

"Well, prepare to get stomped. I thought you were going to help me nail whoever engineered Mr. Max's fatal fall at the Neon Nightmare. I guess you do not care that your so-called Miss Temple is missing one major boyfriend in action."

"My Miss Temple has plenty of action to handle these days. Our esteemed landlady, Miss Electra Lark, is suspected of murder one in this very hotel on this very day."

This news forces Miss Midnight Louise to sit on her highly haired tail to think things over for a change.

"So that is why you are here. *Hmm,* two disasters in two days, both connected to the Circle Ritz. You might want to think about relocating, Pop."

"Just when I have gotten Ma Barker and her street gang moved to the CR for some TLC of a human sort? No way."

"Speaking of 'CR,' is Miss Lieutenant C. R. Molina on this new murder case? And what is with all the dames in purple wall-to-wallow T-shirts and scarlet wide-brims. You would think this was a vintage car convention."

"It is a vintage *person* convention," I tell Louise, "and there has already been a murder. I did intend to concentrate on Mr. Max's sudden fall from grace, quite literally, but I have had my mitts full on this end."

Oddly enough, Miss Midnight Louise does not jump down my throat for once.

"I have been over the Neon Nightmare for the past day and a half like a spider on a web, and that turns out to be an apt figure of speech. The place is riddled with secret rooms and passages."

"I am not surprised, Louise, having already explored that territory. The building is designed as a pyramid and you know what mazes of treasures and dead bodies lay hidden inside those for centuries."

"That is exactly it, Daddikins."

I cringe at her latest sarcastic endearment for me, but I listen to her report.

"Mr. Max's gear and illusions are housed up under the pointed inner roof, but the angled walls have all sorts of rooms, visited by all sorts of persons."

"Such as?" I have some insight into the inner workings of the Neon Nightmare but want to see what the chit has discovered on her own.

She leans close and whispers in my ear. Too bad she is not an Ashleigh sister. "Other magicians. Some of them had seen him fall and they are not alarmed."

"How so?"

"They think it was a ruse, that he is not dead."

"Glory, hallelujah. The newspaper item reported he had died, but perhaps the press rushed to judgment. You cannot believe everything you read in the press. Sometimes you cannot believe anything."

"*If* the Synth is right. They also think Mr. Max was the Phantom Mage. That he robbed the exhibition of the Czar's Scepter, and then vanished to avoid the pursuit of the law."

"Makes sense in the usual devious Mr. Max manner."

"They think he will return in time, to join them in their aims."

"Which are?"

"Do not ask me. They were not about to lay them out for whoever might be eavesdropping. There are aims, and these people have them. Mr. Max was supposed to be part of all this and they still hope that he is merely a clever criminal who will return to their treacherous bosoms."

"And you think, Louise? That he is still alive and will return?"

"I think the jury is out on that one, but if he is dead and anyone is to blame, it is one or more of those so-called magicians who own, operate, and haunt Neon Nightmare and may have secret plans of their very own."

Chapter 10

Mad Hattery

Temple was still super pleased with herself for having aced Electra out of the Lalique Suite without any charges being levied.

When they rendezvoused again by the registration area, Electra cooed over the dainty charms of Temple's new pink hat.

"Enough girly noises," Temple said. "We've got to sit down and hammer out this murder situation. The police may be playing hands-off at the moment, but you're still their most viable suspect. The woman was your long-ago rival, after all."

Electra grimaced. "As I said, I didn't know who she was until I saw the name tag and then I did feel like decking her. You notice that I said 'decked,' not 'killed.'"

"How reassuring."

"Are you mad at me, Temple?"

"No. I'm mad at the cops. I thought Alch knew better. Su is always ready to roll at any hint of guilt, but I always thought of Morrie Alch as a favorite uncle—"

"I am not interested in your favorite uncle, dear girl! I need an alibi. I need a sharp defense lawyer." Electra took a deep breath. "Sorry, I'm frazzled down to my purple roots. What now, Pink Pussycat?" she asked.

"We go home and you tell me even more about your third husband and his second wife. In fact, it wouldn't hurt if you told me about all your husbands and any other wives in common you might have out there.

"Then we discuss every second of your involvement in this convention and the Red Hat Sisterhood."

"Oh, my, just those two subjects are a book and a half."

"Then we need to figure out how the cops found out the victim was your ex's wife so fast."

"Oh! That's right. Someone must have squealed on me."

"We say 'prejudiced the authorities against you.' 'Squealed' went out with Edward J. Robinson and Jimmy Cagney."

"Well, those boys may be dead, but I'm not. We dames outlive 'em."

"Sad but true," Temple said, "and very interesting."

"How so?"

"Maybe your ex died and something's at stake, like his estate."

"I wouldn't have any interest in that."

"No, but maybe your successor did."

"Oh! Elmore always was a hustler. Maybe he hustled himself into something lucrative and she inherited."

"Who would stand to gain by her death?"

Electra's skin took on a lavender hue to match her purple hair.

"That would be Elmore's and my only son, Curtiss."

"Oh. I guess we'd better look elsewhere then, Electra."

"Yes. He's a good kid, Temple. Well, good young man."

"And where does he live now?"

"Tucson, last I knew."

"And Elmore?"

"Reno."

"I thought you met and married him in Florida. He moved to Nevada, really?"

"Last I heard from Curtiss. We usually only talk by phone on holidays and birthdays."

Temple nodded sympathetically. Families were far-flung nowadays, although she could wish that young Curtiss was more far-flung from the Las Vegas scene of this crime than Tucson.

She'd have to get Electra home to the Circle Ritz, sit right down, and draw out a family tree. With five ex-spouses and assorted offspring, that would be a big job.

"The way it was," Electra explained in her cool, shadowed penthouse living room, "is that my dad ran out on the family. I was raised by my mom and a stepdad, and he was funny."

"Tell me you don't mean 'funny' the way I think you do," Temple said.

"I do. Only back then nobody admitted it. I ran away from high school before I graduated. First there was Darren. That fizzled mighty quick. I then married Billy on the road to Daytona Beach. We split about six months later. I kept finding guys who were going to take me 'away from all this,' except 'all this' was myself and my background. Elmore Lark hit me in my early thirties. He was a cardsharp and hustler, but he cleaned up good in those days. By the time I found out he was a two-timer, I was ready to escape with my sanity and his last name."

"Was he unfaithful to you with this dead woman?"

"Hell yes, the little hussy. And they—or she—had the nerve to send me a wedding notice. That's what got me into the wedding chapel business when I moved to Las Vegas later, that tacky card from a chapel out on Highway 95. I decided I wanted to give people ceremonies to remember. Maybe it would keep them together longer."

"You think so?"

"Maybe not, but at least they might have some nice memories. I didn't have nice memories of most of my marriages, and I finally realized it was because I didn't have nice memories of my family life."

"Gosh, Electra. I've always seen you as this energetic entrepreneur, not as a desperate housewife racing from marriage to marriage."

"You mean you always thought I was a free spirit, not a Stepford Wife. Why do you think I evolved into a free spirit?"

"So you knew about her becoming the new Mrs. Elmore Lark?"

"Yeah, as I said, from the cheesy wedding announcement photo she just *had* to send me almost thirty years ago. But she didn't look at all like herself in her Pink Lady outfit here and now."

"Not a great alibi. Okay," Temple said. "What about the other ex-husbands? Don't you want to know where they might be?"

"No," Electra said. "Tasmania or Outer Mongolia would be good."

"You are not a great advertisement for the Lovers' Knot Wedding Chapel attached to this very building."

"Maybe not, but why are you so interested?"

Temple twisted a pale blond bleached lock around her forefinger. "I might want your services. Sometime."

"You? Married? When? I thought Max, your main man, had to remain undercover and under the covers."

"He does. Nothing's changed there."

"Oh, then. Oh. My dear!" Electra grabbed Temple's right hand and crushed it to her large, soft, purple-knit bosom. "It's that darling boy Matt! At last!"

"Darling, but not a boy, Electra." Temple extracted her hand. "We really don't have time to discuss my love life when your formerly wedded life could get you tried on a count of murder one."

"Irises. No canna lilies. Violets? No, something showy, bird of paradise! Music. He loves Bob Dylan, did you know? Say, there's that one with a wedding march tempo! The one about his love speaking in silence—"

"I've never spoken in silence, Electra."

"You could start. Certainly you'll have to be silent for the wedding vows until called upon." Electra's blue eyes teared up. "I feel like . . . a matchmaker."

Temple was remembering the song Electra had mentioned. "Love Minus Zero/No Limit." It did have a solemn, ceremonial tempo, and the singer's "love" was "true" as fire and ice. That line made her squirm instead of smile. She'd warned Matt: breaking up was hell to do.

"Electra! Forget my fantasy wedding. Your ex-love walks in anonymity and where is the dirty dog if his second wife is dead? I'd love to make him suspect number one."

"Elmore? He wouldn't hurt a flypaper."

"Not what we want to hear, or say. I want to know the name of all of your exes, and all post-you liaisons they had, including wives, and any descendants."

"That's a lot of family tree to come up with on the fly, my dear."

"Your family. Your tree. Your job. I'm heading back to the Crystal Phoenix to find out what the gossip is. With that many women flocking around, it's got to be choice."

Electra had sat herself down at her forties blond mahogany dining table, lined note sheet and fountain pen in hand.

"You go ahead, dear. I'll alert my Red Hat Sisterhood chapter to rush to the scene to assist you."

"Really, Electra, I doubt I need their help when I've got the Fontana brothers at my beck and call. And my aunt Kit."

"But my chapter members will fit in where the Fontana boys won't."

Temple sighed and headed back. The last thing she needed was to be drowned in red and purple until death-solved did them part.

Chapter 11

Old Flame-Points

I must admit that middle-aged human dames in extreme colors are not particularly attractive to me, unless they are wearing feathers.

And most of these Red Hat Sisterhood attendees are.

Hubba hubba!

There is enough feather flaunting around here to keep me on the prowl and ready to pounce for a month.

I cannot share this personal peccadillo with my partner in crime solving at Midnight Inc. Investigations. Miss Midnight Louise is the straitlaced sort who disapproves of shenanigans. And all these Red Hat Sisterhood ladies have come to Las Vegas to have shenanigans.

Me, I am a shamus and we shamuses like shenanigans.

So I bob and weave through this plethora of feathered feminine pulchritude milling in the Crystal Phoenix lobby and beyond. Alas, my short stature often gets me overlooked. Who made tall dudes king? Besides some Big and Tall Man shop?

Well, that "man" part is a bit of a handicap for me too.

Although my heart goes out to my Miss Temple as she struggles to keep this major celebration event happy despite the intervention of ugly human emotions resulting in murder, I have my own fish to fry.

Now that Louise is off following up on her Mr. Max fixation, I make my way over miles of casino floor to the pool out back again, where once I hung up my shingle as house detective, and where under the towering canna lilies, I received clients.

Of course, my old stomping grounds are only a huff and a puff away from the Crystal Phoenix pool area. I cannot admit a partiality to coconut oil. Fish oil is another kettle of . . . well, you know.

I gaze into the limpid depths of the carp pond. I watch the mermaid seductions of fluid fin and tail. Koi. Each one worth a month or more of my Miss Temple's employ. Once I hunted here, simply hungry, and their worth was the equal of my survival. Now that I am established, I understand that I cannot dine on EpiKorean delicacies unless I pay for them in advance.

Such is the price of success.

Still, I miss the good old days of daring survival. I miss hankering to move above my station in life.

What reminds me of this is the sight of Miss Savannah Ashleigh sunning her silicone and collagen in a string bikini. "String" is the word for MSA. I am more attracted by the two pink canvas carriers under her lounge chair and her coconut-oil dripping body. That woman needs an oil pan change!

I edge over the hot tiles despite my worries.

Two carriers, sizzling hot pink. Two residents, both pink at the ears and nose, or just hot-tempered.

I approach on velvet paws, sniff carefully. I look in one carrier and see my once-smitten now-snooty diva passed out colder than the Crystal Phoenix's buffet-line salmon.

I butt canvas with the other carrier.

A brick-red purebred nose pushes against its black mesh side.

"Louie?" a low voice whispers on a hint of pure Persian purr.

"Solange?"

"Louie!"

"Solange!"

It is your classic noir dialogue. Full of unsaid . . . little nothings.

"Yvette is in the adjacent carrier," Solange points out, literally sticking a pale scimitar of nail through the mesh in the right direction.

"I saw. So I should care?"

"She will not waken. She is so high-strung that our mistress gives her Prozac for her nerves."

"I do not approve of doping animal companions, but in this case it permits us to conduct our affairs in confidence."

"Oh, Louie."

"Oh, Solange."

"I am sorry. I do not want you to see me now. I am forced to wear this pansy hat of red and purple. I do not think it flatters my coloring."

"Your coloring goes with everything, especially . . . black."

"Oh, Louie."

"Oh, Solange."

"I cannot . . . betray my sister."

"Betray? No. I merely need an on-event guide."

"First, you must free me."

I do not have these mini-saber-tooth canines for nothing. I use one to pull down the zipper of her container.

Miss Solange steps out, a muff of glorious golden fur tipped with the divine color, black.

Her petite face is surmounted by a bonnet of purple straw covered with purple pansies and crimson roses. She looks like a Victorian Valentine's Day postcard.

I tell her so.

"My, you are well traveled, Louie. I do not believe that I have ever seen a Victorian Valentine's Day postcard."

"They are all very feminine and elaborate, like you and the Red Hat ladies."

"My mistress will be distraught about my unauthorized liberty."

I snort, despite the delicate company. "Your mistress is sucking up to those annoying Mexican hairless dogs, the better to pass as Paris Hilton and her ilk. Taco Belle indeed! Cheesy, cheesy, cheesy!"

"We *have* felt relegated to second place of late."

"You and—?"

"My sister Yvette," she whispers in my ear, so close that her vibrissae exchange feints with my vibrissae. (*Whiskers* to you human types out there.)

This is a very titillating conversation. "Your sister Yvette," I tell her, "is in my bad books now."

"You mean for her slurs against your associate who may be a blood relative?"

"Right," I say, knowing that the only way Miss Midnight Louise will be an admitted blood relative of mine is if we mix it up.

However, since Miss Midnight Louise now has *my* job of house detective at the Crystal Phoenix, the only way we could come to blows is if she got between me and my koi. And I have sworn off the expensive show fish. Too big and chewy for the refined palate of a dude-about-town.

"I find Midnight Louise very pretty and agreeable," Solange says.

Well, that is Solange's generous take on a brutal world, and who is to say it is not superior to my own cynical point of view, honed by my sharp incisors?

"If a guy has got to have a partner," I concede, "she is pretty okay."

"Louie!" Solange shivers until her thickly furred coat collar tickles my shoulder. Somebody ought to outlaw that move. "You play the tough guy but you are all pussycat underneath."

Not all, baby. Oh, well. I am supposed to be the gentleman here, not to mention the private dick enlisting a house spy.

"Now, here are the names I need you to recognize, Solange. Just let the ladies pick you up and pet you, and keep those shell-pink little inner ears perked and recording what they say."

She nods soberly and follows me over the hot tiles to the air-conditioned dim interior of the Crystal Phoenix.

Cacophony and voices echo off all the hard lobby surfaces, marble, wood, granite, glass. Scooters bearing Red Hat ladies dart over the shiny marble floor like water bugs.

We need to be on our toes, making like Mexican jumping beans to avoid getting our nether members run over.

"I see what you mean, Louie. This place is a death-by-misadventure waiting to happen."

I begin to worry that Solange is too sensitive a soul to do undercover work.

Then a scooter wheels past and she lofts up to the seat like a Hell's Angel mascot born.

"Oooh!" cries a passing Red Hat lady, gawking at Solange in her flowery and feathery chapeau. "What an adorable cat! And that hat! Where did you get her?"

The rider shrugs purple shoulders. "She just jumped aboard."

"What a darling! I'll walk along with you a little so I can pet her."

"Be my guest."

"Did you hear what happened off the lobby yesterday?"

"No, I just got in."

"Someone got killed!"

"No! Not one of us?"

"Yes! And they're saying another of us did it."

Off goes the Gossipmobile, Solange installed like a beauty queen on a parade float. A PI never had a sweeter eavesdropping machine!

Chapter 12

Old Acquaintances

If anything, more Red Hat ladies crowded the Crystal Phoenix lobby when Temple returned from the Circle Ritz.

If anything on earth was purple, or red, or purple *and* red, it was gathered in this lobby. Rolling luggage bags boasted these royal colors, as did clothing, tote bags, purses, scarves, shoes, hose, nail polish (red or purple), and eye shadow (only in purple, thank God).

The gaudiest women, dripping red and purple feather boas and scarlet lace, plume, and rhinestone-swagged Victorian-size hats, posed on a huge photo poster announcing "Candy Crenshaw and the Red Hat Candies," Candy being the lead singer and "clown princess."

Pink-hatted ladies, like herself, stood out, but there still were a fair number. It occurred to Temple that a mad serial killer of pink-hatted ladies might be at work here. If so, she had firmly put herself among the potential victims.

This was not a new feeling for her, but she had a new significant other now. Matt might not be as easy about that as Max had been, because he was tied to a job and couldn't watch over her the way Max had.

The feeling of total responsibility for herself was heady. She'd sometimes resented Max's omniscient ways in regard to her life and how she lived it. And risked it.

Yet she worried that Matt would be a lot less liberal than Max about the times her PR work turned into PI work. Still, he'd recognized her sleuthing tendency almost as soon as they'd met.

So if she was so liberated, why was she standing there dithering about what Matt *or* Max would think? She needed to know what *she* thought about the problem at hand.

There were many reasons someone might have killed Oleta Lark, none having anything to do with the Red Hat Sisterhood or Oleta's skimpy relationship to Electra.

Temple strolled into the ballroom housing all the Red Hat shops. Oleta's body was gone now, but the murder scene might not have been "released" yet.

As always in Las Vegas, any major Strip crime scene was quickly concealed. A uniformed Crystal Phoenix security guard in a tasteful black-and-tan uniform kept the public from wandering behind the freestanding screens. A pair of Fontana brothers cruised the area, easily drawing away the eyes of arriving Red Hat Sisters.

A third Fontana brother buttonholed Temple, recognizing her despite her new pink hat.

She didn't think of Nicky Fontana as one of Fontana Inc. He was the youngest, cutest Fontana brother, but cast in the same winning mold of olive skin, black curly hair, deep brown eyes, and supernaturally white teeth that probably had inspired the rush to whiteners in the rest of the population.

He was also married and fixed in position as owner of the Crystal Phoenix, while his brothers still rambled the Strip and painted the town red hot nightly.

"You sure got literally undercover on the scene quick," Nicky said. "Nice disguise. What was also nice was finally getting to meet your aunt. I can see where you get some of your spunk. But a little birdie rumor has it that that this relative of yours might be breaking up that old, brotherly gang of mine. Any truth to that rumor?"

For a moment, Temple didn't get it. Then she nodded, forgetting that would set her wide hat brim atremor.

Nicky ducked getting nicked in the chin by the coiled organdy.

"Sorry," she said. "I should renounce head gestures while wearing this getup. You must be referring to my aunt, Kit Carlson, and your eldest brother, Aldo. I might have introduced them. Sort of."

"My uncle, Macho Mario, is hearing wedding bells. We haven't had a wedding in the family since I married Van. I don't know what got into Aldo, except seeing that red hair that you usually sport on your aunt. I hardly see him anymore."

"Well, that'll change, because Kit's joining me here to infiltrate the Red Hat Sisterhood. It's likelier that some out-of-towner killed the Pink Lady, don't you think?"

"Maybe. It would suit us all better if that were the case. Your landlady doesn't look like a crazed killer."

"Neither do any of these attendees. That's why I think someone used the cover of this convention to mask the criminal and the crime."

"Great. Van will love that angle. Good for the hotel. We frown on homegrown homicidal maniacs. But a tourist . . . not our fault."

Temple smiled. Nicky and Van made a great couple and better bosses, which was what Temple cared about. Nicky would always give her a long leash when needed. Van would always make her expectations precise.

"Let's go see the bossy lady," Nicky suggested, "and discuss this stuff in private."

Temple had always liked the easy, affectionate way Nicky deferred to his wife on the job. It was Nicky's vision but Van's execution that had made the Crystal Phoenix Las Vegas's classiest hotel, what would be called a boutique hotel anywhere else, but was just "classy" in Vegas.

But it did make Temple wonder about their sex life: fire and ice sounded good on paper, but in real life . . . Maybe she was dwelling on their sex life because hers had taken such a sudden, earth-shaking turn.

Back to business, Barr. Matt doesn't get off of work until 2:00 A.M. . . . Tomorrow is another day. Oh, yeah.

She and Nicky whisked straight up to the fourteenth floor where Van had her ultra-modern office. She was on the phone when they arrived so they arrayed themselves on the Italian leather chairs in front of Van's desk and waited for her to get free.

Only Van von Rhine would dare to have a glass desktop. Not a paper or a paper clip was out of place. Her pale straight blond hair was smoothed into a tiny French twist at her neck, but everything else about her was Italian. *Furniture, clothes, shoes, purses.*

Husband.

Temple didn't know if Van had developed the design addiction after she'd met Nicky or just had always had good, expensive taste.

She waved a manicured hand at Temple, gave Nicky a cool, inciting glance, and wound up her call in twenty seconds flat.

"Temple, that hat is a bit much, but you've always been able to carry off a lot for such a petite woman. Are you going to nail our Pink Lady killer while fending off the press?"

That was Van, multitasking with a vengeance.

"I thought I'd start," Temple said, "by finding out what the police told you."

"Nicky, I think the male detective enjoyed interviewing you man to man. I suspect he has too many women on his tail already."

Temple collapsed into laughter, freeing her impish self. "You must mean Detective Alch. A sweet guy and a good detective, but he does have a hell of a lady lieutenant to answer to."

"God, she's good, Nicky," Van said, eyeing her husband. "That's the guy. Tell us what we girls weren't up to knowing."

"Can I help it if I inspire police confidence?" Nicky said

with a shrug, spreading his hands like Marlon Brando in *The Godfather.* "The victim was Oleta Lark from Reno."

"A Nevadan?"

"According to her IDs. Forty-eight. Strangled with an official Red Hat Sisterhood scarf."

"Wait," Temple said. "The Pink Lady was strangled with a Red Hat scarf? So the killer is fifty or older?"

"That's the assumption. But anybody can buy those scarves online or at all sorts of shops. That's my observation, from watching Van's shopping habits at the Strip malls and on eBay."

"I do not shop on eBay, Nicky!"

"Just kidding, Duchess. Our credit cards alibi you on that one."

"What are you going to do to keep the publicity on the upside?" Van asked Temple with a frown.

"Accent the positive. Female empowerment. This is a significant woman's movement from a generation that was expected to shrivel up and go quietly on a diet of Maalox and calcium tablets. Instead, they are out there, having fun and making great role models for all of the younger women coming up who aren't going to lose it because they turn thirty or forty or fifty or sixty or seventy or eighty or ninety or a hundred and twenty. There was a time when turning thirty was a day of mourning for women. Now they want to turn a hundred."

"Most inspiring," Nicky said, fanning himself at that fiery speech. "Whew. Put keeping us guys around on that to-do list, please."

"Always," Temple said. "Las Vegas wouldn't be Vegas without the Fontana brothers, each and every one."

"Agreed," Van said, stroking Nicky's ankle with the toe of her Jimmy Choo stiletto.

With a glass desk, you can see everything, Temple thought with a smile. That was Van von Rhine. Nothing to hide.

She was an unofficial Red Hat lady already.

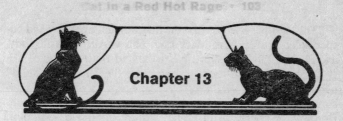

Chapter 13

The League of Extraordinary Gentlewomen

Temple arrived back on the main floor ready to rumba and roll.

An unknown woman in a purple micro-fiber knit pants suit and a red pillbox hat covered with matching feathers headed toward her.

"Pink Hat with the pink marabou band?"

"Yes."

"All right." She turned and nodded to the massing red-and-purple feathered mob. Several separated from the flock, tossing their red or purple, or red-*and*-purple, feather boas over their shoulders.

Temple felt like a wimpy, skinny, young pink person surrounded by a queenly moat of P and Rs, as she decided to call the Red Hat Sisterhood colors for short.

"This is super-secret," said the first woman, a chubby and bespectacled brunet. "I'm Mary Lou. This is Alice, Starla, Judy, and Phyllis, Phyll for short. We're the Red-Hatted League."

Temple expected them to burst into the "Lollipop Guild" number from *The Wizard of Oz*. She was a very puzzled newcomer to this colorful kingdom of exotically attired women: Dorothy, of course. And Louie was the right size and color, if not species and temperament, for Toto. All the scene needed was a witch or two, good and bad. Temple had a feeling they were already milling among the colorful crowd.

"The Red-Hatted League," Temple repeated. "Electra said that was the name of her Red Hat Sisterhood chapter. Um . . . wasn't that a Sherlock Holmes story or something?"

Alice, a tall, angular blonde, tipped her red-and-purple hound's-tooth-pattern deerstalker hat. "No. That story was 'The Red-*Headed* League.' We're told that phrase has some special significance for you," she added.

"Yes." Temple looked around for eavesdroppers. Only Red Hat Sisterhood members filled the lobby, embracing, comparing clothes and insignia, cooing. Looking harmless.

Don't believe it! Temple told herself. The whole point of this organization was that midlife and beyond women weren't inactive, weren't invisible, and weren't the harmless biddies some people liked to think and say they were.

"Yes," Temple repeated. "I used to be a natural redhead, and soon hope to be one again. At least my current blond hair doesn't clash with the convention reds. How did Electra get the word out to you all so fast?"

Starla, who resembled an aging chorus girl (in other words, she would look sexy at any age), hoisted a—what else?—purple cell phone.

"We're all wired, inspired, and ready to kick criminal butt. I used to be a bounty hunter in my younger days."

Phyllis did *not* look hot, but she did look like the world's most efficient librarian with her gray hair in a bun under her scarlet marabou-edged bridesmaid hat. She pulled a P and R folder from her P and R tote bag.

"And I was a dispatcher for the police department while

getting my library degree. I copied the registrants and guest list from the computer at convention central and copied it for everyone. Here also are copies of the various official badges, in case you spot any phonies wandering around. I have everyone's cell phone number but yours, Miss Barr, including my old pal Morrie Alch's. If you'll give us yours now—"

Temple watched five red ballpoint pens topped with long purple ostrich plumes drawn from Red Hat Sisterhood tote bags in unison like Musketeer dueling swords.

She stuttered her phone number and it was duly copied down on the various sheets. Phyllis handed her a set, with her own cell number added.

"Judy and I have already fanned out and gathered info about the vic and her chapter."

Temple eyed Phyll and Judy, a feminine version of Mutt and Jeff: Judy was a tall, thin woman in drapey red ankle-length gown and vest. Some might call her homely and others dignified; Phyll was gray-haired and brisk. On the other hand, Mary Lou was a rhinestone cowgirl: short, curvy, and all fake fingernails (R and P, of course), tight purple jeans, and red jeans jacket, slathered with appropriately colored rhinestones.

"We'd better talk in private," Temple decided, hustling them to the first-floor conference room Nicky had assigned to her during the conference.

A Fontana brother, probably . . . Emilio, stood guard, a single gold ear stud the only visible metal on his person, although the concealed Beretta elsewhere was what would alert a metal detector. There weren't any of those here . . . yet.

"Ladies," he said with an appreciative bow, opening the door to usher them all inside.

And didn't they love that! As a matter of fact, Temple did too. There was no resisting a Fontana brother with his hot young *GQ* looks and his elaborate Old World ways.

"Love the hair," he whispered under Temple's hat. "And the lid."

She was last in the room and the women were still cooing over Emilio.

"Do you know him?" Starla asked.

"He's a brother of the hotel owner. They sometimes work security here."

"A boyfriend?" buxom Mary Lou asked coyly, all her rhinestones twinkling like a flutter of winks.

"Not mine." Max flashed through her mind. Not a boyfriend anymore. An ex. Don't waffle. Move on.

"I'm . . . I'm engaged."

She heard her own words with an inner gasp. She *was* engaged. To a man who would marry her at the drop of a red hat at any Vegas chapel. The thought took her breath away.

Her announcement brought a half-dozen murmurs of congratulations and as many surreptitious glances at her left hand.

"I'm not wearing my ring here. I don't want to attract any attention."

"That big a ring, huh?" Starla's purple-shaded eyelids lifted.

"Not that," she said, although it was that. Partly. "Nobody knows yet, not even Electra. I wanted to surprise her, now—"

"Now," said Phyll, sitting at the conference table and whipping out a notebook, "we need to make sure our founder isn't facing a murder one rap."

"Electra is your founder?"

"Right," Judy said, sitting and still looking as tall as a stork. "Electra brought us together for our love of mysteries, but the fact was, we were all retired or semiretired and lacking things to do. Many of us don't have husbands or adult children in the area. The Red Hat Sisterhood is our support group. Now Electra needs our support and she's going to get it."

"Amen," said Phyll. "You're the shamus here. Electra's told us all about your cases, every one. Just tell us what to do."

In no time, Temple was gazing at a conference table ringed by very silly hats with very serious women under them.

Talk about undercover operatives!

"All right," she said. "First, I want to know about the, er, vic." These dames were more up on crime TV slang than she was.

Judy flipped back about twenty notebook pages. The Red-Hatted League had been busy.

"Oleta Lark. Member of the Reno Scarlet Women chapter for six years. Ex-wife of Elmore, 'the rotten dickhead.'"

Temple almost choked on the news. Oleta was an ex herself? This put things on a whole new level. Judy was so tall and ethereal-looking to be laying down such blunt terms. "Um, ladies, ah, Judy. Who said that?"

"All her chapter members reported she said that, all the time."

"Is he living?"

"If you could call a rented room by the week at the Araby Motel living."

"The Araby Motel? In town here? How'd you find that out?"

"Oleta's hateful remarks about Elmore got us curious," Phyll said. "Never get a librarian on your tail. We easily got an address in Reno, but I decided to check every hotel/motel along the Strip, starting at the bottom. Saved me a lot of checking. He's been in town for a week."

"So he's essentially a recent Las Vegas resident?" Darla asked.

"He's also Electra's ex-husband," Temple announced.

"No!" Alice started scribbling furiously in her notebook. "One of us had better check out the Araby Motel and Mr. Double X in person."

"Two of you," Temple cautioned. "And take a Fontana brother with you. Pick one you like the looks of and go."

This caused a ripple of anticipation among the feathered hat brims.

"There are *more* Fontana brothers?" Starla batted metallic purple false eyelashes.

"Several," Temple admitted. "Just ask Emilio outside for a name. Tell him where you're going, and why, and that I said you need an escort. Alice and Mary Lou, you'd better do that."

There were pouts all around the table, but not on Alice and Mary Lou.

"Meanwhile," Temple said, "what else do we know about the victim?"

"Well—" Phyll leaned forward. Her tone was the familiar

one of a woman letting her hair, or hat, down to give the real story.

"Oleta Lark had written a memoir, her local chapter tells me. About her lousy life, before and after Elmore Lark. A New York publisher was willing to pay big bucks, she said, but it was going to investigate her, now that everybody knows people make up things about their lives, as why wouldn't we? Given how boring things can be?"

"Any copies of this memoir?" Temple asked.

"Large chunks of it on e-mail, to assorted Red Hat Sisterhood members. Nobody knows who all was on the list, but there were a lot of them."

"I suppose her friends were encouraging her."

"Right. And she was leading them on with juicy detail after juicy detail."

"Like what?" Temple said.

"This isn't good for Electra."

"Like what?" Temple said in a sterner tone. "We have to investigate, whoever it hurts. Or seems to. The truth is like the Lone Ranger. It's always out there, it's often masked, and it always sets you free."

"Oh, that's deep," Starla breathed.

"Not really," Temple said modestly. "What was in her memoirs about Electra?"

Judy cleared her throat. "I've interviewed several e-mail recipients. Oleta said Electra couldn't give Elmore the hot sex life he needed. That she cared more about their son and was always after him to father the kid. I guess Elmore was a wild and crazy guy. Party animal."

"No doubt that's where he met Oleta." Starla pronounced *"Oh-leeet-ah"* in an exaggerated catty tone.

Everybody laughed.

Not Temple. If the dead woman was running Electra down not only in her memoirs, but in leaks to other Red Hat Sisterhood members, that only upped the ante on Electra's being a credible suspect.

"And then there's that reference to Oleta having married a bigamist," Phyll said.

"A bigamist? Let me see that e-mail."

This was bad. Bigamy, and exposing it, was no laughing matter. It affected a lot more people than the victim and perp.

Such as her dear landlady who was soon to find out that her long-gone ex may not be an ex.

Chapter 14

Film Noir

The meeting with the Red-Hatted League had Temple walking on figurative Airsteps instead of Argenti for a change. That was an investigative team!

She merged with all the other hatted women milling in the lobby, jazzed by their energy and verve.

Kit, a symphony in lavender and pink, came skittering up to Temple like a glamorous water bug.

"Kiddo! I've got a hot lead."

"I'm all hat."

"There's a woman here."

"No kidding."

"And she's *filming* the event."

"Filming?"

"Yes. You get it. She might have filmed something suspicious. She might have even filmed the murder."

"Wouldn't she know it?"

"That's just it. She's running around with this cute little camcorder in front of God and Her Royal High-Hatness and all, but she's *also* carrying a tote bag big enough to smuggle in a Spielberg track camera."

"And you think—?"

"I think the cute kitty-eye on that bag front could go head-to-head with your Midnight Louie."

"Another camera? A hidden camera?"

"You ever see TV news show exposés? Besides, I've seen the indie filmmakers use that trick dozens of times, when they want 'authenticity.' It's very easy to record people surreptitiously nowadays."

"Why would she do this?"

"You're the shameless shamus, not me. Find out. Anyway, I'm due for a drink with Aldo in the Crystal Court."

"How will I recognize her?" Temple asked, eyeing the sea of red hats surrounding them, along with islands of pink.

"She's wearing the uniform, although her colors are burgundy and eggplant, but her shoes are green snakeskin platform espadrilles. So appropriate, I suspect. You're the shoe maven. Follow the green snakeskin road."

Kit dashed away like she had someone tall, dark, and handsome . . . and Italian to meet.

Temple sighed. She had someone tall, blond, and handsome . . . and betrothed to meet. When she could get away from this chaos.

So she did what she did best, wandered and looked hard.

Most of the footwear here was low, well padded, and comfortable. Red Hat Sisters had pizzazz, but they weren't fashion victims.

Temple's heart thrummed to the thrill of the hunt when she spied a pair of hot pink Ferragamos, but that was just Savannah Ashleigh doing her media thing.

Green. Either Irish or jealous. Or both.

It took a couple of hours of dedicated foot watching for Temple to find the shoes in question.

The woman wearing them was the incarnation of Little Mary Sunshine. Everywhere she went, her cooing voice coaxed celebrating women into standing and delivering a great group shot.

And every group shot was backgrounded by something not so wonderful.

Like HRH getting into a face-to-face with a *Vanity Fair* magazine interviewer who was obviously gay in the Truman Capote mode. Seeing over-the-top females and flagrantly gay men together made Temple wonder why some gay men identified with often-troubled ultra-female women divas like Elizabeth Taylor and Marilyn Monroe. And they all made great drag queens.

Maybe because being "different" was a universal badge. And expressing yourself completely was only human.

Even Electra had been "different" for her time. She'd pulled loose from a bunch of husbands and had ended up running her own unique little world off the Strip here in Las Vegas.

Aha! There were those grass-green snakeskin six-inch-high platform espadrilles again!

Temple dodged out from the mob and turned on the threadbare charm for Snakeskin Stilts.

"Hi, there. I'm a local PR woman. You seem to have a good handle on this event. What's your secret?"

"Empathy," said the woman, turning and scanning behind Temple as if expecting a network camera to be focused upon her. "Isn't empathy always the secret in the media game?"

"Or the scam."

"Aren't you the little cynic?"

Temple hated it when taller, older women pointed out her size.

"My name is Temple Barr. I really need to ask you some questions someplace quiet."

"Around here?"

"How about the Crystal Court bar? I bet you could stand to get off those high-rise shoes. I know I could use a break from mine."

The woman eyed Temple's pink pumps and nodded. Curtly. "Natalie Newman. What's this about?"

"The murder."

"Oh." Natalie was about forty, an angular, skinny woman who adeptly substituted urban chic for natural beauty. "A freelance stringer can always use a lead on murder. Lead me to this island of peace called a bar. It'll probably be standing room only."

It was, except Aldo spotted Temple at the entrance instantly. He abandoned Kit to snag a small table tucked under the Hawaiian-lush greenery that surrounded the bar area.

"Who was that dishy maître d'?" Natalie asked, gluing her eyes to Aldo's back as he left.

"The owner's brother. I do the PR here."

"Why didn't you mention that before, darling?"

Natalie pulled out a gold cigarette holder and matching lighter, then ignited one of those long, slender "women's" cigarettes that always reminded Temple of emaciated tampons.

"You mentioned stringing for someone?" Temple prodded.

"I've reported for the AP, *People*, *Newsweek*, the usual."

The Associated Press and *People* magazine were not the usual print media a regional stringer would work for.

"You're not based in the area?"

"Vegas, are you crazy? No, I'm an East Coast baby. I'm actually a documentary filmmaker, on the side, when I don't need to eat."

"I get that," Temple said as a waiter appeared. She nodded at her guest.

"I'll have a Cosmopolitan." Natalie blew smoke past Temple. "So last wave, but I got hooked on them."

Temple ordered her usual white wine spritzer. It would taste like Chablis-flavored Kool-Aid, but that was the point. PR people really shouldn't slosh down the liquor, not on the job.

"So some TV folks are interested in this Red Hat Sisterhood convention?" Temple asked.

"Not directly. I'm hoping. You know, freelance."

Temple nodded sympathetically, but those green snakeskin platform espadrille shoes had her suspicions set on "liar alert." The shoes, and especially the tote bag Kit had so astutely mentioned. Temple was a tote bag addict herself, but hers was crammed and messy.

Natalie's seemed heavy to sling around, but betrayed no overflow of tissues, breath mints, morning papers, scarves etc. And that one eye of the cat in the red hat on the front looked pretty glassy. Like a lens. Why would a newsie, freelance or not, video record *two* versions of a convention? One upfront and obvious, the other concealed?

Their drinks arrived, giving them both sipping time to regroup.

"What do you think of this Red Hat phenomenon?" Temple asked. People always liked to air their own opinions.

"You said it. It's a phenom. Plus it's colorful. Look at all the local TV crews around. Great for a minute-ten on the evening news. Women making spectacles of themselves is always good copy in the good old U.S. of A."

Temple sipped, weighing that comment. It could be worldly. It could be bitter.

"These women seem to be having something we all could use."

"Cocaine?" Natalie lifted penciled eyebrows.

"I meant fun."

"Well, aren't they the same thing? Listen, Temple, you seem like a nice working girl. Wanna bet that you'll be up to something a bit more serious when you're their age?"

"Sure, it's fun and games. And that's pretty healthy for the aging population. But there's more. Read the press kit. The chapters also join marathons to raise money for breast cancer and visit nursing homes—"

"Single-handedly save the ancient profession of clown. You've obviously gone over to it above your eyebrows." She nodded at Temple's beautiful hat.

"This is to blend in, but what's wrong with it? Men are going to say older women are silly anyway. Why not enjoy the bad rap? Why not reverse it? Embrace it? Disarm the opposition?"

"Now you're talking old-style civil protest. Face it; in this day and age, the only thing that counts is what gets on the media. And that's me, baby; that's me."

Boy, did this woman make Temple see red without even looking around. Still, she needed to pretend to be a media-savvy peer. To be someone Natalie Newman might be able to use, because that's what would keep this so-called stringer on a string.

"The Red Hat Sisterhood," Temple said, "is lucky to have the kind of national attention you can get them."

"Damn right! And they won't know how much until this convention is long past."

A pair of bright red spots on Natalie's cheeks revealed that the Cosmopolitan was getting to her discretion. Her words implied that she had something very different in mind than what she claimed.

Temple tried to calm her anger. This group meant a lot to Electra, and now she was in serious trouble. Temple had never found Electra clownish because she sprayed her white hair fun colors or wore tropical print muumuus. Las Vegas was a place that allowed for a lot of diversity.

She didn't mind a bit when Natalie lurched up on her reptilian stilts, grabbed her bigger-than-Temple's tote bag, and swaggered away.

Chapter 15

No Longer in Service

After Natalie left, Temple stayed at the table and speed-dialed Max's number again.

She didn't really expect him to answer, Mr. Invisible now turned Mr. AWOL, but then she heard that wailing banshee yowl over the line. Temple's stomach plunged into the Pit of Despair. An unreal female voice said that she was sorry, but that this number was no longer in service.

No longer in service?

Temple had been worried about not making contact with Max. Now she was sick-anxious.

She redialed. Listened again to the impossible message. Checked the stupid little LED numbers with slashes through zeroes that made them look like eights, so maybe somehow the wrong number had been entered on her speed-dial. Right.

No, everything was correct. She knew this number by heart.

By heart.

But maybe she didn't deserve to know it anymore. Maybe that alone was the message. Max had cut her off.

"Temple?"

Kit and Aldo were standing by her table, then Kit saw Temple's face and took Natalie's vacant seat, and Temple's hand.

"Temple, honey, what did that tacky woman say to you?"

"Lots of stuff, but that's not it. Kit, Max's number is disconnected."

Kit got it. Her other hand clenched Temple's arm. "Oh, no!"

"Max," Aldo asked. "Your Max?"

Not anymore. Temple tried to swallow a sob and ended up hiccuping.

"Don't say another word," Kit told Aldo. "Just listen and let me handle this. Honey. Temple. Numbers get changed all the time."

"But it rang through the whole time. He hasn't been answering for the past three days!"

"You said yourself he's been juggling a whole lot of career obligations."

Like saving her bacon on the last PR job? Temple thought.

Aldo had been listening to all this in affable Fontana brother mode: laid-back, but with a don't-tread-on-me air, and decorative in the extreme. Now he shot his jacket sleeves in preparation for extreme action.

"Where does he live?" he asked Temple.

"In town, but it's . . . a secret."

"Not if the number is disconnected. I'll drive you there."

"In the Viper?"

"It's my car."

"It doesn't have room for three passengers."

"I'll drive *you* to this secret place. Your delicious aunt will wait here to thank me properly when we get back. You can trust my discretion, because I myself have a lot to be discreet about, right?"

"Aldo—" Temple didn't know what to say. "You are a brick."

The British expression zinged right past him. "No, I'm Italian."

Kit rolled her eyes as Aldo ordered her a second Pink Lady cocktail, kissed her hand, and murmured indecipherable promises that made the tiny hairs on Temple's neck perk up with interest, and she was not only firmly unavailable, but under severe emotional distress.

Then Aldo took Temple's arm and hustled her out the hotel entrance faster than a house detective escorting a lady of the night off the premises.

The parking valet already had the low black sports car growling at the entrance portico, so Temple had the whole ride to berate herself for being a Weepy Worried Wanda.

"You're the Fontana who owns the Viper," she finally said to make talk.

"No, this is the, er, Family car."

"How do you arrange who drives it when?"

"Not the car, the model."

"You mean you *all* drive Vipers?"

"All but Nicky. He's a family man now. He drives a Land Rover." Aldo made a face that screamed "canned ravioli."

"The Fontana brothers run a fleet of Vipers? Isn't that a bit"—she hated to use this word with a Fontana, just in case it really applied—"overkill?"

"Not at all. It gives us an instantly recognizable presence in the community. Sometimes you want people to see you coming and . . . sometimes you don't. Then we drive Saturns."

Awesome. She'd never thought of the Fontana brothers as "Enforcement R Us."

"Besides," Aldo said, the gold hinges of his designer sunglasses glinting as he turned the car onto Max's street, "the ladies like it. This the place?"

"Almost."

Temple clutched her tote bag. Max would kill her for leading a Fontana brother here, leading anyone here. Then again, maybe she'd *get* him killed by coming here now.

What made her think that, other than insane worry?

Aldo was not impressed by the surroundings. "Jeez-Luisa, this neighborhood doesn't look like it needs to be kept secret. It looks like an accountant lived here." He eyed Temple over his glasses frames. "*Your* accountant. Not our accountant."

"I don't have an accountant," she answered. And maybe she didn't have an ex-boyfriend either.

Aldo walked around the parked car and bent to spring Temple from the black leather passenger seat. This was a car that would fry you alive in Las Vegas, but apparently Aldo kept the air-conditioning blasting as much as the multispeaker sound system that had been blaring Italian opera all the way. One more sorrowful aria from *Pagliacci* or Pavarotti and Temple would strangle the nearest tenor.

Aldo followed her clicking heels up the familiar sidewalk.

"No uncollected milk bottles on the doorstep," he mentioned.

"Nobody delivers milk anymore."

"That's my point. So why is that black cat lurking in the Hollywood twist, then?" Aldo, well, pointed.

"Louie!" Temple gasped, glimpsing a dark feline face in the door-side plantings.

Except it wasn't Louie, but a fluffier, younger version of Louie. The gold eyes gave it away.

"Looks like the black cat that hangs out at the Crystal Phoenix," Aldo said. "Of course, all black cats look alike."

As if Fontana brothers didn't?

"Maybe it's an omen," Temple said.

"Aw, Miss Temple. Tell me you're not superstitious?"

Aldo escorted her by the elbow up the rest of the walk.

"Watch it!" He seized her to a stop. "There's a crack. You don't wanna break your mama's back. Especially *my* mama's back. Any more than you wanna shave her mustache." He glanced at her dumbstruck face. "Just kidding. Trying to jolly you up. You are getting grimmer than a grandma at a mob funeral these days."

Lord, she wasn't even a peri-menopausal woman and here was a man comparing her to his grandma! Kit had been right: all downhill from thirty. Except for the Red Hat ladies and her red hot aunt.

"So," Aldo asked, standing in front of Max's ultra-secure door like the pale ghost of Fuller Brush salesman from the days when housewives were at home and hucksters went from door to door instead of unsolicited e-mail to e-mail. "This is where the Mystifying Max hides out. He had the coolest disappearing onstage act in town."

Temple quailed at that "had," but rang the doorbell.

Need any red-feather dusters here? Beat-up Purple Hearts still beating? A memory-erasing vacuum that really doesn't work very well? All returns guaranteed.

But nothing happened, which was a huge relief to Temple. The house was unoccupied. Quiet. Empty. The way Max had designed it to be seen forever. A movie-set facade that only the initiated could see behind.

Temple was sure she wasn't the initiated anymore.

And then the faceless front door opened.

"Yes? You *did* read the NO SOLICITING sign out front?"

Temple was speechless.

Speechless.

"So sorry, miss," Aldo said in whipped-cream-on-cappuccino tones. "We were seeking the previous resident."

"I have no idea who that was, handsome. The Realtor found me this perfect place and the price was so very right that I couldn't refuse."

Temple had used Aldo's charm time to survey the apparent new owner: a leggy brunette about six feet tall with a dangerously curved figure that screamed "showgirl." She was not only stunned, but madly jealous. Go figure.

"Ah," Temple managed. "So you've only been here—"

"A week, sweets. I got this place at a bargain bistro price, and wasn't gonna waste time taking possession before somebody recovered their sanity."

"Was the previous owner . . . was the furniture—?"

"Clean as Whistler's mother."

"No . . . equipment in the extra bedroom?"

"No, I brought my own home gym."

Temple had been thinking of Gandolph the Great's and Max's retired magic props. "No opium bed in the north bedroom?"

"Hey, I don't do anything heavier than Starbucks, sweetie. You want to come in and sit a bit? You look a lot green around the gills."

"That would be very nice." Aldo grabbed Temple's elbow and swept them both inside, understanding that any peek inside would be insightful. "Miss, uh—?"

"French. Dolly French."

Oh, please! Temple thought. Pseudonym City in a city made for phony monikers.

The woman batted her double-wide false eyelashes at Aldo. "And you and your lady friend?"

"Aldo Fontana, at your service, Miss French." He somehow made "French" sound mildly obscene, which of course the rest of the world had been doing for centuries. "Miss Temple Barr is an employee of my"—Aldo cleared his throat like an operatic baritone—"Family."

"Say, I've heard of you Fontana brothers. Want a drink? Your brother's employee looks like she could use one."

"That would be delightful. Would you permit me to mix it?"

"I'd permit you to do a lot of things."

While this B-movie dialogue was unrolling, Temple'd had time to eye the premises. Oh, man! Oh, Max! Everything was gone. Every bit of furniture or wall decor that she knew. Even the super-security touches, like metal interior shutters, were only a dream in Temple's head.

She toddled after Aldo into the kitchen, which was the whole point in him playing bartender: seeing more of the house.

The stainless-steel appliances and countertops were the same, but the high stools were a whole different breed and the stone floor now echoed to Dolly French's stilettos stomping around on them.

"You in the entertainment biz, sweetie?"

"No, public relations."

Dolly stopped on a dime, holding three footed glasses expertly in one long-clawed hand and a bottle of vodka in the other.

"Not that kind of public relations," Temple said through her teeth. "I represent the Crystal Phoenix hotel's publicity and promotional interests."

It was all some ghastly nightmare. A familiar place taken over by unfamiliar things and people. How could what Orson Welles, Garry Randolph, aka Gandolph the Great, and Max Kinsella had created here become so quickly a staging area for a stereotypical Las Vegas woman of iffy morals?

Aldo, as cool as Italian . . . gelato, was making some sort of stirred not shaken martini and trying to catch Temple's eye with sympathy, and caution.

"Did you know," Temple heard herself saying, "that this house originally belonged to Orson Welles?"

"Orson who?"

"He was a boy genius, a noted gourmand, writer, and film director. But he's dead now, of course."

"I thought you said his first name was Orson?" Dolly blinked her fuzzy lashes.

"I did."

"Now you're saying it was 'Ormand'? Isn't that French?"

Ormand Welles. Well, it had a Las Vegas ring to it.

Ring. She thought of Max's little emerald one tucked into her scarf drawer now that she was otherwise "engaged," and the gorgeous one she'd forced Matt to hide in a floor safe because she wasn't ready to come out as his fiancé.

Maybe now was the time to "ring" in the new, "ring" out the old. Max was gone. Only her memories of Max in this house remained.

It was as if a brutal hand had erased everything here in the most hurtful, sweeping way to make her face the facts, and the present, not the past.

Nothing here to cling to, but regret. She sipped the drink Aldo had made while he "allowed" Dolly French to take him on a guided tour of the house. Temple kept staring at the Sub-Zero refrigerator like the Abominable Snowman it was: a lurking vision in a mist, once an old friend, but now mostly an old and fading legend.

"Max, wherefore are thou, Max?"

He had appeared in her life in another place at another time like an answer to a dream. Now the dream had ended, and Max was gone. All trace of him. The perfect exit for a magician.

Maybe she'd better get used to life without everyday magic. Maybe she'd better concentrate on making sure Electra didn't face a nightmare of her own too real to write off.

Electra's Larks

The Circle Ritz penthouse where Electra lived and presided always felt like it was off-limits, even when you were expected.

Temple had only been up here a few times, so she knocked gingerly on the door, then rang the doorbell right after that, convinced that her petite knuckles wouldn't rouse a flea.

The door jerked open to reveal Electra back to wearing her usual wildly floral muumuu.

"What's happening at the convention?" she asked.

"Not much," Temple said. "There's more going on in that hot jungle print you're wearing."

"I don't feel up to wearing imperial purple at the moment. But you look pretty in pink. You never used to wear that color."

"I wasn't planning on masquerading as a Pink Hatter before, and it never went with my natural red hair color."

"It goes great with your new blond do. Come in, dear."

Electra's entry hall was a hexagonal affair lined in mirrored blinds, so multiple muumuus greeted Temple's eyes. Also multiples of her still foreign-looking blond self.

Maybe if she dyed her hair back to its natural red shade, she'd find Max. That was superstitious thinking, but desperate people turn to symbolic notions.

Temple passed herself coming and going in the mirrored blind slats. Now that she was clad in Pink Lady hues she looked as nauseatingly sweet as a tropical drink to a beer buff.

Electra's living room was the usual dim and mysterious, not to mention occupied by hulking pieces of forties-vintage furniture.

Temple loved vintage, but one had to draw the line somewhere, and for her, oversize forties jungle florals in shades of forest-green and chartreuse were it.

She sat gingerly on the only floral-free chair in the room, a plain maroon mohair lounge chair. Mohair was a stiff, buzz-cut wool texture as welcoming to the epidermis as falling into a native stake pit.

Electra sat with a grateful "*oof* " on the long lumbering sofa hunched against the wall. Lights were dim here, but a green glint caromed off the huge glass ball sitting atop the vintage blond-wood TV set. A pair of small, eerie red lights blinked like Christmas bulbs at Electra's ankles.

Since this was firmly spring, as much as Las Vegas ever admitted to such a pleasant, moderate season, Temple assumed the red lights were the reflective eyes of Electra's psychotically shy cat, Karma, the mystic Birman.

Come to think of it, the atmosphere up here was thick enough to slice with a chain saw. Electra might very well be a Las Vegas strangler with a gender-bending mission . . . Instead of the literal lady-killer Bluebeard, she could be a blue-haired lady killer of husbands.

"Did you get the family tree written down?"

"I tried, but I just can't concentrate enough right now. Finding a dead woman, even if she turned out to be someone I had no sympathy for, is very discombobulating."

Temple picked up the notepad and pen that Electra had only managed to doodle on.

"Okay. We'll do this as an interview. You said you had five husbands." Temple asked, pen poised, "Where are they all now?"

"Goodness, dear, I don't know! What's the point of leaving them if they're still on your Christmas card list?"

"You must have known Elmore and Oleta were in Reno, though."

"Nope." Electra gazed at the green globe over the dead TV as the red lights danced at her ankle level. "He was easy to forget."

"I imagine most of them were, from what you said, but I need to know the who, where, and when on all of them."

"Not the why, though?"

"No. That would be prying," Temple said demurely, as befitted a Pink Lady.

As soon as she got through with this convention she was going to ditch this ditzy hat for something red, even if it was a wig the color of her real hair.

"I'm glad you're leaving something for me to have and to hold," Electra said dryly. "Just how serious do you think this being under suspicion is for me?"

"Very. It turns out your next Mrs. Lark was writing a memoir and mailing bits and pieces all over the Internet."

"What would Oleta have to write about? Elmore was dull, dull, dull."

"Not according to one tidbit gleaned from Oleta's compulsive Internet confessions, or maybe it was just canny book promotion: she said her long 'marriage' ended when she was abandoned in a ghost town in Nevada by a bigamist."

"Bigamist!" Electra jumped up as the little Rudolph-red noses at her ankles vanished under the sofa's swaying cocoa-colored fringe.

Her shock reassured Temple. She hadn't heard it from Oleta, then.

Electra was still in angry orbit. "Oleta is saying that bastard didn't really divorce me? Where is he? I'll kill him now if she didn't do the job first before coming here."

"Am I glad this is just between us and the fire-eyed feline under the couch, because murder suspects must never threaten to slay new victims in public. Unless you're a third-world dictator. Are you?"

"Of course not? What are you getting at?"

"The fact is, I don't really know anything about your private life. When a murder happens, no life in the vicinity is private anymore. In this case, especially yours."

Electra sat again in the dimness. Her sigh almost stirred the dark floral draperies at the doors to her patio.

"Well, darn, Temple. I came here to forget all about my past life. It wasn't that successful."

"But you're an entrepreneur. You own and operate this building and the attached Lovers' Knot Wedding Chapel. You've got energy, singular style, and tenants who adore you."

"Really, you guys adore me?"

"What's not to adore? You're patient, creative, fun, and always listen. You're our dorm mother."

" 'Dorm mother.' I like that." Electra's hands curled together on her chest.

Temple realized for the first time that she'd never seen any rings, nary a one, on those busy, plump fingers. And here was Temple with a seriously significant ring she wasn't quite ready to flash, like a novice stripper with a G-string and no nerve to wear it. At least Temple had a couple thoroughly painful thong panties in her lingerie drawer.

"You already know Elmore was number three," Electra was saying in a monotone, subdued voice. "You put that in your notebook. I never bothered to write any of this down—unlike dear, dead Oleta!"

"Whenever you talk to the police again, none of these theatrics. Pretend you're a Stepford wife. Only say what you have to and without any emotion whatsoever."

"When, not if?"

"When, not if, Electra. You were too darn convenient to the

body. Somebody else probably figured that out too. But don't worry, the Red-Hatted League is on it."

"I want to be there *with* them!"

"We'll see." Temple found the pen slipping between her fingers and rolling under the sofa fringe. "Electra, what *is* that under your couch?"

Electra looked down. "Ah, besides dust bunnies? Maybe my cat, Karma."

"Is she declawed?"

"Never!"

"Thanks, I guess I won't risk patting around down there in the dark. I'll try to remember what you say and write this down later."

"Try to re-mem-ber," Electra quavered in a thready soprano.

"Husband number one," Temple demanded.

"I've never really counted him."

"Electra!"

"That's what we girls did in my day, my dear. We either married any man who ever kissed us, or we never married at all and got known as hippies. Darren and I eloped in senior year of high school, and he then further eloped with a bottle of rye a few weeks later. I've never seen or heard from him again, and am the better for it. I don't think that minister was real, anyway, and I never thought to ask to see the license. Boys would do anything to get into your girdle in those days."

"*Girdle?*"

"Tubes or panties with industrial-strength elastic you had to spend ten minutes getting on. They were tight enough to bite like a snapping turtle, believe me, if any roaming fingertips roamed too far. I didn't lose my virginity until my second husband."

Temple cleared her throat. "Darren must have really liked that bottle. It's awfully dark and hot in here. I may swoon."

"That's all right. All the floors are covered in Persian carpets; lots of nap."

"So who was number two?"

"Another elopement. Billy was a filling station attendant with an urge to—"

"Don't say it!"

"—go to refrigeration school. Between his double shifts, I somehow got left out. I divorced him and I moved yet again to forget."

"And then came Elmore."

"Not a moment too soon. I actually had delusions about him."

"You mean 'illusions.' "

"No, just delusions. I had so many delusions that Curtiss actually came along a full nine months after them. I really enjoyed being a housewife and mother. Elmore was always on the road, selling insurance policies. Curtiss and I had six happy years together before Elmore came home one day and said he'd found another woman. What he'd meant was that a conniving cheerleader had found him and his house payment and steady job and little family to fling out on the stoop."

"That was Oleta."

"Yup. She always was a little—"

"I get the picture," Temple said quickly, trying to evade hearing another rough word from her landlady's mouth: slut.

"—snip. That's why I kept the last name 'Lark.' Just to annoy her. And it did."

"Why? You had moved on to Vegas and the Elmore Larks were in Florida."

"By then, I was old enough to start getting mad about being betrayed."

Temple bit her lip and thought about feeling like a betrayer, which she did now. She'd always taken Electra at face value as a free spirit. She'd never guessed how many decades it had taken her to get that way.

"Men and women," Temple said, "seem to have a hard time getting in sync with each other in any era."

Electra's face lost its pained, in-the-past expression and resumed the sweetly sharp look Temple knew so well. And relied upon. She was two thousand miles away from her mother, but they'd never quite evolved into girl talk, anyway. Kit and Electra made excellent stand-ins.

Electra pursed her lips, as if to say: *Enough about my little murder rap and me.* "You care to discuss what's happening on the Max-Matt front? I've been dying to know. Really. Dying."

Temple didn't care to, but she could feel herself blushing, which was a dead giveaway in a modern girl that *something* was happening.

"How much do you know?"

"I'm a landlady. I always know more than I'm supposed to."

Temple nodded and wished she'd been an old-fashioned girl with a handkerchief to knot.

"I know," Electra said, "that our darling boy Matt Devine has made major updates to his bedroom decor. About time! And that you've been up there admiring the changes."

"Electra!"

She shrugged. "You've always had an interest in interior design. And I know Max hasn't been around lately. Except for the time he called and you weren't in, so he took me for a ride on the Vampire."

Temple was stunned silent. Max had been *here,* at the Circle Ritz? Recently? When she hadn't been? And he'd taken Electra for a ride on the vintage motorcycle he had traded to Electra for a down payment on the Circle Ritz unit back when he and Temple had been almost-marrieds?

"The Vampire," Temple repeated. "Max took you out on the Vampire?"

"You weren't here at the time, dear," Electra said gently. "I think . . . I think it was a farewell spin; that I do. He's a knight, Max, in shining midnight-black. Can give an old lady a thrill ride as well as a young one. And, I admit, I was thrilled."

"When? What day?"

"Why, I don't quite remember. Maybe four or five days ago. It felt like a sentimental journey, and I'm sure he'd have much rather had you riding pillion. But you weren't here."

And now Max was not "here" at all.

Temple tried to make sense of the timeline. Did Max have time to squire Electra around on the Vampire and still shut down his house, sell it? Or had all that happened before he came back to the Circle Ritz for one last dashing surprise visit?

Only . . . Temple hadn't been there to be surprised, or kissed good-bye, or driven around the block. So Electra got it in her place: the cryptic, fond farewell. All Max, only Max, all the time.

"Temple. Dear. It's not all tragedy. Haven't you and Matt been—?"

"Yes. But it's tragedy if I never see Max again."

"I've never seen most of my husbands again." Electra leaned back into the sofa. "And you and Matt?"

Temple gave a deep sigh. "We may want a Lovers' Knot ceremony sometime soon."

"No! Really? I'm honored."

"Electra, Max is missing."

"Wasn't he always?"

"Not like this. For real! As far as I know, you're the last person to see him."

She got it immediately. "*Me,* not you."

Temple nodded.

"Then he doesn't know about you and Matt?"

"He's Max. He knew about me and Matt before me and Matt knew about us."

"That makes it worse."

"Right." Temple leaned forward and knotted her hands together. "I don't feel right about this. This is not the way Max would have bowed out, and I think he was probably ready to bow out."

"He was a little . . . the last time I saw him," Electra admitted.

"A little what?"

"A little . . . nostalgic." Electra leaned forward to take Temple's hands in hers. "Listen, hon. If Max is as omniscient as you think he is, there's nothing you could do that surprises him. Maybe this was his graceful exit, like Sherlock Holmes falling into Reichenbach Falls. Maybe he thought people would want to forget about him."

"Like we could?"

Electra shook Temple's intertwined fingers. "He knows that. He knows that he'll be resurrected, that we won't stand for him being gone. Not even you and Matt. He'll come to your wedding. Trust me. He could never resist a surprise appearance."

Temple sighed, shakily. Electra was right. You had to have faith in Max. That was what made him such a peerless magician. Now you see him, now you don't. But you will.

"Meanwhile," Temple said, "we've got to deal with your crisis."

"Right. So how is he?"

"Who? Max? I told you, I don't know and it's driving me crazy."

"No. Matt! I don't know and it's driving me crazy."

"He's fine. He's still here."

"No, I meant, how's he in bed?"

"Electra!"

She shrugged. "It was a natural question, given his priestly history."

"I'm not asking you how Elmore Lark was in bed. Not that I'd ever want to know."

"It's no secret. He wasn't, so there's nothing to tell."

"You must have slept with him to have a son from the marriage."

Electra pulled a face. "No, I was not a virgin bride in that instance. Curtiss was the only good thing that came out of that marriage. With the next husband, Gerry, I got a herpetologist."

"As in helping people with herpes?"

"No. As in snakes. I have a daughter with a fascination for reptiles. Now it's her career. Maybe she was trying to tell me something about my choice of husbands."

"So there was Darren, Billy, Elmore, Gerry . . . who else, and any more kids?"

"Weldon the Winn-Dixie manager and Tom, who couldn't even manage to hold a job. Terra in Indianapolis is a teacher and Rob in St. Louis is a car mechanic. Curtiss sells insurance in Tucson, which is lucrative. Sandy's the herpetologist in Texas. All grown and good kids and nicely on their own. They can't believe I married such a string of losers, though."

"In which case, you could be a suspect in a lot of deaths."

"No. The only one of my exes I might wish dead is that jerk Elmore. But I suppose I should wish him far away so I'm not tempted to confront the bum." Temple decided against telling Electra that her supposed almost not ex was here in town. She also was glad that she managed to get Electra's always-busy mind off of her and Matt's nocturnal adventures.

Better that she dwell on dead people.

"Can I go back to the convention now, Temple?" Electra inquired in a small wee voice. "I was supposed to be helping with registration."

"I don't see why not. Oleta's dead. How much more trouble could you get into?"

Sob Sister, Soul Brother

Matt was finishing his afternoon laps in the Circle Ritz pool.

One thing he loved about working nights—and there were a lot of things he didn't—was having uncrowded daytime access to things that normally would be unpleasantly crowded. There were usually seven or eight after-work visitors to the pool. Now he had it all to himself.

He'd come here late at night too, before or after his "Midnight Hour" stint, which was now two hours and no longer accurately titled. Temple had recently confessed to watching him then, sometimes. That innocent little voyeuristic admission had been wildly . . . stimulating. But so was everything she said and did these giddy, sexy engagement days and nights.

He was smiling as he swam to the side to pull himself up on the pool's tile edge when he heard the cell phone "ring." Temple had helped him program the call signal, a paid-for download of Bob Dylan's "Forever Young." He liked the way the song echoed the New Testament Beatitudes. Once a priest, always a sucker for biblical phrasing.

Not a lot of people called him. His agent. His immediate boss at WCOO radio. Temple.

So he raced for the cell phone, dripping on the hot concrete, snatching it up from the towel, and sitting on the lounge chair.

"Yes?"

"Matt! I'm so glad I reached you."

He lay back in the soothing sunlight, letting his skin and the sunscreen protecting it soak up rays. "Me too."

"I mean now."

There was more than banter under her words. Matt sat up again. "What's happened?"

"Everything! I'm at the Crystal Phoenix. They're holding a huge convention here, and they almost were holding Electra for murder. I just got back from the Circle Ritz talking to her around two. You weren't there."

"Just got back now myself, in time to slip in some laps before the five o'clock crowd hits the pool."

"Oooh, what are you wearing besides a light tan?"

"Light tan swim trunks."

"Are you alone?"

"Yeah, apparently."

"Could I get you to take them off?"

"Hardly!"

"Phone sex is something we haven't tried yet."

"I can wait."

"Oh, don't mind lascivious me. I'm just trying to take my mind off all the really terrible things that have happened already today."

"Electra, under suspicion of murder? What on earth is that about?"

"It's too hard to explain over the phone: hundreds of women

in red hats, some of them in pink hats. One strangled with a Red Hat lady scarf. Electra found her dead, and the victim happens to be the vixen who stole her third husband thirty years ago."

"I am not following this."

"You don't have to. I'm on it. The Fontana brothers are on it. Our old friends Alch and Su are on it. What's really wigging me out right now, selfish as it is, isn't Electra's and the Crystal Phoenix's PR troubles. It's . . . oh, dammit, Matt. It's Max."

He'd really, really hoped to hear as little of that name as possible.

"I needed to talk to somebody about it, and I know you're the last person I should, but Electra's in no state to deal with my petty problems—"

"I'm the first person you should come to. Always. About anything."

"I know. And I love you for it. Here's the thing. Aldo Fontana, who's dating my aunt Kit, believe it or not, drove me out to Max's top-secret house location this morning."

"I could have done that."

"It just came up. I haven't been able to reach Max by phone for three days. I just wanted to say . . . you know, about us. Sorry, good-bye, and good luck. It seemed the decent thing to do."

"I agree." Of course he'd hoped she'd never see Max Kinsella again, that she'd never want to, but that was totally unrealistic.

"Matt, the house was gone!"

"Gone?"

"Not physically, just all the furniture, everything that was so 'Max' about it. This floozy named French opened the door. She'd bought it at a terrific price a few days ago, she said; moved right in. All her ugly condo unit stuff was everywhere."

"You said he'd been acting . . . distant lately."

"And now Electra just told me that he'd visited the Circle Ritz four or five days ago, but I wasn't here. And then he, he—"

Matt waited for her to battle back tears. His heart was sinking like the *Titanic*. Damn Max Kinsella! He always managed to draw the spotlight, create a scene, make Temple's tender heart ache.

"He . . . took Electra."

Matt waited.

"For a ride."

He waited, not guessing the next line.

"On the Vampire. Way out on the highway, really fast. That was supposed to be me, Matt. But Electra got that last ride. It's as if he was saying good-bye to the Circle Ritz, to the Vampire, to me. And now he's really, really, missing. Not like before, just for a while. And I missed saying good-bye."

Matt waited, but Temple didn't say anything else. Probably couldn't. Okay, Counselor Guy, what do you say to the woman you love and adore when she's cracking up over your rival?

You say to yourself: she came to you with this. And that's a very important thing.

"I'm sorry, Temple. Everything's crashing down all at once for you. But I'm not. I'm here. I'll help you. I'll do whatever it takes to find out what happened to him, if you can't."

"I'm sorry for laying this on you. I've got to go back out here and play perky PR woman with everything in hand, and get Electra off the hot plate on the side. What do you think, though, Matt? Why is Max doing this to me?"

"I think Max is doing what he has to, for those undercover reasons nobody has a need-to-know about. I do think he'd given up on being able to offer you the open commitment you needed. I picked that up from him, lately, you know, an ebbing away. I think he foresaw that we would happen if he stepped out of the picture. I think he let that happen.

"Temple, if you don't mind having Max Kinsella for a matchmaker, I sure don't. Trust the man. You always have."

She laughed, shakily. "Thanks. I told you breaking up was hard to do, I just wish I could do it. Formally. I'll see you, later?"

"Later."

"Sorry to be such a weak sister. I'm lucky I didn't short-circuit this stupid cell phone."

"You can come home and short-circuit me anytime."

She laughed. "Thanks for the motivation. Back to the hubbub and the funny, tragic, lethal human circus."

"Love you."

"Love you too, Matt," she whispered back.

It was some comfort that she'd used his name.

Chapter 18

Vanishing Powder

"It was bad," Miss Midnight Louise says, "very bad."

Well, these girls. Always exaggerating. I cannot believe that Miss Midnight Louise, usually as hard as nails, is even a tad breathless as she reports back to me.

Then again, she has hightailed it from Mr. Max's home on the city fringes back to the Circle Ritz by means of sneaking into the six inches of space behind the passenger seat in Aldo Fontana's Viper.

I am not sure whether it was the squeeze or the speed that put a kink in Miss Midnight Louise's tail. I do know that I am not going to yank her chain farther by asking which.

Either way, she has returned to the Crystal Phoenix agitated and expecting me to do something about it. She does not even care that I have been nosing around her turf in a criminal matter.

We have rendezvoused under the tropical greenery edging the lobby bar.

"Listen," I tell Louise. "The scene of the crime as far as we're concerned is now here at Crystal Phoenix Central. Midnight Inc. Investigations can no longer afford to have you gallivanting from the Neon Nightmare club to former residences of former Miss Temple squeezes when our beloved landlady's reputation and freedom are at stake."

"You mean your Miss Temple's and your landlady. I live here at the Phoenix, thank you. So you are willing to give up on investigating Mr. Max's whereabouts and condition—or lack of living condition—after the terrible impact he made on the Neon Nightmare side wall?"

I am indeed disturbed about that, but I am more concerned right now with restoring the Circle Ritz's landlady's reputation. I have just moved Ma Barker and her gang of feral felines to the Circle Ritz. There is not much sustenance around there unless the place's residents get on with the program. Miss Electra Lark is the best general for the job. Ergo, my task is to get her off the homicide hook.

So I answer Louise in a way to take her mind off the current obsession.

First, I reassure. "Mr. Max knows how to take care of himself and about six others at once, and always has," I say. "And he is forever doing things that are not what they seem. That is the magician's credo." Then I tempt her weakest spot, her curiosity. "Anyway, it does not look like his long frame will be jousting me for comforter space in the future. Miss Temple has embraced the light."

"No! You mean Mr. Matt? He is the best-looking shaded golden human I have ever met, but I think you would dislike seeing a black alpha male unseated from the communal bed, even if you did knock toes and claws sometimes. When did this new set of sleeping arrangements happen?"

"Recently. They conducted their courtship off the premises, but there is a ring with enough carats to keep Bugs Bunny for life and they almost forgot themselves on the zebra-striped comforter in Miss Temple's boudoir the other day. With me in the next room, mind you."

"In the daytime! With you present! That is indeed serious," she agrees. "Mr. Matt is the most diligently serious human being I have ever seen. Does he not require papers and witnesses to take a mate?"

"Oh, they want 'papers' for everything these days, including us. Big Brother is watching even the cockroaches now. But I know how romance can turn a dude's head. And my Miss Temple's head is pretty turned too. Frankly, Mr. Max was not making the scene often enough lately to preserve his territory."

"I am thankful I have been fixed to prevent such unpredictable periods of insanity," Louise sniffs.

Although I always aim to use the utmost courtesy with the females of any species, the chit does claim to be a descendant and has recently forced me into making our purely professional association formal. Midnight Inc. Investigations, of course, is mainly me.

I return to our most satisfying bone of contention.

"So you say that my Miss Temple and Mr. Aldo Fontana paid a visit to the house formerly known as Mr. Max's. And so you saw that it was occupied by some foreign dame with a great figure. So what is new in Las Vegas? The city is all about great figures, on the stage and on the list of house gambling rules."

"That must have been a terrible shock for your roommate. It would be like your returning to the Circle Ritz and finding that no one you knew was there."

"With Miss Electra Lark suspected of murder, that could happen."

"Your Miss Temple would be missing, her furniture gone."

"My living room sofa? The zebra-patterned comforter on the bed? My litter box under the sink in the second bathroom? No!"

"You are certainly the self-sacrificing sort, Pops. And you do not even deign to use the litter box in Miss Temple's digs, which is a mighty inaccurate name for her unit, given your habits."

"Where I go is my business, and my business only."

"Thank goodness," she says, swiping a dainty claw over her

eyebrow hairs. "Anyway, Mr. Footloose and Fancy Free, I am sure you have seen some pretty swift set changes on a Las Vegas hotel stage."

"For sure. And the ones at Mr. Max's magic shows, when he used to perform at the Goliath, were faster than a cardsharp's deal."

"Well, that is the way it was at that house of his. After I checked out the Neon Nightmare from top to bottom and learned some very interesting and alarming things, I nipped over to the house you had told me about."

"Only Miss Temple is supposed to know that address."

"And you? How did you manage that, then?"

"I make it my private business to know where my Miss Temple goes."

"And you dropped mention of it to me."

"When?"

"Long ago, when you were thinking I was a stupid unrelated female and not listening."

"I did not do that!"

"What? Think I was a stupid, unrelated female?"

"No. That 'thinking you were not listening' part."

"Trust me, Daddio. If it were not for you dominant males forgetting to remember that we listen, half the stuff in the world would not happen, except thanks to us stupid unrelated females."

"Louise! I cannot follow your flawed logic, not to mention your Sin Tax."

"I know that Sin Tax is very big in Las Vegas," she answers, exposing her fangs in one of those so-called Cheshire Cat grins that toney Brit cats affect.

"Okay, kiddo," I say, knowing Louise hungers for acknowledgment as a relative of mine. "Tell me what you have learned on your little foray."

Does she bend my ear! And whiskers.

I must admit that I am impressed. Wait! I do not have to admit it, and I do not. I just simply let her spill her guts, as girls will, and will figure out later if she is just dreaming or is really on to something.

It turns out the other half of Midnight Inc. Investigations is all hot and bothered by a whole lot of things I thought only I had discovered and was not worried about. Like, as we have discussed, the fact that the Neon Nightmare club is built like a pyramid-shaped hunk of Swiss cheese, with more hidden rooms and shafts than a pharaoh's funeral home in the Egyptian desert.

It makes sense. Las Vegas sits in the middle of the Mojave Desert. A lot of folks died here during the mob wars long ago. Bodies and treasure are buried in these forgotten sands of time.

And . . . those secret areas were not just so the Phantom Mage could rappel down on bungee cords nightly. There are rooms occupied by a hidden coven of magicians with ambitions.

Maybe the kit is right. Maybe Midnight Louie had better take a break from murder one at the Red Hat Sisterhood convention and ankle on over to the Neon Nightmare tonight to see what Mr. Max's former confreres are up to now that the Phantom Mage is MIA too.

Chapter 19

Ding-Dong Daddy

Temple had convinced herself that letting Electra return to the literal scene of the crime was a good idea. An innocent woman would hold her head and hat up, and carry on.

And Detective Alch was okay with it. Simply finding a body was not a crime.

Of course all traces of the late Oleta Lark were gone, conveyed to the Las Vegas coroner. Still, Temple could tell from the subdued note of the lobby chatter that the news of her death was getting around, and hung like a purple-haze pall over the pre-opening activities.

It was most evident in the sidelong glances Electra attracted, even when surrounded by her welcoming Red-Hatted League chapter members. Noticing Detective Su cruising

nearby, it occurred to Temple that the police had okayed
Electra's return because they wanted to *watch* her, and the
reaction of everyone else to her. If so, she was letting Electra
play right into their hands. Great! Temple believed in sup-
porting her local police, but not in railroading her landlady
for murder!

"Electra! You look great," Alice squealed, the first to spot
their missing member. "We are on the trail around here like
bloodhounds." Alice brushed back the bill of her purple-and-
red-checked deerstalker.

That assertion made Electra blink.

"Well," Phyll added, "*blood*hounds are officially red, aren't
they?"

Temple was glad to leave Electra in the friendly custody of
her gal pals and be about her PR person's business, which was
to clear the Crystal Phoenix of any taint, as well as firmly affix
the murder rap on anyone other than Electra.

She still had to wear the cursed Pink Albatross (its brim
span must have been as wide as that doom-bearing seabird's
wingspan) to pass unchallenged in these main hotel areas now
declared the Queendom of Hattitude.

As an unofficial "squirt," Temple felt like a tugboat cruising
among a port thronged with ships of the line. Most of the women
were taller and broader than she, so Temple sometimes felt like
a child lost at a fairgrounds.

The fact that so many women of a certain age had attained a
certain comfortable and even powerful size made Temple realize how easy it would be for one to commit a tidy job of strangulation.

Once the victim's throat was encompassed, it would surely
only be a matter of ruthless compression, of indifference on a
murderous scale.

People often threatened to "wring" someone's neck, but how
many could follow through on such a vow for the two minutes
or so that it took for the action to complete the impulse?

Not her!

She heard a distant mutter like the cooing of pigeons. Standing on tippy toes on her vintage Beverly Feldman spikes, Temple

spotted a male presence cleaving the crowd of red and purple furbelows.

So far only Aldo Fontana had managed that honor. This guy was as tall, but that was because he wore a hat in the sea of hats.

A fawn-colored ten-gallon cowboy hat.

When Temple was able to glimpse the whole man, she saw he was tall but lean in that ready-to-blow-away mode of old cowboys.

His sun-leathered face was cadaverous, with a long, prominent jaw. His jeans were so weather-washed they looked designer-fashionable and his belt buckle was almost as big as his hat.

Of course, Temple was not the only one to have spotted this out-of-place person.

An agitation of red hats surrounded this iconic Western figure.

Then came a shriek.

Weathered Cowboy Guy turned in that direction, then shouted out, "Puddin' Puss! Is that you?"

Another shriek.

Temple clawed her way through the crowds to the scene of unseemly behavior.

The Red-Hatted League was at the center of it, forming an honor guard around Electra, who had plucked a four-inch-long hat pin out of her double-wide red chapeau and was aiming it at the Stranger in Town.

"Elmore Lark," she said, "you stay away from me."

Temple jerked her head back to the guy. This was Electra's third husband, the bigamist? Well, he *was* big. Tall, anyway.

"Now, Puddin' Puss, calm down. I'm jest here to hear what happened to my Pearly Poochie."

Temple was starting to think Elmore Lark would shortly be found strangled by a pet leash.

"Cain't we jest talk?" he asked.

"If we had 'jest talked,' Elmore Lark," Electra retorted, sheathing her hat pin in red felt with the panache of a Musketeer, "I would have had a lot happier life."

"But no darlin' baby boy Curtiss," he said with a grin.

Electra grimaced. "And when did you last have contact with your son?"

Elmore shrugged. "A while. Boy needs his mother. A daddy's jest a ding-dong bother."

"Well, *you* were," Electra said. "You really think I'm gonna sit down meekly and talk to you after all you did, and didn't do, years ago?"

"Waal, no, Puddin' Puss. Except I may be the only man in the state of Nevada who jest knows you didn't do in Miss Pearly Poochie."

He raised bushy gray eyebrows. "Whatayah say? I came down here to give you an alibi."

This Temple had to hear. She elbowed her way through a cotton-knit cloud of purple tops to take Electra's elbow and turn to Elmore Lark.

"The hotel has made an interview room available. Let's go there. Follow me."

"Now who are you, Little Lady?" Elmore asked.

"Your worst nightmare or your best chance. Follow me."

"Yessum. I'd follow your behind anytime anywhere, Little Doggie."

Electra managed to elbow him, hard, in the bony ribs, while she scampered ahead to catch up with Temple.

"You really want to talk to this scum, Temple dear?" she whispered.

"I'll talk to anyone who knew the dead woman and might have had a motive to get her that way. He's the man in the middle, Electra, and they make good witnesses, or suspects. Can you can the vitriol, however deserved, for a while?"

"For you, sure. Besides, I want to watch this worm squirm."

Hotel conference rooms are depressingly similar: large central wood-grain table surrounded by huge, heavy, impossible-to-move leather chairs. A table along one wall usually holds coffee and hot water urns, foam cups, plastic stirring straws, fake sugar, and fake creamer.

This was the Crystal Phoenix, though, Las Vegas's classiest

hotel long before the Bellagio, Paris, Venetian, and Wynn went arty and upscale.

The central table was a slab of granite topped with inch-thick glass. The sleek Herman Miller office chairs didn't take a World Wrestling Federation champion to move them.

The thick-piled carpet boasted a Chihuly-like design that would both wear well and perk up spirits.

And the coffee and tea services were sterling silver. The sugar bowls held sugar. An exotic wood box hid packets of exotic teas and Temple's favorite sugar substitute, Splenda. The matching creamers held—heavens!—real cream and skim milk, the best of both worlds.

That fact may have been why not one, but two black cats had preceded them to the conference room. That Louie! He respected no boundaries, human or feline! She had to wonder if he was after more than filched cream. Everything he did was reasonably catlike, but it often seemed to have a second purpose. He had a definite penchant for death scenes, always *someone*'s unlucky black cat. *Hmm,* Midnight Louie as furry albatross . . .

Seeing the two cats together, Temple could tell that Louise's furrier frame was much smaller and her tail hair was much fatter than Louie's muscular buzz cut.

She also had old-gold eyes rather than green ones.

Despite the differences, Temple still wasn't sure which cat had mixed it up with Savannah Ashleigh's entourage. She had at first assumed it had been Louie, because he had no liking for the Ashleigh woman. But the Crystal Phoenix was Midnight Louise's territory now.

"Waal, Puddin' Puss," Elmore boomed out. "I see the cats still come to you like rats to cheese."

The cats eyed him with the same dubious gaze Electra gave him.

"Don't keep calling me that, Elmore Lark, or I will commit murder."

"See why I came down, PP? I knew you'd lose your cool. Even if you did knock off Oleta, you'll need a character witness."

"You're only a witness to my bad judgment decades ago."

"Sit down," Temple suggested. Ordered. "If you two keep sparring in public it won't do either one of you any good."

"That what you brought us in here to say, Little Lady?"

"And you can drop that nickname too. As long as you're here you can tell me why *you* didn't kill Oleta."

He laughed long and loud about that, then filled up a coffee cup with six teaspoons of sugar before coming to sit at the conference table across from Temple and Electra.

"I'da stood out a little in this Little Red Hen party, don'tcha think? Besides, me and Oleta's been quit for, oh, three, four years now."

"Were you officially divorced?"

"As much as God and Reno can make it so."

"Then why did she describe you as a 'bigamist'?"

"Haven't any idea." He spread his hands wide, his scrawny chest swathed in an innocent checked cowboy shirt with plastic pearl snaps down the front. A plastic cowboy.

Temple turned to Electra. "How did you know for sure you were divorced?"

"I filed the papers before I left. And a couple weeks later I got them, all stamped and signed."

"By the county, or by Elmore Lark?"

"They looked official, and I was so glad to be quit of him."

Elmore Lark was tapping his ten-gallon hat on his angular, bejeaned knee. When the women looked at him, he looked away. And whistled.

The sound brought the two black cats lofting onto the tabletop, sighting on him like a pair of hounds from hell, eyes narrowed, hair raised, and hissing.

Temple shook her head. "The divorce never went through. He sent you forged papers."

Electra was stunned to learn she was still a married woman, and a bigamist herself on top of it.

"Why? Why on earth? He already had hot young Oleta waiting in the other stall?"

Temple narrowed her eyes at the utterly selfish old man. What had he gained by tricking Electra, and Oleta?

"You bore his son."

"And Curtiss turned out fine," Electra said, "because he was with me only from the age of six on."

"You weren't likely to come back."

"That's for sure."

Temple gave her take on the situation. "Elmore wanted Oleta, but not her greedy claws in him. She was entitled to nothing if it came out the marriage was bogus, and it would if he wanted it to. If something happened to him, when the courts asked for documentation, his worldly goods would have still gone to you and Curtiss."

Elmore had stopped his irritating whistling and hat-tapping. He looked sheepish.

Electra looked like a little purple teapot with a red cover who was about to blow its top.

"Elmore Lark! *Why?* Do you realize that I'd remarried since then?"

"Several times," Temple put in with a "so there" emphasis.

Electra didn't even hear that. "Is she right? We're still . . . married?"

"That little filly Oleta. She wanted the whole deal. I don't trust women like that. I trust women like you."

"Stupid?"

"Trustin', Puddin' Puss. That little girl sorta ran me over. I wasn't thinking, but I knew enough to make it so she couldn't get ahold of my horse ranch." He turned the hat in his bony hands. "Curtiss is my only son."

"For all you've ever seen of him."

"I'm not the raisin' father type, but I am the leavin' father type."

"That's for sure," Electra said, standing up. "I could kill you for what you've done to me, and especially to Curtiss."

Some people found women in purple outfits with red hats amusing and a little silly. Electra's fervent tone would have convinced them otherwise.

Certainly it convinced the people just entering the conference room.

Temple cringed inside as she noticed and identified them:
Detectives Su and Alch.

Chapter 20

Truth Has Consequences

Detective Su's first name was "Merry," which Temple had always found incongruous: Merry Su, a homophone for Mary Sue.

She understood that second- and third-generation Asian Americans often bore delightfully trendy American first names nowadays. It was a mark of assimilation, while maintaining pride in the family name of origin.

And Detective Su was another petite woman in a man's world, even more petite than Temple's five-foot-zero, size three and five in clothing and footwear. Su probably wore 0 and size four shoes.

So Temple totally sympathized with such a small woman making it in such a man's world as law enforcement.

But . . .

Sometimes . . .

Sometimes Temple thought Su was a mini-Molina, a female bully who liked to throw her badge and her figurative weight around. In C. R. Molina's case, Temple was talking about an almost-six-foot-tall woman homicide lieutenant with the cojones of a pit bull and the open mind of a shut-tight miniblind.

This was one of those Su-Molina times.

"We don't often walk in on a confession of murder," Su said, folding her arms. She wore a black pantsuit over a white shirt. Her expression and mind seemed to be in an equally black and white mode.

Detective Morrie Alch loomed behind her, a symphony in gray, especially his hair and mustache. From him came a vibe of mature sympathy for all involved.

Not from Detective Su.

"What's this?" she demanded. "An alternative on-site interrogation room? The hotel has asked us to be discreet. It didn't require that we be co-opted by an amateur detective with two alley cats for backup."

"Backup" was the word. Louie and acquaintance obliged by humping their spines like Halloween cats at Su's approach.

Never duel a cat for attitude, Temple thought, watching Detective Su observe the animals' fierce united feline front and wisely swagger around them to confront Temple.

"You are not Las Vegas's answer to Veronica Mars," she told Temple. "You had no business diverting this man, whom I take to be Elmore Lark, from the long arm of the law."

"Oh, ma'am," the man in question couldn't keep from intervening. "She hasn't been diverting at all. In fact, I am delighted to be released from the presence of my, er, ex-wife and associates, into the custody of such a fine member of the Las Vegas Metropolitan Police Department."

"Shut up," Su said. "And sit down, hands on the table. Away from the hat."

Elmore shrugged at Temple and Electra, and the cats, and did as ordered.

Alch came up behind Su on little cat feet. "Let's take him upstairs for questioning," he suggested.

"I suppose you think this is funny," Su said, her dark eyes fixed on Temple.

"No," Alch said, intervening. "I think you're right. This is police business. We're the police and we've got the right to question Mr. Lark. Let's do it someplace private, is all I'm saying."

"Yeah." Su turned away from the table. "Do you want to tell the old broad not to leave town, or should I?"

Alch's eyes shut for an instant. They opened to regard Electra. "Miss Lark, we'd advise you to stay in town, in case we want to talk to you again. It would be even better if you didn't abuse your permission to be at the convention by getting into arguments with the victim's ex-husband. It could look suspicious."

Electra had really appreciated that "Miss." Especially now. She began beaming at the start of Alch's speech but gradually lost her glow and was fervently glum by the ending word "suspicious."

"Thank you, Detective. You can count on me concentrating on Red Hat Sisterhood activities that are completely amusing and innocent."

Su snorted like a horse. Or a Shetland pony, in her instance. Luckily, she didn't stamp a petulant hoof.

From the rubber-soled clunky Mary Janes she wore, Temple thought the petite thump she could produce would lack a certain heavy-metal pizzazz that horseshoes and tap shoes share.

"Lightweight," Temple muttered under her breath as Elmore Lark left the room under the oddball escort of Alch and Su.

Beside her, Electra let out a deep breath and let her head droop to the tabletop. "Holy hypocrite! That bastard lied. About everything. I'm amazed *he* isn't the dead body in the morgue."

"You better hope he's not, because you have police witnesses to wishing him dead."

"Not seriously—"

"Everything here is serious now, Electra. Don't let the happy high of the Red Hat Sisterhood lead you astray. We are hip-deep in trouble."

It was only then Temple noticed that the black cats had

slipped out of the conference room on the heels of Elmore and Merry and Morrie.

Oh, shoot. She and Electra weren't even serious enough players to keep the attention of a couple of cats!

Louie and Louise, how could you?

Chapter 21

The Third Degree

"That was not very nice," Louise observed as we shimmied through the air-conditioning vents.

The Las Vegas summer was firing up for the main event, and I have to admit that my seasoned joints were not doing the horizontal crawl with youthful enthusiasm.

Miss Midnight Louise, of course, was going for a world record in on-land airshaft-swimming.

"What was not nice?"

"Leaving the ladies behind so we could tail the cops. That Detective Su is as mean as a Persian queen in heat."

"She is just annoyed with our Miss Temple for beating her out on the undercover job at the Teen Idol competition. They are like feuding sisters and Miss Lieutenant Molina is their mama."

"Do not let Miss Temple hear that idea. She would take you off at the tail."

"Tut. I know how to handle these human females, unlike most human males. A little purr and rub here, a little manly huff and puff there, and they are all eating out of the palm of my paw."

"Especially Miss Detective Su." She is being sarcastic, and I forbear to reply to that comment.

"That is why we are going over ground. Once we reach the vent into the Lalique Suite, we will hear and see all while remaining not seen and not heard."

"Like very lucky human children."

"Hush! We are almost, *hah!* There."

We hunker down, side to side and face to face, all the better to see and hear through the grille.

"I am jest an innocent bystander," that heroic lonesome cowboy, Elmore Lark, is whining to the two detectives. "I jest came down from Reno to check on my little fillies."

Even a good ole boy like me can see that the phrase "little fillies" is not going over with Miss Detective Su. Even Mr. Detective Alch winces at that one.

"Look, Elmore," Su says. "I can call you 'Elmore', can I not?"

"Sure, lady. Uh, Lieutenant."

Alch chuckles.

"Detective will do," Su tells him. "Are you saying that you never divorced Electra, wife number one?"

"No, not exactly."

"Divorce is a very exact thing, like murder, Elmore. Which is it?"

"The papers were not quite right."

"And you did this because—"

"Oleta was a hot potato." He glanced at Alch for backup, but Alch was too savvy to do more than look as stony as a new president on Mount Rushmore.

Elmore shrugged. "Fun, but . . . touchy. I figured I could always get Electra back—"

Su put a trouser leg up on the chair next to Elmore. It was a fancy Italian leather chair, but she had no shame at resting her mall shoe-shop ersatz leather boot on top of it. (I have learned

a few things from my Miss Temple and her extensive shoe collection.)

"You are a dirty dog, Elmore. I bet there are a lot of women
who would like to see you swing for murder."

"Ah, they do not hang people anymore."

"You know what I mean."

"Ye-ah."

"And the worst part of your cheesy operation is you set one
woman against another and then slip away all innocentlike. You
are not innocent, are you?"

"Of murder, yes."

"So who do you think offed Oleta? Between us." Su's boot
swiveled like it was about to crush out a cigarette. Elmore's
gentleman's area was directly across from it on the next chair.

I swallowed in fellow sympathy. Even the sinister Hyacinth
had never touched claw to my, er, play balls.

"She has got him on the run," Louise chortled next to me. "Or
having the runs," she adds with that peculiarly feminine zest for
certain forms of violence against men who done them wrong.

"I do not know what has gotten into the China Doll of the
LVMPD," I say, truly amazed.

And that is when my man, Detective Morrie Alch, rises to the
occasion.

"We will need to see your marriage and divorce papers," he
tells Elmore Lark. "To both women, and any others you may
have promised to love and obey for all time."

"I am not the greatest housekeeper," Lark says. As if one
could not tell that from the wrinkles in his checked shirt. "Aren't
there records you people can check in the blink of a computer
cursor?"

Su leans closer, all glare. "Sure. But we want to see what
you are flashing around, claiming to be genuine."

"And where were you yesterday morning?" Alch asks.

"At home in Reno. I drove right down when I heard about
Oleta on the nightly news."

"We had not released her name to the press yet." Su is re-
lentless. "Not enough information about next of kin. If you were
on any lists in that regard, you sure did not show up."

"We divorced too. A few years ago."

"So why are you *really* in town?" Alch slipped that in with such an easygoing tone that Lark was answering before he thought about it.

"Some old business with Electra."

"She knew you were coming?"

"Nah. I did not even know all these red-and-purple ladies would be in town."

"Then how did you end up at the Crystal Phoenix?" Su pounced.

Elmore Lark winced and fingered his cowboy hat on the tabletop. Sometimes even your props will let you down. "Oleta e-mailed me to come. Said she knew something of interest to me. About Electra. And I had other interests in town."

Su and Alch sat back in their chairs as one.

It looked like the long-ago romantic triangle was still plenty alive and kicking . . . until someone had throttled Oleta.

At least there is another suspect on the scene besides Miss Electra Lark.

I hiss as much to Louise.

Below us, the humans are leaving the room.

"Why do you always refer to your human lady friends as Miss when some of them are actually Mrs.?" Louise asks in that annoyed tone females and relatives get when they have nothing better to do than pick on some innocent nearby dude.

"It is a courtesy title, Louise. I even use it with you, at times, though Bast knows you have given me little courtesy. All human females were 'Misses' at one time and I honor their eternally youthful origins by using that honorific. And, as you have seen and heard, these 'Mrs.' titles come and go nowadays."

"Do you think that your Miss Temple, now that she is about to become Mr. Matt's Miss Temple and maybe his Mrs., will soon be a 'Miss' again?"

"One never knows in this town," I answer grimly. If my Miss Temple does decide to reside in a state of holy matrimony, I would hope it would be permanent. I do not like to move from pillar to post office. "And you have made my point, Louise. A man is always a 'Mr.,' no matter his marital status. Ergo, I do not see why a woman should not always remain a 'Miss.' "

"I get that, but who is this 'Ergo'?"

"Merely an expression referring to some Latin lover type, no doubt. Speaking of which, it might behoove us to look up Mr. Aldo Fontana and his doings with Miss Temple's aunt. They are on the case too, and those Fontana brothers are very well—"

"Built?"

"Connected, I was going to suggest."

But I admit I am disappointed that even the fiercely independent Miss Midnight Louise can fall prey to a tall, dark guy with a world-class tailor.

Chapter 22

Midnight Madness

Matt Devine sat behind the mike at WCOO-AM, listening to other people's problems.

His own sounded miniature by comparison: a newfound long-lost father in his hometown of Chicago. A mother who wanted to run from a past too traumatic to remember, including an abusive ex-husband, except that Matt's real father had been the only good thing in it. And now that Matt had found that man by happenstance and whatever saint presided over happy endings, she wanted to run from him.

Parents. Way overrated once you were past twenty-one.

But he was only four years past thirty, and way too many of those years had been spent as a dedicated Catholic priest. He didn't regret those years, not even the celibacy. He'd done some good. But time had made clear that he'd run to the priest-hood in search of a more perfect father than his abusive step-father, Cliff Effinger, even if he had to become that "Father" himself.

He'd come to Las Vegas to track down and confront Effin-ger, but the man he found was too small to fear or hate, and was dead now, anyway. Meanwhile, Matt had stumbled from hotline counseling into a radio shrink job that made "Mr. Mid-night" a hot syndicated property.

He'd also met an empathetic, energetic fireball named Tem-ple Barr who'd made him glad he'd waited seventeen years for her . . . and her heroic significant other, charismatic ex-magician Max Kinsella. Now the men's roles had changed.

The Mystifying Max, as his stage name promised, had been in—and out—of Temple's life for so long that the stifled attrac-tion between her and Matt finally had flared. And how. Matt breathed hard each time he recalled every word, every kiss, every touch, every move. With more to come. He'd been infatu-ated with Temple since they met, but now the cat was out of the bag and it was ravenous.

And still his happiness didn't feel guaranteed. Max was a powerful presence even when he went AWOL . . . and Matt?

It was past midnight in Las Vegas. Matt had a $48,000 vin-tage engagement ring in his coat pocket because his betrothed didn't want to wear it "yet" and he couldn't bear to inter it in the new floor safe in his newly redone bedroom . . . where he'd done and redone his betrothed even though that was against every rule for an ex-priest maybe on the road to becoming ex-Catholic.

Come to think of it, "Mr. Midnight," on-air shrink extraordi-naire, had plenty problems of his own.

And still freight cars full of free-floating anxiety and angst poured in from the featureless night. From phones in cheap motel rooms and in ticky-tacky box houses, at bars, in dark liv-ing rooms, dialed secretly.

"He/she is running around on me."

"No one can know I'm pregnant."

"No one can know I had an abortion/adoption/stillbirth."

"Why does he hit me if he says he loves me?"

"Why doesn't he boff me if he says he loves me?"

"Why does she run around with every dude on the block?"

"Should I marry him/her even if he/she is physically/sexually/verbally abusive?"

Sometimes, lately, Matt, the most levelheaded of men, wanted to scream, "How should I know?"

But they thought he did, so he tried to give them honest, supportive advice. Sometimes he hung up the oversize foam-padded earphones for the night feeling that he had.

Not tonight. He got into his Crossfire outside the station and drove back to the Circle Ritz on autopilot.

He needed to confront Temple about what wasn't happening between them. Two-thirty in the morning was a lousy time to do it, but he needed to know.

Besides, he ached to see her again. He'd spent so long subduing all the crazy throbs and fevers of first love, and now it was combined with the wonders and passion of first sex. He was glad they'd been forced to be just friends so long, so they knew each other deep down. Now she'd become a drug he couldn't get enough of, and that felt so right.

Matt stood in the dim hallway, wondering whether to knock.

He sure wasn't about to ring the old-fashioned doorbell. That would wake the whole floor.

Max Kinsella, he knew, had made a habit of coming and going unannounced via the patio doors, an unpredictable and dazzling second-story man to the end.

Matt still felt he ought to knock, which was maybe a pretty bad sign. He pulled out his cell phone and dialed Temple's number, feeling like a fool.

The ringing stopped. She sounded groggy, of course.

"Yes?"

"It's me." Stupid line.

"Matt? Oh." He could hear the rustle of sheets as she settled up against her pillows. "It's been so crazy. I'm so glad to hear your voice."

He could have admitted he'd been crazy too but that didn't seem wise at the moment.

"Where are you?" she asked. "Just home?"

"Yeah. Just home." He leaned against the wall. Her wall.

"I've been running around all day at the Crystal Phoenix."

"Still chaos there?"

"A convention of five thousand divided between the Phoenix and the Goliath? Yes. And . . . well, the usual, at the Phoenix, unfortunately. Listen, if you're not too tired, and could come down for a while—?"

"I am down."

"Down?"

"I'm at your door."

"Oh." There was a silence. Had he overstepped his bounds? "*Oh!* Well! Wait just a sec. I need to put something . . . off."

The cell phone died in his hand, but he'd definitely detected a perk in her interest level.

Two minutes later the door opened. Temple was wearing something long and red and filmy and dotted with rhinestones that was amazingly deficient at covering her breasts.

She couldn't miss his appraisal. "One great thing about being a blond now is I can wear red. Vintage fifties nightie. We femmes fatales knew how to do it then. Come in, wandering voice of the night. I could use a sympathetic ear."

"Your aunt isn't here?"

"Apparently she has found a roost elsewhere for the duration of her visit. Can you spell F-o-n-t-a-n-a?"

Matt raised his eyebrows, but was rather glad to hear Temple was home alone again. They settled at the stools by the kitchen eating counter. Temple's gaze settled on Matt, and it was unsettlingly fond.

"It's so good to see a sane face."

"Um, 'sane' isn't the adjective I was looking for."

"It's so good to see your handsome, wise, sexy face. Can a girl these days just say, 'Kiss me'?"

Matt found his niggling doubts vanishing as he complied. He wondered if a guy could just say, "On the couch, the floor, or the patio under the stars?"

"*Hmmm.*" Temple smiled at him from six inches away, so her eyes were as adorably crossed as a Siamese cat's. Speaking of which?

"Louie?" Matt asked.

"Kind of you to inquire, but he's not in. Not on the couch. Not in my bed. Anywhere else of interest?"

"I was thinking the patio overlooking the pool."

"You know I loved to watch you swim from there. Lustfully. Maybe there," Temple said.

"Electra would see."

Temple sighed. "Not nowadays, lover boy. That's what I needed to tell you."

"Something about Electra?" Matt was confused. He still expected every other sentence out of her mouth to be about Max, not a good sign in her or him.

"She was discovered leaning solicitously over a dead body at the Crystal Phoenix yesterday."

"You mentioned that, but come on, Electra a murderer? She was just trying to help someone, obviously."

"The victim turned out to be the woman who took her third husband away from her, so the 'help' defense is a bit thin."

Matt bit his lip. "Not good, but I stand by my first diagnosis. Electra wouldn't kill a fruit fly."

"I agree. But that's something to worry about tomorrow, Rhett." She leaned forward and took his worried bottom lip in her own. "You tell me: on the plantation porch, by the plantation pond, or in the master bedroom?"

Matt's heart stopped beating for about twenty seconds. She meant it. Here. Now. Them. The bedroom once co-owned by Max.

He reached in his pocket and pulled out the ring.

"You've been carrying this around?"

"I couldn't leave it in a cold metal safe when my whole heart's in it."

"Mine too." Temple beamed and put it on her third finger, left hand, but her eyes never left his.

Matt made his choice. It was late. They were both a little

weary. They deserved a pillow-top mattress. Max was gone. Louie was out.

Matt led Temple into her very own bedroom to make it into a marriage bed.

At five in the morning they awoke. Temple laid her head on Matt's shoulder and her left hand on his chest while she got something off hers.

"He's really gone this time," she whispered, relating all the details about the complete changing of the guard at Max's former home. "He'd been hinting that this was it, but with Max you never knew."

"So you can't ever tell him it's over?"

"I think he knew. Maybe he had somewhere urgent to be. Maybe he thought cutting the cord was the kindest thing to do. The thing is, I don't owe him an apology. I did my best to offer him one, but he's gone again, and I have a brand-new life to live with someone I've always loved very much."

"Always?"

"From the moment we met. I just didn't dare know it then."

"Me neither."

"Now we can dare anything."

"Except for friends and neighbors and close relatives," he said with a laugh, lifting her hand to kiss the ring on it.

"It's about time they knew. We'll get through it."

She didn't say the thing she'd decided during the night when Matt had made her bed theirs.

Once Electra was cleared of murder charges, Temple wanted a civil wedding ceremony in the Lovers' Knot Wedding Chapel downstairs, with all the soft-sculpture people and their Las Vegas friends present, in front of God, state, Elvis, and everybody.

And then they'd decide in which church in which city, and when, they'd do it all over again, to placate the parental demons. And because she really, really wanted to wear her Austrian crystal Stuart Weitzman Midnight Louie spikes with a wedding

gown. On the red carpet to the altar. Catholic, Universalist Unitarian, or whatever their relatives would compromise on.

She wanted to meet Matt's mother. See her parents endorse
their youngest child's adult choice.

Max had been way too big bad wolf, too alpha, for their cau-
tious Midwestern conservatism. Matt still broadcast good boy
gone diffidently successful. He would go down much better,
if anybody would.

As her family's youngest child and sole daughter, she could
only hope.

Chapter 23

Diamond Razzle Dazzle

The buses, vans, and taxis from McCarran airport rolled up to the red carpet the Crystal Phoenix had laid from lobby to porte cochere. Today, Wednesday, officially began the Red Hat Sisterhood convention, even though a couple thousand early arrivals had been in occupancy for a day.

Temple, irreverent PR flack that she was, wondered two things: if she and Matt should get married here instead, or if the Red HAT Sisterhood had ever considered the acronym, RHATS.

If six hundred Red Hat ladies had seemed overwhelming, five thousand seemed like a revolution, a mass of well-dressed, cheerful lemmings leaping off a cliff into all things Las Vegas.

Temple watched the onslaught with mixed feelings.

Several months before, the performance artist Domingo had arrived in Las Vegas to swath the Strip's iconic buildings with a million pink plastic lawn flamingos. The hot pink plumage had indeed been spectacular . . . until the searing Las Vegas sun faded them all to pallid pink.

At first the project had seemed over-the-top for an over-the-top entertainment destination. Then the massed flamingos had attained an odd sort of dignity in numbers. Humble but universal. Colorful, eccentric, unashamed . . . everything Las Vegas. That was Domingo's point. Life is art. Art is life.

Today the Red Hat Sisterhood swarmed over the larger-than-life artfulness of Las Vegas, and conquered.

Red and purple outshone the Strip's neon. They were colors of vigor and assertion, yet available to one and all, if they only had the nerve.

Watching the rivers of crimson and purple flow into the Crystal Phoenix on that royal red welcoming carpet, Temple decided that she had lost her own nerve lately, but she was getting it back.

Matt's gorgeous diamond-and-ruby vintage ring blared from her left hand. She was engaged! With love, with life, with making sure everything in her purview went well. And that included freeing Electra from suspicion by nailing the person who'd strangled Oleta Lark.

Temple, now proud in pink, joined the Red Hat Sisterhood river flowing into the Phoenix. In the lobby, the Fontana brothers, suited in tones of cappuccino, cream, ivory, bisque, and generally well-tailored, naturally tan Hunk, were out in full force, all nine of 'em.

They directed the red-and-purple tide to the check-in lines exclusive to their group. They bowed to kiss plump, beringed hands. Their guiding fingers paused ever so briefly but memorably on curvaceous midlife torsos, merely to direct, of course.

"*Whew*," someone whispered in Temple's ear, under her wide hat brim. "If anybody had told me aging gracefully was this much fun I'd have skipped right over menopause to the good stuff."

Only one person was capable of whispering under Temple's

hat brim. Well, two. But she didn't think petite Detective Merry Su was up to such an incisive summary of this scene, even had she been here.

"Kit. My elusive ex-roommate! Come to think of it, I don't see Aldo among the Brothers Nine."

"Brothers *Eight*. Counting was never your strong suit in kindergarten. And you *won't* see Aldo. He's been forbidden to minister to any midlife needs but mine."

Temple laughed.

Kit went on. "You're looking in the pink, girl, even aside from the hat. Any unauthorized hanky-panky happen while I've been AWOL that I should know about?"

Temple flashed her left hand, feeling as shallow as a sorority candidate.

"*NO!*" Kit shrieked like a Teen Queen. "Major commitment. Fabulous taste. I want him. Whoever he is."

"*Et tu, Auntie?*"

Kit's eyes drilled into Temple's. "He's not my darling Max?"

"He's my darling Matt."

"Oh. Well, he's the bee's knees and wings and striped jailhouse suit and stinger too."

Temple felt a laugh gurgle up from between her extravagantly shod toes to her hot pink hat. It was such a relief to know that there was Life Galore After Fifty. Or Sixty. Or Seventy.

Or even Thirty.

"Are these ladies cool, or what?" she asked her aunt.

"The cat's pajamas," Kit said. "Speaking of which, I'm seeing black cats . . . double."

"Louie's here, and he has a little friend."

"Don't tell me he's gone and gotten monogamous. Some things don't need to change."

"All I know is that he's incapable of putting a female in a fix now. I had to go head-to-head with Savannah Ashleigh to clear him of an 'unwanted littering' charge."

"That woman. Somehow I'm going to out her as a Red Hatter at this convention."

"You're also pretty in pink, but an illegal," Temple pointed out ungenerously.

"Aldo likes me in pink," Kit said, "and what Aldo likes, Aldo gets. A lot of. Lately."

Temple eyed her ring finger. Under these hothouse hotel lobby lights the diamonds shot out serious wattage.

"I'd watch that," said a male voice that had sidled up.

She turned to find Morrie Alch looking at her with a decidedly paternal twinkle. It was the second-nicest thing that had happened to her in twenty-four hours.

The old folks at home in Minnesota were more likely to narrow their eyes in suspicion at any such major alteration on their overprotected only daughter's anatomy. And its worth would only be another dire danger sign to them.

Alch was chuckling. "Did Molina's favorite magician finally spring the big question?"

It was a natural question and Temple knew she'd be getting it a lot. She'd better have a pat answer ready.

"Magicians never do the predictable," she said. Airily. "No. You've met him, though."

Alch was looking abashed for his faux pas.

"Matt," she said, and watched his paternal beam return to high intensity.

"Good for you! Him, rather. Swell guy. If my own daughter had brought home someone that superfine I'd have done the first Highland fling of my sadly ground-bound life."

"Thanks." Temple eyed him slyly. "Is this gonna frost Molina's cornflakes?"

"Just a teensy bit," Alch responded.

"Don't you tell her."

"Staple-gun torture couldn't squeeze it outta me." Alch sobered. "But I do need to talk business to you for a moment."

"Come into my 'alternate interrogation room,' aka 'parlor.' "

Temple waved good-bye to her aunt as she and Alch headed toward the conference room.

"Sorry about Su. She gets a little gung ho." He opened the door to let Temple enter first.

Some woman was missing a good bet in Morrie Alch. Temple had a hunch it might be Molina.

Inside the room, Alch sat on the table end while Temple

took one of the chairs and twirled around in it just because she could. The diamonds and rubies sparkled like state fair glitz while she did it.

Alch chuckled again. "I hate to rain on your parade, but the police have a problem here."

Temple stilled herself and listened.

"Elmore Lark is a tin-plated asshole, but he has an iron-clad alibi for the late morning, the time Oleta was killed. Was meeting some buddies who all swear to it. Background checks don't find anyone else with a motive, except your landlady. The only thing keeping Electra Lark from being taken into custody is Molina."

"Molina?"

"She's with you. Thinks the setup is too pat. My hands are tied. I no more think Electra killed Oleta than she ran the half mile in sixty seconds flat. Su is eager to wrap this up. Over-eager. She doesn't want to give you an inch."

"Because she thinks she should have gone undercover for Molina last time out."

"Maybe. She's a sharp young lady, but she gets all that impressive forward motion from wearing blinders. No side vision. In my experience, crime, and particularly murder, is an oblique sort of thing. It slips in at an angle, does its damage, and slithers away at an angle. Like a sidewinder snake."

Temple thought about it. Alch was right. Murder was not a straightforward act. It probably sneaked up on the murderer too. A bit of natural fury mixed with what seemed a reasonable sense of loss or betrayal. Human nature operating as usual. And then the same old ingredients that had resulted in a little flurry of aggravation suddenly escalated to an unthinkable act.

"What are you saying?" she asked Alch, right out.

He told her, right out.

"I'm saying our real Las Vegas CSIs didn't find any DNA evidence on the body but Electra's."

"She found Oleta. She tried to undo the scarf."

"Perfectly natural. Perfectly suitable for framing. No one needs to look further. They had the same husband, for God's sake. No one else remotely comes to mind for the crime, much less has any evidential link to it."

"You're saying that's all that Las Vegas's finest can come up with."

"Yeah. Unless you can provide some evidence that changes our minds."

"Me? That's your job."

"Our job is done, says procedure and history and everything we go by, which is hard evidence."

"Electra would never—"

"You believe that. I believe that. You prove it."

Temple took a deep breath. "I've just . . . gotten lucky around some previous crime scenes. I'm not a professional."

"That's what Electra Lark needs now. A professional. It ain't the police." He took her left hand in his. "Sorry to rain on your parade, Princess."

"No. Thanks for telling me. Su sure wouldn't."

Alch narrowed his eyes. "I like Su and I respect her, but she's still young and needs a lesson. You give it to her, Red."

"I'm a blonde nowadays, haven't you noticed?"

Alch shook his head. "A woman can change her hair color like she can her nail polish these days. But not her heart. You've always had that redhead rage for truth, justice, and the American way. My money's on you, kid. Don't let me down."

His words made her smile long after he walked away.

Not much was expected of her in her family except staying way too safe.

Maybe that's why she stuck her nose into crimes on her turf: she had something to prove. Just because her frame was slight, she wasn't short-sheeted in the brain or heart department.

Even Molina had tacitly admitted she had a gift for detection. That's why Su was annoyed with her. And why Alch was rooting for her to clear Electra for good and all by finding a better candidate.

And that's why her parents and older brothers had been a teensy bit right to worry about her.

You want to look for the truth in a case of murder, you're bound to annoy somebody much more threatening than Detective Su.

Chapter 24

Bad Boy, Bad Boy, Whatcha Gonna Do?

Temple returned to the field of battle, i.e., her most stable job assignment, to find TV vans and crews crowding the Crystal Phoenix Hotel's porte cochere, filming away like paparazzi at a Paris Hilton or a Tom "Crazy" Cruise sighting.

Neither of those publicity-worthy figures honored Las Vegas at the moment. Temple guessed with a sinking feeling in her gut that the Red Hat Sisterhood was somehow in the news again. Another murder? If so, the death of someone unrelated to Electra would be nice. . . .

Then she saw something poking above the lofted mikes and cameras. A cluster of black hats, not red or purple ones.

Hmmm. Natalie Newman! Miss Snaky Shoes was cruising

among the local media in the general film-at-six and -ten feeding frenzy.

Sometimes even three-inch-high heels could not make a five-foot-zero woman tall enough to see what she desperately needed to view in the performance of her job.

"Here," a baritone voice said behind her.

Waist-encompassing hands lofted Temple two feet off the ground for the bird's-eye view available from a ballerina lift. For a moment, to Temple's gut and heart it felt like Max was back, taking charge.

Then she glanced over her shoulder and down on a dark-haired male head, and it was all too plain to her.

She patted her dancing partner's shoulder—nice padding! Was it muscle or tailoring? Only her auntie knew for sure. Aldo Fontana lowered her back to ground zero again.

But she'd seen enough.

The hats that had become the center of attention in a sea of Red Hat Sisterhood ladies were black, masculine, and surmounted by protest signs.

WHAT FILM STARRED PRINCE? PURPLE HAGS! read one.

RHS: RAGING HORMONE SISSYHOOD read another.

MEN JUST WANTA HAVE FUN. GET THE GUN!

That one was outright threatening.

Temple had been thinking that her pert pink hat was giving her a headache. Her forehead wasn't used to being bounded by a hatband. Now she knew that those black hats would give her an even bigger headache. As would the lunkheads under them.

"Everything okay?" Aldo asked.

"Nothing's okay. Can you plow a path through that mob?"

"My dear lady, I *am* the mob."

He put his hand into his left front suit coat, like a squat little-Caesar type Corsican named Napoleon, only Aldo was a tall Las Vegan. He then shouldered forward, earning a lot of turned heads, nasty looks, and suddenly pale faces as they spotted his hand on heart (or holster) posture.

Temple trotted in his wake, ducking all the mikes and cameras, until she and Aldo had a front row seat.

If there was an opposite number to a Red Hat Sisterhood

woman, several of them were picketing the Crystal Phoenix.

The men all wore black and blue: blue jeans and blue work shirts and black cowboy hats, belts, and boots. And huge tin belt buckles bearing the initials BHB.

Their signs announced them as the Black Hat Brotherhood and said they were for men's rights. Temple the PR maven didn't think that a black-and-blue color scheme was a really wise choice for men asserting rights over women.

No matter. They were all middle-aged and mostly shy on hair, except the facial sort, and big on beer guts. Or beer-nut guts.

They didn't offer the glamour of the Red Hat Sisterhood. No dye jobs, tummy tucks, or false eyelashes here. But their cowboy boots had high heels and they broadcast a certain down-to-earth malcontent swagger as they marched back and forth. And they made dynamite copy and great sound bites. Those black cowboy hats made for instant visuals.

Natalie Newman had cornered their apparent leader and was eagerly asking questions. Several TV station videographers were capturing his answers over her shoulder.

From the quality of her questions, she was clearly way more tuned into the Black Hat Brotherhood than the average local reporter.

"Is this your first public protest?" she asked.

"Right. We're the Men Left Behind. We been run-around-on, run-out-on, and just plain run-down. What's so special about a bunch of women dressing up like freaks and having a high old time while their husbands and kids are untended at home?"

"*You're* not at home," Temple pointed out, raising her voice to a far higher profile than her frame could ever attain.

The cameras zoomed in on her for an instant, then fixed back on the spokesman.

"Well, now, that's a good point, little pink lady. We're just here in Las Vegas to have fun, like those Ragin' Hormone Sisters. Sounds like some New Age vocal group to me. Anyway, we men are here in Las Vegas to gamble, smoke cigars, and watch naked young women who're worth the view."

Boos and hisses from gathering Red Hat Sisterhood women answered that statement.

Natalie Newman raised her voice so the looming multistation mikes could capture it.

"When and why did the Black Hat Brotherhood form?"

" 'When' was at the previous Ragin' Hormones hooha last year in St. Louis. 'Why' was because we men are tired of being used, abused, and put out to pasture when the women get their change of life."

"Don't men undergo a change of life?" Temple asked.

"Only because the women go crazy then, Hot Pink. You better come on over to our side. We can use a pretty little blond filly like you, instead of these old gray mares most of us are stuck with."

Like all protesters, they meant to inflame.

The Red Hat Sisterhood started up their own chant: "Two, four, six, eight, you old guys discriminate."

The Black Hat Brotherhood retaliated in kind: "Two, four, six, eight, you old dames are full of hate."

It was a PR person's nightmare. The Crystal Phoenix marquee would star in the local news on every station tonight. Temple had to do something.

She used her high heels to stomp her way through the crowding media reporters and videographers. With a trail of *ows* in her wake, she seized the media attention from Natalie Newman by projecting her voice.

"All right, ladies and gentlemen," Temple declaimed. "In this corner we have the Black Hat Brotherhood." She pointed like a carnival barker. "In this corner we have the Red Hat Sisterhood." She pointed again. "I propose a no-holds-barred debate on these issues tomorrow at 2:00 P.M. right here."

Her bold proposal had hushed the contending factions. Temple racked her brains. Who would make a media-friendly moderator?

"The debate will be moderated by . . . Mr. Midnight himself, Matt Devine, syndicated host of Las Vegas's own WCOO-AM radio's 'Midnight Hour.' "

A series of *ooohs* among the assembled media and onlookers told Temple she'd hit publicity gold.

She just hoped she didn't lose a fiancé over it.

Chapter 25

Hot Water and
Cool Tequila

Or a major client.

Temple was called onto the carpet in Van von Rhine's office, only it was all bleached wood floors and no carpet.

Nicky was there, with his brother, Aldo, as a witness.

Van was tapping one sleek Italian designer pump on her high-end wood floor, very audibly. Temple was thinking that Van could wear a bath towel to work if it was Italian-made and be just as happy in it, as she was with her easygoing husband, on whom Temple was banking with every instinct in her.

"Pardon me, Temple," Van said, maintaining her natural blond cool. Or ice. "I don't see how transferring a distasteful media brawl from the Crystal Phoenix's front porte cochere to our meeting rooms inside is an improvement. But you're the public relations expert."

You're the one whose baby-blond bleached head this is on, was the message.

"The media was eating us up for the five, six, and ten P. M. news," Temple said. "I had to do something to stop it for the moment."

"But they'll be back tomorrow, hunting for blood. For red ink for the hotel. We've worked very hard to establish a reputation as a first-class destination in Las Vegas. Not as the equivalent of World Wrestling Federation contest between middle-aged men and women."

Nicky lit up. "Hey, maybe we can get all the debaters to wear those Stingy Dingy underwear like they do on the wrestling shows."

"You mean tighty whities," Temple said.

"Oh, my God!" Van hid her face in her hands. "There is no way out of this but disgrace."

"Matt will lend an air of dignity," Temple suggested.

Van looked up to skewer her with a steel-blue gaze. "Are you sure he'll be willing to go along with this tasteless stunt?"

Temple stretched out her left hand and wiggled the heavy-duty engagement ring on it.

Van blinked at the high-end glitz. "Congratulations. Okay," she conceded. "He's just a fool in love. I still don't think he'll do this, even for you."

"I would," Nicky said.

Van lifted a pale eyebrow. "You'd do it for Temple if you were Matt, or just on principle?"

"I'd do it because it makes sense."

Temple released a hot, long-held breath. Van was the head of this operation, but Nicky was the guts and the heart.

"Look," he went on. "The damage was done. Our clients were being attacked by a rowdy protester group. Someone sicced the media on that and I'd sure like to know who."

Nicky eyed Temple, who nodded. She had media contacts all over town and they were going to get roasted on a red-hot grill until she knew who'd masterminded that ugly scene. She had her suspicions. She'd get to that just as soon as she got to Matt and did what Van von Rhine rightfully thought was going to be a hard sell.

Three nights tied to his four-poster bed ought to do it for a fiancé. Also for her.

But Matt had scruples, and those were very costly indeed.

Maybe five nights.

"So who do you think did it?" Nicky asked.

"Huh?" Temple pulled her imagination and libido back to the problem at hand. "I have my suspects," she said mysteriously.

Actually, it was "suspect" singular, but she wasn't ready to go on record for that.

Temple raced back down to the holding cells.

Wait a minute! She'd been doing too much unofficial police work lately. They weren't holding cells, just neighboring conference rooms.

A pair of Fontana brothers stood guard outside each set of double doors. Aldo was waiting for her, and he introduced her to his siblings, just so she wouldn't get embarrassingly confused about names.

"Ernesto and Rico are keeping the Black Hat Brotherhood bottled up with lots of beer," Aldo said, rolling his eyes. Italians preferred wine to beer and hard liquor.

"Armando and Julio, on the other hand, have been trying to keep the Red Hat Sisterhood from unnecessary stress."

Temple could hear female hooting inside. "What did you have them served? Tea?"

Aldo winced. "Texas Tea, I was told. I was also told it would knock a mule-headed beer-drinking Black Hat Brother back on his ass."

Texas Tea, Temple thought. Wasn't that Jack Daniel's and lemonade? She braced herself to enter the conference room to meet with the Red Hat Sisterhood on ninety proof.

Once inside, the double doors snapped shut, locking her in.

There wasn't much choice of debaters. Whoever had been in

the unruly crowds on both sides had been swept into swift custody by the Fontana brothers at Temple's instructions.

She was surprised to see two pink hats among the red.

Holy Hattie Carnegie!

One was her aunt Kit, sure to be a strong debater, and one was Savannah Ashleigh. Talk about a loss leader.

Looking around, she was relieved to see that two of Electra's Red-Hatted League members were among the group, Judy and Phyll, the Mutt and Jeff librarians. And of course she'd had to invite Jeanne Johnson, Her Royal Hatness, the founder and head woman. That pretty much made up a debate team, if she could ditch Savannah.

"Traitor!" the woman in question now spat at Temple.

"I beg your pardon?"

"You named a *man* moderator. Why not me? I'm much better known nationally than some local radio personality."

"The title is 'moderator.' You're not moderate."

"I'm as modern as the next Teen Idol."

"Moderate. Like the weather."

"Oh." Savannah trout-pouted, which collagen treatments to her lips had well qualified her to do. "You mean dull, boring. Bland."

"Exactly," Temple said.

"Well, I certainly am not that!"

"I agree," Temple said with a broad smile.

HRH spoke next. "This could be a good publicity opportunity for our message," she said, "but I'm worried about lowering ourselves to debate these rowdy protesters. This is our convention. We were violated."

Temple sighed. "I agree, but protesters have a habit of taking over the news media. At least a debate will even the playing field."

Temple then set up the debaters: HRH Jeanne Johnson; "clown princess" Candy Crenshaw, recommended by HRH; Kit; and Phyll, one of the two Red-Hatted League librarians. (Never argue with a librarian; they know too much.) She designated Savannah Ashleigh as official emcee and note-taker. The ersatz actress would know how to pose and fidget to draw the cameramen's attention. It would still effectively gag her. That was fighting dirty, but Temple worked for the Crystal Phoenix, not the Black Hat Brotherhood or Savannah Ashleigh.

Speaking of fighting dirty, Temple next headed to the roundup of Black Hat Brotherhood members.

Armando and Julio Fontana were concerned about allowing her entrance.

"These men have been drinking beer for an hour and a half," Armando warned.

"I've been binge drinking upset-stomach acids," Temple answered. "We're about even."

She went in, bowled over by a yeasty reek. About fifteen cowpokes glowered at her from under the brims of their black felt hats. Holy Hopalong Cassidy! One was Elmore Lark.

All Temple could think was that this headgear must be mighty hot in a Las Vegas spring. At least the women had been inside and air-conditioned.

Temple introduced herself. "I need four candidates for the debate team, pronto," she said. "You can draw straws or duke it out."

The men murmured approvingly at her brisk directions.

"I'm the head man," one said. "The BHB founder." He stood and nodded at her. "Mike Crenshaw."

"Oh. That's the same last name of the lead singer and jokester of that group, Candy Crenshaw and the Red Hat Candies."

"They call me Cal, and the Big Hat Breaker," Crenshaw said with a tight grin.

Temple had lost her smile, suddenly realizing that she had another pair of warring exes on her hands. Crenshaw was a burly man in his sixties. Having plunged into a whirlpool, Temple thought it might be interesting to muddy the waters. "And Mr. Lark, I see you're a member. Want to the join the debate?"

She was thinking he'd never do it, not with bigamy charges against him. In fact, coming down here had put him into the teeth of his two ex-wives and risked bringing up his dicey marital history. Was he really that ticked off at a group that encouraged older women to embrace their ages and not "act" in the ways society expected? Maybe. The Black Hat Brotherhood was a strong reminder that a lot of men of a certain age didn't like change, especially in their wives.

"Damn right," he said, tipping his black hat without rising.

She just knew his long legs in cowboy boots were stretched out under the conference table. Temple shrugged her acquiescence. It wasn't her hide the media would nail to the wall if someone tipped them off about his marital record. She was acting as a PR person and a friend now, not a so-called objective reporter.

If these Black Hat Brotherhood guys were too smug and naive to finesse their big media opportunity, tough. Which, of course, was their whole raison d'être. In their minds, Real Men would rather bomb than be caught being reasonable.

"Hey," Matt said, walking up the short hallway to his door at the Circle Ritz late that afternoon to find Temple holding up the wall with a pitcher of something pale, cold, and alcoholic.

God, he looked good!

Oops. Sorry, God, I know he used to be all yours, but you made him this way.

Since they'd broken the sex barrier something tentative in Matt had vanished, given way to a new ease and confidence that was as sexy as hell. *Sorry, God! Again.* She supposed releasing his held-back feelings had done that. Now he looked her deep in the eyes, ready to see everything she could show him. A guy couldn't glow, but he could simmer, and Matt simmering for her was irresistible.

She smiled back at him, and they just stood there basking in each other's pleasure with the other.

Then he pulled her close for a long, deep kiss. Not a word said. Not a word necessary.

"You've been waiting for me?" he asked, sounding a little smug and a lot satisfied. "How long?"

What girl couldn't play along with a moment like this. "All my life."

He paused, then laughed. But his brown bedroom eyes were melting like the ice in her pitcher. "And you want—?"

"You. When was it ever different?"

"For a lot of months when you were busy elsewhere, but let's not count that."

"I thought so too." Temple edged away from the door so he could get his key in the lock.

He started to open the door, then paused. Took her and the pitcher into close custody again. "What do you want?"

"Number one or number two?"

Matt's eyes squeezed shut to consider. "Number two?"

"Shucks. Your help."

"That's it? My help? Not my love, my support, my endless passion."

"You asked for 'number two.' "

"So I did. Come on down then." He opened the door to let her eel through.

She put the pitcher on the nearest kitchen counter. Her hand was icy and it was heavy.

"What am I being bribed with?" he asked.

"Margaritas. You brought two to my door when we first met, remember?"

"I remember when we first met, but not the Margaritas."

"It was after I solved my first case, when you altered my TEMPLE BARR, PR card to read TEMPLE BARR, PI."

"You've got a long memory."

"You've got a long . . . never mind," Temple said, getting out a pair of vintage martini glasses she'd given him with frosted Art Deco bubbles etching the clear glass bowls.

"I could use a drink," he admitted. "It's hot out there."

"It could be hotter in here," she said, pouring.

"Temple, you are gorgeous and I can't resist you worth a darn, but you're sometimes as transparent as glass. What do you want?"

"Oh, too bad," she purred. "You *could* have milked this one for at least twenty minutes."

"I'm guessing neither of us has the time right now."

She handed him a glass, then lifted her own to chime rims. "Okay. I'm in a really, really tight spot. It could cost me the Crystal Phoenix account."

Matt stopped sipping, his forehead corrugating with worry. "That's not possible. They love you. Almost as much as I do."

"Yeah, but one disastrous round of bad publicity, and love ain't enough in the PR biz. I am hoping, praying, it is in the Personal Relations biz."

" 'Praying'?" You must need me bad." He sounded pretty pleased about that.

"Matt, I promise, just this one time!"

"Really bad."

"I'm on record about it. Sorry! The cameras were rolling, I had to do major spin control. You just popped into my mind. Maybe because you're always on it."

"Sure, flatter me. Into what?"

"A great media gig. Really. It'll be huge for your radio show."

"My radio show doesn't need to be huger."

"You can always use the right good publicity. The crowd just *oohed* when they heard your name."

"This crowd heard my name because—?"

"I gave it to them. I needed an instantly recognizable moderator for a live debate tomorrow on the roles of aging men and women in our society."

"Temple!"

"You'll be perfect. The media are chomping at the bit. Your radio station will love it. Better phone 'em to start hyping it now. They'll probably want to cover it live."

"Temple."

"Five nights."

"What?"

"Tied to your four-poster. You can do anything you want."

"I'm new at this. I don't have five nights' backlog."

"I'll help."

"You don't have to bribe me. You just have to explain the situation."

She did, while they sipped the first Margarita.

Matt heard her out. He finally nodded. "I'm thinking a week."

"Whatever. I'll pull the whole thing together. Get you a list of possible questions, panelists, everything."

He glanced at his watch. "In less than twenty-four hours?"

"That's why I gotta get going. I can count on you, then? *Salud!* Skoal! Cheers! 'Bye now. Adios. Au revoir. Ta-ta. Gotta fly."

She pecked him on the lips. He caught her before she could dash away and made a minute of it.

"Tomorrow," she said. "The Phoenix lobby, 1:00 P.M., to get you up to speed. I'll be the 'little blond filly' in the pink hat. Thanks a million!"

She skittered away on her festive slides, heart flying too.

This was the first time that Matt, and not Max, would be assisting her, not only in a skin-saving PR capacity, but maybe in a crime-solving one. Who knew what could come out in a heated debate between these warring men and women?

Temple hit her own place, kicking off her heels and skating barefoot over the slick wood floor to her office, where she riffled through her trusty Rolodex and started making a list and checking it twice. Everything was on computer, but the Rolodex kept her grounded.

Her first calls were to her best sources, so it was easy to slip in a casual question about who alerted them to the protest.

"One of the Red Hat women," Sunny Cadeaux, a sister PR woman-around-town, said. They hadn't talked in ages, but it was instant girl chat.

"You're sure?"

"She didn't leave a name. Just said they were all meeting there and it was very upsetting."

The anonymous Red Hat tipster proved to be a universal source, until Temple got tired of hearing it. She punched in a number she usually didn't have much reason to use.

"Pete," the woman on the phone yelled to a passing colleague, "how'd we end up sending a videographer to that nothing mini-protest at the Crystal Phoenix?"

Temple held her breath as she heard a muffled answer.

"One of our stringers," the reporter reported, sounding disgusted. "Usually is more reliable."

"You have a name?"

"You flack the Crystal Phoenix. I don't want to get an associate in trouble."

"Actually, I'd like to thank whoever it was. I've set up a debate between the Red Hat Sisterhood and the Black Hat Brotherhood moderated by Matt Devine, Mr. Midnight at WCOO-AM."

"No kidding. Mr. Midnight, *hmm*. Nobody ever gets to see him in person. When is it?"

Temple told her, listening to the faint scratch of pencil on paper.

"Good thinking," the reporter said. "People are dying to see what he looks like off the syndicated airwaves, given that dreamy voice. Probably bald and three hundred pounds, like your usual radio personality."

"Decidedly *not*," Temple promised.

"Okay, we'll send someone. Oh. The tipster was someone who hadn't worked for us in a long time."

Temple crossed her fingers.

"Natalie Newman, Mark says. She goes back with us to before she got married and was Natalie Markowitz. She used to be a lot savvier than to call us out on a silly story like this."

No, Temple thought. She was still savvy. And a lot of other things.

Temple thanked the woman, then cut the connection to listen to the lullaby of the dial tone.

Natalie Newman clearly had a double agenda at the convention. Her two cameras proved that. But maybe she had a triple one, and maybe Oleta Lark's murder proved that.

Proving *that* would be a tough assignment for Temple, but she suspected it involved something in the past, something she wasn't seeing yet. She'd keep her eyes and ears on the alert and on Natalie Newman.

Maybe by the time she was through, the local media would think she was Santa Claus, offering the gift of exposing a murderer.

Chapter 26

Mr. Midnight
Sings the Blues

Matt showed up for his usual midnight talk radio gig half an hour early, whistling.

He felt this boundless energy nowadays.

Love was a many-splendored thing and way more than an ex-priest like him was equipped to deal with. He understood that his euphoria and repressed upbringing would soon have to slug it out, but for now, now that he was reassured that all was right with their world in bed and out. It was all gravy with truffles.

"Matt, my man!"

Leticia greeted him during the two precious minutes she was off-mike. "You're lookin' fine, honey. Happy and oh-so-hot. Tell Auntie Ambrosia all about it."

She did resemble an aunt: Aunt Jemima crossed with Queen

Latifah, both comfy and glamorous. Ambrosia was her on-air name and it fit what she dished out over the late-night airwaves. She did a heartfelt oldies and goodies show, full of the songs that made people forget old wounds and work their way through new ones. She coaxed the callers into expressing deep feelings as they recalled some person lost or found, emotions old or new, painful or joyful. Ambrosia cooed the introductions to the songs she picked, always exactly right whether they targeted angst or euphoria. Matt was the station's midnight shrink. Ambrosia was its pre-midnight guardian angel.

Now she grinned at him. "Matt, my bro, you are acting way too happy for the Evening Emperor of Angst. Don't tell me Mr. Midnight is losing his melancholy, baby!"

"Sorry." Matt smiled and sat on the desk's edge. "I just won the personal stakes lottery."

"O-o-o-oh?"

There was nothing about an engagement for a man to flaunt but his happiness. "I asked. She accepted."

"Why shouldn't she, honey, whoever she is?"

"I don't know, because she has free will?"

"Aw, all that Cat-lick stuff. That isn't exciting, man. That isn't entertainment."

"I asked her to marry me."

"Now, that's entertainment. And—?"

Matt shrugged. "She accepted the ring."

"Now, that's just entrepreneurial. The girl want the ring, or you?"

"Me. I think."

"Whatcha doin' *thinkin'* at such a time? Hey. Wait. Gotta get back on the air. Here's a song, just for you, Jude dude."

The Beatles' "Hey, Jude" hit the airwaves with the press of Ambrosia's long, false fingernail painted tangerine.

Matt listened to the classic lyrics, finding them new and, now, personally significant. He was remembering to let her into his heart so he could start to make it better. He wasn't afraid anymore. He knew he was made to go out and get her under his skin. And she was. And he didn't have to carry the world on his shoulders alone anymore. Well, not entirely.

"She had a good guy," he couldn't help saying as the song ended. "Before."

"But he wasn't somebody like you, Mr. Midnight Heartthrob. You think you get all those lovesick females callin' in 'cause you talk pretty? Station didn't put out all those billboards of you lounging on that red suede sofa to bring in the blind, baby."

Matt still felt squirmy about that ad campaign.

"Her former guy *was* somebody: rich, good-looking, dazzling performer, smart, and really a decent guy."

"So?"

"So, I don't feel free to give away his name."

"Now let me see, Matthew."

"Matthias."

"Whatever. *Handsome. Humph.* I get that you got that. Rich? I know what your new two-year contract was, honey boy, so don't jive me there. *A dazzling performer.* And just what do you think we both do night after night on the airwaves? *Smart?* Yeah. *A decent guy.* You are a way more than decent, guy."

"And he was a lot more experienced than I am."

Letitia blinked her Oprah-size double set of false eyelashes at him.

"You know what I mean," Matt said. She did. He'd confided in her over the months like an emotion-blitzed call-in. "With women."

"Are you getting better, honey chile?"

"Oh, yeah."

"*Hmmm.* In that case that new fiancée of yours had better watch out. Ambrosia might be on her tail, or yours."

Matt knew that Ambrosia's worldly bluster was another insulator, like the three hundred pounds her body wore, from the aftermath of childhood sexual abuse.

He'd just been celibate by choice, trying to hide unhappiness behind a vocation. She'd been molested.

He lifted her hand and kissed it. "Any gal or guy'd be lucky to call you girlfriend."

"Well." She beamed at his tribute. "That's what I'm here for, baby, to soothe the troubled soul. When's the wedding?"

"We haven't decided yet. We don't know whether to go for a Vegas quickie or drag the relatives up north into it. Or both."

"Me, I'd want that white dress and long, long train, and everybody lookin' on."

"I suppose most women would."

"Your girl?"

"She'd say no, but probably. Besides, I might like to see her like that myself."

"Every woman wants to be someone's angel for a few hours, honey. Hey! Enough jiving. You gotta go on in fifty seconds."

Letitia scooted out of the literally hot seat to let Matt take her place. He just had time to put on the foam-padded headset, pull his notebook and pen to center spot, and watch the director through the glass window, counting down.

His intro echoed in his ears.

"It's the Midnight Hour with Las Vegas's leading man of mellow advice, the divine Mr. D, Matt Devine."

Chapter 27

The Scene of the Climb

Getting into any nightclub is a snap for those blessed with the ebony coloring and effacing stature of Midnight Louise and myself.

Getting into a nightclub that has reflective black Lucite floors and walls is almost too easy to be ethical.

So the kit and I do the Neon Nightmare Slink and are soon among the merrymakers crowding the bar and the dance floor. If we can avoid some clumsy human foot doing the salsa stomp on our tippy toes or rear members, we will soon melt into these shiny black walls like licorice ghosts.

Well, that comparison leaves something to be desired (mainly that we are not edible like licorice, unless there is a pit bull in the building). Anyway, we do our patented pussyfoot past all the carousing humans to a place that Miss Midnight Louise has earmarked as a "secret entrance."

"It is probably just a janitors' closet," I tell her.

"A tad jealous that *I* have found my way around this maze when you have not?"

"Nonsense, Louise. I always appreciate the efforts of under- lings. *Ouch!*"

That girl spends hours honing her nails to saber-sharpness, not to mention a spit polish.

In the meantime, she has leaped up to trigger a pressure- opening door, like you see on some TV cabinets. We tumble on through as it bounces shut behind us, leaving us in total darkness.

Darkness is never total for the feline nation.

My trusty, long, supersensitive vibrissae (you thought I was referring to something else?) fan out on either side of my noble nose, feeling the air currents, searching for boundaries. Only Santa has whiskers as famed, and mine are white as snow, just like his.

"Forget the white-cane act," Louise hisses at me. "I know the way."

As we mush along my eyes adapt to the almost nonexistent light.

We now spot the whisker-thin vertical and horizontal pres- ence of light leaking from door frames that are not quite tight.

I even hear the distant murmur of human voices.

Alas, I do not recognize the deep, dark timbre of Mr. Max's baritone among them. But I do hear his name mentioned! Both of them.

Louise and I pause outside the pale outline of a door, ears and noses twitching our vibrissae.

We hear the name "Kinsella." We hear the name "Phantom Mage." The people within do not appear to think that they are one and the same, at the moment, or in group discussion. We need to get into that room!

But we are stuck on the outside looking in. Okay. That is not quite as accurately stated as the experienced shamus should put it. We are stuck on the secret inside of Neon Nightmare looking into the even-more-secret inner sanctum of Neon Nightmare. There is obviously no way that a couple of hip black cats are going to bust into a room filled with light and humans and not attract unwelcome attention.

Sure, we will be underestimated, as usual, but we will also be worthy of note, as always.

"I am dying," Louise says, "to find out what they are saying."

Hey! That might be a way. People do not expect dead cats to eavesdrop.

Uh, no. Ma Barker would not want Miss Midnight Louise to sacrifice herself just so I could get an earful. Ma Barker does not have many known maybe-grandkits.

The narrow beam from one of those tiny, high-intensity toy flashlights comes roaming down the hallway. Louise and I flatten and play dead, or background.

The flashlight does not illuminate much, but it does reflect off the satin folds of a full-length black cloak lining.

Eureka! It is an excellent thing that I have kept my coat licked to shiny perfection. Midnight Inc. Investigations sweeps through the now-open door swathed in cloak folds. We melt separately under the nearest chairs and take a deep breath.

"Cosimo!" our savior is hailed. "We were just talking about our current conundrum."

"Conundrum" is a funny old-time word that means "puzzle."

If you are talking "conundrum" in this town, you are talking Mr. Max Kinsella, the most enigmatic magician and counterspy guy on the planet. If he still is *on* the planet, which is what Miss Midnight Louise and I have risked our mutual extremities to find out.

"Where are the odds leaning today?" Cosimo asks, throwing his cloak over his chair back and smacking me in the kisser with several woolen folds sharp enough to eviscerate an eel.

"I think our scintillating Max has offed the Phantom Mage and is lying low until the caper with the Czar's Scepter is history." The voice offering this opinion is darkly female, spoken by a real devil-dame from the heyday of Noir.

I must admit that voice makes my most adaptable member sit

up and take notice. Hubba Hubba Hussy! Louise's foreclaws in my shoulder remind me to keep a low profile. Is not that always like a female?

"Why would he kill the Phantom Mage?" another voice asks.

"The guy ripped off his act. Kinsella acted like he was indifferent to that, but he was an alpha magician in this town not too long ago, and we alpha magicians do not forget, or forgive."

"It would have been a splendid parting gesture," the woman says. She is a Cleopatra-style temptress lounging into a red leather chair like it used to be the skin of her favorite lover before he disappointed her.

"Maybe you are right, Serena," says an old dude in plain civvies, "but he also turned the tables on us, my friends, by undoing the criminal act we required him to perform as a membership ritual. I agree that he is a first-rank magician, but he also has a first-rank ego."

"And you do not?" Serena asks.

"Touché. Still, I find the man too mercurial to be entirely trustworthy. No one knows where he has gone now, for instance. Or why he both did our bidding, rather spectacularly, and *un*did it. Or if he has indeed murdered this lesser magician-acrobat called the Phantom Mage, or if that demise was an accident. Max Kinsella strikes me as a man ever-ready to take credit for accidents."

"We thought at one time that he might *be* the Phantom Mage," suggested an older, heavier woman than Serena, but one no less dramatic. "Perhaps he is missing because he is dead."

The first woman stirs on her chair like a cobra easing into a striking posture. "I doubt it, Czarina. He left me a note."

"A note? What did it say? Let us see it."

"I am sorry, Czarina." Serena preens on her sofa like a purebred with a velvet catnip mouse. "It was rather personal."

"Personal?" The man called Cosimo sounds sharp. "We are all Synth members here, and that dominates such minor matters as concupiscence."

"Concupiscence," Serena derides. "Leave that Latin beating-around-the-bush word to the bishops. Lust is not alien to our gathering. Max wrote that he finds it useful to drop out of sight— a rather cheeky turn of phrase after recent developments—for a while. But that . . . the rest is personal."

It is a gathering of magicians. The white note in her fingers wafts into the man's hand next to her.

"*Hmm.*" Cosimo reads the message with rolling diction. "In his self-imposed exile he will fondly recall your satin skin, the . . . the tattoo of a bat on your—?"

"Enough, Cosimo." Serena had risen and struck, snatching the paper from his hands. "You see that he is alive and definitely kicking."

"I did not know you had found the time to test our new recruit with your charms."

"It was a hasty but memorable encounter. I can assure you that he was interested. Of course, I didn't allow him any real liberties. Not until we were certain of him."

"And now you think we should be."

"Certainly." She settles back into her chair, circling the palms of her scarlet-nailed hands on the arms. "Unless he is really dead, which would be a shame now that I am authorized to screw him."

"He will return, Serena," Czarina assures her. "He is not a fool and I doubt that Death has claimed him. And any normal heterosexual man would return to do obeisance at your thighs, Goddess of the Nile since days of old."

Serena purrs like a Persian of my acquaintance in heat. Too bad I have never been around this Persian of my acquaintance when she *was* in heat.

While I am being enthralled by all this sexy talk, I have let down my guard.

My neck ruff is collared by four shivs.

"This conversation has degenerated," Miss Midnight Louise hisses in my ear. "We are outta here."

And, yes, before I can stutter a fond farewell to the magicians of the Synth who are so busy congratulating themselves,

I am whisked out into the corridor by Louise, who has taken a dislike to sexy talk on many other occasions.

This is a side effect of the process known as "fixing."

I do not know why it is called that.

But I think that Miss Serena could use a bout of that herself.

Chapter 28

Debate to the Death

Five thousand Red Hat Sisterhood members pouring into the Crystal Phoenix and the Goliath hosting hotels made the Black Hat Brotherhood vastly outmanned for the day's debate. Luckily, only a few hundred Red Hat women showed up for it.

Even so vastly outnumbered, the fifteen men entered the hotel like a posse surrounding a wrestling favorite. In fact, overnight the golden oldie boys had come up with American-flag-blue rhinestone hatbands and red-dyed pheasant feathers to stick in those glitzy new bands.

Matt stood beside Temple at the back of the debate room, watching the Red State dudes in Blue and the Blue State dolls in Red file into the hotel's small-event auditorium. The Red Hat Sisterhood outnumbered the Black Hat Brothers a zillion to one, but on the raised dais, at the neutral white-linen clothed tables featuring a small tabletop podium for Matt, it was four black-and-blues against four red-and-purples.

"I can see why the TV stations sent so many videographers," Matt murmured to Temple, blinking at the colorful and sparkling gathering. "Makes me happy radio is my medium. Saves me a lot of eye strain and headaches."

"TV loves people willing to make spectacles of themselves."

"Which is why you counseled me to wear an ivory shirt and blazer, no tie. Not even a blue and red one."

"You do get the association?"

"It's a neutral color scheme for a moderator," he said, eyeing his bland facade.

Temple raised her eyebrows and said nothing.

"Oh, I get it! Red, white, and blue, reading left to right. That is 'spin' with a capital *S*."

"Plus," she said, adjusting the collar of his open-necked shirt, "you look so dreamy in off-white."

"The PR maven is making decisions based on how 'dreamy' the moderator looks?"

"Absolutely. Perk of the job."

"I just hope I can keep these extreme debaters from each other's throats. Maybe you really needed Jerry Springer."

"I do have some Fontana brothers muscle lurking in the wings." Temple nodded to her own version of bodyguards standing at the extremes of the debating platform.

"Good Lord, I'm dressed like a Fontana brother clone," Matt realized.

"Northern Italian, where the blonds come from, not southern. Those natives are brunet."

"You're also going for a revival meeting look here too, aren't you?"

"My dear man, I'm trying to touch on numerous subtle cultural nuances."

"I never knew PR was so manipulative."

"Or that I was?"

"If I weren't so nervous about doing this moderator gig, I'd probably have a long answer for that one."

"You'll be great. You improvise six nights a week live on your radio show. How could this be any worse?"

Matt forbore to say anything more.

"Oh," Temple added. "There is one thing."

"Yeah?"

"You look somewhat suspicious."

"It's that 'one thing' element you mentioned."

Temple grimaced. "We have a prima donna on board."

Matt waited.

"Savannah Ashleigh, fading D-movie actress, is a celebrity emcee for the Red Hat Sisterhood. She's really hard to hold back. I had to allow her to introduce you."

"I don't know her and she doesn't know me. How can she introduce me?"

"She's show biz. I gave her a bio. How much damage can she do? It was that, or have a bloodbath offstage, like in *Macbeth*."

Matt sighed. "I thought one always called it 'the Scottish play' or it would be cursed by some new death."

"This isn't a play performance," Temple said. "And it will actually boost your career. You deserve more than radio exposure."

"I don't need it."

"But your panting public does." Temple went on tiptoe to demonstrate what his panting public needed with a quick but thorough kiss.

Then she backed off.

She felt like a nervous matchmaker, as she always did at a full-press media event. Now she had to sit back and watch all the ingredients blend into some powerhouse super-salad of hype no one could predict, least of all her.

Especially unpredictable was Electra's red-hatted presence in the audience. Temple was uneasy about that, but maybe seeing Elmore make a public ass out of himself would be cathartic, which was a fancy word for feeling self-justified. Temple understood that this was so traumatic for Electra, having her past zooming back at her like a motorcycle out of control.

Temple had been there recently. . . .

Matt would be the sane, neutral bridge between two volatile

substances: manly men and womanly women. Both had enough years on them to add up to media TNT.

Temple prepared to bite her nails as Savannah Ashleigh did a Marilyn Monroe wiggle to the podium to start the show. Even her voice was MM breathy.

"Ladies and gentlemen. I am so proud and happy to introduce your host for this event, the yummy-on-the-tummy and even ears and other areas too—Mr. Midnight! Matt Devine from 'The Midnight Hour' on station WCOO, that's pronounced W-'cooo,' and we will when we hear him over the microphone. I must say that he looks as yummy as he sounds, so voice isn't everything."

Temple felt her eyes crossing, but the TV cameras zoomed in on Savannah's cleavage and then on Matt's face as he approached the podium.

Claps and whistles faded.

Matt leaned toward the microphone, looking boyishly mischievous. "I would like to thank the pulchritudinous Miss Ashleigh for her extremely wholesome delivery of the introduction."

The paraphrase of JFK's response to Marilyn Monroe's notoriously inciting "Happy Birthday" serenade spawned another round of hoots, applause, and catcalls.

Temple let out a long-held breath. Matt would do just fine.

Now, let the games begin!

"Girls just want to have fun," Candy Crenshaw was saying into her microphone. "Boys just want to have guns." The Red Hat Sisterhood's clown princess was ready to crack wise.

Only four minutes into the debate, tempers were already boiling over.

"Just a minute, Ms. Crenshaw," Matt said. "Let's get this straight. "You're saying that grown men can't indulge their fantasy personas, but that women can?"

"Women can-can," Cal Crenshaw shot back, leaning to look around the moderator's podium to glare at his ex-wife. "I happen to know this woman is sixty-three and a half years old. Why is she got up like a saloon girl from the Old West?"

A titter stirred the audience, for the feather boas did scream "saloon floozy."

"Thank you, gentlemen and ladies," Crenshaw went on with a tip of his Western hat brim.

"Why are you got up as Wyatt Earp?" Kit asked quickly.

"To match you gals," another BHB panelist said. "Anything you can do we can do better."

"Can you get five thousand soul brothers to meet in Las Vegas?" Candy Crenshaw asked. "How many of you disgruntled dudes are there? Fifteen in all?"

"That's enough to ruffle your feathers," Crenshaw bragged.

Matt intervened. "Let's have a duel of the membership numbers, ladies and gents. Gentlemen?"

"Mmm*ble-mmmble*," Crenshaw muttered into his mike.

"I didn't quite hear that," Matt prodded.

"Forty-five," he answered.

"Must be their waist sizes," Candy Crenshaw quipped.

The audience roared.

"Look who's talking?" Elmore Lark riposted.

"Enough," Matt said, "or we'll all think you're comparing IQs."

Laughter came from the audience and both sides of the debating table.

"Look," Matt said, "can't you Black Hat guys admit you get a kick from dressing up in an over-the-top 'uniform' and parading around in public?"

"We have points to make," Mike Crenshaw growled. A little.

"So do the ladies." Matt was now firmly in the role of peacemaker.

Things were getting so cozy that the water pitcher was crossing the dividing line of the podium and snaking its way from the red-and-purple side to the black-and-blue side.

Temple felt like a diplomat. Both sides were kind of cute, really, the flamboyant middle-aged folks playing dress-up. Even the issues they raised were mostly moot. People their age could hardly care that passionately about the sexual one-upmanship one-upwomanship games anymore, could they?

She eyed Matt with fond pride. He'd been perfect for this

delicate assignment. Maybe, when the clips ran on TV, he'd get some master of ceremonies gigs out of it. Not that she wanted him out of town any more than he was . . .

Even Electra's ex, Elmore Lark, appeared to be mellowing. He coughed into a Western kerchief, then stood up to wave at the crowd, doffing his hat and putting hand on heart.

That was a bit much. He was an unadmitted bigamist, no matter the excuses he made, not some hokey Buffalo Bill Cody impersonator waving at the audience like a star performer. . . .

Oops. He keeled over onto the table.

He must have been drinking, had a concealed pint of something in the back pocket of his jeans.

Oops.

Temple started running to the front of the room, but by now the whole audience was rising and buzzing. TV videographers were crowding like crows with camcorders around that end of the table.

Elmore Lark had been taken ill.

Or . . . killed. Right in front of God and TV cameras and everyone.

Chapter 29

Lark to Lark?

The sirens wailed away down the Strip.

Elmore Lark lay in the back of an ambulance under the intense care of two emergency technicians.

Temple was about ready to ride along with them as a patient.

Her first job after alerting hotel security to call an ambulance was to drag Electra out of the room to the nearest Fontana brother.

"Home, James," Temple had said. That smooth, olive-skinned Fontana brow had puckered.

"I'm Armando, Miss Temple—"

"She needs to vanish. Fast."

"Ah. Just the job for a Viper. Madame?" He bowed and offered his arm to Electra, who promptly forgot all about the clear and present danger to her loathed not-really-ex-husband.

Temple was left unescorted, and uninspired.

The Crystal Phoenix continued to be the site of homicide most bona fide. The Red Hat Sisterhood's "Big Wheel in Las Vegas" convention kept coming up corpses. Temple's best and biggest client kept showing up on the evening news in less than a positive light, and Max was MIA.

Matt, however, was standing by his woman. Right now. And he was way more bracing than even a Fontana brother.

"What a rotten break," he told Temple, massaging her iron-hard shoulder muscles. "Although the way those panelists were snipping at each other during the debate, it's a wonder *I'm* not finely chopped liver."

"Thank God," Temple said. "I really don't know what to do. This convention seems primed for trouble, not to mention murder. Every time I try to turn the thing around, it gets worse."

"I'll say," Matt said, sounding grim.

"What? What don't I know now?"

"The cops can't guarantee I can leave in time for my 'Midnight Hour' show. Lark's collapse could be medical, but the EMTs didn't detect anything obvious. So it could be anything, including murder. So that's how they're treating the scene and every 'actor' in it. It seems the water pitcher passed through my hands to both sides of the debating table."

"The water pitcher? They're thinking poisoned water? Do you know how impossible that would be?"

"Obviously, you do." Matt waited.

"Water is tasteless as well as clear. It'd be almost impossible to doctor with strong poisons, which smell, taste, and look bad!"

"I doubt I'm a serious candidate. The police just need a candidate and I was up there on the podium with all those unknown quantities."

Temple wrapped her hand through his arm.

"It's that pale Fontana Brothers suit. It made you *look* suspicious."

"It made you like it, so it's not all bad."

She leaned her head against his upper arm. "I am so

flummoxed here. It's bad enough that Electra is a suspect for the first murder. If her bigamist non-ex-husband dies, she's a shoo-in for the role of serial killer."

"That marriage, real or not, was ages back in time. People today don't hold on to the bitterness of a failed marriage as long as they used to."

"That's true." She looked up at him. "But your mother did."

"They weren't married."

"That's why she's so bitter."

"What does my mother have to do with it?"

"It just made me remember that the body may age but the emotions don't."

"That true for you and Max?"

She reared back. "He's out of my life. I just want it to be because I said so, not because something bad happened to him."

"So now you're God?"

"You won't get this, or how your mother feels, unless you become a girl."

That made him pause. "You're right. My mom's furious because my father was finessed out of her life, and mine, by trickery. His relatives just told this pregnant young girl that he'd died 'over there,' and they'd give her a two-flat to live in and rent out the other half to keep her and the baby, and good-bye. When he was just fine! She never had any say in it, and neither did he. Now, when I found him and he wants to talk to her—sincerely, I think—she hates *him*, not the people who kept them apart. If that's girl-think, I don't get it, but I guess it makes sense to her, at least emotionally."

"Said with the total clarity and sensitivity the adoring public, including me, expects from Mr. Midnight."

"Temple, I've never had a girlfriend before, much less a fiancée. Max must have had several, starting way back with Kathleen O'Connor. You have to cut me a lot of slack."

"But I don't want to cut you slack." She grabbed him by the creamy Fontana Brothers lapels. "Not one bit. I want you on your toes, working to make me a very happy girl."

"That's not work."

"That makes me want to make you a very happy boy."

"I think we're in sync on the personal front. What can I do here and now? I have to put in my time with the detectives, but then I'm yours."

"Report back to me on everything they want to know about. Meanwhile, I'm going to cruise this crazy, mixed-up crowd to see what I can find out."

When Matt had vanished into the frantic stew of milling red-and-purple women, Temple began to circulate. She often did her best work—in PR and as an unofficial PI—while eavesdropping.

Rumor was making the rounds, but benignly. Word was one of the Black Hat Brotherhood guys had suffered a heart attack. Poor fellow, but that Type A behavior no doubt brought it on. Why won't middle-aged ever men *listen* and slow down?

The Black Hat Brotherhood was slowing down *now*, after the shock of Elmore's collapse. Temple had seen their hats lined up at the Crystal Court bar, as they knocked back some high-octane liquid tranquilizers. Elmore's attack had unnerved them as well as the women in the audience.

Many of the women here were widows. A man collapsing at the debate table revived their memories and losses.

Several women were zooming around on motorized scooters, lacking mobility but making up for it by driving as if racing in the Indy 500. Everywhere, she spotted signs of female zest. These seasoned women were not going to let themselves become invisible, just as they weren't afraid to look bizarre while clinging to the epitome of feminine accessories despite sagging chins and boobs and butts, varicose-veined legs, drawn-on eyebrows, purple and red wigs, every exaggerated feminine grace that age was assumed to strip away. And they reveled in flouting the politically correct act of fading into a corner and dying.

Temple had never seen so many sparkling eyes, whether under white hair or gaudy wig. Every gal here was a one-woman support group for every other gal here. One, in her late eighties, had driven in from California, Red Hat regalia packed in her red convertible.

The red and purple colors everywhere made even the feeblest woman look vibrant. Temple was soaking up energy. *Zap!* That she had even for a moment thought thirty-one was a significant birthday seemed so incredibly shallow now that she wanted to run around the block thirty-one times in penance, and a Las Vegas Strip block was gigantic!

And penance was a Catholic concept, Matt's hang-up, not hers.

And yet. She was beginning to see that she'd be as baffled by Max's instant and unhailed defection in thirty years as now. And that a sixty-something her would still have a thirtyish heart, and memory, as these women did.

So. This killing and perhaps attempted killing weren't silly senior citizen affairs, but possibly came from the still-living heart of what may have happened decades ago. Our bodies aged, but our deepest, dearest . . . and darkest . . . emotions didn't.

How could a callow, thirty-going-on-thirty-one filly like her solve mysteries of the heart leading to murder at the other end of the age kaleidoscope?

Chapter 30

Mad as a Hatter

"I am so humiliated," Miss Midnight Louise says.

I am so amazed. I did not think anything could humiliate this feline Gloria Steinem.

Gloria Steinem is a passé name in the media world now. Have you noticed what rare birds major media feminists are nowadays? Myself, I could not be happier about it. After witnessing the brouhaha outside the Crystal Phoenix, I am thinking my sympathies lie with the Black Hat Brotherhood. I do not wear a hat, but I am black.

Miss Midnight Louise is black like me and she does not wear a hat, but I sense that we have our differences, as usual.

"Those Black Hat Brotherhood thugs," she fusses. "Turning my turf into a circus act."

"You think that the Red Hat ladies were not already doing that?"

"Only in the sense of admirable joie de vivre."

Okay, my "joie" is about to go DOA. Dead On Arrival. "You have to admit that they are a rather . . . feathery . . . lot," I say.

"It is all in the name of fun."

"The last time I looked, pursuing feathers was in the name of survival for our species."

"Only in the wild. And in the wild, the male of the species is usually the more colorful and flagrant. That is so unfair. It is only right that these Red Hat Sisterhood ladies opt for a brighter plumage in their mature years."

"So what can I look forward to you wearing in your mature years, which are admittedly a fair ways off?"

"*Not* a flamingo fedora," she says, referring to my unfortunate brief stint as a cat food commercial huckster wearing that obnoxious article.

Gadzooks, Midnight Louie is cooked! I did not think anyone remembered my ill-fated venture into TV stardom. The greatest and most effective weapon of a female, what makes her indeed deadlier than the male, is a long memory.

"This was a put-up job," I comment.

"I thought so too. Your Miss Temple was caught flat-footed, which is hard to do with a person as prone to wearing stiletto heels as she is."

"Flat-footed *at first*. That is permissible. The last I saw, she was flying around like a madwoman trying to put a lid on things."

"I see we are back to the subject of hats," she notes.

"Yes. It is odd that no one much wears hats today, and yet they are so central to this case."

"Central how?"

"A plethora of hats at a convention can hide a lot of things."

"Identities," she suggests.

"Yes."

"Weapons?"

"Could be. The crown of a hat can conceal a lot. Not to mention all the hatboxes being toted into this hotel."

"*Humph.* The best concealing headgear so far is the high-crowned ten-gallon hats those would-be cowboys affect."

"Yup," I say.

"They are the loose cannons in this convention."

"But they are not *in* this convention. They are convention-crashers."

"I wonder why."

"They have grievances, or think they do."

"Still, why make a spectacle of themselves?"

"Their so-called ex-better halves are having all the fun?"

"That is a silly motive. Men are used to going off and drinking beer and shooting things all on their own. Why should they deny the women in their lives the harmless hobbies of shopping, spending money, and looking outrageous?"

"All those things you describe could be addictions to the weak human personality."

"As if you are not addicted to catnip and female gullibility!"

"Females? Gullible? Louise. Please."

"Some are," she says softly. "And these women with their red chapeaux and Chardonnay and brave spirits are fighting off what could be a lonely old age with others of their kind. Ma Barker is such a one, with no mate, no certain home, and many dependents to look after."

"She will have a home," I growl. "At the Circle Ritz. I just have to get my people's attention off the hullabaloo and homicide here so I can enlighten them on what is needed under their very noses and on their doorstep."

"That is very noble of you, Dadster."

I cringe, as usual, at the impudent form of address.

She muses on. "I am not about to let Mr. Max go gently into that dark night. I find the doings at his address most suspicious and intend to stake it out indefinitely. So I guess *you* will have to spring Miss Electra Lark from suspicion, or Ma Barker and her gang will have traipsed the length of Las Vegas, at your recommendation, from Nowheresville to Nothingsville for naught."

Sigh. Miss Midnight Louise sure knows how to sand the luster off a guy's topcoat.

But the kit has it right. If I wish my easily distractible Circle Ritz gang to get on with the program and help my disenfranchised kind, I will have to solve this murder for them. Again.

Amazing. I take on a little job of rehabilitation for the homeless. Then, suddenly, I am whiskers deep in homicide and red hats and it is not even a Vatican conspiracy thriller. Call it my Givenchy Code.

Only in Las Vegas.

Chapter 31

E-mailed to Death

While musing about murder and the middle-aged woman, Temple was almost run over by a red scooter manned . . . womaned by a P and R lady with a gorgeous golden Persian cat riding shotgun.

Hey! Wasn't that one of Savannah Ashleigh's Persians? Louie had been sweet on the silver one, to the point of earning him a false paternity suit. The golden one had been sweet where her sister and mistress had been sour.

But . . . would Savannah Ashleigh really allow one of her precious Persians to hot-rod around the convention floor on a hot red scooter? Nah. Not if she knew, and maybe her attention these days was all on Taco and Belle.

Meanwhile, Temple's hot silver cell phone text message

revealed a call to order. The Red-Hatted League required a "confab," having dug up lots of "sensitive info."

Temple returned to her designated conference room, the door still manned by a Fontana brother, just a different one every time.

"The ladies have preceded you into the room," Eduardo said. "I've ordered several light cocktails to hold them. At great personal risk," he added. "They have a propensity for doing weapons searches."

"On Fontana brothers, or the general population?"

Eduardo frowned. "Lamentably, they seem inclined to bless us with the most personal attention. 'Lend a woman a Lexus, and she thinks she owns it. Give a woman a wink, and she thinks she owns *you*.' These are fun ladies, really. Remind me of my grandma Belladonna."

"You don't want to mention that 'grandma' part in this crowd. Trust me."

Eduardo shrugged. "I'm off in two hours. Ralph can watch his own butt."

Temple sighed. She was sure Eduardo meant that last comment literally. Still, good help was hard to find at a major national convention, and she needed nonpolice sources.

Her entrance evoked a round of applause.

"Have we got 'mail,' " Alice said.

"E-mail," Phyll added. "Yup. That stuff never goes away on the Internet, if you know where to look."

At the moment, Phyll looked like an extremely smug purple and redheaded nuthatch.

Temple sat down, ready to take copious notes.

"Here's the deal," Judy said. " 'The Black Hat Brotherhood' isn't just some macho group that just sprang up. Two of its founders are disgruntled Red Hat Sisterhood ex-spouses."

"Elmore?"

Judy nodded.

"So you're saying that some of the women here might be murderers?"

"You do not get it, Little Pink."

Temple took umbrage. To them, she was not only small, she was young and green. And *pink!*

"This stuff is not just sixties' generation carping," Phyll added. "It digs down deep. The Red Hat Sisterhood is fairly new on the scene, only a few years old."

"But the *reason* for its existence is eternal," Judy said, portentously.

Always look for a librarian to be portentous. They'd earned it. They knew what everybody else had forgotten. Temple had never thought of librarians as pit bulls with bifocals before.

But the incriminating information Judy and Phyll had dug up in a few short hours was amazing. They'd returned with reams of printouts cradled on the crooks of their arms like freshly printed thousand-dollar bills.

"There's that much hard info out there on our victims and suspects?" she asked.

"There's that much information out there on you and me," Phyll said. "Hey, don't hyperventilate, Temple. Just kidding. A lot of this stuff is bits and pieces of Oleta's unpublished memoirs."

"That looks like more than enough to publish," Temple observed as the papers hit the conference tabletop. She'd usually only heard papers make such a substantial "smack" when heaving the Sunday *New York Times* to her coffee table top . . . when Max had gotten one as preface to a lazy day of reading in bed.

The memory saddened her. An engaged girl with puzzles to solve shouldn't be sad. Temple picked up the top page and started skimming. It was a digest printout. Oleta's e-mail address had been steamedfemme4311@hotmail.com. That significant numeral made it scary to contemplate how many mad, mad, mad madwomen were out there.

The weird part was that being a woman scorned had come to Oleta after she had made Electra into one. Didn't Oleta and women like her understand that you reap what you sow? What goes around comes around? Though men certainly didn't seem to get that, either.

Temple sat down slowly, reading.

This was disastrous. The current segment described Electra as a vengeful harpy, aching to get into a literal catfight with the tender young innocent that Oleta portrayed herself as having been. Her memoirs made a strong case for Elmore needing to use any means to escape the Electra Oleta portrayed, even to marrying another woman without the formality of a divorce.

Women who made a habit of poaching other women's men often made the cast-off wife the villain. Until it was their turn.

"It doesn't look good for Electra," Alice agreed, reading silently over Temple's shoulder. "It's almost as if Oleta had planted a motive for Electra in these e-mails."

" 'Almost as if,' heck no! That's exactly what she did."

Temple stood up, excited. "What if the wrong victim died? What if Oleta had always intended to kill Elmore here, and blame Electra for it? If the widely distributed 'peeks' at her memoirs were a setup?"

"That would be pretty fiendish," Phyll said.

"But perfect. She mentions Elmore as resenting her Red Hat Sisterhood activities and book project. And he must have been a member of the Black Hat Brotherhood for some time. Why? Ironically, maybe he was going to kill her after she left him? Maybe did? She could have known that the Black Hats would be here protesting this convention, and she knew Electra lived in Las Vegas."

"How'd she know that?" asked Judy.

"Electra runs the Lovers' Knot Wedding Chapel. Those chapels are always making the news. Bretangelo, pop stars Bret Aspen and Laura D'Angelo, got married at her chapel just a couple months ago. That generated press all over the country."

"Isn't a 'tangelo' a hybrid fruit?" Alice wondered.

"There have been rumors about her," Starla said darkly. "That mango-blond hair job!"

"Aren't they divorced already?" Judy asked.

"Well, yeah," Temple said. "Stars marry and adopt and divorce at the drop of a scandal sheet these days. Las Vegas and Reno are conveniently close for both ends of the cycle. I hope those babes keep the third-world kids longer than they keep the Rodeo Drive husbands."

Red-hatted heads shook in agreement and sorrow at what the world of international celebrity had come to.

"Elmore Lark was attacked too. But why *after* Oleta," Judy objected.

Temple thought. "His illness sure could be an attack. Maybe he was meant to die first? Maybe the method, whatever it was, had been set in motion. Poison, say. It had to be that if he hasn't just suffered a stroke or heart attack. Poison is a murder method with a very forgiving timeline."

"How? Oleta couldn't foresee the debate?"

"Maybe the method that made him collapse had nothing to do with the debate."

"Or the water pitcher. That would get your significant other off the hook."

For a second, Temple assumed that Phyll was referring to Max. He sure was habit-forming when it came to scrapes and schemes.

But, no, her SO now was Matt, and she herself had managed to get him involved in a possible attempted murder case.

"Does this look like a real book?" she asked Judy of the print-outs. "Or just random parts?"

"Hard to tell. It does dwell a lot on her meeting Elmore thirty years ago and winning him away from Electra. 'Weaning' was the way she put it."

"Ugh," Temple said. " 'Weaning' a man off his wife. Makes you wonder why she lasted as long among the living as she did."

"Anyway, it's hard to tell whether she was accentuating the negative because she was now bitter and alone, or because she wanted to spill everything and make things hot for Elmore."

"It's hard to believe a legitimate publisher would be that interested in a sad old tale like that. Can you find out how real a deal Oleta Lark had for this so-called memoir?"

"Hey," Phyll said. "If the truth is out there on the Worldwide Web, a librarian can find it."

"I'm not so sure—" Temple began when Judy jumped in.

"The ordinary author wouldn't spread all that material free over the Web, you'd think."

"That's the smart way to market these days," Alice objected. "Tease 'em with a free sample, hopefully scandalous, on the Web. That's how you build buzz."

Temple nodded. "And if you were out to slander someone, that'd be the perfect way to start. Oleta seems to have been a pretty vengeful person."

"She writes a lot," Starla added, "about finding salvation and self-esteem through the Red Hat Sisterhood. The title is *Confessions of a Randy Red Hat Woman*."

Temple the PR maven bristled at that. "That title wasn't going to sit well with the organization and most members. Talk about a million motives for murder."

"Maybe she was using us as the first line of assault," Alice suggested, "but she seemed sincere. She'd joined three years ago and was hugely gung ho. In fact, she planned to debut her Red Hot Hattery Shop at this convention, then open one in Reno."

"She set up shop here for the first time." Temple seized on that. "Just in time for the 'Big Wheel in Las Vegas' convention." Temple considered. "That's savvy marketing, but does it also disguise a different agenda here? We need to ask the other members of the Reno Scarlet Women what Oleta seemed like. Does the Red Hat Sisterhood Web site list all the different chapters in the country?"

"Sure thing, sugar." Starla snapped her cinnamon gum, exhaling a spicy scent. "We're a network. We like to know all about each other. Our Red-Hatted League was even featured in one of the recent magazines."

"Was Electra mentioned or pictured in the national magazine, say, recently?"

"Of course!" Judy said. "Yes! That's right. Oleta would have seen that. Mentioned *and* pictured. She is our Red-Hatted League headwoman, after all."

"*Hmmm.*" Temple was thinking that she ought to look up the Sherlock Holmes short story that gave this particular chapter its name. Might be some vague connection to events in the here and now.

Who knows?

And speaking of that, she needed to find out what the police knew by now about the attack on Elmore, if it was attempted murder. Who was prime for squealing?

The ever-sympathetic Morrie Alch, of course.

Ms. Sherlock Strikes
a Holmes Run

It was amazing what you could find on the Internet, Temple mused for the millionth time when she hit her home computer that evening.

So, thinking of "headed," Temple had typed "The Red-Headed League" on a search engine along with the surname "Doyle." She'd found a version of the story in question as fast as you could say "Sherlock Holmes."

She'd read all the Holmes stories as a kid, but had forgotten most of them. Luckily, this particular tale had been read by a girl already being teased about her "fire-engine" red hair. Some of her sixth-grade classmates, mostly boys, would wail like sirens whenever she came into view.

Her mother said it was because they liked her, but that had

never made sense to Temple. Her older brothers were supposed to like her, and all they could do was ditch her and dis her. Only they didn't call it dissing then.

So when she read the tale of Mr. Jabez Wilson in far-off, old-fashioned London, who was given a mysterious but well-paying job because of his red hair, young Temple treasured it.

Although the notion of a Red-Headed League seeking out red-haired people for easy work and good pay turned out to be a hoax to cover a bank robbery, Temple had thrilled at the idea that red hair was special and valued and would bring her adventure and rewards.

Her mother had previously tried to console her with that "special" idea, but she believed it more from reading Doyle's story. She wished she'd had an interesting name to go with her interesting hair, like Mr. Jabez Wilson in the story. It took her a few more years to appreciate being named "Temple" instead of "Ashley."

For a couple of years, on school documents, she had written her required middle name as "Jazabelle" instead of the hated "Ursula."

That ended in junior high when the phys. ed. teacher, a sixtyish woman built like coach John Madden but with a plainer face, had called her "Temple Jazabelle Barr" aloud when she flunked out of basketball. (Who would put a four-foot-eleven girl in as a guard anyway?)

That whole moniker being repeated twelve times a day by the girls in junior high was worse than the siren shrieks of the boys in grade school. So "Ursula" duly appeared on her school cards again, and thankfully no one ever said that out loud. Even the aunt for whom she was named Ursula went by the nickname of "Kit." Temple wondered if Aldo knew that.

Still, reading the story again had been fun. Like a lot of the Holmes stories, it showed a naive person being dragooned into a puzzling situation because a hidden schemer had a secret purpose.

It was not unwise for a modern-day Sherlock to keep that classic formula in mind.

Chapter 33

Big Wheels

It was 6:00 P.M. and Matt was wondering where his wandering SO was. So he was surprised to hear an alto female voice when he answered his cell phone.

"I need to talk to you," C. R. Molina said without any greeting, as usual, the busy, brusque homicide lieutenant personified.

"Your place or mine?" he asked, determined to be playful in the face of such unrelenting social sobriety.

"Neutral ground," she specified.

"Is there any in Las Vegas?"

"For you or me, probably not. Say, seven?"

"Charley's Hamburgers?"

He was a radio shrink. He could hear the hesitation before

she answered. Apparently, for some reason, Charley's wasn't neutral ground for her.

"Fine." The shortness of Molina's answer showed her annoyance with herself for what she'd felt when she heard that name and location.

Matt would have to try to finesse the reason out of her when they met, simply because it was his job. And it never hurt to know what a homicide lieutenant thought and felt when you'd literally been front and center at a murder scene.

"Seven, then," he said.

"You still driving that silver flash?"

"Yeah. You want a spin in it?"

"Maybe. Just maybe I do."

Matt eased the Crossfire into an unpaved parking spot near Charley's. This was his first real new car, paid for and picked out by him. Being a Catholic priest with a vow of poverty for seventeen years made getting a nice car both a cherished luxury and a venial sin.

He recognized Molina's personal aging Toyota wagon a few spaces over and ambled over to lean down to the open driver's window.

Again, she wasted no time on sentimental greetings.

"The blue cheese bacon burger," she told him. "Hold the ketchup. Mustard, no fries. We eat in my car. When we're all tidy again we take that spin in yours."

Matt lifted an eyebrow, but nodded and went to the window. Charley's was a small, tumbledown shack on a lowly street, no glitz, no glam, just the best darn hamburgers in town. And they were way politically incorrect on the fat and grease meter.

Molina was right. No amount of napkins could save a car from the lethally good grease of a Charley's burger. He ordered the Philly steakburger for himself, then made his way over the lumpy dirt of the lot to the passenger's side of her car.

She had the driver's seat pushed way back to accommodate her almost six-foot frame. Matt scooted the passenger seat, set full forward for Molina's teen daughter Mariah, back all the way so they could talk face-to-face.

First they bit into the huge burgers, chewing them down to eatable height.

"What's new?" she finally asked. "Besides having your fingerprints all over a possibly lethal pitcher of hotel water?"

"That what this is about?"

"Among other things." Molina bucked in her seat.

Probably the semiautomatic at the small of her back felt bulky against the car seat, Matt thought. Packing iron must get uncomfy in this overheated climate.

Molina was an interesting woman, strong, complex, unpredictable. Temple scoffed at her no-nonsense looks. Matt had seen nuns in civvies who dressed with more style. Her dark blunt-cut hair and strong, unmanicured eyebrows suited her. He liked her a lot, but she was a cop and she never let you forget it. And at the moment he was the dork in the center spotlight with a possibly poisoned man two places to the left and languishing in Never-Never Land at the local hospital.

"Tell me why," Molina said after eating her burger. She rolled her grease-soaked tissues into a small hard ball inside a fistful of flimsy diner napkins.

He understood instantly what she meant. "Temple—"

"Oh, God."

"Temple does PR for the Crystal Phoenix. You know that."

"So she's ring-mastering those wild and crazy red-and-purple women around the hotel?"

"The Red Hat Sisterhood has its own homegrown PR force, I understand. Temple got involved because of Electra Lark."

"Alch told me." Molina gave him another "Oh, God."

"So you asked me here for spiritual advice?" he said.

She gave him a narrow look. "You should be so lucky. I agree that you and Electra Lark are two of the unlikeliest murder candidates in Clark County, but you do have the Circle Ritz in common, not to mention the ever-dangerous Temple Barr. So how did you get up on that podium between two warring factions in the battle of the sexes?"

"It was . . . Temple's idea."

"Of course. So now she has two Circle Ritz pals in the bull's-eye for murder."

"Fiancé," Matt said, not knowing why he'd spilled the beans. Maybe that word "pal" had done it.

"Fiancé? Who's the fiancé?"

"Me, I'm told."

"Temple and you are . . . engaged?"

He nodded.

It took a lot to shake the stoic expression off Carmen Molina's face, but that admission had done it. She couldn't have looked more shocked if he had confessed to killing Elmore Lark, or Abraham Lincoln.

She took a deep breath. "Well, that changes a whole lot of modus operandi around this town."

He knew she was thinking of Max Kinsella, but Matt didn't want to go there. He said nothing while she absorbed his new status as if digesting a singularly disagreeable meal.

"I suppose congratulations are in order, but . . . look at you! Now *you*'re in the middle of a murder investigation. That's what squiring Miss Temple Barr around town will get you. I tremble to picture you two as the Nick and Nora of Las Vegas, but this town always did lean to the ridiculous. You done eating here?"

He nodded.

"Good. Take me for a ride in that eye-candy car of yours."

He shrugged and followed her out of the Toyota, which she locked manually after dumping the hamburger leavings in the nearby trash can. He followed suit, beeping the Crossfire open when they were twenty feet away.

"Show-off." She smiled finally, though. "Small, isn't it? Will I fit?"

He nodded, but Molina had to scoot the passenger seat back because it was set all the way forward, for Temple.

"My kid," she commented, "and your pint-size fiancée. At least my daughter will outgrow the full-frontal seat position in my car."

"Where do you want to go?"

"Ninety-three north. There's a speed trap six miles south of one-sixty-eight, then it's clear sailing until Ash Springs."

"You want me to speed, Lieutenant?"

"I want to blow my mind clear, Devine."

"About the Crystal Phoenix death and attempted death?"

"About Fontana brothers and Red Hat dames, and cabbages and queens."

Matt didn't know how to respond to lines from *Alice in Wonderland,* so he eased the low-slung car over the pitted dirt lot and onto smooth asphalt.

He kept the windows down, and soon the wind was whipping their hair around.

"You keep a neat car," she noted.

"Tied down," he suggested.

"Now you really *are* tied down," Molina commented.

Matt flushed in the dark, remembering Temple's teasing promises for his cooperation in moderating this fatal debate. Which had now made him an attempted murder suspect.

"How did this all happen?" Molina asked. They had to shout over the wind.

"Temple needed a likely moderator for the Red Hat Sisterhood, Black Hat Brotherhood debate she dreamed up to defuse the shouting match in front of the hotel, so—"

"Not that. The momentous engagement. You cut out the great and powerful Max Kinsella. How'd that happen?"

Matt was feeling really, really modest. He knew that Max Kinsella had cut out Max Kinsella by not being there for Temple. Matt felt like the lucky man by default.

"I finally asked," he said. "That simple."

"Knee, ring, and all that?"

"Ring. No knee. Is there a reason you want all the slushy details?"

"Maybe." She'd leaned her elbow on the open door with the window rolled down and the wind howling past her face. She pulled herself back into the car again. "So. Is Max Kinsella out of town in some romantic funk, or something?"

"Why?"

"No more stalking incidents for a whole six days, that's why."

"That's a record?"

"Lately, yeah."

Matt mulled the situation.

For several weeks, Molina had discovered, her modest bungalow in Our Lady of Guadalupe parish had been entered by a stalker. Items she hadn't owned had shown up in her closet, then on her bed, then in her daughter Mariah's room. The objects had been harmless, but sexually taunting, including a trail of red rose petals through the house to Mariah's bedroom and then to hers.

She was sure Max Kinsella was behind it. She'd never been able to pin on him a double murder at the Goliath Hotel the night he left Vegas for a year. It was no secret that she had hounded Temple ever since then for information on her missing live-in lover. Even when he came back, Max had resumed a role as Temple's phantom lover, easily evading Molina, though she knew he was in town. Only Temple and Matt knew that Max's suspicious actions were related—not to his cover career as a magician—but to his secret role as a counterterrorist.

Molina's unquenchable suspicion of Max was a problem for Matt. Now that he finally had won Temple to have and to hold, the last thing he wanted was Max and what he was or was not doing at the forefront of his life again.

"He could be out of town," Matt said shortly. "Temple can't reach him."

"Why would she want to?" Molina's expression of amazement felt complimentary. Pride goeth before a fall, though.

"She wanted to say good-bye."

"Wow. He wouldn't want to hear that. Sure he isn't just ducking her?"

"I'm not sure about anything regarding Max Kinsella. Are you?"

She set her lips. She'd eaten off what little lip gloss had ever been on them, but their color was still vivid, maybe her half-Hispanic heritage shining through.

"No," she finally answered. "Except that he could very well be my stalker."

"Temple told me about that rap. I don't think so."

"No? I know *you* don't. Who made you the expert?"

"He runs on pride. It makes him a loner, but he's too proud to sink to such sick, puppyish behavior."

"Lucifer wouldn't crawl, not even to God."

"Something like that. You're a policewoman. I bet you've ticked off a lot of bad actors, not to mention people I know."

She grinned at him, her short chin-brushing hairdo blowing back like a storm of dark, gleeful clouds. Molina should let herself loose more often. He still wondered about Charley's.

"So why'd you dislike meeting me at Charley's?"

Her grin faded. "You are such a wet blanket, Devine. I bet you think that was an insightful question. Shrinks suck."

"Met Max there sometime, huh?"

"You just frigging turn this car around. And drive the speed limit, damn it!"

"No turnoff on this highway for miles," he reported. Serenely. "Kinda like life. So that's it. Deep down, you *wanted* to nail Max as your stalker. A shrink could have a field day with that one."

"No, I did not. I am not that kind of a victim. Deep down I wanted him to be what your Miss Temple always thought he was, worth her time. But now even she's given up on him. Hallelujah. That man has distorted all our lives. How can you even contemplate him being innocent of anything?"

"I don't think he'd stalk a woman. A man, maybe. Sure. He was—"

"Two words very important there. 'Was' and what you were going to say right after it."

"He's out of Temple's life now. Mine too, because of that fact. And because of what he was, a spy. He was a good guy, Carmen. He had been a counterterrorist in Europe since the age of seventeen. While I was in the seminary climbing the seven-story mountain to the priesthood, Max was out there on the line, trying to save lives."

"He was wanted by Interpol. There's a record."

"He planted that record, him and his mentors. He was a teenage counterterrorist. The magician part was always the cover. That's why I don't see him stalking you. Oh, sure, he'd probably enjoy tweaking your whiskers, like he did mine. We've both done it by the book, and he hasn't. And he probably foresaw we'd win in our plodding, methodical ways."

"This is how you won Temple? Plodding and methodical?"

"Probably." Matt shook his head, tossing off her rude questions. That was her job. He just didn't know why she had to do it on his time.

Temple had to deal with it being over with Max. Matt had to deal with there being no Max to act as a counterforce to his own will anymore. He actually missed that.

"He may be dead," Matt heard himself saying, and the thought disturbed him. Would Max really have faded like this on Temple? If he could help it?

"No! That bastard would never leave us alone, and just die!"

"Carmen . . ." Matt slowed the car, hit the button that closed the windows so she could hear every word. "He may very well be dead. That's what Temple's secretly afraid of. He had enemies from beyond Las Vegas. From far away and way back. And, contrary to appearances, he was not infallible."

" '*Was*' again, Matt?"

He nodded. "I'm very much beginning to be afraid so."

"You *want* a live rival?"

"Definitely preferable to a dead one. You know for sure then."

"A little sin of pride, there?"

"Definitely."

"And if he's dead, who done it?"

"That's your job."

She nodded. "If my stalker never shows up again, and Max Kinsella never does, then we'll know the answer to that question."

"Maybe."

"Maybe? That's proof positive."

Matt eyed her quickly. "Maybe. Enough proof for you. If we were talking about anybody else but Max. Me, I'd have to see it to believe it."

Chapter 34

Molina Mia!

Temple had some time to kill the next day before tracking down Detective Alch, so she dropped in on one of the "perk-shops." This one featured the Red Hat Candies Clown Princess vocal group, with Candy Crenshaw performing solo as "Obrah Spinfree."

Really, Temple just wanted to get a load off her Stuart Weitzmans—she was no Iron-ankled Natalie Newman or Iron Maiden Molina—and to think for a while.

The Crystal Phoenix's conference theater made a perfect double for a live talk show set.

After the five hugely mugging Red Hat Candies sang a few song parodies, Candy "Obrah" came trudging onstage in a black curly wig and false black eyelashes two inches long. (Oprah had been wearing glam lashes for some time, so Candy was up to snuff on her impression.) She was clad in tight jeans and a rhinestone bra and dragging a little red wagon behind her, heaped, not with pounds of ugly Oprah fat but with piles of red and purple feather boas.

"You see, ladies," she said, "you can uplift your lives by forgetting about the fat and converting to feathers."

She flapped her elbows like a bird, releasing a pair of feathered helium balloons that hefted the glitzy cups of her O-bra.

"Take a load off, ladies. Go, O-bra. It's not Oxygen, but Helium that will make us free."

The act was corny but won lots of giggles and applause. And, in a way, it emphasized that women were always being converted to something: this diet or that guru or this self-help system or that celebrity role model.

At the end Temple checked her watch. Time to find and interrogate a police detective. But he was nowhere to be found.

She finally spotted him near her special conference room! Good. With Su. Bad. And with, amazingly, the interesting combination of Candy Crenshaw and her estranged husband, Cal, of the Black Hat Brotherhood.

Offstage, Candy truly mixed the clown look with her P and R persona. She was an Uma Thurman–skinny gal who accessorized it with extreme fluff. The curly purple fright wig made her head watermelon-big and her face and neck the small stem of it.

Her purple fishnet hose emphasized knobby knees and ankles. A short skimpy red chenille fabric looked more like a bed skirt than a girl skirt. Her elbows were as bony and gawky as her knees, and the huge purple, red, and black eight-foot-long boa constrictor of feathers draped over her shoulders dwarfed her toothpick-thin body. Candy's limbs looked like they could stab somebody, but her jokes were a lot blunter.

Cal, on the other hand, was a comfortably middle-aged man with billowing belly and double chin.

"You are the cutest little thing," Candy was cooing at

Detective Su despite the glower she was getting in return. "You look like you'd wear a double-zero-size parachute."

Su was not buying. Or laughing.

Alch swallowed a chuckle in spite of himself, more for seeing Su's Great Dane–size dignity tweaked than the effectiveness of Candy Crenshaw's jokes.

"This is not an occasion for levity," Su told the woman. "It is a murder investigation and our field of suspects is very wide."

" 'Wide' is not a word you know the meaning of," Candy cracked.

" 'Suspect' is not a word you know the meaning of," Su shot back. "Alch, I want to talk to her in the interrogation room."

Normally that destination would give Temple an edgy feeling, but here it was just a posh Crystal Phoenix conference room. She was delirious, however, to see slight little Su herding away her giraffe-tall exotic quarry.

"I need a word with you," Temple told Alch.

"Fine," he said, jerking his head at Cal Crenshaw. "We're done for now. No skipping town."

"The Black Hat Brotherhood is here for the duration, Detective."

"The investigation might outlast the convention."

"Great. That'll give us time to get our guys on some of the local talk shows."

Temple and Alch watched Crenshaw stomp away on his black cowboy boots, spurs jingling like reindeer harnesses.

"All spur and no spine," Alch diagnosed. He turned to Temple with a grin. "So what do you want to con out of me now?"

"I think we'll need to talk privately in my interrogation room."

"Yours? You mean the conference room where you've set up shop to irritate Su?"

"You do read my mind," she answered.

"That's only fair. You want to pick my brain."

Temple produced a guilty look.

"With that pink hat on, you could pick the brain of a slug."

Temple had the grace to blush. Morrie Alch was such a smart, sweet guy, and was single with a grown daughter, she'd heard. Why didn't Molina get off her high horse and grab him?

She relied on him at work. Temple supposed a lady lieutenant couldn't marry down, but someone had to break stupid conventions and rules. Temple also supposed that Lieutenant C. R. Molina would be the last woman on earth to do that.

"So what's your agenda?" Alch asked as he sat on one end of the long conference table that had recently hosted red-hatted ladies. Temple turned around from shutting the double doors.

Mr. Affable was gone. The arms folded on the detective's chest indicated that he may be nice, but he wasn't going to be easy.

"Personally? I've got to clear Electra and get Matt out of the suspect picture. Professionally? I need to get the media heat off the Crystal Phoenix. This is their biggest convention ever, and doing it in partnership with the Goliath is a good deal for both hotels, neither of which is exactly the new kid on the block."

"Your Debate of the Sexes scheme only upped the bad publicity," he pointed out. "And upped the possible murder raps around here. And Electra Lark remains a prime suspect."

"I know! And it roped my fiancé into the murderous merriment going around."

"Fiancé," Alch teased. "You sure like to sling that word around."

"Guilty." Yeah, she did. She'd had too long a run as an almost fiancée with Max. At bottom, she was a middle-of-the-country girl, a heartland product. And her heart needed to know it had the hope of a permanent home.

"That's okay," Alch said softly. "Old-fashioned values go good with that hat of yours."

"Molina," she began.

"She's my boss. Don't go there."

Temple reassembled her forces. "I really don't want to, and I don't think any sane man would either." No rise from Alch. "Speaking of insane men, was Elmore Lark really a murder victim?"

Alch nodded. "Only the word is 'almost.' He'll recover. That's top secret, by the way."

"Recover? Oh. That's good news." That was also theory-busting news. Still, Elmore had been murderously attacked, even if he hadn't succumbed. How? "Was it the water pitcher? How could it be? A clear, tasteless substance is a lousy medium for poison. And it had to have been poison, right?"

"I guess you're moonlighting as a technical consultant for *CSI: Crime Scene Investigation* these days, huh?"

"No. That's a bunch of hokum, I know that. But it had to have been poison."

"Why do you think so?"

"The public collapse, while on camera. If the cause of the attack wasn't natural, it had to have been induced by a lethal substance. But not in the water."

Alch nodded.

That was all she was going to get from him, confirmation of her assumptions. That was more than any other detective she knew would give her.

Temple began pacing. "Wait! He had to have carried the poison on him!"

Alch's expression became even more poker-faced, telling her she was moving in the right direction.

She paced again, then stopped right in front of him, saying, dramatically, "A hip flask full of liquor."

"Slightly warm," he said.

"Flasks carry straight liquor. The taste is strong and over-bearing. It would mask almost any poison if Elmore had swigged some down in the men's room before going to the panel and on camera. Even the deadliest poison takes a few minutes to act."

Alch shrugged and nodded. "I'd put you on *CSI.*"

"So." Temple paced some more in her smart hot pink, high-heeled slides.

Her pink hat wasn't the only thing Morrie Alch liked about her, and friendly paternalism only went so far with even the most decent of men. Maybe he missed his daughter at cajoling sweet sixteen.

Temple had never been a cajoler, but she liked to let her imagination loose.

"Elmore didn't carry a hip flask," she both asked and stated outright.

He nodded.

She paced again, recalling the hokey Western outfits he wore.

"Something else he carried was tainted, then. In his jeans' hip pocket."

Alch's expression betrayed surprised agreement.

"I feel like I'm on the old *Family Feud* game show. I have to guess the top five most likely answers. Breath mints or those little strips!"

Alch's expression grew even more deadpan.

She'd missed. "No, I guess Elmore Lark wouldn't be as self-conscious as a computer nerd on a date at this stage of the game, would he?"

Alch chuckled.

"Wait. Tobacco! It can be lethal. Poison-spiked cigarettes. A whole pack of them. It would work slowly, then, bingo, the dose would build up and a quick ciggie to ease the tension of the debate could be the Camel that broke the weak straw that was Elmore Lark's back."

Alch laughed out loud. "Nice way to put it. Yeah, if you're talking Fu Manchu or some other pulp villains of the early twentieth century. This is the twenty-first century, kid."

"But Elmore Lark was a twentieth, even a nineteenth-century kind of guy, especially in regard to women."

Temple sighed. No poison in the water. Or in any liquor or cigarettes Elmore could have carried on him. Maybe he bit his nails!

She said as much to Alch, who bent over double from laughing. "Creative, but he'd need a daily manicure of poison to do the job."

"Some seductive Red Hat honey maybe could have talked him into a harmless clear nail polish, then, wham-o!"

"You think you could talk me into some harmless clear nail polish?"

"If I wasn't engaged, maybe I could."

"No. Real men don't do their nails. Elmore's a real man."

"Yeah. Lying, lazy, deceptive, womanizing . . ."

"Agreed. The guy's a rat. A lot of people like to poison rats. And his kind of rat, the poisoner would likely be a woman. Poison is a woman's weapon."

"But Elmore's a man's man, in the worst interpretation of that."

Temple tapped her toe, beating a fast, impatient beat on the stone-cold floor. That's how cold she felt her guesses were. Alch was still sitting here playing the game only because her earlier guesses had been in the ballpark.

Time to slam something into far left field.

"If it was in his jeans pocket, it had to be as small as a tiny flask or cigarette case. What are both of them? Metal?"

Alch had stopped grinning and was looking ready to be impressed. She couldn't stop now. *Family Feud*. She'd always felt sorry for the players who were last to guess after all the most obvious answers had been taken.

Elmore Lark. Aging urban cowboy. High-heeled boots, big-buckled belt, neckerchief, ten-gallon hat. A man's man while taking women to the cleaners.

"You're right," Alch said consolingly, "that it was something that would fit in a jeans pocket."

"Not cigarettes? Wait. A cigar?"

"Nicotine is somewhat toxic," he admitted, "but not in this amount, and not instantly. Besides, a smoker would have built up resistance."

"And he wasn't a smoker?"

Alch shook his head. "Although nicotine can be lethal in more than cigarettes over years of inhalation, it wasn't in this case. In this case it was a, er, smoke screen."

"So something else was lethal to Elmore Lark? He *was* a drinker. Maybe one of those airplane-sized bottles of scotch was how he concealed it. That would fit in a jeans pocket."

Alch paused. He didn't dare speak too loudly, or plainly.

"Let's just say that Elmore Lark wasn't toasting his own health."

Temple felt she had pushed Alch's envelope to the seam-splitting point. She said her thanks and good-bye, and mulled the detective's parting words as she left the room for the colorful chaos of the Red Hat Sisterhood–populated lobby.

Elmore Lark "wasn't toasting his own health."

A *toast* had killed him? Alcohol? Sure, you could kill

yourself by overusing alcohol, usually over years. But how could someone else kill you with it if not with poison *in* it? And Alch had implied alcohol wasn't the medium.

If something at the debate hadn't poisoned him, the attempt looked much more premeditated and distant. But ifs were all she had. She sure wasn't going to get any more information about it from the LVMPD.

At least Matt and the water pitcher were off the hook.

Except hers.

Chapter 35

Hints and Intimations

Temple eyed the swirl of red and purple pooling around her, the echo of laughing voices exploding from all the shiny hard surfaces that lined Las Vegas hotel-casino's public areas.

If you could hear yourself think in a Las Vegas hotel-casino, they weren't doing their job right. The cheerful clatter and clinks of slot machines kept up that subliminal cash-register chatter, while excited human voices competed with them.

And then she realized, what with all her concentration on El-more Lark's possible habits and many means of poisoning, no one—at least not her—had checked out Oleta Lark's hat habit.

She wove through the crowd, jousting brims with ladies of different colors, red, pink, lavender, until she reached the ballroom that hosted the Red Hat Sisterhood stores, aka the Hatorium Emporium.

Oleta had bought a merchandise booth here, not the one where she was killed. Presumably it had been set up before her death and was still standing. At least Temple would learn something about Oleta's personal taste, if nothing more.

But the convention "store" was a riot of cheerful disregard of taste, at least in the conservative sense. The atmosphere of women-only shoppers jostling each other at tables filled with frivolous fun products jogged more than her body. It triggered her memory, spurring one of those déjà vu feelings of slipping back in time.

That's when Temple remembered *where* she'd bought the costume jewelry ring reminiscent of the one Max had bought her and Shangri-La the magician had stolen onstage.

For some reason Matt came to mind. A flashback slide of him rooting through her scarf drawer. There was something intimate and sexy about that act, that memory. Wow. Her scarf drawer and the rings that resided in it are now a Freudian paradise . . .

Of recovered memory!

Temple stood shock-still as people and conversation flowed around her. She'd been handling PR for the annual women's show at the convention center a few months ago. Such shows were orgies of girly self-indulgence, showcasing products that soothed the savaged soul: massage and bath oils, jewelry and clothes.

Just as here and now, there were how-to sessions on using hairpieces and false eyelashes for fun, and for older women who were getting scanty in both outgrowths. Cooking seminars with kitchen gadgets. New cosmetics. That's where Temple had first seen the Besamé vintage color cosmetics and the mineral-only makeup powders that were now a commercial rage.

And that's where, on the show's Sunday sell-off before closing, she'd spotted the ring uncannily like the one she'd lost and had never stopped missing. The woman behind the display discounted it to less than forty bucks (it had real cubic zirconias) and slipped it into a little box and then into a little bigger paper bag.

And . . . sometimes your subconscious could kick up a long forgotten and buried memory, one not openly noted at the time. And the . . . the bag had sagged a little on Temple's arm as she'd turned to leave the booth.

It had almost felt like the lightest touch snagging her bag, providing a second's worth of drag.

Had that been when the second ring box bearing the worm Ouroboros ring that Kathleen O'Connor had dumped on Matt had found its way into her possession?

Temple was always busy. She'd dumped the paper bag on her dresser top, and later, dumped the ring box in her favorite catch-all spot, the scarf drawer.

Why would anyone lay that sinister ring on her? Who would have had it? Only Kitty the Cutter O'Connor.

People intent on shopping continued bumping into Temple. This was a room of constant movement and female chatter, shopping nirvana. But Temple stood still, frozen in thought, beating the fringes of her memory.

What had she looked and sounded like, that vaguely noticed saleswoman?

Short. Like Temple. Kitty had been maybe three inches taller than she. Still qualified as "short." A typical saleswoman, all perkiness and persuasion. She had "talked" Temple into the first ring, almost as if she had known it would appeal to her. Because she knew it was similar to the real opal and diamond ring? No. Shangri-La *knew* that.

Temple was mixing up her villainesses. If Kitty O'Connor had been masquerading as the saleswoman . . . No, that would have been too difficult to arrange just to taunt Temple with a mock ring. She *was* a saleswoman on that day, for some reason, and she was a saleswoman who had taken advantage of an amazing opportunity. A second chance to snooker Temple. Except it was *Shangri-La* who'd relieved Temple of Max's ring.

Okay, no one had ever figured this out at the time, not even high and mighty Lieutenant C. R. Molina.

Like Sherlock Holmes had said—now that she'd encountered "The Red-Hatted League" she was recalling her childhood acquaintance with the Canon—"Once you eliminate the possible, whatever remains, no matter how improbable, must be the truth." Or something to that effect.

Ah. Temple ignored a particularly intense bump that almost knocked her off her feet. She was almost knocked out of her shoes.

"My sweet Stuart Weitzmans!" she murmured.

Shangri-La was Kitty O'Connor. Or, rather, Kitty O'Connor was Shangri-La. That could be the only explanation if Matt's worm Ouroboros ring had gotten into Temple's possession on the *same* day a double for Max's semiengagement ring had. Who else would recognize that the cheap imitation ring bore a striking resemblance to the one from Tiffany's and Max? It all made terrifying, mind-boggling sense.

Random thoughts, more like twinges, hit Temple then too.

But Kitty O'Connor was dead. Max had seen her die in a solo motorcycle accident out on Highway 61. No, that route was in Minnesota and from an old Bob Dylan song. Kitty must have spun out on Highway 95. Temple had never asked Max where, only accepted the what.

Unless Max had been lying and Kitty *hadn't* died. Or he'd been mistaken somehow. No, she was *buried*.

But Shangri-La wasn't.

Except she had died recently too, in costume. Or had she?

If the two women were the same. They were both dead. Or not.

Temple looked around the room thronging with women squealing and flaunting red or purple feather boas and umbrellas and stockings and satin gloves at each other.

"Look!" they were caroling. "Look. Look at what I found! No, over here! It's fabulous! It's too great to be true! Let me see it!"

Temple turned, blindly, and pushed her way out of the room that had just served as her personal time machine.

She needed some peace and quiet. She needed to escape from the red and purple mania. She needed to figure out what had really happened that Sunday, so long ago, and what had really happened to her.

Chapter 36

Loving Dangerously

Temple went home and poured herself a stiff drink from Max's Millennium scotch. For the first time, she didn't go into a funk over something related to him. To them. She had big-time conundrums to solve.

She then unearthed every item in her scarf drawer. It gave up no more ring boxes.

Then she sat on her living-room sofa, her bare feet up on the glass coffee table and her heels lying askew on the faux goat-hair rug, and sipped really good scotch very, very slowly.

"Once you eliminate the possible, whatever remains, no matter how improbable, must be the truth."

Round and round her mind went. The thought, the suspicion, the idea, was incredible. She tried out the impossible first: *Kathleen O'Connor was Shangri-La*. That was impossible because of what had happened at the New Millennium a week ago. Shangri-La had been revealed as an illegal immigrant and an Asian acrobat. However, ignoring that, it was possible because Shangri-La was all costume and mask of makeup. She was also an acrobat, but a lifelong double agent like Kathleen O'Connor would know martial arts and that was only a skip and jump from being an athletic magician.

Max had found the profession of magician to be the perfect cover for his activities. Why wouldn't Kathleen O'Connor come to the same conclusion, especially since she knew all about him and would have relished using his own methods to track him and bring him down. Maybe Shangri-La wasn't always the same person. Hai Ling was illegally in this country. Maybe Kitty the Cutter forced her into stepping aside at times when it suited Kitty to masquerade as Shangri-La. For criminal activities! Like that designer drug smuggling operation at the Opium Den!

Everything was amazing . . . and fit . . . and, Temple mused, utterly useless. Because Kathleen was dead and buried. Temple's brilliant insight had come too late. It didn't matter, except that it proved that Matt was eternally free of Kitty the Cutter's sick, violent stalking, as was Max.

If she could only find Max to tell him so! He'd be so proud of her reasoning, her revelation. Except he was noncommunicado, as he'd so often been lately. Too absent to even keep her chronic attraction to Matt from finally exploding into consummation. Not that she regretted a moment of that, but Max could have at least *tried* to prevent it, instead of pushing her into Matt's bed like some heroic doomed lover passing her onto a new romance and a better life.

So her elated mood at having solved the biggest mystery afflicting them all dropped like a stone. She was still sipping her way through that one expensive glass when she got up to answer the knock on her door, hoping that it wasn't someone wearing purple and red.

She'd had enough of P and R PR to last a lifetime.

She lucked out in that respect. She faced a wall of plain khaki-colored cotton pantsuit.

Lieutenant C. R. Molina was poised with a fist still raised.

That vision shook Temple out of her fog and into combat alert.

"Should I cringe now or later?" she asked.

"I'm greedy," Molina said. "I want both."

"And you still expect me to invite you in?"

"Oh, that would be nice." Said sarcastically. "Actually, I have some questions that you might really want to know the answers to."

Temple stepped back from the door, resigned. Molina followed her into the living room, but neither woman sat. Their relationship, always at odds over Max, was too thorny for simple actions like that.

"Have you seen Kinsella lately?" Molina asked, eyeing Temple's glass of scotch.

Still the same old tune. Only this time, with Max vanishing again, it really stung. Molina was the last person Temple wanted to know that Max had left Las Vegas, maybe. Had left her, certainly.

"Seen Max? Not recently," Temple said casually. "We've never lived in each other's hip pockets."

"Heard from him?"

"Not recently."

Molina nodded. "Were you aware of a magician working at Neon Nightmare?"

"I know the nightclub, but no."

"He wore a cape and a mask and performed as the Phantom Mage. He bounced around the dark interior walls on bungee cords and did magic effects in literal thin air. I understand he was quite popular."

"Sounds like a comic book superhero act."

"Sounded like Max Kinsella to me."

"He hasn't performed in almost two years."

"Exactly why he might want to polish his skills anonymously. What do you think? Even better, what do you know?"

"Nothing about this Phantom Mage. Why ask me? Why not trot over to Neon Nightmare and interview the magician in question? Surely you and your shield can sweet-talk only a mask off a man."

"I would, except I didn't learn about him until he stopped performing."

Temple rolled her eyes. "This is such a non-issue, then. Guess we'll never know who the Phantom Mage was."

But she was wondering now if it *had* been Max. He'd talked about rehearsing again, about putting a new act together. It had been his excuse for remaining distant lately. Maybe that's why he'd left. To train in Europe or someplace safe. Right, and not tell her he was going?

"Maybe we'll all soon know who he was," Molina said, watching her. "Have you seen or spoken to Max Kinsella since last week? Telling me won't betray him. I know you've been in close contact for months."

Temple had to take a few moments to mentally backtrack. Her mind had been pretty occupied by Matt and his dinner date and engagement ring recently . . .

"No," she said finally.

"That's interesting. You might want to sit down."

Temple remained standing. Molina sat on the sofa's broad arm, a position that put their faces on a level.

"The Phantom Mage left a huge puzzle behind him."

"He's gone, then? He left?"

Molina shrugged. "Hard to say. Witnesses are divided about whether he died on the scene or not."

"Died?" Temple spoke quickly to keep from focusing on her stomach doing a swan dive. *Died?* "What scene? I haven't read anything in the newspaper about the Neon Nightmare."

"There was a small notice, but no follow-up. That's the mysterious part. Witnesses saw him fall. He hit the wall, hard, when his bungee cord failed. An onlooker gave him CPR. Nine-eleven was called, then a pair of EMTs took him away in an ambulance, siren screaming. About four hundred shocked people witnessed it."

Temple felt her knees turn to Jell-O. *Molina must think this was Max.* And she'd come here, to Temple's home, to taunt her with the horrifying, gory details to make her give something away.

"You know," Temple said, her voice shaking, "you're a heartless bitch."

"I did suggest you sit down."

"I won't suggest what I think you should do."

"I still think you should sit down."

"There's more?"

"The onlookers were pretty shaken up. They started calling the police to inquire about the man's fate or condition. Of course we had to look into it then."

"And of course *you* couldn't let a magician disappear on you again."

"Or on you. Again."

Temple swallowed, hard. That's just what had happened.

"When we started investigating it," Molina said, "we found out the magician had really, actually disappeared into thin air. No ambulance had reached any medical facility with an injured or dead man wearing a mask and a cloak. No ambulance service had made a hospital run that night at that time.

"The man who performed CPR never came forward, and never could be found. The only description was medium everything—height, weight, and age—in dark clothes.

"That's when I became interested in the incident. I sent some detectives to the scene. The fatal bungee cord couldn't be found. All the bungee cords hanging from the apex of the interior pyramid at the Neon Nightmare club were fine. Whole. Unbroken, and uncut. Everything was normal.

"It must have been an act, my detectives concluded. It must have been the magician's spectacular exit from a job he'd tired of.

"No unclaimed bodies lie in the morgue. Sometimes, when illegal Mexican workers die, their friends and family stuff the body in a truck or a car trunk and race back into Mexico to bury him. Nobody official in the U.S. knows a thing about it. That could have happened here, except Mexicans are a short-statured people and everybody at Neon Nightmare agrees that the Phantom Mage was tall and imposing, a thrilling acrobat and illusionist. Really too good for a nightclub act at the Neon Nightmare. The crowd misses him. Maybe you do too."

That was such a low blow that Temple wanted to shriek at the woman, but she wasn't giving Molina a shred of information about Max, good, bad, or just damn scary. This might be the last chance she had to shield him from Molina's obsessive desire to find him guilty of something.

She wouldn't spill her hard-won speculations about Kathleen O'Connor and Shangri-La, which Molina would never take seriously anyway.

Most of all, she wouldn't tell Molina about how Max's very private, hidden house had changed, and changed hands, so supernaturally fast, and so finally.

"I'm not Max's keeper," Temple said. "I never was. Maybe he left town to get away from you. I sure would if I were a man."

There! A low blow in return.

Molina stood. "So you won't help me. You won't say if you know where he is. Or even *that* he is."

"I never did before."

"No, you've been utterly consistent, if never utterly convincing. I can't see for the life of me what he ever did to win your loyalty, but it's first class, if blind."

Temple didn't trust herself to speak.

Molina turned and headed for the door.

"What are you going to do?" Temple called after her.

"What it takes," she answered.

Molina was utterly consistent too.

Temple sat only after Molina had left. Sank would better describe the motion.

An elongated chirping sound distracted her, as Midnight Louie jumped up on the sofa beside her. The big black cat paced on the soft seat cushion, leaning into her shoulder to rub back and forth. He pushed his chin against hers and purred.

She wasn't used to him being so lovey-dovey.

Things must be really bad.

It must be true. But then who had sold Max's house, if he was dead? He'd always lived alone after he'd returned from his year's disappearance. They'd never lived together in Las Vegas after that fabulous first year of loving dangerously at the Circle Ritz.

Max fell and had died, and no one had known?

No. Maybe Max fell. Hundreds saw it. But hundreds and thousands had seen Max fly, onstage. And had believed it.

Temple shook her head, surprised by a blur of blond at the edges of her eyes. That did it. As soon as this mess was over, she was going to get her hair back to its natural red shade. There had to be a hair wizard in Las Vegas that could put her hair back where it had been. Even if no one could put her world back where it had been.

And . . . Matt had briefly been under suspicion, thanks to her trying to put PR "spin" on a protest. And Electra still was. She had to concentrate on them. On those present. On the provable living.

Chapter 37

Electra Lite

The oleander bushes surrounding the Circle Ritz parking lot were doing a lot of blowing in the wind these days, Temple noticed as she stood on her balcony overlooking the parking lot.

Funny. The breeze wasn't whipping her longer hair around; it was just stirring the oleander leaves far below.

If she hadn't had so much on her mind—Max's whereabouts, the new scenario she'd dreamed up for Kathleen O'Connor and her alter ego, Electra's pending murder rap, talking marriage with Matt—she might have investigated.

But her mind was on huddling with Electra to get a handle on the two Red Hat Sisterhood convention incidents connected to her complicated past.

If there was anything unusual to see in the vicinity of the oleanders, it bypassed her attention.

The building's small elevator was a wood-lined bundle of fifties charm the size of a confessional, but it sure could crawl up the wall at a snail's pace. Make that a slug's pace.

Temple's pink low-heeled slides danced an impatient jig on the car's parquet floor until it creaked to a stop at the penthouse level.

Ringing Electra's doorbell produced the usual long wait. Temple finally pushed on the door. It wafted slightly open.

Pushing through, she found Electra's pathologically shy cat, Karma, sitting on the threshold. The mirrored vertical blinds lining the octagonal entry hall reproduced a host of Karmas, cream-colored coat, white-tipped paws, and dark brown mask at her eyes.

"Electra?" Temple called.

Karma remained the usual inscrutable. Temple hated to cross into the cat's territory without its mistress present. The animal broadcast an air both eerie and intimidating. Its heavenly blue eyes seemed transparent at times. At other times, Temple had seen them gleam red, like a demon's.

"Electra?"

"Coming," the landlady's cheery voice caroled from deep within the shadowed rooms.

Electra kept the light out of her living area because of Karma's shyness, Temple had been told. Now she wondered if Electra was simply used to living in the shadows of her own hazy past, and husbands.

"What's happening, dear?"

"Elmore will survive and Matt is no longer a suspect in the attack."

"That's wonderful. About Matt, I mean. Who is suspected?"

"You knew him best, they say."

"Not for years. Sit down. You look stumped."

"I am. I don't even know what was used on Elmore. Alch does, but he'll only give me aggravating hints."

"Oh, that charming detective. I should think you could coax more than hints out of him."

"One would hope. But he's raised a daughter; he's personally dealt with a teenage girl. He is no longer susceptible to coaxing from females. He did admit that Elmore was poisoned."

Electra gasped. "Oh! That's a terrible way to die. Elmore was a lying creep, but he didn't deserve death by poison. Maybe a jalapeño enema, but not poison."

"Electra! Talk like that will not get you taken off the suspects list."

"Why not? I'm not threatening any lethal damage, just a whole lot of pain."

"The object is to look and sound as innocent as the early morning rain."

"I am, Temple, that's why I can afford to tell the truth about the bum. The world wouldn't have missed him much. I never did. And that's why I wouldn't wait all this time and then try to kill the jerk."

"The question is how the poison was administered. I've suggested every method I can think of to Alch. He just beams like Buddha and says I'm not even warm."

"What did you strike out on?"

"A hip flask. Alcohol is strong enough to disguise a lot of lethal substances."

"No." Electra shook her purple-sprayed head. "He liked his liquor well enough but I wouldn't see him as the hip flask sort."

"I thought maybe nicotine, but he didn't smoke."

"No, never smoked."

"You're no help. Alch admitted, implied, that if it was something he carried in his back pocket, it could be metal like a cigarette case." Temple kept silent for a moment, stumped. "Why would Alch say that Elmore wasn't toasting his own health? He wouldn't anyway, because he wasn't a known drinker."

"Toast. Now there was an Elmore Lark weakness. The man adored French toast. I had to make it every morning when we were married. Can't stand it to this day."

"Food? Food was Elmore's poison? They must have examined the contents after the hospital pumped his stomach. You can't stash a piece of French toast in a tight back jeans pocket. He could have had it for breakfast, and someone had doctored it. Maybe one of those middle-aged ladies he preys on now invited him to breakfast and, presto, poison powder sprinkled on his French toast like . . . powdered sugar! That would work!"

Temple jumped up.

Electra looked around as Temple glimpsed Karma's fluffy tail vanishing under the sofa fringe.

"That must be it! What Alch meant."

"Whatever you say, dear. But I left Elmore long ago. I don't care who sprinkles his toast or anything else with what."

"Don't you see? Whoever attempted to kill him knew his habits, and used them. And must have known him *after* you did."

"But the police won't believe that. That's a 'someone' and I'm right here to blame."

"I'll just have to find who did know his habits and used them to try to kill him."

"That's nice, dear. Now can you sit down and have some Crystal Light so poor Karma will be reassured that no one will be leaping up unseemly and shouting and she can gather her psychic thoughts and come out from under the sofa?"

Subdued, Temple complied, wondering all the while how she could nail a killer with a doctored powdered sugar theory. Maybe "Spoonful of Sugar Helps the Medicine Go Down" Mary Poppins could, but Temple wasn't a magical English nanny. She was just a PR woman with a strong sense of protecting her friends.

Chapter 38

A Kick in the Karma

Usually I can count on my Miss Temple to lock up a case of murder in four days flat. Double murder, or second attempt. Five days flat.

But my esteemed associate (*not* Miss Midnight Louise) is not her usual razor-sharp self, partly because our beloved landlady is in the hot seat, but mostly because she herself is trying to be this human insanity called "faithful" to two tomcats. (Not to mention myself, who has always been her steady fella and only real roommate, night-in and night-out. *My* nights out, that is.)

It is so simple in the feline world, as I tell Miss Midnight Louise again and again. One hot young queen. Two potent neighborhood toms. You are talking a litter of adorable goldens and blacks, not a shabby combo for a mama of any species.

But, no. Humans have to make a pair out of a possible full house. Any gambler will tell you this: the more players, the better the odds. And the more fun!

Still, I have cast my lot in life with my Miss Temple, and I generally have no complaints. I must admit, now that push has come to shove, that I am already missing the always-impending presence of Mr. Max. That guy knew how to build an audience's expectations onstage, shatter them, and then show up behind them with an armful of tame doves. Yum-yum. I am talking about the doves, not Mr. Max.

But Mr. Matt is an okay guy. If you want sincerity with a Capital S, not to mention that smoldering sort of sex appeal that comes from a restrictive upbringing, my Miss Temple could do no better.

But, see, I have always thought that she could do herself the biggest favor with both. What is so wrong with that? It has been the feline way since before we bit the hands that fed us. Since before there *were* hands to feed us.

Speaking of which, I am standing in the Circle Ritz parking lot fretting about human behavior, when I am suddenly held up to dry on my own impeccable good intentions and behavior.

"You slug!" I hear hissed from the nearby oleander bushes.

Something snarled and black (and snarling) rushes into my face.

It is my purported mother, Ma Barker. Jeez, I wish *she* had a couple of consuming tomcats on her mind. But no. She has her whole damn litter of a gang on her mind.

"We are starving. You said down-Strip would be the Promised Land. Free food from gullible humans who would not try to trap us."

"There are no traps."

"There is nothing in *our* traps, either, fool! We have walked off all the spare fat our spare frames could spare."

Okay. I could edit that sentence. Eliminate redundant "spares." Okay. That would not be life affirming in this current situation.

"What about the Free-to-Be-Feline piles I have led you and the Chosen Felines to in my own domicile?" I ask.

"That stuff sucks, my son," Ma Barker responds.

I cannot disagree.

"Okay," I say. "But that is all I have for now. It will get better later, I promise."

Ma Barker gets a bit dewy. "You sound just like your father."

"I mean it! The head lady of this place is too busy to cook for the gang. She does not even know you are here yet. She is facing major murder charges."

Ma Barker desists her howling and lays back into a purr. "This place is run by a head lady, human style?"

"Right."

"And she is up on murder charges?"

"False, of course."

"My kind of human. Except for the false part. So what are you going to do in the meantime, sonny?"

"I will . . . ah, consult the resident, um, goddess."

"It is human or feline?"

"A bit of both, I fear. Just settle down here."

"We no longer have the energy to climb that arch of rugged trunk for a few nuggets of dried green rabbit dung."

"I agree! I will see about getting you something more succulent."

"Succulents are watery cacti, son. Not nourishing."

"I meant moist, meaty, thick, tasty."

"Like lizard tongue."

"Ah, more like a major cat food brand."

"I prefer baby food."

"That too," I sigh, my work cut out for me.

I take the despised palm tree route to the Circle Ritz's fourth floor, then claw my way up the exterior to the penthouse.

Panting outside the French doors, I finally see a ray of light. A scimitar of claw has pulled a door ajar.

Now, I suppose, I must do obeisance to the resident goddess, Karma.

I roll into the desirable shade inside, hearing the soothing wheeze of the air-conditioning device. The dimness is also soothing. I could have a nice nap.

"Slug!" I hear in dulcet sacred Birman tones.

I bet the Dalai Lamas did not have to put up with this, but they are mostly extinct these days. As I may soon be.

Miss Karma is circling around me on her miraculously white-footed feet.

"Are you responsible for that low-end, homeless riffraff in the parking lot being here?"

"Yes," I am forced to admit. "They were starving uptown."

"What makes you think they will not starve downtown?"

"As soon as the human Circle Ritz denizens can get their attention off of your . . . roommate's survival, I am sure they will all see the need around them and meet it."

"*Hmph.* You are a lowly mixed breed."

I hold my tongue. And teeth.

"You have served the lowest desires of both kinds."

I hold my tongue, but it is hard.

"You have delusions of being a force-about-town."

I hold my shivs.

"You hold to no guiding principle but self-interest."

I growl.

"And that of a favored few humans of your acquaintance. No mystical human figure has blessed you with its favor."

Well, there was Elvis. Or his ghost.

"No miracle has occurred to paint your outer coat to celebrate your inner courage."

Okay, so these Birmans got their coloring centuries ago from dying to protect the Dalai Lama of their time. Did not work, did it? And the current Dalai Lama, cool dude as he is, may be the last of his kind, while *their* kind gets exhibited in fancy cat shows. *Huh!* They are all just hand-me-downs. I am one-of-a-kind, because I am no kind in particular.

"No miracle occurred for you, Louie?"

"No," I say. But then, my just being here after having been abandoned in an alley is some kind of miracle to my way of thinking. Which is not divine. Or Birmanish.

"Very well. I will beseech Buddha for loaves and fishes for your wandering kin."

Uh, that was the other guy.

Karma thrums her shivs on the carpeting. I think I hear a temple bell ring, but then I realize it is a microwave tinging.

"My obedient servant has left a warm meal for me. If your followers can get it, they are welcome to it."

Hmm. Warm, meaty, fishy, not-Maurice-endorsed product. At least two bowls full.

I bump the patio doors open with my sturdy rear quarters and signal the corps. Ma Barker's rangy, somewhat raccoon-customized form comes scrabbling up the palm tree trunk, everyone but poor three-legged Gimpy after her.

I look at Karma. "I can work the microwave. You think your Divineship could transport a little grub down to the three-leg waiting below?"

Those celestial blue eyes blink. In a wink, shy, reclusive Karma has a napkin full of Á La Cat's best between her sharp white teeth, and is sliding down the palm trunk like it is a magic carpet.

The last I see, she is laying it all out for Gimpy, and pitching tasty nuggets into his tuna-hole. Meanwhile, I am the chef du jour, clambering to the countertop, teeth tearing packets open, kicking them into the microwave, then using fifteen-second bursts to release their full, fishy aroma.

Manx! Cooking for a crowd is murder.

Chapter 39

Dangerous Curves

Dirty Larry hunched forward in Molina's visitor's chair, his hands loosely clasped.

It was an oddly tense posture for a man with a style cool enough to chill ice. Maybe he sensed that she wanted to know something she didn't want him to know she wanted.

What a tangled web undercover work involved! If Max Kinsella really was the super-spy Matt claimed he was, he must have been one hell of a multitasker. She knew she was too direct and authoritarian to match wits with a seasoned undercover operative like Larry Paddock. But she needed to do just that.

"My favorite redhead-gone-blond is up to her tiny tush in the murder and attempted murder at the Crystal Phoenix," she told him. "I dug out the surveillance report you did on her for me a couple weeks back."

"You want a vintage shop sized-up, she's your woman."

"I know her routines look all girly and innocent, but I don't buy appearances." Her hard look implied that might apply to him as well.

Larry shrugged. He had that inborn indifference to authority of any kind that made him such an apt candidate for a drug runner or other specialist in the criminal arts. Molina figured it was a native talent, honed through a prefelonious boyhood in some urban slum. Then military, probably special branch, then undercover in L.A. or Las Vegas where crime was as spectacularly intense as the scenery and social ambiance.

"Anything innocuous could be a cover," she told him. "You didn't give me the addresses beyond the general locations."

"You want addresses of local vintage shops?" He grinned crookedly. "I thought Carmen the chanteuse habituated those places."

"Not for years. Her thirties and forties era is out of fashion in the vintage shops now."

"Too bad. Them's ritzy rags." He gave her a male once-over that stripped away the khaki pantsuit and attired her in dark liquid velvet.

Darned if she didn't mind that. There was something feral and sexy about Dirty Larry. What used to be called devil-may-care in the torch song era. He'd aimed that at her when no one else dared. She hadn't made up her mind about who was using who here, or if either of them cared.

She did care about getting a deeper interrogation of him on the matter of Temple Barr's movements around Las Vegas, without him catching on, which was tricky.

"Mind this store for the moment," she admonished him, lightly enough that it sounded as much like a come-on as a rebuke. "This is police business."

"Sure, Lieutenant, you can pull rank on me anytime." The tone was insolent.

"Like you'd ever take that."

He shrugged, his smile tight. Then he shifted in the chair

and pulled out a small cheap notebook, half the pages pulling out of the spiral binding.

"I took down the addys, just figured you didn't plan on stopping by these nothing places."

He started by spitting out the date, then shop names and addresses. Molina could barely jot them down fast enough.

"That's the vintage shops, all along or near Charleston, as you know. The residence was 1200 Mohave Way, kinda like *High Noon*. The hotels I think you know well enough to dispense with street addresses. And the funky round residence—"

"That one I know all too well," she said, waving a hand as she finished jotting down the vintage store addresses she didn't want or need as if they were manna from heaven.

"What's the deal with this old stuff?"

She looked up to see that the notebook had disappeared. She bet Dirty Larry had a lot of stashing places on his person, almost as many as a magician.

She felt her face flush. Guilt maybe. But Larry was good. He'd read every flicker of her expression, her thoughts.

"You want to search me, Lieutenant?" He spread his arms and hands, inviting.

"Not today."

"Tonight?"

"Maybe." Damn it. She needed to distract him. Sexual banter might do that.

His head tilted, like a bird who'd heard a worm wiggling underground.

"I was thinking Carmen needed to put in an appearance at the Blue Dahlia," she said.

"Tonight?"

Now she would have to. "You've been a good boy with your math questions. But I hope you weren't using a crib notebook."

He laughed, easy and contented, all male satisfaction. It'd be hard to lose him tonight, but she had to. "Admit it. Those velvet gowns make you hot."

"And they don't make you hot?"

He rose, leaned forward, tapped the top of her hand with the pen in it. "I'll be there."

Some emergency with Mariah. That would be her out.

Dirty Larry paused at the door to her office. Cut her a dirty blond Sting look. Maybe she didn't want an out.

It was too bad her appearance at the Blue Dahlia was a sham.

The trio was really smoking and her voice had been just unused enough to have a throatier edge that matched them.

Dirty Larry had been lounging at a corner table drinking Madeira on ice like it was cough syrup meant to be taken by teaspoons, sober but undressing her with his eyes.

He was impertinent, unprofessional, arrogant, and oddly attractive. Maybe it would take an outlaw like him to breach her formidable defenses.

But not tonight. She had other business in mind.

She was crooning out the song's endless last bars when the slimy-looking guy who was as twitchy as a coke addict sidled up to Larry's table.

Larry frowned, big time. He gestured the lowlife away, brought his eyes back to her so she could breathe the last "you" of "It had to be you" right at him.

His lips pantomimed the word "Shit." Then he rose and made a royal wave with one hand that meant "and all that stuff we cops do."

And left.

Thanks to the inside info she had on the drug deal at the Opium Den going down, he was outta here. And so was she.

Molina bowed her head slightly to the enthusiastic applause, winked at the guys in the band, and beat a retreat to her tiny closet of a dressing room.

In front of the big round mirror on the vintage dressing table, she wiped off the dark carmine forties lipstick shade from an online company of vintage cosmetic shades called Besamé. *Kiss me.* Not tonight. She dusted her face with dark brown face powder in a random camouflage pattern. The velvet gown, peacock-green, went on a hanger. She was wearing black yoga pants underneath. The dark green satin platform forties sandals gave way to black high-top tennis shoes. Black turtleneck. You'd think she was a Max Kinsella fashion clone.

If she was lucky, thanks to that Mojave Way address from Larry, she'd be invading Max Kinsella territory tonight. The Glock was too heavy for this gig. A small black Beretta nine-shot semiautomatic, perhaps in tribute to the Fontana brothers, was in her black nylon ankle holster.

She glimpsed herself in the round mirror before she ducked out of the dressing room and out the Dahlia's back door. She looked lean, dark, and dingy.

Maybe this wasn't Max Kinsella. Maybe this was more Midnight Louie, Allah bless his tribe.

Because she was going to solo as a cat burglar tonight, God willing. Not exactly what Larry'd had in mind, but what she'd planned from the first. Her lips managed a tight feline smile.

Chapter 40

Dead of Night

Molina had to agree with Larry's reported opinion.

Bland, boring neighborhood. One-story, ranch-style houses. Only the Asian rat-tail sweep up at the roof's corners gave the place some flare. Not that it didn't cost three times what her modest bungalow in the Latino area did.

The house was fifties vintage, dark and shrouded like all the firmly middle-class homes in this aging subdivision.

The traffic swish of the Strip was almost audible here, it was so close in compared to more modern suburban developments in Henderson and environs.

No garage out front, but discreetly tucked at the back, as functional things were then.

The shrubbery was low and trimmed, unlike its neighbors.

Someone knew the rules for discouraging lurkers. The lights at the corner eaves were motion-triggered.

She'd be better off to climb the cedar-wood six-foot fence at the side and try entering by the back. It had been a long time since she'd scrambled over a wall in pursuit. Desks didn't require much scrambling.

But she kept her martial arts up and should still be fairly limber . . . shoot! Literally. She'd almost snagged her ankle holster on one of the pointed boards.

The backyard was lit on the fringes by rows of low lights. Probably solar-powered. She quickly padded out of their glare toward the house and the bulk of a hot tub on a patio.

If this place was what she thought and fervently hoped it was, she could dream up some steamy scenarios for that now-covered aquatic playpen. She had to crouch along the hot tub's bulk to near the back door without triggering the corner lights.

And then she saw the red gleam near a potted hibiscus plant, matched by one from the opposite pot.

Right. Laser light security. Or guard cats. Given her suspicions, the cats wouldn't surprise her. But if she wished to surprise anyone still in residence, it was up the fence to the roof, like a cat, and over the tile shingles to the back door, then down. Where she expected to find other barriers.

She did.

Steel shutters. And on the windows too.

She pulled out the small computerized device she'd "borrowed." Max Kinsella was making her break a lot of rules, not to mention laws.

The device ran through endless codes from the major manufacturers of security barriers. Kinsella might have modified and customized the codes, but this probability device was tireless.

And she knew this was the right place now. The security level screamed that fact. This was the one innocuous residential address at which Temple Barr had stopped the day Molina had asked Larry to tail her.

Her heart was beating with the excitement of a hunter who might suddenly become prey. If Matt was right, Kinsella was an international-level spy. Breaching even a few of his defenses meant only that more awaited her.

This was way out of the range of her normal operations. She'd been a desk jockey for too long. Still, she loved being back in the field, flying on nerve and adrenaline. She loved . . . breaking the law in the law's cause. One-upping Kinsella. Proving him guilty of something. Proving him the lying bastard she'd always seen him for. Proving Temple Barr a deluded little girl.

Matt an idealist.

Herself right.

Kinsella wrong. Dead wrong.

The device blipped and then the flashing light stayed red. The back door shutter opened slowly, with a low, grinding sound.

She tested the outer glass door, twin to a million others. It swung ajar.

She stepped into the black empty hole the shutter had left in its stead, into the heart of darkness.

Nothing is as haunting as the landscape of an unlit, presumably empty house.

Every breath you take sounds like the wheeze of an iron lung. Every soft, hesitating step crushes minuscule grains of sand underfoot, as if you were smashing shells in a driveway.

She passed through some utility room or pantry onto a hard-surfaced floor, probably the kitchen. She had a small, high-intensity flashlight in the tiny inner pocket of her supple knit pants, but she left it there.

The house seemed to breathe with her. Someone could be here. *He* could be here.

She hoped he was.

Step by step, she edged around the altarlike bulk of a kitchen island, her eyes adapting to what little light sifted through the back door into the interior dimness.

Ovals of metal pots glimmered above the island and her head. This was a reflective, metallic chef's kitchen, so unlike her expectations of Max Kinsella. Crook, yes. Never cook.

Was she wrong? Was this the wrong place? Was it some paranoid citizen's bunker against imagined assault?

No.

The slim scimitars of light glanced over a butcher block impaled with an expensive array of long, dangerous kitchen knives, something odd about their presence here.

The refrigerator was a matte silver mirror of stainless steel. She glimpsed her own figure as an impossibly narrow fencepost of wrought iron, moving out of range.

From the kitchen she moved into utterly dark inner space, probably a dining room. She edged outward until her hand felt a stucco wall and followed it. A waft of air told her a door or a hall intersected it.

She was moving on primitive instinct now, mostly sightless, her ears straining at every sound she made. It had taken maybe seven minutes to get to this point.

And she sensed a presence. Someone besides her was in this house, in these rooms. Nothing proved it. Nothing could deny it.

She moved even more cautiously. Yes, into a hall. Her long arms could span it, touch each side. The long arms of the law.

You can run, but you can't hide, Max Kinsella. You are mine!

A floorboard creaked ever so slightly.

To her right and behind.

Molina flattened against one wall, felt down it until a doorknob butted against her hip. Had she been moving faster she would have collided with it and huffed out an audible breath of pain.

As it was, she felt the small round disk, the kind you find on louvered wooden doors on closets, and pulled. A panel opened silently. She slipped behind it into folds of clothing. A closet, yes. She pulled the flimsy door shut. It was too light to creak.

Some light sifted through the louvers, striping the darkness with horizontal bars. A jail cell on its side.

Shelter? Or trap?

She heard sounds, motion. The subtle grind of footsteps not

hers on the hard-surface floor of the kitchen. A subtle, scraping sound, faintly shrill, reminded her of something she couldn't name. A faint bellows of someone else moving and breathing now that she was still.

Her heart was thundering in her veins and chest, at her ears and throat. Bending down to draw the Beretta would be damned awkward. She'd butt her head on the louvered door so close. She should have drawn it when she was in the larger hall, damn it!

She heard a door opening, a solid-core door across the hall. Then a tiny sound, minute but long, like . . . like something tearing. Again and again. There was a rhythmic, sawing motion to the sound. Across the hall, in another room. Someone breaking into something? A cabinet. A magician's cabinet?

And breath. Getting louder as the small gnawing sound continued. Heavy. Breathing. Someone else was definitely in here. And not a resident.

Someone secret, like herself.

Who?

The tearing sound stopped. The minuscule grains of outdoor sand crushed again. Breathing, harsh, passed her louvers. She held her own breath until her chest burned and she feared an exhalation would sound like a tsunami.

She clapped her hand to her mouth and used her singer's strong stomach and chest muscles to expel the air, silent bit by silent bit.

Whoever was in here was dangerous. And it wasn't Max Kinsella. He wouldn't move like a thief in his own rooms. No one had sensed her yet. Yet she knew she wasn't alone.

She felt as if some giant slow-slinking serpent was moving from room to room, about some very vicious business.

And then her mind fixed on the impression of what had been wrong in the kitchen like a grade-school student clinging to a flash card recognized a fraction too late to count.

Metal being honed.

The knife block.

One had been missing in the regular ranks of dark hilts glinting with steel rivets.

A big one.
The biggest one.
The butcher knife.
Holy Saint Ginsu Jesus!

Chapter 41

Transportation

The senior partner of Midnight Inc. Investigations is not the all-knowing oracle he thinks he is.

In fact, there are times when I deeply hope that he is not the dirty dog who sired me and my littermates on my unknown but obviously easily duped mother and took off for other venues.

I admit that I have always had a soft spot for Mr. Matt Devine.

For one thing, he offered me a temporary home for a few days back when I was known as "Caviar," and had not yet beat all comers to become house detective at the Crystal Phoenix. And I have always felt something in common with the dude, given he was searching for two absent fathers: a mean step-father and, unknowingly, his birth father. I fear his quests have been as disappointing as mine was.

And Mr. Midnight Louie, dude about Vegas (I would say "dud" about Vegas were he here to hear me), is not the only one wont to drop in on Karma at the Circle Ritz and get up-to-date on the doings of its human occupants.

Anyway, I have a bone to pick with him on what is more important: sheep-dogging his Miss Temple through murder among the feather free-for-all at the Crystal Phoenix, or figuring out what is going on with the Mystifying Max.

That dude is sure living up to his performing moniker lately, or maybe not.

So instead of hobnobbing with the chic chapeaux set, I have taken on the thankless job of sitting outside Mr. Max's residence waiting for something to happen.

Stakeout detail is ungrateful work. You have to sit still until your tail goes numb, both of them in my case. You have to hang out in the shrubbery where the ants crawl in and the ants crawl out and the ants play pinochle on your snout. And these are fire ants!

You have to ignore taunting lizards at your feet and birds chirping and pooping in the bushes above your head. Through heat of day and dark of night, nothing can distract you from your eternal duty.

And, on top of it all, nothing is happening at Chez Max.

I am beginning to think my possibly paternal partner is right. Nothing of interest will happen here and I am wasting my time as another endless day draws to a close and the crickets come out to chatter.

Last night, however, things got interesting for a few hours.

A crew of ninjas pulled up in a train of dark vans about 3:00 A.M., which is when humans are most deeply asleep. Also when my breed is more alert and active, as humans who decide to keep us as indoor domestic pets soon discover.

When I say "ninjas," I mean ninjas. I have glimpsed those Asian action films. These men were all in black spandex, including hoods and masks. Imagine Spider-Man in mourning. They were nimble, they were strong, and they were fast as a firefly.

Each van was emptied on the lawn, filled with furniture abstracted from the house, and then driven away with suspiciously quiet care. Then the furniture from the lawn was borne silently inside. I watched this surreptitious exchange program go on until the sun was starting to curl its claws into the horizon and pull itself up over the edge of the world.

Not my favorite time.

Twelve vanloads must have been carted out, and in.

Then all was quiet as the sun started getting bold and hot and the lizards stirred and the birds chirped and pooped and nothing happened all day.

No doubt the senior partner would have been off eating and snoozing in his cushy haunts.

I stayed by my post, dining on the occasional grasshopper, until the sun tired of broiling all living things on the surface and slunk behind the Western Mountains to infest the other side of the world.

Except for a few drops sucked off the early morning sprinklers in the neighborhood, my throat was as parched as the sandy dirt surrounding the house, but my curiosity was stronger than my thirst. What would the next night bring? I intend to find out.

So here I am, waiting unseen, when it seems that everybody in the Western world has decided to break into the Kinsella domicile at once. I hunker down, ready to watch and wonder, and draw conclusions. And report back to my partner. If I feel that he deserves to be in the loop.

Chapter 42

Lost in Space

Molina understood that she was no longer the invader.

She was now the resident, and she had been interrupted by one nasty unlawful entrant.

At least that made her home invasion look justifiable.

And made her wonder where the hell Max Kinsella was.

He wouldn't be slinking through his own quarters.

He wouldn't tolerate anyone getting this familiar with his territory, or her breaking in. He wouldn't have left it this easy to get in. Maybe the bastard was dead, as Matt feared.

Matt *feared!* That man had no normal negative emotions, like jealousy, or wishing a rival dead. Kinsella was no loss. He was her stalker. And now, in a case of poetic justice, he apparently had his own stalker.

Or could he be, God forbid, innocent? Could her stalker and his be the same person? Could she and Max Kinsella both be victims?

Molina rejected that term as violently as she knew Kinsella would. He hadn't been an innocent since his teens, if Matt's revelation about the counterterrorist past was true.

So maybe Kinsella was really gone. At least from this house. And maybe someone else had the same hankering as Molina to violate and solve its secrets. Except . . . Molina was a pro. She was textbook careful, as silent as possible.

The other intruder was breathing hard now, obviously. Angered by something found, or not found, possibly Kinsella himself.

He had left. For real, this time. Molina was suddenly sure about that. The magician had left the building.

Live or dead.

The idea reminded her of the old "she left" case. The killer of the murdered woman found lying with that phrase painted on Molina's own car at the Blue Dahlia parking lot had been tracked down, tried, and convicted.

But the case of the murdered woman found in the church parking lot about the same time, on whose body the phrase "she left" had appeared at the morgue, that was still open.

Unsolved.

What was the victim's name? Gloria. Gloria something. Retired showgirl. Or something.

Molina shook her head free of old cold cases. No time to stroll down a murderous memory lane. She had to contend with whoever wanted into the house as badly as she did, and that gave her pause. Okay. She was a trifle obsessed. She was risking her whole career by being here. Right now she couldn't think of one good reason why if she had to answer to a higher authority.

That man was why! That "demmed illusive Pimpernel," as the old swashbuckler novel put it. Kinsella drove everybody around him crazy. Temple Barr had apparently shaken loose of that old black magic, but now she, Carmen Regina Molina, had been caught in his abandoned web like a fruit fly on honey.

She pushed the louvered door open. Slowly, cautiously. Bent

to touch her ankle. The Beretta rasped as she drew it from the holster. That was the same snakelike, slithering sound the other person in the house had made.

So small.

But all other sound stopped, even the impatient breathing.

Molina stepped out into the hall. And saw a descending glint of steel. Where was the shrill music from the infamous shower knife scene in *Psycho*? She was suddenly Janet Leigh, wasn't she?

Except she was armed and dangerous, and forearmed too.

Molina's forearm cracked into the descending arm attacking her. Arm bones were the human body's strongest.

She blocked the blow, which came in lower than she'd thought, but the knife blade burned along her right side, a thin, shallow slice.

It didn't hurt now, but it would bleed.

Molina's long leg lashed out, tangling with someone's ankle. An explosive breath huffed into the dark as a body stumbled and fell. Then stuttering steps pounded in the hall, running by the time they hit the slate floor of the kitchen with muffled thumps.

Sneakers.

Hot blood ran down to her hip as Molina bounded in pursuit.

She passed the vague reflective doorway of the stainless-steel refrigerator as she heard the back door bang open and shut.

Lights from the left blinded her.

She blinked wildly in that direction, finding the source in an adjoining room, maybe the den. Two table lamps, probably on timers, but controlled by yet a third person in the house.

And she glimpsed the operator.

A man standing by a chair. Wearing pants anyway.

A silhouette.

She aimed the Beretta, but didn't dare shoot a "what if." What if he was a civilian? A security firm guard? Even a resident, even Max Kinsella? So she'd made herself into a deer in the headlights.

A bleeding deer in the headlights.

Damn, damn, damn.

The man laughed softly.

Love and Hate:
He Said, She Said

"I hate him and he won't get out of my life!"

"I love her and she won't let me into her life."

The phone lines for the "Midnight Hour," which ran for two hours now, it was so popular, were dishing up double doses of he-she angst tonight.

Matt was riding on the edge of his nerves. The whole male-female apache dance was getting to him.

He couldn't help personalizing tonight: *I hate Max Kinsella because he won't get out of my life. I love Temple and she didn't let me into her life (check that: bed) for so long.*

But those declarations weren't true in his case. He'd never hated Max; he'd even sympathized with him. He'd always understood why Temple hadn't seen his fresh young sapling of first love for the significant redwood forest that was Mighty Max. Matt had been reared to see two sides, even to his own life and loves.

Sometimes lately that felt downright wussy.

He watched the clock. The program's two hours usually flew by as he probed the callers' hearts and minds. Now he was impatient, as if something important was going on out there in the night he ought to know about, be in on.

Maybe it was the call that afternoon from his mentor in seminary-turned-FBI agent, Frank Bucek. He was in town to speak at some law enforcement seminar. Wanted to check in with Matt.

"I work really late."

"You think I'm too old to stay up past midnight? I'll catch your radio show, then we can hit one of the high-end hotels. Must be bars that serve cocktail menus all night long in this town."

"Yeah, sure. I guess we can meet at the Venetian," Matt had said like an old Vegas hand.

The idea of his former religious counselor hearing him on the radio advising the lovelorn and co-dependent unnerved him. Also, uh, his current ecstatic state of living in sin.

Father Frank had been his confessor all through seminary. He'd left the priesthood too, but at a much older age. Matt pictured him as staidly courting an ex-nun and marrying immediately, before any test runs, and having kids right away. Lots of kids that only stopped because the wife was menopausal pretty quick. No birth control, for sure.

Forgive me, Father, for I have sinned. On all counts.

Matt had never regarded his radio gig as a performance, but tonight he did. Afterward, just past 2:00 A.M., he drove the Crossfire to the Venetian, rehearsing what he'd say. If asked.

Frank was at the bar, wearing a good gray suit that the Fontana brothers could probably nail as to designer and price level. Receding hair sharpened his features, and an intelligent, energetic air never failed him, in Roman collar or out of it. Matt realized as he approached that this was the father he'd always wished he'd had. Now that he had an image of his actual father, he still preferred Bucek. The man was brilliant. Why had he left the church after so long? And for the FBI?

Frank stood, holding out a hand with a crippling grip that Matt finally knew how to resist and return.

"Matt! Good work! You always were a remarkable diagnostician of the human soul. No wonder even Elvis called in to your show."

"That was some pathological impersonator."

"Not according to Quantico's top sound analysis people. You could probably exploit those audio recordings."

"Not my job."

"No." Bucek's quick smile was pleased. "All restless souls deserve privacy, at the end. I ordered you a scotch."

"Fine. How was the conference?"

"Both boring and exhilarating. The world runs on these things. Half the time I hate them, but half the time I love them."

"You're good in front of people."

"And you're not?"

"I fake it well."

"*Hmm.* You fake the least of anybody I've ever known. That's your problem. So what's up with you?"

Matt sipped the straight-up scotch. It was almost as good as Max Kinsella's Millennium brand that he'd shared first with Matt, in a private, bitter wake for Kathleen O'Connor. Almost. Nobody beat Kinsella for taste, especially in women.

"I'm engaged to be married," Matt said.

"Well! A toast then, to the blushing bride. Who is she?"

"Temple, of course."

"Not 'of course.' Nothing in your life has been 'of course.' Hard sometimes, but ultimately rewarding."

Bucek clinked glass rims. "I must confess that I have mixed feelings about that young woman."

"How so?" Matt asked cautiously.

"She's bright, honest, gutsy. I'd be proud to be her father."

So far, so good. Father "Frankenfurter's" favorable opinion was always hard-won in seminary.

"And I couldn't help noticing that she is one sweet and delicious girly little number."

"Am I blushing?" Matt asked.

"Nope. You're too far gone already."

"You're probably right."

Matt welcomed the combo plate of appetizers Frank had ordered coming down between them, hot and fried and distracting.

"So when's the wedding?" Frank asked after they'd each dipped into the cheese and crab and chicken wings.

"We don't know. We haven't met each other's families yet."

"You're from Chicago, right?"

"Right. Temple's family is in Minneapolis."

"One quick trip, then, should do it."

"You don't know my family, especially since I found my birth father."

"That's wonderful, Matt." Frank clapped him on the arm.

"Not for my mother."

"Ah."

"Anyway, you don't need to hear all that. Did you get married soon after you left St. Vincent's?"

"Lord, no! I shopped around some first."

Matt nearly choked on a chicken wing. "Dated, you mean."

"Sure." He eyed Matt. "You've been hooked on Miss Barr from the git-go, haven't you?"

"Yeah. Knocked over, but she was taken. I tried to see other women. They were nice, attractive, but—"

"But no fireworks. So you outwaited the competition."

"We've always been friends. I've always suspected she sensed we could be more."

Bucek nodded. "You'd have been an idiot not to have been interested in her. Single gals of her quality aren't out there at your age, and at mine. So, what is she?"

Matt understood the question instantly. "UU, but she's not practicing."

The older man's sharp guffaw made all heads within twenty feet turn their way.

"Sorry, Matt." Frank was trying to smother his laughter with the linen napkin. "She *is* independent. Well, UUs are very easy with ecumenical anything. The ceremony shouldn't be a problem."

"No."

"Spit it out."

Matt glanced at his small plate of wing bones and crumpled batter.

Frank smiled. "I'm not asking about what you're eating, I'm asking about what's eating you."

"That transparent?"

"You're as edgy as a seminarian with a question about wet dreams."

Matt looked around, but everyone was chatting and drinking and ignoring them again. He lowered his voice. "I'm living in sin."

"Do you like it?"

Matt felt Father Frankenfurter had let him down with the blunt, almost jovial question. "Obviously, yes. And no."

"What's not to like?"

"I can't receive communion at mass."

"So don't. Everyone will just think you didn't fast, if they think anything."

"But we may not get married for months."

"Didn't we priests always advise young couples to wait?"

"Frank, you're supposed to be the voice of authority and wisdom here."

"Nope. Not my deal anymore. Come on, Matt! You were a parish priest for years. How many beautiful nuptial masses did you officiate at where the lovely young couple moved into separate apartments after months, even years together, just before they showed up in your office to discuss wedding plans?"

"A lot, I suppose. Some wanted advanced degrees before marrying. Many had been 'dating' for several years."

"Sounds sensible to me. Why can't you do likewise for a few months?"

"I was a priest. I'm supposed to follow the rules more than anyone."

"You were supposed to be compassionate too. How about having a little compassion for yourself. Look. You are in love with a great young woman. You know she's had another lover—"

"It wasn't just that. They'd planned on marrying eventually, except his . . . job got in the way."

Frank waved a dissenting hand. "I'm not slamming anyone. I'm saying that people who love each other should express it the best way they know how. There are way too many people in this world expressing hate. They're in the headlines every day. Jesus associated with the common people who felt love, not the control-freak hypocrites who ran the temple. Oops, your girlfriend has a name made for double entendres in our game. Are you hurting anyone? Then chill."

"But—"

Frank raised that commanding hand again. "You came here to Las Vegas hunting a man, right?"

"Looking for."

"Hunting. I know a bit about that. Your abusive ex-stepfather. What drove that?"

"I stood up to him when I was in high school, but it wasn't enough. I wanted to see what had become of him, I wanted to . . . scare the crap out of him, take out on him what he'd taken out on my mother. Not me, my mother."

"So you had an agenda of hate."

"Anger, more."

"And did you catch up with him?"

Matt nodded, taking a slug of scotch.

"What did you do?"

"Slammed him against a wall. Told him what I thought of him. Tried to beat him up back, but he was such a loser, so truly small after I saw him again. He wasn't worth my rage."

"You're a lucky man."

Matt gave him a questioning look.

"You had every natural right to hate and harm that guy. And that would have been a mortal sin. You would have been taking on his evil, perpetuating the chain of hurt and retaliation. You stopped. So, forget it. I'm not the one who's going to call love a sin for you. Yeah, I know the church has confused love with sex, for centuries, but I'm out of it now, and you are too. My advice: Don't overthink it, kid. Love needs to be embraced with open arms and eyes and no damn guilt, just as we all do, God bless us everyone. So enjoy."

Temple lay awake in bed, running the events and questions of the day through her head, when she heard the floor above her creaking as Matt came home.

Late. Three-thirty.

She wondered what had kept him out. Whatever it was, he must be wide-awake still, like her.

She'd heard the sounds of his movements above her rooms before. This was an old building; floors creaked, faucets squeaked. Now the sounds of his motions drew her. She'd fought so hard for months to ignore their attraction, to *not* think about him. Now she didn't have to. She could lie here getting turned on. She could think about doing something about it.

When she spun her legs out of the bed to the floor, Louie, arrayed by her feet, meowed his protest.

"It's all yours, fella. Spread out and enjoy."

She was wearing her favorite sleep T-shirt, which was as unflattering as a Mother Hubbard dress. But she didn't plan on keeping it on long anyway.

She ran barefoot up the stairs and knocked on his door.

It took a minute or two to open. He must have been in the bedroom already.

No, he still had his open shirt and Jockeys on.

Not for long.

"Hi, I'm your nonaddictive sleeping pill," she said. "Better get in bed and let me start acting on you."

"Temple!" He was laughing as she backed him up into the bedroom, onto the bed.

"What? I'm too much for you?"

"Never," he said fervently. She liked fervent. "It's just that I never dreamed that you'd come up here like this, to visit me."

"What *did* you dream?" Temple asked.

"Oh, God. That you'd suddenly really look at me. See me. Love me. I was needy, I guess."

"I don't think so, Matt. I think you were hot. That's the way it starts when you love someone. You want them too."

"One? Them?"

"Making general subjects agree with verbs is the writer's worst chore. Cut me some slack."

"I don't want to cut you some slack," he quoted her. " 'Not one bit. I want you on your toes,' working your heart and soul off, 'to make me a very happy' guy."

"There's no way we can be on our toes in this position," Temple pointed out, wriggling her bare ones.

She knew she shouldn't tease him. He buried his face between her neck and shoulder. She giggled.

"That tickles!"

"This is bad?"

"This is good." Temple sighed.

She felt a little guilty. Not about Max, for once, for about luring Matt from the rules of his church.

She felt like an older woman. My God! Her. She, the woman, was the more experienced. It wasn't supposed to be like this. The woman on top. Society said there was something unnatural about this inversion of the "natural order." Women were supposed to be anxious and ignorant. Innocent, they called it. Duped, others might call it.

But it was her responsibility now. To be gentle with him. To admire and encourage his intensity, his unfurling lust. Whew. She could shatter him with a careless word or gesture. Make him doubt himself, what he felt. It was a tremendous responsibility.

And . . . wow, really exciting.

He was responding with even more intensity tonight, kissing her, covering her. Matt was tireless, passionate, in love with love.

First love. Could it really be *only* love? She wished, wished, wished that was so. It would salve his always raw Catholic conscience. God must have wanted this, because it was so exulting, so personal, so ecstatic. God needed sex, or else there'd be no universe, no natural world, no creatures great and small.

And Temple believed that when they were together, as she never had before. She knew love; she knew sex. Max would have been enough, had his world let him be.

She was everything to Matt, as he was to her now. And so far the world was letting them be.

And it was . . . divine.

Chapter 44

Red Hot Mama

"Step into the light or I'll shoot," she barked out, although if he was armed he could have shot her anytime before this.

That he hadn't was promising.

The knife assailant was history, though.

"Now," she said in the same brusque, mean-business tone. That didn't mean her heart wasn't pounding from the attack, the escaped perp, the new mystery.

He obliged.

Oh, my God.

Not Max Kinsella, at least, but the only other man capable of laughing at her when she had a Beretta aimed at his heart.

Her eyes began to adjust to the bright headlights of the table lamps. If this man was an enemy, he was one who relished her discomfort more than her death.

"I like you even better in this outfit," Dirty Larry said from the dark side of the living room. "You are a lady with more secrets than a Swiss bank account. Maybe now is the time to tell me some."

"What are you doing here?" she demanded, just as brusque, even if a bit relieved.

"When a woman leads me on and then ditches me, I find out why. I'm a cop, Carmen. You can't play me like a junior-high swain."

She lowered her gun, and tried to calm her pulse.

The uplighting from the table lamps cast Larry Paddock's face into a creepy, half-lit mask.

"So you're really ticked?" she said.

"No." He sat down in the chair. "I'm turned on. Always love a good chase. And curious."

She edged nearer, the gun lowered but still clutched in both hands, although the knife wound was starting to throb now.

"So you let a perp escape to get one up on me?"

"The fence is a cinch to scale. You know that; I know that. I'd just got in the front when that scuffle broke out in the hall. That was one gone break-in artist. Besides, I was more curious about why *you* were here than *he* was."

Dirty Larry stood and came toward her. "And I was *really* curious about if you would actually deliver what you were promising tonight if whatever this was hadn't been on your mind. So I really came here after you."

His words and tone could have been sinister or sexy. Molina wasn't sure which motive was scarier. She was sure her heart was still beating like the proverbial trip hammer and it should be slowing down by now.

Was it Dirty Larry or dirty tricks?

The two table lamps were beginning to spin around each other and the gun was sliding from her hands. She managed to push the safety on as the bright lights circled her head. That damn knife wound must have been longer and deeper than she'd thought.

"Jesus," she said, meaning the prayer.

"Christ!" she heard him say, meaning the swear word.

And then she went to heaven.

Molina woke up, immediately aware that she'd passed out and not happy about it. If word about the "swooning lieutenant" got around the department it would be way worse than being outed as the "crooning lieutenant," fourteen years of blood, sweat, and rank were cooked.

She was on her back.

Bad.

On a bed.

Worse.

On a strange bed.

Worst.

Maybe on Max Kinsella's bed.

Unthinkable.

She focused slowly, ignoring the burning pain in her side and the ugly pull of adhesive tape along her ribs.

The nightstand lamp was blinding her, but she made out that old devil silhouette in a chair by the wall.

Dirty Larry.

He lifted a forefinger to catch her attention. It was hovering over an open cell phone.

"One button punched," he said, "and the EMTs come to deal with your knife wound. You want?"

"No!"

"Okay, it's your funeral. I don't think the wound is that bad, but you should get better medical attention than me."

Molina patted her side. Her turtleneck sweater was down and her yoga pants were up, holding on a long expanse of gauze and tape, but they certainly hadn't been while she was out cold.

"You can carry a lot of dead weight," she told him.

He chuckled. "More like drag, but you didn't know the difference at the time. Whoever lives here has a hell of a lot of first aid stuff in the bathroom, which looks like the ones at the Luxor."

"You mean like a fancy, dark tomb fit for a pharaoh?"

"Right."

"Figures."

"You know the resident?"

"Maybe 'knew,' maybe 'ex-resident.' A magician."

"Yeah, that was a magician's bathroom. It felt like being pent-up in one of those tricky disappearing boxes. So. How do you feel?"

"Still woozy."

He lifted a glass of water. "Here's some Tylenol. Sure don't want to give you aspirin. Can you sit up to take it?"

"Sure," she said, then tried. "*Oof.*"

He came over to pull her upright against the pillows. It hurt.

"Sure you don't want medical help?"

"Would you?"

"No."

She took the pills and the water glass and choked down the three caplets. Then she swung her legs to the floor.

"You ready already?"

"I'll have to be by tomorrow morning. Might as well be now."

"What's the deal here?" he asked. "This is the house I tailed our little former redhead to. Now I tail you here."

"I thought the person who lived here might be my stalker. I decided to find out."

"Who lived here?"

"A missing magician."

"Isn't that redundant?"

"Not in this case."

"So who had broken in before you did?"

"I don't know." Molina put down the water glass. She wasn't sure if her attacker had broken in before, or after, her. "Help me up and let's go see."

He came to pull her up. It got as near as close dancing, and he enjoyed that.

"You like having the upper hand, don't you?" she said.

"Always." He leaned near and whispered in her ear, "I've seen London, I've seen France, I've seen—"

She laughed. "Shut up." But she thought: *Sinister, or sexy?*

Somehow that question seemed even more appropriate in Max Kinsella's ex-house.

Because he was gone for good, one way or another; that she knew now, no matter the props still stored here.

Able to lurch around on her own power, she first visited the room across the hall from the closet where she'd hidden.

She paused in the doorway to aim her high-intensity flashlight over the huge piece of furniture looming against one wall, almost a room in itself.

"What the—?"

Larry ambled into the flashlight beam to eye it up close. "Shit! This is right up my alley."

"What do you mean?" The flashlight illuminated a vivid brocade surface, fret-worked uprights, and a brocade canopy.

"Opium bed." Her light caught his grin. "Now that's a crib fit for taking one of your velvet gowns off in, Carmen."

She ran the light over the massive outlines, grander and larger than a four-poster bed. A small flare in the pit of her stomach said he was right. *Madre de Dios!* What she didn't need to deal with right now was a crazy UC guy for a lover. But she sensed something perversely sexy about getting it on with Larry in Max Kinsella's abandoned digs, and Larry was picking up on that like a good cop should.

In fact, the place reeked of hidden sex. She was sure Temple Barr was a phantom of the erotic opera that had occurred in some of these over-the-top rooms. Now the rooms held a darker ambiance. Whoever had broken in tonight had broadcast a subtle, homicidal presence. And that wasn't sexy, just sick.

She limped over to the wall of doors and jerked back the first of several mirrored sliding doors.

"Oh, my," Larry breathed in her ear, having followed her. "Lions and tigers and bears have been busy in here."

She instantly saw what he meant. The ranks of solid black clothes inside had been shredded into clownish tatters, some dangling from their padded black satin hangers, others fallen to the floor in piles like charred autumn leaves.

Larry bent to run his fingers through the ruins.

"Cashmere. Silk. Italian wool. This guy knew how to dress."

"Yes."

"The magician?"

"Yes."

"And the slasher was—?"

"I don't know who, but let's check out the kitchen next."

When he stepped close and put her good arm around his shoulder, she didn't object. Her other side was on fire. She needed more than Tylenol, but she wasn't going to get it just yet. She couldn't contain a small moan as she felt her lifted arm stretch the wound on the opposite side.

"Scars give a girl that lived-in look," he said.

"Don't make me laugh. It hurts too much."

He ran a finger down her good side. "I think they're sexy."

"Everything hurts too much right now for nonsense, Larry."

But he was right. She'd have a helluva scar from this. That reminded her of the thin straight razor scar Matt Devine's manly side carried, courtesy of the woman Temple Barr had christened "Kitty the Cutter."

Payback time. Now Molina had her own Cutter Anonymous. Could the home invader here be her stalker? But what link did she have to Max Kinsella other than an itch to pin some crime or other on him?

When she and Larry shuffled into the kitchen, he turned on the overhead fluorescents. No point in being discreet. That time had passed long before.

He spotted the knife block. "One gone."

"I sensed that coming in, but didn't fully register what it meant until I heard those clothes being slashed, although I didn't realize what that sound was until I saw the evidence."

"Yeah. Our minds are like cameras. They record everything on a crime scene, but the whole picture doesn't snap into full focus right away. It's pretty plain. You were right on his heels. Someone must have a real bad hex on this missing magician."

"The magician might be more than missing. He might be dead."

"Really? You don't know?"

"He probably is dead. He'd never allow his stuff to be trashed like this if he were alive. Let's look around some more."

They visited every room. One bedroom was stuffed with stage props and conjuring chests. Larry looked around and sniffed hard in there.

When Molina raised her eyebrows, he shrugged. "Checking to make sure no dead bodies are ripening here. This would be the perfect place to stash a dead magician."

"Yeah." She could barely focus even though they had all the lights on. She still wasn't sure the invader had arrived before her. Surely, she would have sensed movement from the git-go. Larry already had shown up inside. The slasher could have been him. "How'd you get in the front door?"

"Drug lords use this same level of high security. If I didn't know how to work it, I'd be dead."

"So this place is high-level secure."

"Right. Except that you got in the back. I got in the front, which was a lot harder, no offense. And an unknown actor got in somehow just before you did."

He sure kept stressing that. Police instincts, or planting his own scenario? It was hell to be too jaded to trust anyone.

"That was—" she began.

"What?"

"Creepy. Like shadowing a snake."

"Sick. I agree. And whoever it was had a hankering to slice up a human as well as a high-end wardrobe."

"The resident vic was pretty hate-worthy."

"The magician."

She nodded.

"You?"

She nodded. "Among others."

"Anybody love him?"

She nodded. "That little blonde you saw at Mariah's Teen Idol gig, who I had you tail."

"She was making pretty innocuous rounds, but she led me—and you—here. And the tail was also pretty tasty."

"That is so sexist."

"Why? Because it's not your tail I'm talking about?"

"I don't have one."

"Yeah, you do." He grinned. "I just peeked."

With as much blood as she had lost, Molina had enough left to flush. "Not funny."

"I was being serious."

That was what she was afraid of. Thing was, Larry knew too much, way too much, about her recent, atypical acts of skirting the law, her own standards, everything.

Thing was, she couldn't decide whether that was sexy . . . or sinister.

Chapter 45

Toodle Who?

I must say one thing for my partner's basic instincts.

She sure does have a female knack for uncovering a crime in progress, even if it is only some poor dude trying to take a catnap.

I feel four shivs in my shoulder and hear a voice hissing, "Wake up, you layabout! I have been noticing some unwarranted activity around Mr. Max's supposedly sold and occupied house."

"Are you still playing that sad old tune, Louise?" I ask, unrolling from a warm and comfy ball in my own previously private quarters, i.e., Miss Temple's bed, sans Mr. Matt for once. "I thought we had decided to permit your Mr. Max to fade into the sunset until my Miss Temple's current domestic and on-the-job problems were settled."

"Her worst enemy has been prowling about the premises while I had it under surveillance."

Well, that made me sit up and take notice. I cannot have mere shirttail relatives (maybe) taking over my primary job of protecting my Miss Temple!

"I wish you would get off this Mr. Max crusade, Louise. Gone is gone. Even Miss Temple has accepted that."

"Not to mention accepting a shaded golden into her bed where you black-haired boys used to loll at your leisure."

"I wish you would not refer to Mr. Matt as if he were a certain color of Persian," I snap. Literally.

"Aha!" She jumps back like a ninja. "Methinks a certain color of female Persian has soured your milk. Your so-called Divine Yvette is a shaded silver."

"I call her the Supine Yvette now," I say airily.

"Not for her bedtime manners, I bet," she answers.

Little does Miss Midnight Louise know that it is because of her alley cat origins and rumored relationship to me (rumored mostly by herself) that I have been untimely dropped by She Who Was Formerly the Divine Yvette.

She eyes me slyly. "I would bet that there is not much peaceful resting space there for you on Miss Temple's zebra-striped comforter now. At least Mr. Max had the decency to absent himself frequently on impossibly dangerous secret missions."

Her words sting like a cat's-claw cactus.

The fact is my various extremities have been subjected to certain heedless rollings and pinnings, as if I were mere bread dough to be mashed and smashed, on what should be my supreme sprawling space, the California king-size bed. Not to mention all the sweet nothings that I have been forced to overhear, which would be enough to curl the ears on a Swiss chocolate cat who did not even understand English.

So I admit to Miss Louise, "There may be some who enjoy kittenish caperings, not to mention squeals and mews and purrs, and find them amusing and even adorable, but I am not one. Not if it disturbs my sleep."

"Speaking of disturbed sleep, I have been spending my nights outside Chez Kinsella. I can tell you that what has been going on there lately may not be as titillating as late-night TV in your Circle Ritz boudoir, but it has been fairly puzzling, and . . . now . . . mind-blowing."

"Please, Louise. Do not resort to such uncouth and vulgar modern street expressions as 'mind-blowing.' "

"I believe that is the only way to describe Miss Lieutenant C. R. Molina breaking into Mr. Max's ex-digs with that scruffy cop guy from her daughter's Teen Idol idyll hot on her heels. And I do mean hot. He is seriously after the crooning cop. And so may be an anonymous perp, who stuck her with a butcher knife before exiting the premises. Or so I learned from eavesdropping in the dark. I am thinking Midnight Inc. Investigations should ramble on over to examine the scene of the crimes."

Molina. Hot cop guy? Mr. Max's former premises? Butcher knife? Unapprehended perps?

"What happened to the leggy veteran chorus chick you yourself witnessed in possession of those fabled premises not two days ago?" I ask.

"Good question, Pops. That is the way your Miss Temple escorted by Mr. Aldo Fontana may have been meant to see it. Now it is full of all the old furnishings and as busy with trespassers coming and going as a park marked 'Do Not Step on the Grass.' "

"Aha! That order is usually because there are already snakes installed on the same grass."

"Apparently one was loose in Mr. Max's former quarters. His clothes were slashed into fringe, from what I overheard."

"They did not catch you?"

"No. Miss Lieutenant C. R. Molina had been so badly clawed she had to lean on Mr. So-called Dirty Larry, the undercover narc."

"No! She would not lean on a crutch if both her legs were broken. Where is she now?"

"He said he was driving her to medical care of a top-secret nature."

"Then the house is empty."

"That is why I am here, Rip Van Wrinkle. You want to take a stroll through Mr. Max Kinsella's formerly secret domicile and figure out how it changes from sold and inhabited to not sold and vacated in forty-eight hours?"

I push my muscular legs into four inches of cotton batting, seeking to gain purchase. It is a cushy venue I am deserting, but something very strange is happening at the house formerly known as Mr. Max's.

"We will have to hitchhike," Louise warns me as I land with an impressive *thump* on the wooden bedroom floor.

"Fine. I am sure we can catch a ride on somebody slinging *Review-Journals* to the driveway at this hour." Louise flicks her tail in annoyance at yet another ride from heck. "Where is your usual resident tonight?"

I jerk my head heavenward.

Miss Midnight Louise gets my drift immediately. "Maybe you can bunk with Ma Barker's gang if you cannot stand the bedroom antics anymore. Are they getting any free grub here yet?"

"I have told Karma to implant the idea in Miss Electra Lark's noggin while she is sleeping, but the Sacred Cat of the Dalai Lamas claims our landlady's head holds too much 'static' these days and nights to be influenced subconsciously. I guess you could call that, I suppose, 'bad Karma.'"

"Well, Miss Electra Lark is suspected of murder. That is enough to braise any mere human's brain. We are going to have to raid a Petco for free food if your humans do not come through."

"Actually, I have found a temporary solution myself."

"Really?"

"Really."

"And?"

"I have plenty of Free-to-Be-Feline around the place. I have been inviting the gang in via the palm tree trunk to have a nibble of kibble now and then. They may loathe the stuff as much as I do but these beggars aren't too choosy right now, thank Bast."

"You are 'palming' Free-to-Be-Feline off on a gang of starving street cats?"

"It is very nutritious. So say the label and my Miss Temple." I dampen a mitt and run it over my rakish eyebrow. "And she is absolutely delighted that I am eating the swill down to the crumbs so well these days."

Chapter 46

Sewed Up

Imagine a barrio doctor having access to dissolving stitches, Molina thought as Larry drove her home from ninety minutes of patching up on the sleazy side of town. And of sheer hell medicated only by some straight shots of cheap tequila.

Her blue eyes had fooled the doctor and the various gang types lounging around getting knife cuts sewn up too. They spoke in quick, idiomatic Spanish, and she got every word. Far more than Dirty Larry.

Larry had managed to find her a separate room: the tiny laundry room rather than the kitchen table. For his trouble the doctor assumed Larry had done the deed in a domestic dispute.

"This was a nightmare," she told Larry in her car, which he was driving. "How are you going to get back for your vehicle?"

"'Vehicle,'" he mocked. "Six shots of tequila, a knife wound as long as a ruler, and you still use cop talk."

"Listen. I wouldn't dis me if I were you. They were spilling their guts both ways in that place, literally and conversationally." Only she said it "convershashionally."

"Right. I got some of it. What'd I miss?"

"Big score going down in the Mercado parking lot tomorrow night."

"Great. Not another wild cocaine chase, I hope. Thanks." He pulled the car into her driveway. "Mariah?" He'd first met her thirteen-year-old daughter-turning-diva during the dreadful Teen Idol stage, and case.

"On a class trip. End of school year. End of grade school. Junior high, ready or not."

"Sure. I see you planned for everything but a maniac killer. Can't blame you for being caught napping."

"I was *not* napping. I am not napping now."

"Sure," he said, helping her out of the car. "I'll check the house in case your stalker was busy here while you were busy getting stalked in the magician's house."

That hadn't occurred to her. Between the pain and the liquid painkiller, she could only nod sagely.

Larry used her garage-door opener to enter the house and left her on the living-room sofa while he did a room-by-room and closet-by-closet check. He was fast and thorough.

"Clear," he reported, stuffing his hands in the pockets of his nylon windbreaker and looking down at her on the couch. "I can get you into the bedroom."

She regarded the fistful of big white tablets the doctor had given her for pain. Probably Vicodin. She wouldn't take them.

"No."

"I wasn't ever going to get you into the bedroom tonight, no way, no how, was I?"

"No. Not tonight. But thanks anyway."

His eyebrows were so blond they disappeared unless he frowned. He was frowning now. "You didn't say not ever."

"You didn't ask."

"I guess we should leave it at that."

"Right." She waited until he was in the kitchen, behind her back, on the way out.

"Thanks for the backup, though."

The kitchen door shut. She heard the garage door rattling closed a few seconds later. And then nothing.

She supposed he'd hitch to where he was going, or catch a bus, or call a snitch.

She didn't worry about it. She worried about getting herself and the house right for Mariah's return in the morning. And getting herself into work looking unhurt and unfrazzled. She'd need a giant bottle of Tylenol for that, and a really good acting job.

And then she needed to think about Max Kinsella's house. A shiver snaked down her spine. She'd been there, in that legendary hideout. With someone who apparently disliked him even more than she did. *She* wouldn't have slashed all that expensive clothing.

Who would? And if he *was* being stalked, even after he'd pulled a disappearing act, could it be the same person who was stalking her?

Or was it all a Kinsella sleight-of-hand act to erase her suspicions and put her out of commission and off his case? He was capable of attacking himself to put her off the trail.

Molina put her hand to her head. Her forehead was feverish and damp. Even MIA, Max Kinsella was the biggest headache in her migraine-ridden life lately.

What more could go wrong?

Mop-up Operation

Were there still milkmen, we would have arrived with them at the humble, or at least low profile, abode formerly known as Mr. Max's.

As I predicted (call me *Mr.* Karma!), we hopped a lift in a newspaper delivery van. The night was still dark, but to our feline eyes a faint glow of dawn was creeping over the edge of the world.

I must say having another pair of eyes and feet on the job so Midnight Inc. Investigations can cover two fronts is pretty handy. Uh, pretty mitty.

Miss Midnight Louise leads me around to the back, where the evening's earlier cat-and-mouse game has resulted in, according to her, multiple home invasion, confrontation, and escape events.

I am beginning to think that Miss Midnight Louise gets all the down-and-dirty action while I dither among the much more civilized Red Hat set.

I recall my Miss Temple remarking in the past that it would take a tank to break into Mr. Max's house. These super-heavy safeguards seem to be mostly disabled, maybe because the original furnishings had beat a retreat and then been installed again.

Obviously, my Miss Temple was meant to think Mr. Max was long gone. This raises my hopes that the newspaper article was a rush to judgment and that he is not really dead. Or maybe the returned furniture was meant to make someone else think that he was *not* dead, when he really is.

My Miss Temple's visit was predictable, but the subsequent visits of various dark-clothed intruders was not. I would love to know who they all were and why they were here.

Despite all the nighttime action, the house smells deserted when the chit and I eel through the broken screen on the outer back door and the slightly ajar solid wood door itself. The inside is dim, but I can scent my Miss Temple's previous trails through here, and so I tell Louise.

"You are no bloodhound," she scoffs.

"Nevertheless, I have cohabited with Miss Temple for more than a year now. I know the scent of everything from her hair preparations to her foot powder."

"Well, I may not know those trivial scents, but I can tell you one thing. There is a trail of fairly fresh blood in the hall and in the adjacent room."

Blood! I trot along and do indeed find a dried trail in those places. Unfortunately, unlike the ignoble canine, I cannot recognize people by their blood trails. Besides, I would need blood samples to compare this trail with and I am not up to scratching random Las Vegas citizens in search of a similar taste. Yes, different people's blood tastes different to my tongue. I do not know if all of my kind are similarly sensitive, but it works for me. In fact, if I do encounter someone who strikes me as a suspect for these break-ins, I might just give them a full-frontal, full-shiv whack to check it out.

"You are sure that my Miss Temple was not among the cat burglars?" I ask Louise.

"I do not think so, but I cannot be certain. You know how hard our signature color is to differentiate from the darkness? The other two I saw were large and likely male, like Mr. Matt."

"You are not suggesting—?"

"Of course not. I only meant that neither larger figure was as tall as Mr. Max. So we cannot console ourselves that he was sneaking back into his own house. The first one turned tail and ran when the other two came, but those two arrived separately. One of the second two was hurt, and the third escorted that one out. I heard voices then. One was female, the other male."

"Maybe these are former associates of Mr. Max. The movers' ninja costumes you mentioned sound like something from a magic stage show. It is not easy to come up with so many so-called cat suits in a short time."

"They did move as if choreographed," Louise concedes. "I can see that Mr. Max's associates would wish to remove his belongings after his demise, but why would they replace them?"

"Demise!" I huff. "That remains to be seen or, rather, the remains remain to be seen, and no one has, have they?" Miss Louise blinks old-gold confusion at my rather convoluted phrasing. "The answer to your question is clear. The house was changed like a stage set for Miss Temple and Miss Temple only, to convince her that seeking Mr. Max here was hopeless. Why would that be necessary unless he was *not* dead?"

"I do not know. You have pulled a big disappearing act in your life, Pops, on my mama and all us kits. You just wandered off, never to return. You did not need to stage anything."

"Now, Louise, do not be bitter. We guys all wandered off in those days."

"Apparently you still are doing so."

I ignore her, always a good policy, and slip through the empty rooms again. My sniffer is not at the level of a professional like Nose E., the Maltese drug- and bomb-sniffing dog. But I have something better than a canine sniffer. I have experience.

Hence it is that I discover the really shocking piece of physical evidence on the premises.

"Louise! Take a look at this. It is right up our alley."

She hisses a little, but soon pads into the hall to pause in the doorway of the room I occupy.

"What is it? A garbage can?"

"It is something certainly ready for a garbage can. Get over here and look for yourself."

She does, her eyes not as adjusted as mine to the light level, and peers through the open closet door.

"It looks like a fine nest for a nap. Count on you to lie down on the job."

"Look again. Go on, run your shivs through it."

She ventures into the closet, acting like she thinks I might slam the door shut on her any minute. If my moseying down the road after a short round of hanky-panky with her mother has made her the eternally suspicious little dame that she is, then maybe I have something to answer for, after all.

Her mitts are testing the dark stuff on the floor, then moving it around and sniffing the pieces, her tail slashing back and forth hard enough to swipe the whiskers off my kisser.

I step back. "Well?"

"These are remnants of wool. Wool is subject to the attacks of moths, but these garments have been destroyed by slashes. Maybe Lucky and Kahlúa, the Cloaked Conjuror's black panthers, came by for an exercise bout. The Fontana brothers wear the finest lightweight wool from Italy, so I ought to know. These are from a black sheep, though, whereas they wear only white sheep wool."

"Black sheep wool. A signature of Mr. Max. The person you saw helped out of here last night was not the only victim of knife work."

"A human was sharpening his claws on Mr. Max's clothes?"

"Or hers. Maybe the same person who engineered his fatal fall came here later to gloat."

"Great. And we have no idea who all these people coming and going here were and where they are now!"

"But we know enough to keep an eye peeled for them in

future. You had better stay here on watch outside. I need to get back to the Crystal Phoenix until that crime scene is resolved."

"And what will I do for breakfast?"

"I'll, ah, see what I can pick up in the neighborhood."

With that I dash away like the busy CEO I am. I sure hope the refuse collectors have not hit the trash cans around here yet.

Chapter 48

Knife Act

"Lieutenant?"

Molina looked up from her desk, trying to keep her face smooth and untroubled. The knife wound felt like a pack of gerbils were gnawing at her side, trying to exit her chest cavity.

"Yeah, Morrie?"

It would have to be Alch, whom she not only owed common courtesy, but who had a way of seeing beneath surfaces.

"It's not looking good for Mrs. Lark over at the Phoenix. I don't think she did it, but the local media is all over this Red Hat event and the department is looking bad for not making an arrest."

"We can't just arrest the most likely suspect. We have to make it"—the word really stuck in her craw right now—"stick."

"You're right. I'm right. I'll try to hold back Su and the entire West Coast media."

"The media you can handle. Su, I don't know."

"You okay?"

"Why not?"

"Look a little gray around the gills."

"Mariah. Out all night."

"No!" Alch, the single father of an only adult daughter, had watched Mariah growing into her teen years with delight and an empathetic pinch of despair.

"A parentally approved sleepover, Morrie. All girls. Only who knows what those girls will get up to today?"

He chuckled. "So *you* didn't sleep a wink during Daughter Darling's sleepover."

"Not a wink," she answered with absolute conviction.

"That's me all over again. Say listen, I'm gonna come down hard on that big convention scene and come up with some other suspects, so help me, Sleeping Beauty."

"Thanks, Morrie." Her voice had faded at the end there.

He raised an eyebrow. They didn't call her the Iron Maiden of the LVMPD for nothing. Her voice never faded.

"Kids," he said. "You kill 'em with kindness and they kill you with worry."

She didn't try to answer this time, just nodded briskly. That was the Molina they all knew and tolerated while leaving her personal life alone.

She breathed a big sigh of relief when Morrie left . . . and nearly shrieked at the pulsing, splitting feeling all along her side. Knife wounds hurt like hell until they fought off the infection and started closing. She'd have to move like a real iron maiden around here until the stitches took hold.

The phone rang.

"Yes," she barked. The pain helped her stay in character better than anything.

It was the desk sergeant. A tipster named Hyde was asking for her, and her alone.

"Freak or geek?" she asked.

"Looks like a fairly solid cit."

"Send him up."

Molina wanted to sigh, but she swallowed the gesture. Anything from coughing to hiccuping would be agonizing for a few days, maybe a couple weeks. So much for Dirty Larry's bedroom fantasies.

Minutes later a shadow loomed in the half-open maple-blond door to her narrow office.

Dark.

And then in walked Rafi Nadir. Just the last person in the whole wide world she'd want to see on her office threshold right now.

"Impersonating a snitch?" she asked. "You used to impersonate an officer."

They were fighting words, and they shot out of her current pain and wariness, and from some old unhealed wounds as well.

She pulled her forces together: observation, and that old police authoritative attitude that controlled anyone who might resist or bribe or cry wolf at the drop of a shield.

Despite her own problems, she saw that Rafi had a new resoluteness. That's what had conned the desk sergeant. How? Maybe the black denim jacket paired with black denim jeans and a burgundy T-shirt that read SUPPORT OUR TROOPS. He was thinner, harder, more pulled together. Maybe even confident. For a so-called police confidant. Confidential snitch.

Every muscle in her body tightened at her own assessment. *Danger, Wilhelmina Robinson!* Rafi was looking in control while she was running on anemia, adrenaline, and nerves.

"Can I sit?" he asked.

"May."

"Can. I speak real life, not off some blackboard. You always wanted me to pass as something you weren't."

She shrugged. *Ouch!*

"I know why you look like you swallowed a peach pit," he said, sitting before her desk.

"Why?"

"You know why I'm here, admit it, Carmen."

She had no idea. Her side and head ached abominably and

Dirty Larry was enough encroaching male to deal with in one week.

"Why?" she asked.

His face puckered in disbelief, maybe disgust. "The kid, of course. Like you didn't expect this. I can count, Carmen. I know when you left L.A. I know how old the kid is."

"I didn't leave L.A. I left you. And she isn't 'the kid.' "

"No. She's my kid too."

Odd, how a chair she'd sat in for years could just melt and vanish. How the distance between her desk and the door could suddenly telescope in and out, as if she were being jerked forward and backward in time like a yo-yo.

How her fingers could curl into the papers on her desk and still not find anything solid to dig into.

How her side felt the swift, long score of a sharp knife blade, and also pulled at stitches like a seam splitting, morphing into a splitting headache. A head wound.

"That came after," she heard her voice say from a long distance away.

"Naw. I don't think so. I can see myself in her."

"No."

"My eyes."

"No. My mother's eyes."

"You got your father's eyes. Anglo. Northern European blue. Why shouldn't Mariah have gotten my eyes, Middle Eastern brown? Don't that fact make your blue eyes bluer?" he paraphrased the old hit song. Bitterly.

"You didn't want *her*, Rafi. A daughter. You wanted me tied to her, tied down, off the force."

"Wait. We talking L.A. here? I didn't even know you were pregnant. And I didn't want her?"

"You made sure I was pregnant. Daughters aren't valued in Muslim society. Remember that suicide? The Anglo girl who got involved with an Arab foreign student and jumped off a bridge because her baby was a girl, and he completely rejected it, and her?"

Rafi was leaning nearer, his almost-black eyes intent, shocked.

"That was a shitty case, but I'm not that foreign student. You wouldn't even have known what gender the baby was in those days, so can that excuse. I'm a half-breed, sure. Like you. Did I resent it, being Arab-American? Yeah. Every day. It wasn't a fashionable mix, nobody was fighting to get my kind represented on the force, not like Latinas and black chicks, and that was years before 9/11. Then it really got fun. The looks. The stops. I used to stop people when I was a cop. Now I'm a stopee."

Molina started to put a hand to her forehead, to block the overhead fluorescent glare that felt like the lights of a third-degree interrogation room in the bad old days, but the hand started up, then stopped. A weak, hesitant gesture. Not a good message in a situation like this.

"I won't discuss this on the job," she managed through the throbbing in her head and side.

"Then where? And when?"

"I . . . don't know. This is not a good time."

"It wasn't a good time fourteen years ago when you walked out on me without a trace. Without a reason."

"You were a bastard!" Was it her shouting? "That's all the reason I needed." Was that her lurching over the desktop and collapsing?

Even Rafi Nadir looked shocked. Concerned. Right.

"Hey." Morrie Alch was in the doorway. "You're outta here, fellah."

Nadir rose, spinning, ready to fight.

"I can call for reinforcements," Alch said, standing his ground, "but I'd rather beat the crap out of you myself."

Nadir was ten years younger and a lot taller, but Alch was all infuriated street cop at the moment. Both Nadir and Molina knew better than to tangle with him just then.

"I'm gone," Rafi said, spreading his empty hands. "Just like she was all those years ago."

Alch shut the door behind Nadir and came to the desk.

"Carmen? What the hell's wrong? Oh, Jesus."

She looked down at her desk, where he was staring.

Her side was bleeding all over the crumpled paperwork.

Chapter 49

Getaway

Molina was under the glaring fluorescent lights again, feeling a lot weaker and with a lot fewer places to hide this time.

This time she sat on a bathroom toilet.

And yet another man was trying to get into her clothes.

Dirty Larry, the Dirty Doctor, now Morrie Alch of all people. At least it wasn't Rafi Nadir.

"Stop fighting me, Carmen," he said firmly. "I've done more scraped knees than are on an octopus. Jeez, who sewed this up, Dr. Frankenstein's assistant, Igor?"

"Barrio doc. Dirty Larry was"—she didn't want to say "with me," because it wasn't precisely accurate and she didn't want Morrie ragging on her like an overprotective dad about hanging out with a narc. They were known to be wild cards.

"Dirty Larry came along afterward. He realized I couldn't go to a regular facility without answering questions neither of us wanted to answer."

"Where'd he take you from?"

Actually, Alch had looked more like the trustworthy family doctor than a cop as he'd gingerly pulled the blood-sopped bandage off the wound. She hoped he'd follow through on that impression.

"From the scene of a B and E."

"You the breaker and enterer?"

"Yeah. *Ouch!* You don't have to pour half a bottle of rubbing alcohol on it." She hissed in pain again.

"Yeah, I do. Those stitches aren't pretty. You're gonna have a really ragged scar, Carmen."

"Like I care?"

"Wouldn't want my daughter treated like that. Do a doting father a favor. Before you return from your flu absence, see a plastic surgeon. They don't have to report anything to the police, and in your case, they'll just think you got this in the line of duty. Looks like bad ER work."

"What flu? I've never missed work for a cold or flu."

"Flamingo flu! Bird flu. You know how to pull a con. You're gonna need at least three days off."

"No."

"Yes."

She glared at him as the alcohol sting ebbed.

"Easy." Alch was looking as hard as Clint Eastwood in a Dirty Harry movie. Also like the Man Who Knew Too Much.

"Yes, Daddy," she conceded unhappily.

He resumed cutting lengths of white adhesive tape and attaching them to the edge of the bathroom sink.

"You need to be taped all around for a long knife wound like that. That doc was a total quack. Is Mariah able to take care of you if you're in bed for a couple of days?"

"Don't know. She's not exactly at the 'taking care of' stage."

"I'll stop in when I can. Change your dressings. You order in. Watch TV. Keep down and as still as you can."

"I'll die of boredom."

Morrie pulled a huge roll of gauze out of the medicine cabinet. "You'll kill your career if you don't lay low for a while."

"Oh . . . shoot."

"Believe it or not, that would have been worse."

"You don't know what, why—"

He gave her a grave smile. "You'll tell me, though. Eventually."

"*Aiii!*" The gauze was hitting the raw wound.

"Maybe now, huh?" he asked.

Morrie knelt to roll the gauze around and around her bared midriff. She wanted to sigh and protest. But any movement was like red hot lava rolling over her bare skin.

Morrie was, damn him, right. She needed to stay away from work and heal enough to function. She needed help. Someone between Mariah and her and Rafi Nadir. And maybe between her and Dirty Larry. Someone she could trust. Utterly.

"Stay there," he said when her middle was wrapped like a mummy and starting to feel supported and better.

She buttoned her blouse when he left, feeling unexposed despite everything. The single father of a teenage daughter knew where not to look. She smiled. Morrie was a true sweetie of a guy. Wait! She must be sick. She didn't think of any men that way.

He returned, bearing gifts. Two lowball glasses, a little smudgy, and a nice tall bottle of Johnnie Walker black.

"Now we use the good alcohol," he said, sitting on the tub edge and pouring.

"Don't make me laugh, Morrie. Don't even make me chuckle. Please."

"You got it." He handed her the glass.

"I need to call in."

"Nope. I called in on the way over here and said you had a real bad case of flu and I was taking you to the doctor."

"You did! I didn't hear—"

"You were way out of it, Carmen."

"Oh. My papers—"

"I stashed 'em in your desk drawer. I'll get new forms and refill them out on your computer when I get back."

She sipped a mouthwash-large bolt of scotch. Ran it over her teeth and gums, then swallowed that bracing fire.

"So." Morrie sighed and relaxed for her. "Where, when, and why?"

"You don't often have a chance to get your collars drunk before you interrogate them."

"Nope."

"This really isn't fair, Morrie."

"Nope."

"I'm your superior officer."

"Yup. But us privates sometimes have to look out for the looies for their own good."

"We're not in the army, Morrie. Just law enforcement."

"It's a war anyway." He clicked glasses with her. "To iron maidens and good sense."

"If I'd had good sense I wouldn't be in this condition."

"So tell me about it."

She sipped the drink again, feeling the fire of the wound retreating before the inner fire of the straight scotch. That's the way the firemen did it: set a fire to stop a fire.

"First, I have to say you have a really cute bathroom, Morrie. I never dreamed."

He looked around at the seashell-patterned wallpaper, the sage-green and pink guest towels. "My daughter redid it when she was in college. Domestic phase. Then she went and got married and left me with this sea foam dream."

"Don't make me laugh, Morrie."

"Tell me about it, and you won't laugh."

"No. I won't laugh."

So she told him about her stalker, which made him angry. He'd had a daughter to look after too. She told him about her suspicions about Max Kinsella being her nemesis. And he looked skeptical, as Matt did. Damn! That magician conned everyone around him, even grown men who should know better. Even when it looked like for all intents and purposes that he was dead and gone.

She described the last home invasion the stalker engineered, the trail of rose petals to Mariah's bedroom, then hers.

Morrie stood up, tried to pace in the tidy little bathroom. "That should have been reported. You can't do this all on your own."

"I had no proof . . . until I got a print from Temple Barr's place that matched the one print left on all that sick stuff the stalker planted at my place."

"A print. Just one?"

"One is enough."

"So Temple Barr's your stalker?"

"Don't. Make Me. Laugh." Confession and scotch were making her edgy, confrontational.

"It wasn't her fingerprint," she admitted, "but you know whose prints would be all over her place, especially on those theatrical, egocentric Vangelis CDs in the bedroom."

"Vangelis, huh?" Morrie chuckled. Was it admiringly? "Guy must have had some stamina."

Molina felt her face burning almost as much as her side at the implication.

"So," he said, "you have a set to match your one print with?"

"No. But when I catch him—"

The threat rang hollow even in her own ears. That house had been abandoned, ownerless. Certainly it had held only a shadow of the dark charisma of its likely resident. It was a ruin the snakes had come to take possession of. One particular resident snake with a fang that was eleven inches long.

So she told Morrie of her unauthorized entry. The invader she'd accidentally interrupted. Larry showing up. That part was touchy.

"What was Larry doing there?"

"He was following me."

"Your stalker, maybe?"

"He's one of us."

"No, he's not. He's an undercover guy. They're loners. They get freaky. Sometimes they turn."

"I'm sure that wasn't it."

She eyed Alch. He was looking kinda blurry now, through a glass, smearily. She wasn't used to anything stronger than a beer and an occasional social cocktail. She wasn't used to a secret, pulsing pain that never backed off. Never had been plagued with menstrual cramps. Always had been strong. Hardy.

She wasn't used to a fatherly gaze. Her real father had vanished before she could remember him, a piece of history that labeled her mother's shame. Pregnant by a blue-eyed Anglo. So she made up for it by marrying José Quintera and bore him seven black-olive-eyed *niños* and *niñas*. Carmen babysat her stepbrothers and sisters all through her school years, and then she shocked everyone by getting a junior college law enforcement degree and turning cop.

And by keeping her mother's surname. After all that kid sitting, she never intended to have any of her own, church ban on birth control or not. Then Rafi Nadir had pierced that life plan with a pin though her diaphragm. Or not. Maybe he wasn't lying. Either way: exit Carmen and, later, enter Mariah. Even her family didn't know about Mariah. She'd thought it was safer that way. Had she been fleeing a ghost, in L.A., and chasing a ghost here in Vegas?

Her mother had never talked to her about her father. A shame and failure better forgotten. Like Rafi Nadir. Like mother, like daughter.

She'd made sure to spare Mariah the humiliation of a wayward father, or an indifferent stepfather. Matt had suffered from one of those stepfathers, unfortunately not indifferent, just mean and violent.

Molina shuddered and took another slug of scotch. She may have been wrong about Rafi's motives, but he still wasn't a candidate for Father of the Year.

The pain inside was getting more insistent than the pain outside.

Morrie put a hand on her shoulder.

"You just rest, kid." He was only ten or eleven years older than she was. How'd she end up outranking him? He was a good cop, a better detective, and a great human being. Burned past him with ambition, that was how. Had a reverse edge, like Rafi claimed. Women barred for so many years, then suddenly becoming a politically correct carnation in the PD's buttonhole.

Pain and—*Dios!*—helplessness made you think and rethink things. People. Events. Your life.

"I'll handle the Crystal Phoenix case," Morrie was saying. "I think we've got a couple leads to look at if Su doesn't get too eager and tip our hand."

Molina nodded.

"I'll take you home now and get you settled. I'll be looking in on you, so lay off those unauthorized B and Es and keep Dirty Larry out of your laundry for a while."

She was nodding, agreeing, nodding off.

Morrie took the glass from her hand because it was weighing her arm down to the floor and dribbling yellow liquid like a two-year-old on the clean white tile bathroom floor. At least she wasn't dribbling blood anymore.

And thank God Mariah was on a three-day school trip to the Grand Canyon. There was a Grand Canyon in her gut. She'd lied to Morrie. Shouldn't have. Lying got to be a habit.

And the next thing she knew, she was staring at her bedroom ceiling, gently lit by the time from the bedside clock floating in red numbers on the ceiling.

Twelve-oh-one.

Thing was, was it twelve o'clock high, or twelve o'clock low?

Chapter 50

A Paler Shade of Pink

Temple had decided it was time to take the pink satin gloves off.

First, she'd been diverted in the store area from looking for Oleta's booth by recovered memories of the whole Shangri-La/Kathleen O'Connor tangle.

She'd come to terms with those speculations. They had nothing to do with this place, this time, and this crime. She could fret over them later when she and Matt could talk long and privately again.

Now, she had to get Electra off the police list of suspects. This convention would be winding down shortly. Everybody would be scattering to the far four corners of the country. It'd be all too easy for the police, even earnest Detective Alch, to stick the at-hand local with the whole rap.

This time Temple refused to let anything purple or red distract her on the way to Oleta's booth. She stopped only to ask directions.

"Oh, yes, that poor woman!" said one purveyor at the Red-Hat-to-Toe booth.

This specialized in head and footwear, including rhinestone-studded reading glasses and red-and-purple anklets and sneakers, not to mention the ankle bracelets and huge hats.

The stork-tall seller herself was festooned in as many of her wares as possible, which made her resemble an overdressed emu, like songstress/clown Candy Crenshaw.

"Poor Oleta's chapter decided to sell whatever many of her wares they could, and take the rest back to Reno to benefit the chapter."

"They're selling her items?"

Temple felt a sudden panic. Something *key* could have been among that merchandise, maybe hidden among that merchandise. Like Oleta's tell-all book manuscript. Temple just knew that while Oleta might have spilled some of the juicy beans about her love life on the Internet she would have saved the best for the actual publication of her tell-all.

"Oh, don't worry, dear," said Madam Big Bird, "I'm sure it's not all gone. You can still buy a memento."

Eek! The stuff was probably selling like red, white, and purple hotcakes because people always like souvenirs from a murder.

It still made Temple shudder that O. J. Simpson's two kids by Nicole Brown had opened a lemonade stand to serve the media and crowds besieging the O. J. estate after their mother's brutal death. Maybe they were too young to realize that cashing in on their mother's murder was awful. Or maybe they were just too much O. J.'s and not enough Nicole's children. When a wife is abused in a household, the children can choose the abuser's side to protect themselves.

So Temple really hated to join the three-deep crowd around

the booth clawing for goods. She had to stretch, even on her three-inch pink patent J. Reneé heels, to see what everybody was competing for.

Apparently Oleta was serious about being a writer. Her booth was piled with commercial diaries and notepads and stationery slathered with red and purple hats, heels, feathers, and cats dressed in all of the above.

The usual feather boas hung from corner racks, as did red hats by the brimful. No pink and lavender items that would attract Red Hat ladies-in-waiting decorated the booth.

Temple suspected that Oleta Lark, having displaced at least one older woman, didn't like to cater to the younger women coming up behind her now that she was "an older woman," and almost a Red Hatter.

Temple, with the tenacity of an entire life spent being too short to see anything, edged around the crowd to the side of the table and then peeked under the floor-length tablecloth. This was where extra items were always stacked.

She dearly wished she'd known enough at the Women's Exposition to peer under the table skirt of the woman who had possessed among her stock-in-trade rings related to the two men most dear to Temple.

Temple felt another chill. She'd spotted something big and bulky under the table. Not a body this time, thank God! Yet it was an item peculiarly appropriate to the convention, and apparently unique at the booth.

Temple wasn't proud. She got down on her knees and dove for the prize, pulling it toward herself with much effort over a tidal wave of empty boxes.

When she wrestled the huge round hatbox close enough, she lifted it. Cardboard. She shook it. Nothing shifted or rattled. Empty. Drat it!

"Say! What're you doing down there! Get up this minute."

Temple crawled back out from under the purple table skirt, dragging her prize with her.

"I just saw something perfect for my new pink hat," she wailed in a Mariah-like tone of aggrieved excuse.

She'd also just patted down the suspect hatbox in secret and now was mighty interested in conducting a private interrogation off the premises.

Temple rose from the floor, clutching an item that she knew would be the envy of all eyes: a crimson hatbox as big around as the bottom layer of a wedding cake, topped with a high mound of purple net flowers, and circled by a purple silk scarf with a design of red flowers. The exact same scarf design as the one that had wrung Oleta Lark's neck.

"That's *the* scarf!" a nearby woman shrieked. "You said you were all out," she shrilled at the saleswoman.

That lady glanced from the screamer's scowling face to Temple's expression of innocently sincere greed.

"We *were* out. This young lady has found one we didn't know about."

"I'll pay you fifty bucks for it," Screaming Woman told Temple.

"I can't sell it. I don't own it yet, but I want to. This is for my very first pink hat." Temple let her voice and chin tremble a little, like a scared Chihuahua's.

"Shame on you," the saleslady told the gathered shoppers. "You're all a bunch of turkey-necked vultures gobbling up poor dead Oleta's stock only because she *is* dead. This young lady is new to our organization and simply needs a hat box.

"That will be twenty-seven-fifty, miss."

"Oh. Gosh. Thanks. This will look so great in my bedroom. It's all pink with red and purple accents."

"Cash. Thanks."

The member of Oleta's group leaned near as she handed over the change. "Love your hat."

"Thank you!"

Temple escaped in girlish triumph, aware that the brouhaha had caught the attention of everyone in the room.

She hurried through the lobby toward the conference room that Nicky and Van had declared hers, shut the double doors, untied the scarf with the dignity the facsimile of a murder weapon deserved, then tore the lavender net roses off the hatbox's mounded top.

Broken basted-on lavender threads sprouted like blades of

grass from Oz on the red velvet top. Temple ripped off the glued-on purple braid around the lid, and lifted the red velvet.

Beneath lay a snowy mound of printed paper.

Oleta's manuscript.

She'd brought a copy with her. To show it, sell it, or use it for blackmail?

Didn't matter. Temple had the whole story in her hands now and an all-night reading assignment that even Matt couldn't interrupt.

But that was later. This was now, and she still had a lot of tasks on her to-do list.

Chapter 51

The Flirting Fontanas

"You see the woman in the green shoes?" Temple asked.

"Yes," Emilio said. "She Irish?"

"I rather doubt it," Temple said. "Those are six-inch plat-forms and she always wears them."

He stared. "Isn't that excessive?"

"Darn right. Especially for covering a convention on these hard floors all day."

"Agreed. I don't wear high heels and my feet are killing me from this guard duty. So why would she do that?"

"I thought all Fontana brothers knew all women inside out."

Emilio's dark eyes grew wary. He knew women well enough to realize that Temple was angling for something. This inno-cent game of Twenty Fashion Questions was the lead-up to the jaws of the trap crashing shut. On his fine silk-clad Italian calf.

"Like you, Miss Temple, she wishes to be taller and show off her ankles, which are not as world class as yours."

"Nicely put. What is it with men and ankles anyway? Surely they're one of the most awkward parts of the human anatomy, along with elbows."

"It's always a matter of what you do with them." His eyes narrowed at Natalie Newman's high-rise footwear. "Those are much too high for anything other than Milano runways or entering and exiting limousines."

"I know that six-inch heels are the coming thing in *InStyle*. That's not real life, though, and Miss Newman is a working journalist and filmmaker, doomed to be on her feet all day. Do you think Michael Moore would wear shoes like that to out a politician?"

Emilio choked discreetly at the idea of Michael Moore's three hundred pounds on Natalie's high platform shoes.

"You are leading, Miss Temple, but I'm not following, although this is a most enjoyable ride."

"That woman is wearing those ridiculous stilts for the same reason that I like my three-inchers. *She needs to be taller to see.*"

"But she's already tall for a woman."

"Exactly. She doesn't need her eyes to see, but something else."

Emilio digested that one. "She does lift that handheld camcorder over the crowd frequently. It's clever, actually, to make herself into a giraffe the better to film the convention."

"What about the tote bag?"

"Not even a Gucci knockoff," Emilio noted with a slight sneer. "Otherwise not much different from your ever-present bag of the same sort, sensibly purchased at T. J. Maxx."

"You do know women inside out," Temple marveled at his accurate call.

He looked down at her through sexy, half-closed eyes. "I can get you a great deal on the real Gucci if you yearn to go upscale."

"Sorry, Emilio, shoes are my thing, not bags. I'm happy with Target or Steinmart in that regard."

Emilio winced to hear such anti-Italian talk.

"No," Temple went on, craning her neck at the Newman woman as she moved through the crowd, "it's what is *in* that bag that I want a good look at. That I want copied without her knowing it. Of course not even the fantastic flying Fontana brothers could manage that."

"Such a thing is impossible. When do you want it?"

"It would have to be done without alerting her, and it would require special equipment."

"All of us Fontanas have special equipment," she was told fiercely. "And we all can move like leopards if necessary."

"I'm happy to hear it for my aunt Kit's sake," Temple continued, unflustered. "Because I know in my bones that there's a second camcorder in that tote bag and I want the video in it copied and returned to the camera with Natalie Newman completely unaware of that."

"*Hmmm.* I'll have to consult the family. A simple seduction might be the easiest way"—he glanced at Natalie's severe features—"but, despite the sexy shoes, her ankles predict that she's a plate of cold spaghetti sans sauce in bed and even Fontana brothers can't sacrifice themselves to a pleasureless charade. I'm afraid we can't rely on charm in this instance. Let me get back to you on this."

"Of course," Temple said. "But make it snappy."

Temple returned to the Crystal Phoenix the next morning to find Red Hat ladies eagerly lining up to the right of the lobby.

She was about to walk around the impediment when a Fontana brother appeared with the smile of the maître d' at the Bellagio's Le Cirque restaurant on his handsome face.

"'Scuse, miss. Hotel security. Due to recent unfortunate events that are the talk of the convention and the town, we are conducting a spot check on items being brought into the hotel. Your most attractive tote bag has been selected for further looking into," he murmured in a way that would lead one to offer tote bag, body, and soul to the inspector if she was not careful. "Please join the other ladies awaiting inspection. We promise to be thorough, but, alas, quick."

"Just like a man," the Red Hat lady who was last in line chuckled as Temple fell into place, mad with curiosity.

She spotted Natalie Newman's hatless dark hair eight places ahead and realized the genius of the plan. Another Fontana brother was looming over the reporter despite her extra-high heels and slathering on Fontana brother charm an inch (of Alfredo sauce) thick as he slipped the precious bag from her custody.

"There's camera equipment in there," she protested, quite rightly.

"Exactly why my brothers in hotel security will hand-check your bag. We will handle everything with the most delicate of touches, and return it to you in perfect working order."

An *oooh* from the entire line of women within earshot made Natalie look like a cur—or worse, a frigid fool—for objecting to anything a Fontana brother might wish to do with her bag.

"Do you think they do pat downs?" the woman in front of Temple giggled.

"Only of bags," she replied, "and of course you don't want to be taken for a 'bag.'"

Natalie had been plucked from the line to be queried on the exact nature of her job and her work here, as if that were a rare and special activity of tremendous interest to the interrogating Fontana brother.

Her sunken cheeks began to pinken at such intimate and solicitous attention. She didn't even notice that the other women shuffled past, allowed to proceed far more quickly than she.

Temple was soon the only woman behind her. No others had been recruited after her.

Everything was very airport: the beige wall dividers. The sounds of a big machine churning out of view.

Natalie turned to watch Temple's tote bag being whisked out of her custody with the same charming patter as her own had been.

"This is ridiculous," Natalie whispered to her, suddenly a partner in being subjected to bureaucratic idiocy.

"It looks like they're targeting oversize bags," Temple whispered back.

"These other silly cows seem to actually *like* being examined by these greaser gangsters!"

"Well, they're here to have fun and I suppose this adds a bit of drama."

"These are the same silly, stupid women who watch soap operas and read romance novels. They're making idiots of themselves and don't even know it."

"Isn't it hard to record the convention when you despise the attendees?"

Natalie's pale lips pursed. "I'm not a PR flack like you. I'm a journalist. I can . . . be objective about anything."

"Except Purple Cows," Temple said innocently.

Natalie's unplucked brows clashed above her nose like broadswords.

"It's fine for you girly little things to think you can slide through life on your looks without any moral or social conscience. Some of us aspire to more than easy money and the attentions of"—she glared at the Fontana brother handing her tote bag back with a small bow and a big smile—"gigolos!"

Temple and Armando watched her depart, driving those porn-film high soles into the marble floor like flatirons.

"It was a pleasure," he mused, "to pick the pocketbook of such an unpleasant female undetected. We will have video in fifteen minutes in your conference room. Julio will fetch a chilled bottle of Asti Spumanti for your viewing pleasure."

"It's only 10:00 A.M. I don't need wine."

"But we do. It really is necessary to rinse the taste of that unhappy woman out of our mouths."

In the conference room, Temple's tote bag awaited her atop the long conference table opposite the dead-body-long television that had descended from the ceiling.

A DVD player sat like a centerpiece at the exact middle of the long table. Temple wasn't even going to ask what it had taken to extract and copy the media in Natalie's hidden camera, and then replace it as if nothing had transpired, but technical boxes of unknown abilities crouched along the sideboard.

The four Fontanas active in the operation took seats along either side of the conference table, one using a remote to darken the lights and start the player.

Immediately the buzzing chaos of the convention-goers filled the room. Snatches of conversation. Laughter. The footage had a film verité feeling.

The screen was filled with deep purple. Then the camera's eye zoomed out to reveal the very large purple butt of a woman bending over a wheeled canvas bag.

The camera roved at hip level, zooming in on swollen ankles in laced-edged red anklets, then swooping up to creased and folded middle-age faces wearing blobs of red and purple on lips and eyelids.

"You look darling!" a female voice caroled as the camera closed in on another, decidedly not-darling close-up of an unsuspecting woman.

"Jeesh," a Fontana murmured, "this is character assassination."

Temple nodded in the dark. "She's using a fish-eye lens to distort their faces and bodies. Natalie's pretty good at operating that tote-bag camera blind. She must have done a lot of this."

"What's the point?" Eduardo asked. "She's getting paid to film the convention."

"As I suspected, her real agenda is mocking it. Paid to undermine. Nice work if you can get it. I bet she's done this before. Time to ask the Internet to cough up any references on her."

"If she's using her real name."

Temple glanced at Eduardo. "She's been a stringer for national news magazines, and I hear that's her married name. And she doesn't care how angry the Red Hat Sisterhood is, organizationally or individually, once she's got what she wants in the can, or on the DVD, rather. Amazing how technology is outdating all our expressions."

When the recording had run its course, Temple refused a glass of wine, but lifted her water glass in their honor.

"To the Fontana brothers. Long may they wave."

"*Cin-cin*," said Armando, pronouncing the Italian toast "Chin-chin."

"*Salud*," said Eduardo in turn, using another romance language, Spanish.

"*Prosit*," said Emilio, resorting to German.

"And *Skoal*," finished Ralph, going Nordic.

"*L'chayim*," Temple finished in Yiddish, saluting life with her water glass, hoping they'd recorded a clue to untimely death with this session.

Temple eyed her co-conspirators for one last toast in English. "To the Red Hat Sisterhood! Your inspection line not only may remove a murderer hiding in their midst, but it was a high point of the day for all the women I overheard raving about their time in the 'Guy Line.'"

"Those," Eduardo said, obviously leaving Natalie Newman out, "were charming ladies. They have a zest for life that is quite Italian."

"We will have the proper equipment delivered to your Circle Ritz domicile so that you can see both recordings completely."

"Thanks, but I think I know what's she up to now. About six-three with those shoes."

"Those are knockoff Versace," Eduardo sniffed, opening the double doors to release Temple back into the noisy flood of P and R adherents. "Just as she is a fake."

Ms. Apprehension

Temple returned to the lobby to be greeted by a shrill, Hitch-cockian film scream. Before she could triangulate on the direction it came from, she saw the flock of Fontana brothers behind her racing past, cell phones glued to their ears.

She spun on a resale Jimmy Choo spike heel and trailed them through a crowd of excited, muttering women that gave way as the Fontanas charged past.

What the women muttered wasn't encouraging.

"Another murder—!"

"Strangled."

"Boa?"

"No, scarf."

"Are those guys hot! D'you think they're undercover cops?"

By then Temple was weaving in and out of the gathered conventioneers, trying desperately to catch up to the Fontanas.

The crowd around the entrance to the Hatorium Emporium was particularly thick. Temple found herself using elbows and heels to pick her way through, leaving a chorus of *ows* in her wake.

"It's another Pink Hat," someone cried.

Her own pink hat got several tugs.

"Don't go in there!"

"It's death to Pink Hatters."

Someone swiped the hat off her head, but Temple snatched it back and carried it.

No way the police would be on-scene for this latest attack. She and the Fontana brothers were the first responders. Maybe they'd catch the perp.

Suddenly she'd caught up with them, but they were a ring holding everyone back.

"Ernesto!" she asked the first one whose attention she could snag. "What's happened?"

Their expressions were as grim as death, their locked jaws and forbidding arms braced to hold back the mob.

Even her.

Especially her.

"You don't wanta rush in," Ernesto warned. "Aldo's there."

Aldo? Well, of course, if they were all on red alert. He would be there. He was the eldest. He was . . .

Temple's heart and jaw dropped in concert.

"A Pink Hatter?"

"She needs air," Ernesto said gruffly as Temple strained to see past him.

She could hear sirens screaming down the hotel driveway again.

"K-Kit?"

"Coming out," someone shouted with such authority that the babbling mob fell back.

Ernesto swept Temple out of the way, holding her close to some really great Italian tailoring covering a body of steel.

Aldo raced past, carrying Kit swagged in his arms like a

doll, her arms swinging with the motion, her soft strawberry-red hair bare.

"You won't want to be a Pink Lady anymore," Ernesto muttered.

"She's—?"

"Alive, but someone sure tried to change that."

Armando raced past, carrying a pink hat and purple scarf with red flowers on it.

"That scarf design sold out," Temple told the Fontana brother who was providing her spine at the moment, choking on the words. "They were all gone. I got the last one. I'm storing it in the conference room."

"We'll see if you still have it there," Ernesto suggested ominously. "But first, we've got a hospital run to make."

Temple was swept out of there almost as limply as Kit, thrown into the front seat of a black Viper, just one in a train of the powerful sport cars.

With a roar like an Indy 500 race, a cortege of Vipers shot out from under the Crystal Phoenix porte cochere.

They caught up to the ambulance in no time, but Temple was too woozy and worried to notice how'd they'd managed to weave through the clogged Strip traffic at 4:00 P.M.

All she could think was *Kit . . . Kit . . . Kit* like a pulse pounding in her forehead, interrupted by a *my fault . . . my fault . . . my fault*. For who'd want to kill Kit? But killing a nosy ex-TV-reporter turned PR person was another matter.

The Fontana brother driving—Giuseppe, she thought—had her left hand in tight custody and was rotating the steering wheel one-handed. The brakes pushed them almost into the windshield when the car stopped under another, smaller, plainer porte cochere.

Ernesto opened the passenger door and pulled Temple out. With a conjoined roar, the black Vipers growled away to the parking lot.

Temple's ankles were wobbling on her Choos, but Ernesto took her arm and rushed her inside. Aldo was slumped in one of the plastic shell waiting-room chairs.

Temple had never seen a Fontana brother slump before.

The pink hat was turning in his flaccid hands, around and around. Ernesto left her standing beside him and rushed to the desk.

"We have a relative here now, yes," he was saying. "Niece."

"Aldo," Temple asked, gasped, "what happened?"

"They won't let me see her. Not related."

"What happened at the hotel?"

He still stared into the distance, turning the frivolous hat through his hands.

"I did CPR. Got her breathing again."

"Again! Who—?"

"Disappeared into that mob. No one realized what had happened at first." He pulled the scarf from his side coat pocket to show her a tight knot with a slashed end. "No one had a pocketknife to cut the garrote until I got there. I don't know how long—"

"Oh, God. And that's the scarf I got with Oleta's hatbox. Someone snatched it to do this." Temple wanted to sink down on the chair next to him, but she was afraid to bend her knees for fear she'd never stand up again.

A hand caught her elbow. "You can go in," Ernesto said. "The doctor will see you."

Aldo was still brooding over the murder weapon. The attempted murder weapon, God willing. He knew a nonrelative couldn't see Kit.

Temple put a hand to her mouth to push back any emotions and let Ernesto lead her to a closed door, where a nurse on the other side said, "Come in, miss. It's only a few steps."

A few steps were about all she could manage. She was led through another door into an office, and given a clipboard of papers.

"How is she?"

"The doctor will tell you. First, you need to fill these out."

Temple tried to focus on the questions, half of which she didn't know answers to. Kit was her New York City aunt she'd only seen again in the last year. She didn't know her exact street address, so she put in her own at the Circle Ritz. She didn't know her health history or her doctor. Not even her age! Not exactly.

The nurse came to collect the sheet.

"I don't know. So much. She's visiting from out of town."

The nurse's eyes flicked over all the empty lines. "Doctor will be right in."

"Doctor" was never right in. It was always an eternity later.

Temple jumped at the sound of passing footsteps in the hall, however muffled. Her door remained shut, until she wanted to leap up, open it, and gaze rudely up and down the hall.

But her role was to wait until called upon.

And poor Aldo in the waiting room outside had no role at all.

Temple ran her fingers into her hair and let loose a mental scream. What would she tell her mother? What *could* she tell her mother? Kit was single and lived in the country's biggest city. She must have dozens of New York friends, and no significant other there. No one but Aldo here, and he was a sudden fling. New, unexpected. Likely not permanent. Temple was the only permanent next of kin available.

The door cracked open so suddenly she twitched. Could a thirty-year-old have a heart attack?

The doctor was an Indian woman. A woman of Indian extraction. She wore glasses and a warm expression.

"This is your aunt?"

"Kit. Yes. Um, Ursula's her formal first name. Carlson the surname. Kit's the nickname. Kit Carlson."

The woman in the white coat smiled and consulted the clipboard she carried.

"We are missing much data, but that is not critical. Nor is your aunt's condition. She lost her consciousness, but it was restored in time. She will be weak. Her voice will be . . . rough. She may have forgotten the incident that led to this condition. But she will recover. Would you like to see her?"

"I would. God, yes, I would. And so would the man who gave her CPR."

"A quick thinker. Certainly. Remember, she will not recall what you think that she should just yet. And I'll keep her overnight here for observation. Merely a precaution."

Temple could hardly keep from jumping up and down.

"Yes. I understand. Can I get Aldo now?"

"Aldo?"

"Her . . . significant other."

The doctor smiled. "A very good idea at such a time." She turned to leave, then turned back. "This was an attack. The police have been notified. I don't know if they will assign her a guard."

"I can assign her a guard."

"You?"

"Aldo. If you'll permit him to stay overnight."

"He is too involved, perhaps. And someone with law enforcement experience is needed."

"He has that. He's a member of the Fontana Family."

The doctor's eyebrows lofted high above her upper glasses rims. "Oh. I see. I suppose there is no choice in this matter, then?"

"He would be solo."

"And you?"

"I'm going to go home and have a nervous breakdown."

"Excellent idea." The doctor smiled. "You and Mr. Fontana may join me in Miss Carlson's room. If I decide your plan is suitable and will not interfere with operations, Mr. Fontana may occupy a chair outside her door for the night."

Temple didn't mention that her idea of a nervous breakdown was reviewing all footage taken by both of Natalie Newman's cameras, then reading Oleta's memoir and laying out every page of the Red Hat Sisterhood convention material.

Then she would grill her brain for anything she might have done that could have led a murderer to believe that she was almost ready to name a killer.

Chapter 53

Drop-Dead Red

Late that evening at the Circle Ritz, Temple determined to go back to the convention first thing tomorrow, Fontana brothers be darned!

She would, however, ditch wearing the pink hat on advice of counsel. She'd return in a hot red hat from her vintage collection even though that was "illegal." At least it would help disguise her from the convention strangler. And she wouldn't leave until she'd fingered a killer and an attempted killer.

In fact, she had a hat-brained plan to smoke out the killer, one that everyone she knew would object to on grounds of insanity, hers. So she wouldn't tell anyone. Most of what she needed was locked up in the conference room, but it required a slight modification.

Working on a craft project is supposed to be relaxing. As Temple assembled her materials she hummed to herself. Nothing special, just an absorbed, happy sound.

The Fontana brothers' playful toasts of yesterday echoed in her mind: *salud, prosit, skoal*. Those guys were true bon vivants, French for high-livers. What would that be in Italian? Toasting with a good drink was a universal trait from sunny Mediterranean climes to the frozen northlands. *A Vôtre Santé*, toasted the French. To your good health. Most countries' toast word or phrase was used in other languages as commonly as *Joyeux Noël* or *Feliz Navidad*.

Wait! Alch had said Elmore Lark "wasn't just toasting his health" on the panel when he fell ill. Was the detective implying a foreign substance, or that *someone foreign* was a suspect? Or was it the toast? What had the Fontana brothers fallen back on after using the Italian variation yesterday? *Prosit. Salud. Skoal.*

Common variations . . . "Eureka!" Temple said, nearly slicing off a chunk of her forefinger before she dropped the scissors.

Something small that would slip into a jeans pocket in a bottle or a . . . tin! Something easily doctored with poison. Something that other people knew about or saw Elmore using.

Temple abandoned her coffee table craft project to take her home office computer for a spin on the Internet. She couldn't help wondering how Sherlock Holmes would have ever impressed anybody with his instant store of vast but specialized knowledge if he'd had to compete with Google.

She typed in the suspect word and came up with usual 3,869-plus sites.

The top entries were most enlightening.

Skoal, she read, was a leading manufacturer of chewing tobacco, along with Copenhagen, Red Seal, and Rooster. My, but the color red came up a lot, if you considered that roosters had that scarlet coxcomb.

She didn't know any users, thank goodness, and understood women's distaste for that male affection for the stuff known as "spit" tobacco, or "dip" (as in "dipwad"?), or "chew."

That "pinch between your cheek and gum" she'd seen

advertised now and again (and had ignored) offered a nicotine rush and a risk of mouth cancer to go with it.

Hmmm. Other effects were increased heart rate and blood pressure, not to mention decreased smell and taste, which would make a man a prime candidate for poisoning.

And the stuff came in "compact little tins."

That Alch! Had he led her on, without ever lying!

Her eyes nearly popped out of her head when she read the next paragraph. Spit tobacco contained such lethal additives as arsenic, cadmium, DDT, formaldehyde, and hydrogen cyanide, the poison used in gas chambers.

Wasn't that what Cold War spies had implanted in their teeth for instant suicide if caught? Cyanide capsules. A clever person with access to cyanide certainly could "roll" his or her own. Empty a harmless pill capsule, fill it with cyanide, and dump the poison in Elmore's ever-present tin of chew.

Temple remembered him hawking into a handkerchief at the debate table. He probably used the tobacco in the john before and after appearing in public. Maybe that last chaw was already disagreeing with him. If enough cyanide to fill a tooth could be instantly fatal, so could a dose taken in a wad of tobacco.

She looked up "Skoal" as a toast, just for fun. It didn't seem directly relevant, but the entry she found was certainly grisly.

It seemed that at the full moon, in early northern European caves, the priests of the Norse god Odin would toast him using the skull of a fallen foe as a sacrificial cup.

Well, wasn't that special?

She quickly called Electra on her desk phone.

"I have two questions. Where were you at 2:20 P.M. yesterday?"

"Assisting in a perkshop demonstration of hair extensions. Is that important?"

"Important and good. That's when Kit was mistaken for me and attacked."

"I heard about that, also that she's going to be all right. Such a shame. You had to ask me?"

"Yes. That puts the kibosh on the police's suspicion of you.

It doesn't clear you of Oleta's death, but it sure upsets the Railroad Electra trend."

"I should hope so! Although I'd never want anyone to be hurt just so I was cleared."

Temple decided to keep mum about her upcoming brilliant hokey plan.

"What was your second question?" Electra asked.

"Did Elmore use chewing tobacco?"

"Not when I knew him, or I'd have never 'married' him. He always was a sports addict. Don't a lot of athletes use chewing tobacco because it doesn't affect their wind the way cigarettes do?"

"Skoal!" Temple crowed.

"Ah, have we got something to celebrate?"

"Yes, I know now what almost killed Elmore. It's not 'Skoal' as in a toast, Electra. It's a brand name! Elmore's now hooked on chewing tobacco, and that's where the poison was placed. Remember the cyanide capsules foreign agents had built into their teeth in all those old spy movies? This was to be a vintage death."

"Whatever you say, dear. But I left Elmore before he had any such disgusting habit as chewing tobacco. I can put up with a lot of things, but stinky brown spit every few minutes isn't one of them. There are spitting lizards I could cohabit with if I'd wanted that."

"Don't you see? Whoever tried to kill Elmore knew his nasty habits, and used them. And must have known him *after* you did."

"But the police won't believe that I never knew him to use that vile stuff."

"I'll just have to find out who did know he used chewing tobacco, and used it to try to kill him."

"That's nice, dear, but do be careful! Now just go get some Crystal Light to toast yourself and use some other word than Skoal, and calm down. You sound really overheated."

Subdued, Temple complied and returned to her living room, wondering how she could nail a killer with a small tin of chewing tobacco. Still, she only had to figure out who wanted Elmore Lark dead and knew enough about him to hit on the perfect method.

Meanwhile, her first trick to trip up the killer was a corny scheme, but centered on a hat and would attract attention. What more did she need for bait at this particular convention? Except maybe herself.

Ouch.

Would that stop Viking stock? No!

Temple lifted her glass of Crystal Light and envisioned the recent computer graphic of Viking warriors chug-a-lugging from a dead enemy's skull.

"Skoal!"

Chapter 54

The Red Hat Rage Brigade

My partner is still off on her own private crusade working the missing Mr. Max Kinsella case when it becomes clear from eavesdropping on the recent hullabaloo that my Miss Temple has plans to put her life in danger.

I see her set the bait this morning and soon the word gets all around the convention. People come to gawk and spread even more word around. By the time all the conventioneers exit to attend the two simultaneous banquets tonight, Miss Temple's bait will be left for someone bad to come sniffing around it.

I expect her to be lying in wait, and I intend to be lying in wait with her, unbeknownst to her, of course. I am your unbeknownst go-to guy.

What good will it do if Miss Midnight Louise finds Mr. Max

alive and in the meantime Miss Temple has been offed? That is what you would call an ironic situation, although it is more of a moronic situation, in my opinion.

I know it is up to me. As per usual. Because, of course, the Fontana litter are off seeing to Aldo and Miss Kit Carlson. Even the police are no longer hanging around here as much. The Red Hat ladies will be tuckered and tucked away for the night while visions of purple plums dance in their heads after the evening's banquet.

This being Las Vegas, plenty of patrons and hotel personnel are stirring on the Crystal Phoenix's main floor, but the Red Hat Sisterhood's public spaces are shut down.

I realize I will need reinforcements before this case is over, but have nowhere to turn. The police are not expecting more mayhem on-site. The hotel security forces are top-notch, but they are only human.

What is needed here is the superhuman sight and hearing of my kind. I am ready to gnaw my nails in frustration, except that I will need them later, when a bright idea occurs to me.

It is not only fresh and exciting, but it will improve my status among the desirable ladies of my species.

I dash through a moving parade of feet to the elevators. How convenient that I was hanging about the lobby when the first convention-goers arrived, for I then burned a particular suite number into my inboard memory device.

The first carload only takes me a few floors up before emptying. I prance with impatience waiting for another elevator to stop where I have been marooned. Several stop, because I have leaped repeatedly at the call button until it depresses. I hang out of sight behind a cigarette butt stand while riders grouse about thoughtless people who call the elevator, then decide to walk and leave the doors opening on nothing.

Oh contraire, grousers! It is actually a very thoughtful feline who has summoned you to this floor. I wait until a car opens that is crammed with people yet to disembark, for I seek the hotel's top floor. Too bad the particular guest I seek is not top-drawer to match!

Of course, I must time my leap aboard to the second. While

they are all craning their necks looking left and right down the hall, I slip among their pant legs, trying not to brush my softly furred sides against any sensitive bare female gams. (Not for personal reasons, of course. Normally, I am only too happy to massage female gams. Here, however, I am trying to remain undercover as well as underfoot.)

It is my good luck that only one highly intoxicated (a redundancy, I fear) gentleman remains aboard when we arrive at the top floor containing the suites.

I follow his lurching path out of the car onto purple plush carpet.

I was blending into the bellman's dark pant legs four days ago when I heard him instructed to take Miss Savannah Ashleigh's gaudy luggage cart to the Baccarat Suite.

Knowing the Crystal Phoenix layout from my days as house detective here, I leave the amiable sot playing with his room key card outside his quarters and speed to the address in question. And they say we cannot be trained!

Something also in question is whether Miss Savannah is in residence at the moment or not. Although the time is late, past my namesake hour, it would best serve my emergency plan for her to be making merry elsewhere right now.

I scratch softly low on the door.

In an instant I am answered by the snare-drum *scritch* of delicate pads on paint. *Pads,* plural. Both Ashleigh sisters are awake and ready to rock!

It is true that I and the Supine Yvette, formerly known as the Divine Yvette, are on the outs, but Solange is still in my little black book. Okay, my large black book.

I can stomach the snobby Supine Yvette if the Benign Solange is in the picture.

I hiss under the door that they need to unlock it.

They plead the deadlock and the safety chain.

I ask if they have a pipe access door in the bathroom.

After a few minutes, Solange reports that they do, but that Yvette's tail has become caught in the opening.

Manx! If I had been installed in a penthouse suite, my first piece of business would have been checking the air-conditioning and plumbing systems for egress. A dude always needs a back door.

But what can you expect from Persians? They are not exactly designed for street smarts. On the other mitt, they are sublimely designed for other purposes.

Speaking of the Sublime Solange, she is hissing at me under the door that there is another interior door at two-jumps level in the bathroom.

I sit down and think. I always think better sitting down, without pressure on my footpads.

Of course, all Las Vegas knows the Crystal Phoenix as a very classy hotel. It was classy before the many new mega hotels made a conscious effort to spend millions on high-end art collections. In fact, the powers that be along the Strip (and there are a lot of them) are eager to disavow the place's gangster history.

But you can't keep a good hood down. Or a good 'hood.

Rumor has it that one obscure room dating back to the Bugsy Siegel era can still be found at the Flamingo Hilton. Bugsy, of course, built the first Flamingo and began the dot on an empty map's evolution into Billionaire's Row.

And here at the Crystal Phoenix, room 711 is still decorated with the forties flair popular in the day of its founder, Jersey Joe Jackson. They say when he lost his fortune he lived on in that small suite. They say he still lives on there in the dust motes that take human shape from time to time.

Me, I like to use the place for siestas. The hotel never rents it. And I may have seen a ghost there while in the twilight state between dreaming and waking up.

Right now I'm daydreaming about how this hotel used to be the Joshua Tree when Jersey Joe founded it. How it sat deserted and ruined until Nicky Fontana came along with mondo millions of clean dough from his grandma's pasta empire and remade the place with the help of an imported little hotel marketing doll named Van von Rhine.

Of course, since then the Phoenix has been redone inside and out, and added onto up, down, and sideways. But its functional core is the old Joshua Tree, with its then-fancy "futuristic" features.

One comes to mind just when I need it. I seem to recall that it has a central vacuum system for cleaning.

No. I am not contemplating sending the Ashleigh sisters down a central vacuum system. That would be cruel, although speedy. And it would really wreak havoc with their hairdos.

However, I also recall from my early prowls of the premises when I was house detective, the old Joshua Tree had a system of linen handling that involved that old-fashioned, low-tech approach of . . . laundry shoots.

Two jumps up. I guess that even the pampered Ashleigh sisters could manage that if motivated. One waiting to bat the hinged door open while the other leaps through; one to perch on the sink surround and open the door manually (mittually?) and leap through after the first has gone.

It will take acrobatics not usual to short-legged Persians. It will take cooperation between sisters of a different color. It will take massive persuasion from Midnight Louie, perhaps with a soupçon of disinformation.

But my dear associate's life is at stake, and species loyalty is worth two tins of sardines and a catnip spray can, under the circumstances.

I need reinforcements below, *pronto!* (To quote the Fontana brothers.) Fire in the hatch! Even if it's a pair of furious felines!

I instruct Solange on how to get her and Yvette launched. I tell them that they will land on Cloud Nine.

And then I race back to the elevators, leap to hit the down button, and hope for the best.

Chapter 55

Red Tide

Temple's connections at the Crystal Phoenix got her easy and secret access to a passkey that allowed her to sneak back into the locked ballroom housing the Red Hat stores.

Nicky Fontana had not been crazy about her doing that, but she explained that she wanted to search the premises without anyone, including Van, knowing.

She told him a small but reasonable lie about smuggling via the shops that might explain Oleta's death, if not the attempt on Elmore's life. She didn't want, she said, to embarrass the hotel and the Red Hat Sisterhood if her suspicions were wrong.

Nicky recognized that as a noble and necessary motive.

So she'd tucked her blond hair under a big red hat resting

atop a red-knit turban and had donned huge gold circle ear-rings. This was not a Temple Barr look. It was more a mini-Carmen Miranda look.

That 1940s Latina entertainer had worn towers of fake fruit on her head. Temple had settled for red chiffon roses and ostrich feathers nestled in veiling. She also resorted to red running shoes in another effort at disguise. It had worked: the mirror told her she resembled a walking crimson mushroom with a very lavish cap.

Nobody glanced at her twice as she left the bathroom off the lobby and headed toward the ballroom areas. Red Hat ladies had been sweeping past en masse en route to the big dinner events at both the Phoenix and the neighboring Goliath. She was just a late-goer. While half the Red Hat Sisterhood attended a program and banquet in the Phoenix's Crystal Court ballroom, the other half made merry at the Goliath Hotel across the Strip.

The Hatorium Emporium ballroom had doors on three sides, one set far down a dark hall abutting the hotel's cavernous service and kitchen areas. Temple unlocked the padlock and chains with no witnesses. Any Marley's Ghost clanking sounds she made were masked by the loud muffled sounds of stage announcements and laughter coming from the hotel's huge central ballroom.

She knew better than to shut the slightly open door behind her. These things could make terrific thumps, as convention-goers who try to sneak out of boring presentations find out. She often wondered if that was meant to keep people inside.

Once she slipped inside the ballroom, she paused to orient herself.

This place was not on anyone's most-wanted list for the evening. The demonstration stages circling the room stood empty and still. The ballroom was silent, as it should be. Yet the air-conditioning gave it the look of a deserted dressing room. All the dozens and dozens of racks of hats and clothes trembled in the interior breeze, especially with so much of it feathered.

So the room seemed occupied, anyway, by a mute congregation of twitchy wearing apparel. Temple felt a bit twitchy too.

She'd promised everyone from Matt to Kit to Nicky to Detective Alch to avoid risks. But the Red Hat Sisterhood would be flowing out of Las Vegas in a giant Red Tide starting tomorrow. And with them might go a murderer.

That would leave Electra to take the blame for the death of Oleta and the attempted murder of Elmore Lark. Temple didn't know if a prosecutor could get a conviction, but she didn't want the matter to come to trial so they all could find out. Despite the offer of Macho Mario's personal defense attorney, Temple did not trust in law and order to resolve these crimes.

So she'd do what none of the people closest to her would understand or approve. But Max would.

If you want to catch a crook, you don't need a crook. You just need some high-profile bait. And it wasn't her, for a change. She was just here to hide and watch.

Because there it was. Her bait. By the light of the ballroom's red exit signs (a rather chilling sight) and the low-level security lights still on in the ceiling high above, Temple glimpsed the giant-size piece of cheese she'd placed in the ballroom this morning. Surely a human-size rat couldn't resist trying to take it tonight.

It was Oleta's lost hatbox that had been stored in the conference room. Its top was mounded high again with computer paper, redecorated and glued. Under that carpet of lavender net roses, lay . . . blank sheets.

That morning Temple, in red hat and heels, had noisily donated it to the booth to raise money for a memorial for Oleta. Everyone could buy chances to win it, and Temple had announced she'd filled the hatbox with ten-dollar bills. She bought fifteen five-dollar chances to start the hatbox rolling.

Of course, all the folks at the stages surrounding the booths had paused in their glamour photos, hairpiece displays, and makeup hawking to announce the "Oleta Lark Memorial Hatbox" prize over their mikes.

At noon luncheons at both the Phoenix and Goliath, Temple was introduced by Her Royal Hatness herself as a "generous donor" of a "magnificently decorated personal hatbox" belonging to "our late beloved sister so brutally taken from us."

Nothing like murder and lavender net roses to stir up a crowd.

Now, Temple was willing to bet, someone would be slinking into the closed ballroom to "win" the prize before anyone else could. Someone who suspected it might contain what Temple had found: Oleta's complete manuscript, not worthy of publishing, not full of clues to her murder, but perhaps inadvertently able to draw out an insecure murderer.

Temple eyed the situation. She decided high ground would help her spot a sneak thief in the semidark. Tiptoeing on her rubber-soled and well-named sneakers, she climbed the four steps to a demonstration area that would permit her to watch the hatbox booth from a height.

A nearby mannequin dressed in full feather was perfect to hide behind. She got into place, then eyed the area she'd chosen. Lots of clothes and hats hung on racks up here too. A table, empty now, sat in front of a folding screen.

Temple couldn't decide what this booth hawked, besides the clothing. Didn't matter. At least it provided a dummy to hide behind. Even better were the curtains behind it. She retreated farther, sticking her head out of the part in the curtains.

No sooner had she settled down to wait than she heard something move. Clothing brushing, feet shuffling. The sound wasn't coming from the distant, locked ballroom doors. It was coming amid the rows of booths.

Oh. An intruder wouldn't be able to beg or borrow a security passkey from the hotel owner. An intruder would have to hide, like Temple, and wait until the room was empty.

Had the intruder heard Temple arrive? Get into place? She'd been quiet about it. The stealthy sounds continued, micelike rustles anybody else would dismiss. The stealth made Temple think the person hadn't heard or spotted her presence.

Temple didn't want to lose her vantage point, but she hunkered down farther behind the standing female mannequin. Those things were always six feet tall with linebacker shoulders, anyway. They could conceal three Temples, four on a day when she wasn't wearing high heels. Like today. Tonight.

Her retreating back heel hit something narrow but hard. She

craned her neck backward. Just a glint of light off the metal legs of a light plastic chair. Another mannequin was sitting there, all dressed up with no place to go. Too bad. Temple could have sat on that chair and watched in comfort.

Ooh. A shadowy figure was moving behind the boas in Oleta's booth.

Temple crouched lower, this time brushing the mannequin's shod foot. The sole slid out of place a bit, making that telltale sandy drag that you hear in a soft-shoe routine.

In this big empty ballroom, it sounded like a spurt of sound from a chain saw.

Temple gritted her teeth and held perfectly still.

Then she glanced back at the betraying shoe, finally realizing where she'd chosen to hide.

This was a Red Hat Sisterhood onstage demonstration vignette. The Red Hat Sisterhood colors were red and purple, with a tad of lavender and pink, shades that were discernible in the twilight of the distant security lights.

This shoe was . . . green.

A six-inch-high green platform espadrille.

Temple's hand reached to check out the mannequin's ankle and calf. Nothing personal.

It was, as expected, cold and hard and stiff.

She lit her micro-flashlight to briefly illuminate the model's face before snapping it off.

That face had been cold and hard and stiff.

As in life, actually. Only it was dead now.

Temple felt the same deadly chill in her bones.

Damn! Her prime suspect for the murder sat there murdered herself. In fact, her dead body was perfectly placed to keep watch with Temple while the real murderer went for Temple's bait a hundred feet across the room.

Temple couldn't think of anything to do but flash her pinpoint light over the moving figure. And scream bloody murder.

Maybe announcing hers. Because who, besides Nicky, had she notified of her scheme who was anywhere around to hear? No one.

She'd always known this was a hat-brained idea that everyone would ridicule, and now it might prove fatal.

On the other hand, this room was one big overstocked clothes closet, and the perfect place to play hide-and-seek until help came. If it did.

Chapter 56

Crack Cocaine for Cats

My sharp ears have been awaiting the signal.

Yvette and Solange are still panting with suspense behind me.

The suspense that has them panting was landing in the giant hotel linen cart at the bottom of the fourteenth-floor laundry shoot. Neither had been on a theme park ride before. Neither understood that such a speedy exit down two stories to a central gathering station was the ride of a lifetime. That people paid for such thrills and repeated them regularly, even religiously.

I had to explain all that to them after I'd clawed them free of tangled 400-count sheets reeking with human foot odors and worse.

But you cannot keep prima donna Persians down. They were

happy to heckle me unmercifully all the way down in the empty elevator I snagged for them, playing hide-and-seek through the hotel's service regions to the back ballroom doors my Miss Temple has so conveniently left ajar. The door is open just enough for her slender self and some super fluffy felines to slip through.

I, naturally, had seen her preparing her rather amateurish little trap at our home base. She sacrificed a half ream of printer paper to create the proper mound on the hatbox cover. I immediately saw through her ruse, but was mystified as to how I could do my duty and provide her effective backup.

Not that I alone am not sufficient for the task, but extra sets of shivs are always welcome when dealing with a rogue human of unknown origin. Miss Midnight Louise, of course, has been stubbornly pursuing the Missing Max case. (If you ask me, she is way too interested in the comings and goings of dudes of another species.)

So it is just me and the Ashleigh girls, who are now plenty riled from their dive and digging out, just as I needed them to be. I realize that I have led them into what would be the equivalent of an opium den to my forebear shamus, Sherlock Holmes. And I have then expected them to contain themselves until the exact right moment.

Even my PI-hardened senses have been twitching at the air of universal prey wafting around this huge, darkened, empty ballroom. Everything our night-piercing eyes view through the crack in the door trembles temptingly with tension.

The air-conditioning wafts the scent of all the things that trigger our predatory instincts. Feathers. Feathers small and coarse, as from turkeys and chickens. Feathers airy and long, as from ostriches and emus. Feathers soft and frilly, as from the elusive marabou, perhaps a relative of the elusive caribou, who knows? Feathers fan-long and colored like deadly poisons, from the stately peacock.

We also scent fake fur. *Umm.* Soft and plush and so clawable. Microfiber! Double-knit! Spandex! Fabrics, not feathers, but also divinely designed by the great Bast for joyful stalking and rending and reducing to tatters.

I am reminded of the stalker whom Midnight Louise said had

shredded Mr. Max's wardrobe. A very sick individual, as humans go, but there was something of the jungle cat in that primitive action. I too lust after the soft dangling attractions inside human closets. Of course we domesticated cats have learned, mostly, to control these primitive destructive urges. However, we never avoid a legitimate reason to unleash them.

Taking down a murderer will do nicely.

My shivs are slipping in and out of their sheathes, eager to impress themselves on human skin and all the intervening surfaces. I can hear the rip and roar now.

But my doughty roommate's scream is our version of the late, lamented blue-light special at Kmart stores. The Ashleigh girls, released from pampered civility by a nod of my sagacious head, surge past me, rapacious streaks of riffling fur.

"Not the one who bears my scent," I remind them with a final snarl, and gallop forward myself, heading for the elevated area where I had earlier spied the tiny light winking as bright as a Birman's eye.

My well-prepared missiles have hit their shambling target on the ballroom floor by the time I leap up onto the stage.

I hear the mingled screeches and screams of two species, the sublime sound of shivs skiing down several feet of snagged fabric, above and below the belt line. In my observation, there is nothing like the dainty and fluffy Persian for ripping the heck out of anything.

By now the arias of feline fury and human pain have summoned reinforcements. Security people thunder through the front double doors. Some thoughtful person has found the lights and put them all on full power.

Human eyes blink in the glaring light, but my pupils shrink to slits as I focus on my Miss Temple, clearly visible on the Glamour-Glo PhotoLaser stage not twelve feet away. Her low-shod, high-hatted red ensemble is enough to put my fangs on edge, but no one else present is rocked by her shocking and unusual lack of taste.

She is conferring with Fontana brothers three who have materialized with the lights, over the pale-painted mannequin in the hot seat.

Meanwhile, I turn to regard the ballroom floor, where the Ashleigh girls have the target down and are voraciously pummeling a pile of red-and-purple rags that appears to be still moving. And moaning.

Since my Miss Temple is surrounded by sufficient human muscle, I hurtle after my accomplices. Much as I would enjoy joining in on the fun, my position in the community as an upholder of law and order forces me to put a damper on the Ashleigh girls' exuberant killer instincts.

"Sit and pummel," I order, moving around to examine our catch.

Whoever described the human female as "a rag, a bone, and a hunk of hair" must have come upon one after a full frontal, two-pronged, thirty-two-nailed feline epidermis workout.

Even I am impressed. I cannot wait to hear what Miss Midnight Louise thinks about the very recent exploits of Louie's Angels.

Chapter 57

The Naked Truth

"Nasty," Julio said, gazing with his brothers and Temple at the seated corpse of Natalie Newman.

Temple was still shuddering, which encouraged Ernesto to put a bracing arm around her shoulders.

If Oleta Lark's corpse had looked unnervingly alive, Natalie was definitely dead according to the TV crime scene stereotype. Her exposed flesh was bluish gray. Blotches of pooled blood streaked her narrow legs like horrible varicose veins.

Even worse, what held her upright was the scarf that had throttled her. Its ends were wrapped around the upright of the wooden chair she sat in. The scarf was purple with a flock of flying red birds. It was not the lethal Oleta Lark scarf design, at least.

"She must have been killed hours and hours ago," Temple suggested.

Ernesto nodded, pointing to the black-surfaced floor of the portable stage.

"Drag marks," he said. "She was killed much earlier and hidden behind this curtain background."

"No one working the photo presentation must have gone back here," Temple said. "Not until I ducked behind the curtain to hide. Darn! With her death, there goes my main suspect."

"For the Oleta Lark murder?" Julio asked.

Temple nodded unhappily.

"Then," demanded Ernesto, "who's that facedown on the ballroom carpeting under the killer cats?"

"I have no idea. Whoever it is was determined to lay hands on the manuscript of Oleta Lark's autobiography. I salted the dead woman's booth with a fake version. I figured that would draw the murderer, but I figured the murderer was Natalie Newman."

Julio eyed Ernesto and Emilio. "We'd better rescue the unknown lady from the feral felines and turn her over to the police for questioning."

"Hey, that's Louie," Temple said as they got closer. "And the frantic felines who shredded everything in sight are Savannah Ashleigh's pampered Persians."

They all paused to study another body, this one definitely alive, but prone and moaning faintly.

Temple took in the purple fishnet stockings and wedgie shoes, red-satin elbow gloves, purple wig, crushed red hat . . . the microfiber muumuu snagged over every visible fold by the Persian girls' fancy footwork.

"Candy Crenshaw," she breathed, "the convention's singing clown princess. I haven't even dug up a decent motive for her yet."

"Good," said a gruff voice behind her. "You'll leave something for the local police to do."

She and the Fontana trio turned as one.

Detective Alch stood there, looking officially severe.

"You four get out of here. You're contaminating the crime scene, whatever it is."

324 • Carole Nelson Douglas

"Scenes," Temple said, pointing out the lethal vignette on-stage a hundred feet away.

It took Alch a few seconds to realize he was gazing on a model corpse.

"Su," he called, "secure the stage and the body."

Temple saw the other detective leaping up on the stage, sans stairs, to do just that. Louie distracted her from that sad scene by swaggering over to massage Temple's calves with his sides.

"The cats stay," Alch ordered. "Our crime techs will need to get their, um, claw prints. So, who do we have here?"

"Candy Crenshaw, a member who heads a girl group of singers here at the Red Hat Sisterhood convention," Temple said.

"Did she kill the woman up there?"

"That's Natalie Newman, aka Markowitz. I suspect so. Somebody did," she answered.

"And why do you suspect so?"

"Well, Natalie's real last name was Markowitz."

"A name like Markowitz or Alch, say, is alone cause for suspicion?" Morrie was sounding nettled.

"Oh, no. But I found out that her mother was a Red Hat Sisterhood member in a New Jersey chapter."

"There are laws against that?" he asked.

"Maybe against New Jersey," Temple said, grinning, "but not against being in a Red Hat Sisterhood chapter. The suspicious thing is that Natalie changed her name just three years ago."

"No laws against that."

"That's also when her mother left the New Jersey Red Hat Sisterhood chapter," she pointed out.

"And you know this how?"

"From her sister chapter members, of course. They're all here. You can confirm everything I say with them."

"I'll have Su do it. She's so good with glitzy ladies like you and Miss Lark."

A Fontana brother snickered. Alch nailed him with a glance.

"I hope nobody here is illegally carrying, because I have

plenty of uniforms arriving to handle even minor infractions of the law."

Temple sensed a wall of absolutely still and law-abiding Fontana brothers behind her.

"I'm not," she said virtuously, "and I can't leave until Louie is released. He's my . . . roomie."

Louie stretched up her side to lick her hand. Right on the engagement ring finger. Cats were so territorial.

"Okay, boys," Alch told the Fontanas. "I won't look too hard at any bumps in your tailoring if you don't remain in view for more than twenty seconds. I'll take care of Miss Barr and her cat. Cats."

Temple felt the faint aromatic stir of Brut cologne as they faded away like old mob soldiers.

Alch didn't leave her long to regret their absence. "Why'd you suspect the convention camera woman?"

"She was an outsider, but she obviously had issues with the Red Hat Sisterhood, and despised them. She was filming a deliberately unflattering view of the women at the same time as she did the standard version. I found out her real last name was Markowitz. It's not unusual for a media personality to take a less ethnic name, but not in reporting. You build a reputation under a byline; you want to keep it. Even if you marry. But Natalie didn't. Newman. She was a 'new man' avenging her father. She also didn't want any members recognizing her last name and remembering the scandal. With e-mail, it was all over the Web. Tracking some Red Hat Sisterhood chapter gossip, I found out a certain Mollie Markowitz was a 'scandalous' Red Hat Sisterhood member in New Jersey. Then it was a question of: if Natalie secretly despised Red Hat Sisters, and her unflattering hidden recordings sure made it look like she did, did Natalie despise her mother too? And if so, why? All I had to do was use the network here to find out more."

"And you found?"

"Mollie Markowitz resigned the Red Hat Sisterhood because of a red hot scandal. She found so much post-menopausal zest after she joined that she also found a new, younger man and left her husband for him. It was during an outing to a male strip club she'd arranged."

"A new, younger male stripper?" Alch's eyebrows rose at this significant piece of news.

"Forty." Temple lowered her voice. "But I'm told that's 'boy toy' age for certain women."

Alch groaned. "Any age is 'boy toy' age for the benighted male of the species. You girls wrap us around your ring fingers. Don't deny it! You yourself have two in thrall. And maybe three," he added, looking down at Midnight Louie.

Unwittingly, Alch had touched on a sore point with Temple. Missing Max. As in Max was missing, not as in she was missing Max, because, of course, she had moved on, and Matt was Divine.

Thinking of Divine, what were Savannah Ashleigh's cats doing here, except having an unlawful rendezvous with Midnight Louie? There'd be hell to pay with Savannah Ashleigh too. It wasn't either her or Midnight Louie's night.

She asked Alch, "Are you serious about the cats being, ah, claw-printed?"

"Yup. They scratched that poor creature on the floor semi-comatose. They could be rabid. Could be a lawsuit in it."

"Even if that woman's a murderer?"

"Civil law is not criminal law."

O Savannah! Temple thought. Her pampered Persians in quarantine would not be the cat's meow.

Alch reacted to squeaking leather and jingling metal over his shoulder as two uniformed officers approached.

"Help the lady up," he ordered. "Let's see what the cats dragged down."

The spindly hose-covered legs wobbled as the cops lifted her in one sustained swoop. Wig and hat fell over her eyes. Feathers from the savaged boa sprinkled down like gaudy ticker tape to the carpet at their feet.

She lifted a red satin-covered forearm to her eyes against the glare of fully illuminated ceiling lights.

"How badly have these cats clawed you, ma'am?" Alch asked, always the gentleman.

At this point, Temple was only a luckless bystander. The hatbox sat untouched three feet away. Temple had no proof that it had lured the woman here.

"Ma'am?" one of the young cops asked, sounding worried.

Something was wrong with the woman, beyond cat scratches. Her head hung like sunflower on a gossamer stem. Her ankles kept turning out so her feet slipped off the wedgie shoes to the floor, twisting the ankle straps.

It was like trying to keep the Strawman from *The Wizard of Oz* in upright custody. Impossible.

Liquor? Temple wondered. Drugs?

"We need to have this lady walk the line," one of the uniform cops suggested.

Alch regarded the three cats still milling around her bony ankles and tattered fishnet hose like they thought real fish might be in there somewhere.

"Off with her hat," he said.

After a tiny pause, one of the cops obliged. The purple wig came with it, to reveal a bald head.

Temple gasped. The poor woman had alopecia or cancer!

She felt terrible that her cat's purebred posse had attacked her. Maybe the poor thing "shopped" the convention store alone at night to select what she needed, not wanting to face exposure by daylight. Maybe she didn't want Oleta's hatbox at all! Maybe it was all a terrible mistake. Hers.

Alch pulled away the boa to reveal bony shoulders and no breasts.

Cancer, surely! This public undressing was cruel!

Why were the uniformed cops chuckling?

"Say, Detective. Guess we have a shemale here. Must be from one of the shows down the Strip."

Okay. Temple turned her expectations 180 degrees around.

Tall. Boney. Ankles like silly putty on the high wedge heels. No hair on head. No boobs on torso. This was not Candy Crenshaw, however thin. This was not a transsexual in transition. This was a regular guy! In disguise.

Temple watched the red-gloved hand pulled down to reveal

badly made-up lips and eyes. Almost clownish. No wonder Temple had assumed the person was Candy Crenshaw. . . .

"Elmore Lark?" Temple couldn't have sounded more astounded if she had tried.

Good thing that Molina wasn't here to hear that amazed squawk. And why *wasn't* Molina here? She'd have to ask Alch before they all scattered for the night.

Louie, meanwhile, was strutting and hissing as if he'd always known the identity of the attackee. Louie was even better than Temple at putting on a show of omniscience.

"You *were* trying to steal Oleta's hatbox," Temple accused.

"It was my life too," Elmore said. It sounded suspiciously like a whine. "I just wanted to make sure she hadn't said any darn damning things about me. Women are so vindictive."

"Some men are so worthy of it," Temple answered.

"I'll conduct this interrogation," Alch said. "First, Mr. Lark. Do you need medical attention?"

"Sure. Those cats' claws are like an arpeggio of needles. Mainly, I hit my head going down after they ambushed me. So I got nothing to say until I reach my lawyer in Reno."

Temple watched the two officers escort their broken-down Red Hat lady out of the ballroom.

Alch was shaking his head.

"Here we have Keystone Kops and on the stage we have a Wax Museum of Horror. We can hold this goofball for unlawful entry and false impersonation, I guess. I want custody of that hatbox, but not the cats. The department can only handle so many silly elements at once. I think we can sort all this out unaided. You and the Pussycat Patrol are outta here."

Temple didn't object as another officer took her arm and escorted her to the now-gaping double doors to the ballroom. The Ashleigh girls, herded by Louie, wafted alongside her ankles like overgrown marabou bedroom slippers.

High-intensity lights and crime scene investigators were flooding the lobby outside.

Temple hadn't even had a chance to fully explain Natalie Newman's motives, which now that she had been murdered, were moot. She certainly hadn't had a chance to read every page of Oleta Lark's book manuscript, but she would now, in what was left of tonight, before Alch discovered the dummy book in the hatbox lid.

Hat. Lid. Box. Dummy.

Temple's mind was in freefall as she passed a shrieking Savannah Ashleigh at the doors.

"Yvette! You're covered with common turkey feathers! And Solange! I thought you were missing. Mummy was so distraught."

The overdone actress squealed with a strange combination of delight and distaste when two put-upon officers lifted an overexcited Yvette and Solange into each of her beseeching arms. Then all four clawed feet windmilled, slashing their mistress's clothes. Savannah began shrieking again. For real.

Louie was no longer making like a wreath around Temple's ankles; he probably had other things to attend to, as did she, and had vanished into the crowd of onlookers.

Temple sleepwalked to the hotel entrance, numbed by the unexpected death and the spectacular public failure of her attempt to set a hatbox trap for a murderer. Elmore Lark looked like a vain jerk for falling for her stupid stunt, but if just being in the ballroom after hours made someone Natalie's murderer, then Temple herself was a prime suspect.

She was so puzzled and upset she wondered if she was up to driving her Miata home.

Outside the hotel the air was hot and still, like warm soup, despite the late hour. The parking valets were inside gawking at Elmore Lark's debut as a Red Hat Sister in drag.

Then a low black car purred under the porte cochere and paused. The passenger door opened. A pale-clad arm and an inviting baritone suggested she needed a ride home.

Temple fell into the leather seat.

She sat speechless, thinking, watching the lights of the Strip speed by like long, electric strands of neon taffy.

Dude with Hattitude

A gentleman always escorts his ladies home for the night.

I am pleased that my Miss Temple recognizes that my first allegiance is to my species, especially to the vixen-clawed hellcats who took down the individual who fell into her hatbox trap.

Imagine. A fully grown human male tripped up by a hatbox and a pair of Persian Mixmasters. Do I know how to pick my associates, or what?

Unfortunately, Miss Savannah Ashleigh comes to her senses as she enters the elevators and notices my presence.

"Out, you foul alley cat!" she screams. "My poor darlings have blood all over their enameled nails, thanks to you, some of it mine! Out, out, damn inkspot!"

I have never been dismissed in such Shakespearean terms

before, so I pause to preen while the elevator doors close and sever me for the nonce from my little razor-nailed fluff puffs. Well, for the night, at least.

But, never fear, sharp-edged femme fatales are never far from Midnight Louie's front, rear, or side view.

"Some excitement at the Crystal Phoenix!" Midnight Louise notes from behind me. "While I am absent following up on your roommate's affairs, you manage to turn a whole division of the Las Vegas Metropolitan Police Department loose in my hotel."

I turn, quickly smoothing my ruffled bib. "I was only discovering another murder victim and unmasking a transgender impostor. All should be hunky dory and the usual peaceful by morning."

Louise sits, shaking her head. "How unfortunate that restraining orders do not apply to rogue male cats."

Hmm. I rather like that "rogue male" soubriquet. Reminds me of an elephant. Something big and imposing and good at crushing impediments.

"Do not get your whiskers in a self-congratulating twist. You can tell me what you *think* went down here later. I have news from the front."

I swallow. Above all, I am my Miss Temple's sworn defender. I know that she remains perplexed by the absence of her former beloved. She does not like to leave any mysteries unsolved, particularly her own.

"Yes, Louise?"

"That house might be a police department training course. When I returned for another exploration, I found that since the dustup with Miss Lieutenant C. R. Molina there, another person has been on the premises. In fact, two."

"This is interesting."

"One is an apparent insurance investigator. He was rather like you: middle-aged, short, somewhat overweight, otherwise nondescript."

"I say, Louise—"

"The other was like me: smooth, silent, slick, and, lamentably, unlike me. Also a human male."

"This is all you have to report?"

"The first man came by day. The second by night. The first

I do not know from Asphodel. The second I have seen with Miss Lieutenant C. R. Molina."

"Detective Alch?"

"No."

I am forced to wrack my brain, which is pretty wrecked by now. "I cannot guess. Like yourself, Miss Lieutenant Molina does not have a lot of friends of the male persuasion."

Louise taps a foreclaw on the marble tile of the floor. It makes a sharp, impatient sound.

"Anyway," I say. "I have no time to sit around luxury hotels and speculate. Ma Barker's gang is back at the Circle Ritz, wondering where their headwaiter is. I need to get home to feed the homeless. Chef Song here at the hotel wouldn't have any tidbits suitable for starving relatives?"

She hisses at me. "You know that Chef Song does not do takeout. I will return with you to the Circle Ritz and help you distribute nuggets of your unwanted Free-to-Be-Feline to your poor relations."

That is not exactly how I would describe my charitable endeavors, but at least I will have company back to the Circle Ritz, where my Miss Temple is no doubt breathlessly awaiting my company and insights. Or maybe I mean Mr. Matt's company.

Chapter 59

Curb Service

Ralph, the youngest Fontana brother next to Nicky, was just
as dreamy-looking as the rest, but somehow his all-American
name didn't convey the same mystique.

However, he was every bit as eager to oblige, which is an
excellent thing in a man.

After dropping her off at the Circle Ritz, he promised to
return shortly.

Temple had barely trundled upstairs, changed into a bell-
bottomed jumpsuit, ditched the red headgear, and settled down
again with Oleta's manuscript, when her doorbell rang.

Ralph awaited without, bearing equipment. She could run
the DVD disc on her computer, but wanted to see the video on
the bigger living-room TV screen. In no time he'd replaced her

outdated VCR (that only Max had heretofore managed to program with a bit of magic). Then he ran her through the new DVD player's workings, particularly the pause, fast forward, and reverse. Finally, he opened the hideously expensive bottle of wine he'd brought, poured the first glass, and put the bottle on a coaster on the coffee table.

Oh, and made a bag of popcorn in the microwave.

A Fontana Brothers Production was nothing if not thorough.

Assured that Temple wanted for nothing (besides a murderer with a cast-iron motive), he bowed and left.

To read or just sit back and watch? That was the modern Hamlet's dilemma.

She and Matt were a new couple. There was no tacit plan to spend their nights together either here or there. Temple, on her own for more than two years, preferred suspense to habit by now. Max had trained her well for his unexplained absences.

Except this one. Was Molina right? Had he been the Phantom Mage? He hadn't missed a beat when dealing with the White Russian exhibition acrobatics. He seemed in peak form. Something may have gone wrong, but Temple couldn't saddle her new relationship with worries about an ex-boyfriend.

She sipped the wine, turned down the lights, and ran Natalie's secret recording, a notebook on the sofa arm, roller-ball pen in hand. The manuscript would be next.

Chapter 60

A Fool and His Honey

Temple woke up with daylight oozing through the sheer curtains on the French doors to the balcony.

A set of those doors were ajar and a trail of Free-to-Be-Feline nuggets—like large, army-green ants—were marching from there to the kitchen. Or vice versa.

"Louie?"

The protesting meow came from the other side of the couch. Louie was coiled there like a furry snake, his one open green eye looking very annoyed.

"I guess you had a big night last night too," she admitted, patting his head.

He barely restrained a hiss.

On the other hand, his access to the Ashleigh girls had been suddenly cut off.

"I didn't get any last night, either," she consoled him.

Oddly, this didn't seem to console Midnight Louie. He yawned to show his fangs and tongue, then licked his whiskers.

"More food? You've been going through that Free-to-Be-Feline like there's no tomorrow lately."

He jumped down to the floor, then stalked to the kitchen, where he turned and glared accusingly at her.

Temple pushed herself up from the corner she'd been curled into and went to open another ten-pound bag. What was going on here? Louie would soon be the size of Nero Wolfe.

While she was up, Temple poured and drank a glass of milk, then dribbled the dregs over the Free-to-Be-Feline.

Louie remained bowed over the bowl, but only making the occasional crunching sound. No wonder he was full! He'd been through three bags of it in the last week.

With him taken care of, Temple went to shower, sharpen her brain, and gather her evidence for a fast trip to the LVMPD Crimes Against Persons unit.

Did she have a crime scenario for them! All thanks to Oleta's manuscript, Natalie's film, and Fontana brother wine.

Luckily, nice Detective Alch was in when she phoned, although he was sure it was unnecessary to see her.

"I have physical evidence as well as theories," she said.

"You've been holding something back from the police?" Nice Detective Alch was sounding sharp.

He'd been looking frazzled lately, come to think of it. Molina must be riding the rag. Okay, that was sexist. Shame on Temple! But she felt no rules of politically correct behavior applied when it came to her, and Max's, archenemy.

"Have you still got Elmore Lark in custody?" she asked.

"No. We don't have any crime scene evidence connected to the murder of Natalie Newman, aka Markowitz, and we don't have any on Oleta Lark."

"But Elmore nearly killed himself trying to make Electra look guilty."

"We don't have enough evidence on her either. And Elmore Lark is an obvious loon, dressing up in that crazy drag outfit to pursue your obvious trap of the hatbox. This whole case is laughable."

"But any other possible suspects are leaving town with the convention."

"We're not closing the case. We just don't have one on anybody yet."

Temple decided arguing with the police was a lost cause. She made her good-byes and hung up. She had a feeling something was distracting Alch these days. Maybe a personal problem.

At least Electra wasn't in danger of imminent arrest, but she wasn't completely cleared either.

Maybe it was time for the Red-Hatted League to take matters into their own hats and swing into action.

Six hours later, Temple and Electra and the core Red-Hatted League members were hunkered down in a minivan way too new for the Araby Motel parking lot. They'd had a lot of fun wetting down the dust in a vacant lot and throwing handfuls at the vehicle until it acquired a disreputable patina.

They were all wearing scruffy clothes anyway, jeans and faded velour jogging suits saved as car-washing rags. Temple even had white tennis shoes on.

The older women were the utter opposite of their gaudy, glitzy Red Hat selves.

Except for Starla. Her lips and nails were a fresh, gleaming crimson color. She was out of her Red Hat Sisterhood red and purple, but poured into denim glitz: low-rise rhinestone-decorated jeans and matching jacket, low-cut white T-shirt featuring a sequined image of a sexy cowgirl on a bucking bronco horse.

Her frankly bleached blond hair was sprayed into a hussy hive of bedhead waves and her painted red toenails peeked out from strappy hooker-high heels.

She was "strappy" someplace else: in the recording wire taped to her torso. The ex-bounty hunter had all the right equipment for going undercover, if not under the covers, with Elmore Lark.

"It's wonderful you know how to get wired," Electra commented.

"When you're a bounty hunter," Starla explained, "sometimes you gotta surprise 'em, or ambush 'em. And sometimes you gotta trick 'em." She heaved her breasts higher in the tight T-shirt, giving the cowgirl a potent buck. "And sometimes you gotta seduce 'em."

"In Elmore's case," Electra said fervently, "I'm glad *you* gotta do that, not me. But I can hear every word in the van, right?"

"You all can. Ole Elmore is not only gonna be recorded, he's gonna be broadcast live. You think that anonymous bottle of Johnnie Walker we sent over four hours ago has done the trick?" she asked Electra.

"He and Johnny must be bosom buddies by now. He was never a drinker, but he never had this much pressure."

"I just hope he hasn't passed out," Temple said.

"If he has, these'll wake him up. When high-tech equipment lets you down, the low-tech equipment never fails." Boosting her boobs again, Starla tested the spandex in her jeans by leaving the van, then minced across the hot parking lot to one of the ground-floor doors.

Temple slid the van door closed as soon as Starla's last spike heel was out of the way. That quick glance around showed an abandoned lot, except for two bejeaned guys with scruffy dark jaws working a junker sixties Impala blistered with Las Vegas sun psoriasis.

Starla's knuckles were hitting a faded, painted door. "Y'all in there, honey? I'm that friend of Johnny's."

Starla turned to wink at the van a moment before the door opened and she vanished inside.

"What do you hope Starla will get out of Elmore?" Electra asked as she and Judy and Phyll and Mary Lou hunkered down beside Temple by the radio receiver. An attached recorder was taping away.

"Bragging. Unguarded answers. I prepped her on where to lead the conversation. *Shh!* We're rolling."

"Sit down, honey," came Elmore's smarmy voice. "Bed's fine. This dump hasn't got a chair you could put more'n a wastebasket on without breaking, and you've got a bod born to break beds, if you don't mind my sayin' so. So you sent me this nice full bottle of whiskey! What was the 'Congratulations' note for? When did you join my fan club, which is purty low on applicants lately?"

"I just thought you got a raw deal. I don't like dames who kiss and tell. That Oleta deserved having her neck wrung."

There was a clink of glass on glass. "I'm glad," came Elmore's slurred voice, "I'da hoped the person who sent me this would show up. I left a little Johnny for you to have some. I ain't got anything personal against Oleta. Or didn't, that is. And I wasn't the one wrung her neck, that's for sure. She just was causing me a bucket of problems with that 'memoir' thing and all those e-mails calling me every kind of whipsnake there ever was on earth."

"Hurts a man's pride," Starla prodded.

"Pride, heck! Coulda flattened my pocketbook."

"Couldn't have hurt that much, judging by this place."

"Hell, this is jest a hideout. Doesn't mean I ain't got a wad or a lot of 'em up north in Reno. Or maybe something big comin' in. Doesn't mean I can't take a hot little number like you out for a real big night on the town. What's yer name again, honey?"

"Starla."

"Now ain't that purty? Almost as purty as Mr. Walker here, he is some flash dude, huh? I kin be a flash dude, too, when I wanta be. What can you be?"

"A lot of fun, honey."

"Waal, my little sweet potato, you sure are cinched in tight to all those sparkly clothes. Maybe I can help ease up the bindings under your saddle blanket."

"That old lech," Electra fumed. "He wasn't any hot stuff when he was thirty years younger."

"Viagra," Judy said, rolling her eyes. "Makes a man into a blowhard."

"First," Starla said over the wire, "I gotta make sure you won't throttle me accidentally in your sleep."

"Nah. I never throttled anything lately but this bottle. I was mad at Oleta, but I never woulda killed her."

The women in the van exchanged glances. This wasn't the damning confession they needed.

Temple leaned forward. "Go, Starla! Push it."

"You were hanging around the convention with the Black Hat Brotherhood," Starla prodded. "You must have wanted something from her, or you'd have stayed away."

"I asked her to can the memoir crap. Nicely."

"And she said?"

"Never."

"You sure you didn't kill her to stop her?"

"I didn't have to, honey. Someone else did it for me."

"Your non-ex-wife, Electra."

"Don't you call her that! Everybody's claimin' to be my ex or my current or my soon-to-be. A guy gets tired of that. His past trailin' after him blightin' his future. I wished they'd all jest go away."

"If Electra had been charged with Oleta's death, that would have happened."

"Yup. But that didn't happen."

"Elmore sounds real regretful about that," Electra commented sarcastically.

"Stop that, you naughty thing!" Starla said, giggling. "I'll have a tad more scotch."

"Me too," Elmore said.

Glasses clinked again.

"This is soooo sleazy," Phyll commented enthusiastically. "It's like on TV."

"Soap opera or cop show?" Judy asked.

"Maybe both."

"*Shhh!*" Temple said. "Sleazy" wouldn't help solve the murders.

"What about that woman who was taping the events?" Starla probed between giggles. "She was dead in that chair in the stores area when you were making like a female impersonator. What on earth made you even try that?"

"Oleta's stupid 'Hat Heaven' booth. See, she'd always fancied herself a writer. Liked to play with words. When that 'lost' hatbox showed up and went out for all to see, I spotted that it was the only hatbox she'd ever had with a mounded top. That was all wrong. See, women stack those things. Oleta had one closet all with stacked hatboxes inside. You don't make the tops mounded."

"Ah, real smart, Elmore."

"Right. I knew right away that would be where she'd hide her tell-all manuscript. It would be with her even when she was outta town, see? By then I was a suspect character, so I figured that if I looked like all those dressed up dolls, no one would spot me."

"It worked."

"Except for that miserable little Pink Hat brat. She's the one who put the hatbox up for bidding, and I bet she found the manuscript before she did it. She deserved a nice little throttle, but—"

"But—?" Starla's voice was tight with hope and tension.

Elmore stayed silent as the women in the van held their breaths and waited for a damning confession.

"But," he finally said after an audible bolt of scotch, "someone else beat me to it. These hands ain't made for strangling. They're made for—"

"Stop that!" The sound of a slap. "Those hands aren't touching anything on me until I know you didn't kill those women."

"I didn't, I tell you."

"That's not good enough. I need evidence. I need to know who did."

"Now, sweet potato, why would I know that?" he wheedled. "You wouldn't starve a man because of what he didn't know."

"He's lying," Electra said.

"Yes, but what about?" Temple said, frowning.

"Come on, girl, you don't want to hold out on your future sugar daddy."

"All the sugar you've got's in your lying words."

"No. Swear to God. I'm gonna have a pile as high as the Luxor. I've got me ranch land up in Reno. Dirt-poor, but it's like you, sweet potato. It's what's under the surface—"

A scuffle was heard. Starla giggled and pretended to pretend to resist, that much was clear.

"We might have to rescue her," Judy said. "I don't know how much pawing a Red Hat woman should have to put up with."

Temple hesitated. This scheme had been a bust, except for the store that had sold them the bottle of Johnnie Walker.

"Wow!" Phyll whispered from the front of the van, peering between the seats through the tinted windshield. "Who's that heading for Elmore Lark territory?"

They all crowded to hunch behind her while the receiver broadcast sounds of heavy breathing and slap and tickle as Starla tried to fend off Elmore without turning off his expansive tipsy monologue.

A tall, thin woman in blue jeans and boots and a plaid blouse was striding toward Elmore's door. She never hesitated to knock, but jerked it open.

Starla screamed on the receiver. A thump sounded as she or Elmore fell to the floor.

"You idiotic bastard!" the newcomer shouted in a deep, disgusted voice. "I leave you alone for a few hours and you're with some drunken floozy."

"Hey, lady. I'm not drunk. He is."

"Even worse!" the woman shouted. "Get out of here."

"I just need to get my things together." Starla was playing for time, wanting to record this interloper who apparently knew Lark well.

"Cheap whore! Go, or you'll be sorry."

"Just a minute. My—my purse."

"Forget it. You're not getting paid for anything." There was a silence where all the rapt listeners could hear was heavy breathing from all parties involved.

"Bunnie, honey," Elmore began wheedling.

"You're not just a little out of it," the new woman said. "You're downright drunk. What did you tell her?"

"Nothin', honey. I told her nothin'. I said nothin', I told her I did nothin' to those women, jest got dolled up a bit in those Red Hat duds. Even Dustin Hoffman does drag sometime."

"Get outta here, you stupid chippie!" The woman obviously had Starla by the jacket lapels and was shaking her. "I oughtta wring your neck."

"And she's the one who did it!" Temple jumped up, only avoiding braining herself on the van's ceiling by being so short. "Come on!"

Phyll and Judy put their weight into pushing the side van door open so all of them could pour out onto the hot pavement.

The two guys fiddling with the car suddenly jumped up and headed for the door, one pulling it open before Temple and company could reach it.

Starla had been leaning against the door. Around her neck was a Red Hat scarf. The strangling ends of it were in the hands of the long tall woman who'd popped in on Elmore Lark.

Losing the support of the door, Starla fell into the supportive custody of the man who'd jerked it open.

The other guy had the strange woman's hands behind her back . . . and tied there with her own scarf in thirty seconds flat.

Elmore was weaving on his feet in the seedy motel room, clinging to a cheap plastic cup still in its plastic wrapper but filled with expensive scotch . . .

. . . which Temple was going to have a big bolt of when she got home.

They'd nailed the strangler, but Temple had never seen her before and had no idea on earth who the hell she was.

Chapter 61

Footnotes

Detective Morrie Alch came into the tiny LVMPD conference room where Temple, Electra, her Red-Hatted League sisters, and the two car guys, aka Armando and Ralph Fontana, were waiting.

He wore his scary, emotionless police face and his first words were: "Elmore sang like—excuse the expression—a lark."

That broke the tension as the ladies laughed and eyed him with interest.

"Is it true, Miss Temple Barr," he went on, "that you have no idea of who the woman who tried to strangle Starla is?"

"True, but I have a footnote."

He chuckled, gazing at her deliberately dirty white tennis shoes.

"You usually have an interesting footnote, but I hope today it's a lot better-looking than those skaggy tennies."

"I'm working undercover, Detective," she rebuked him. "You know I'd never be caught dead in these shoes otherwise."

"At least you weren't in danger of being caught dead this time." He glanced at Starla. "I remember when you were doing bounty hunting, Miss Starnes. You always had a lot of nerve. This was a flea-brained and dangerous scheme," he added with almost-Molina-like severity, looking back at Temple. "Fontana brothers in reserve or not."

And where was Molina anyway? Temple wondered.

"So," Alch asked her directly. "What is your footnote?"

"First, I have some papers to leave with you: my copy of Oleta's full manuscript and my notes on Natalie Newman's recordings, with a copy of both DVDs. But my 'footnote' is in the form of a statement, like on *Jeopardy!* 'Dressed Elmore Lark in drag for his raid on the hatbox.' "

Alch's law enforcement expression thawed again as he threw a wallet stuffed with credit cards and IDs down on the table.

"Right on, Little Red. And the question is: 'Who is Candace Crenshaw?' "

Electra and her gal pals squealed as one. Their reactions were swift and universal.

"But she's a Red Hat celebrity!"

"She performed at the convention."

"She's a star! What did she want with Elmore?" That was Electra.

"It's complicated," Alch said. "And it'll come out at the trial. After Miss Barr found some references in Oleta's manuscript, we checked some sources up north. Elmore was suddenly sitting on some very uranium-rich acres up there in Reno. A vengeful and illegitimate ex, not to mention other not-really-exes, not only confronted him with doing time for bigamy until death did him in at the prison, but the common-law wife and ex-wife legalities—once his good luck got out, and it would have— would tie up the land and the fortune for years."

"What was Candy Crenshaw's stake in all this?" Temple asked. "She seems to have come out of left field."

"Not really, if you dig a bit. We found out she was a member of the same Red Hat group as Oleta. Say she'd become Elmore's latest but secret sweetie up in Reno, so when big money entered the picture, she wanted to be the wife of record with a legal claim to his bucks."

"And Elmore would go along with this?" Electra was indignant.

"He'd always been a weasel and a fool for women. He did what she said down here, like shadowing Oleta. We don't know if he knew she killed Oleta, but when Candy Crenshaw got what legal entitlements she wanted, he'd probably have been strangled by his bolo tie and left to rot in the desert."

"Instead he'll rot in prison," Temple told Electra, who just shook her head, bewildered by both of them.

That was all that Alch was going to tell them for their trouble, so they left the busy, bustling building (murder was big business in Las Vegas) and stood outside in the hot sun, unwilling to just disband in an anticlimax.

The two Fontana brothers were the first to peel off, hunting a change of clothes and a close shave of a different sort than Starla's.

Starla sighed as they watched them walk to the junker Impala. "I almost like the Brothers F more down and dirty and a little unshaven." The other women murmured seconds, but Temple was too exhausted to join the chorus.

"I need to get home and get out of these disreputable jeans and sneakers," Temple said. "And don't nobody say they like me better this way."

The Red-Hatted League linked arms and chanted, "We like you any way!"

"Thanks, doll!" Electra broke free to give Temple a hug that almost lifted her off her feet. "I can finally retire Elmore to the Dump of Dubious Exes."

"Aren't you coming back to the Circle Ritz with me?"

"No, I'm going out for a celebratory drink of Johnnie Walker scotch with the girls. You're welcome to join us."

"No, just bring me back to my Miata at the Crystal Phoenix."

"I'll take her back." Alch was suddenly out on the sidewalk with them.

That broke up the gang.

"I want to talk to you privately," he added, smiling to watch the other women scatter like squirrels in the presence of a cat. "Come on back up."

Temple did.

The main room was still teaming with desks and detectives and intense talk and shrill phones ringing. Alch's corner was just like that, and probably a perk. Even a lieutenant like Molina had only a tiny hidey-hole of an office.

Temple had been on red alert since arriving, but had not spotted a trace of Molina, although Su was glowering at her from another desk-computer setup.

"Get you some coffee?" Alch asked.

Temple had spied the large aluminum urn on her way in. The sides were spattered with dark brown spots and it was surrounded by stacks of foam cups and spilled packets of powder and granules that looked like a dope dealer's rejects.

"No, thank you."

"You look like you've been up all night."

"Gee, thanks. I was."

Alch softened. "That ring of yours still sparkles like the morning dew."

"Thanks." Temple had forgotten it and glanced at the reassuring rubies, red for truth and devotion. The color of love, of blood, of the Red Hat Sisterhood.

She saw her copies of the video recordings on Alch's paper-covered desk.

"Why was Newman making a second set of recordings?" he asked now that no one was around to overhear.

"That's her motive. I told you a little about it. Her mother joined the Red Hat Sisterhood. That was either proceeded by, or simultaneous with, Mollie Markowitz deciding that her marriage was stultifying and over with."

"So. That happens every day all over the U.S. of A. That happened with my own marriage. And beg your pardon, Miss

Barr, but 'proceeded by' and 'simultaneous with.' Are you testifying in court as an expert witness, or what?"

"I'm an expert video watcher now!"

"Aren't we all nowadays?"

"You mean all the live TV news 'chases.' While Natalie was secretly taping another distorted side of the convention, she was inadvertently capturing someone else operating clandestinely."

"How'd she do this secret recording?"

"Like the undercover TV news investigators do it. Concealed camera in a bag. They're so small today. It's a snap."

"Why she'd do it?"

"Her motive. Her mother left her father after she joined the Red Hat group. Natalie was her father's daughter. He'd been a newspaperman back in the days when print media mattered. I looked him up online. Jacob Markowitz, a crusading reporter of the old school, reporter's notebooks and typewriter. Did some noteworthy stories on Vietnam vets when nobody wanted to look at their side of the story the public had sickened of. Sixty-seven years old. Retired. Expecting a calm life. He had a heart attack and died. Not uncommon for a retiring newspaperman. Deadlines will eat up your cardiac system. Natalie must have blamed her mother and the Red Hat Sisterhood, where the longtime homemaker suddenly started wanting to get around with the girls."

"What did getting around with the girls mean?"

"Well, she met this male stripper. I bet it was just some silly, post-menopausal crush. If everybody had left it alone, it would have vanished. The Jersey Lily Redbirds chapter reported that Jacob demanded a divorce and Natalie came home to support him. Before the couple could divorce, or reconcile, Jacob died, the mother inherited the mantle of bereaved widow and the estate, and Natalie had a lot of scores to settle."

"So someone at the Red Hat Sisterhood knew she was doing them a dirty turn and talked about it, tipping off Candace?"

"My aunt Kit, an ex-actress, tipped me off about the camera. But Candace, having murdered once, was probably watching us all like a red-and-purple hawk."

"Your aunt. Aldo's new girlfriend."

"Right." Temple waited for him to comment on the age difference, given that it mirrored what Mollie Markowitz had done.

"Cool lady," was all Alch said. "Might have asked her out myself if I wanted to ruffle some Fontana feathers."

"Don't mention feathers! I have seen enough of them at this convention to even swear off pillows plumped with the stuff."

Alch chuckled. "So what did you find on that video recording?"

"I didn't see it at first, but I was looking at the unflattering portrayal of the Red Hat Sisterhood, which is an indirect client of mine."

He nodded.

"Last night I went through sections frame by frame in that clever stop-action mode that DVD players have."

"You can run a DVD player? This new technology has me beat. Lucky Matt Devine. Can you program a TiVo? I might offer him some competition."

"I can run it because a Fontana brother gave me an extensive short course, Detective. I'm not a techie, either."

"I'm crushed, but you're a credit to your gender anyway."

"I slowed down the segments of them setting up the convention shops, before Oleta's body was discovered, and the segments before the Black Hat/Red Hat debate."

Alch nodded seriously, all joshing over.

"I found some things I think Natalie did too. Only she made the mistake of doing something about them."

"Blackmail?"

"Right."

"That will get a body killed. It's a rewarding crime, because if you shut up the source, the entire problem goes away forever. What'd you spot, kid?"

"Elmore Lark."

"We've processed the physical evidence around Newman's body. Nothing ties Elmore Lark into it."

Temple sighed. "Natalie's video ties him into Oleta's murder scene, and the attempt on his own life."

"How?"

"I didn't see it until several run-throughs, but he's one of the hotel setup guys working on Oleta's booth. He's wearing a painter's jumpsuit and cap, but it's clearly Elmore."

"And—?"

"She caught him on video before the debate, by the hall drinking fountain, gulping down some sort of capsule."

"You mean he didn't chew the poison, but took it before?"

"Right. He could probably control the dose better. And, from the recording, he seems to be faking the collapse. Probably to make it look worse than it was."

"Trying to poison himself is just stupid, it's not a crime. And the Black Hat Brotherhood is a protest group. They might have sent a member in undercover. None of this proves anything."

"It proves Natalie could have tried to blackmail him, which drove Candace to kill her."

"Why?"

Temple had to think about that one. "Maybe Natalie didn't try to blackmail him. Maybe she recognized she had a big story in her little camera. Maybe she tried to interview him, get some more prime video, and gave away that she knew too much. She didn't know when to stop. She'd been pretty heavy-handed about filming the convention.

"Of course, Elmore would tell Candy. He was penny-ante, and so were his schemes. All he wanted, I think, was to keep his errant wives out of the picture up in Reno. He wanted to see and get Oleta's book because the bigamist charge would alert Electra to their legitimate marriage and her stake in his property. He must have searched Oleta's house in Reno after she came down here, for the book and not found it."

"We searched the house after her death," Alch admitted. "There was a computer, but the hard drive was missing."

"Right. Elmore disabled the computer, but didn't find a printout there, so that's why he was hanging around the Hatorium setup hoping to search the stuff Oleta brought down here. When Electra was discovered with her body, he faked his own poisoning to help get Electra sent upriver. He may even have thought Electra did the deed. With both of them out of the way, in his limited way of figuring it, the fortune in uranium was his to splurge on a grasping woman like Candace Crenshaw. Reno's always been a big uranium area; I bet Candy found out about his land before he did.

"His expedition in Candy's clothes to snag the hatbox was his own hot idea, I bet. She may have let him do it, but mainly to muddy the waters about the death of Natalie Newman, whom she'd always recognized as a bigger threat than the police. She attacked my aunt, thinking it was me, to muddy the waters even more, using the scarf I'd bought at Oleta's booth and left in the conference room. Notice how those Red Hat outfits make everyone look alike at first glance? Candy was just another anonymous leaf in a forest, and she could always throw Elmore to the wolves if someone came too close to suspecting her.

"Elmore may never have suspected that Candy was the killer. And he sure didn't know Natalie was dead, or he'd never have put himself in disguise on a murder scene."

Alch was silent while the room hummed around them with reports of crimes in the making.

"All conjecture. Luckily, now that we know about Candy Crenshaw, we can build a good case. What's interesting, though, is that we found Newman's camera and equipment when we checked her hotel room. And there wasn't any recording media in that itty-bitty camera with the viewing eyehole through her tote bag. Nada."

Temple gaped. "Have you tested the bag for Elmore's or Candace's prints?"

Alch smiled. "No, but we will now, though even Elmore may have been smart enough to wipe off the purse, and Candy certainly was. It's one of those big tote bags like you carry, and people don't always remember where their fingertips have been. Our crime lab is almost as good as those pretty TV folks at bringing up latent prints. If we get a good print, we have that copied video recording of yours, which will then be worth something."

Temple nodded, and looked around for Molina again.

"She's under the weather," Alch said. "Off work. I'm sure otherwise she'd be here to congratulate you."

Temple rolled her eyes. "That assumption would not hold up in court, Detective Alch."

"You never know about people," he told her, his gaze both intent and kind. "You never know."

The truism was, well, true, but it made Temple think about Max again, and about never knowing. Never.

But, then again, Molina wouldn't either.

And that made all the difference.

Chapter 62

A Dazzling Engagement

While thousands of Red Hat Sisterhood members and their hatboxes spread through McCarran Airport on their way home hither and yon, confounding security personnel, the Crystal Phoenix and Circle Ritz crowds had taken over the revolving rooftop restaurant known as the Crystal Carousel.

The central head table was reserved for Nicky and Van, Temple and Matt, Kit and Aldo, and Electra Lark. Surrounding tables of four held a mixed bag of guests. Two hosted the black-tie glory of the remaining Fontana brothers. Their uncle "Macho" Mario Fontana and wife and "private secretary" and bodyguard occupied another table. The Circle Ritz residents filled four more tables. At another table sat Detectives Alch and Su. Lieutenant Molina had sent her regrets. She said she wasn't feeling well.

Temple would bet she wasn't, having again failed to lay another crime at the feet of Temple's ex-nearest and dearest.

Even Savannah Ashleigh had been invited, and commandeered a whole table for her Rodeo Drive–attired pair of Chihuahuas. Yvette and Solange, the Persians, were undressed for the occasion. Their magnificent coats shone like actual silver and gold under the restaurant's sparkling mirrored ceiling lined in crystal lights.

Danny Dove was there, with Leticia Brown, aka Ambrosia, Matt's WCOO-FM's producer-personality. And somewhere, on the dark carpeted floor, Midnight Louie and Midnight Louise were doing security detail mixed with a casual nosh offered by various diners now and then.

The Fontana males were resplendent in Gangster-Hollywood formalwear: cream silk ties on black silk shirts with black dinner jackets and cream trousers.

Very near them were two tables of the Red-Hatted League, all glittery in red rhinestones and a crimson rage of satin and flowered and feathered cocktail hats.

Temple wore an emerald taffeta fifties dress that was short in front but had a long bustle-topped fall in back, all the better to show off her Stuart Weitzman Midnight Louie Austrian crystal pavé pumps with the green-eyed black cat silhouette on the heels.

The dress was short at the knee, tiny at the waist, and had a band of vestigial off-the-shoulder sleeves.

Her blond hair was smoothed into a Van von Rhine updo, probably the last time her hair would be blond and sleek.

After dinner she kept her left hand in Matt's under the table. It was cold, something new for her warm nature. Her engagement ring was in its box in Matt's pocket. After the after-dinner speeches, they were going to rise and announce something of their own, their engagement. Some in this room knew about it already, but this would be the formal, public, official announcement.

Temple only pecked at her plate all through the many dinner courses, which kept Louie and Louise at her side, catching the morsels of chateaubriand steak she dropped down to them.

"I've never seen you this nervous," Matt leaned in to whisper. "Not even when a killer was coming for you."

"Killer-schmiller," she whispered back. "They're a dime a dozen in this town. Now, an engagement announcement, that's a one-off for me."

His brown eyes warmed. "Glad to hear that. Happy to be here for it."

She took a deep breath. Nicky had stood and was playing master of ceremonies with the usual Fontana aplomb.

"Van and I are especially happy to welcome you all here for a rather unusual celebration. A celebration of a whole host of things.

"First of all, we celebrate the Crystal Phoenix's successfully *hosting* the largest convention group in our history. They are going, going, gone now, but here's to the Red Hat Sisterhood!"

"Here, here," cried Electra, rising along with her Red-Hatted League members. Her hair was all snowy flyaway flips under the red-rhinestone-dotted cage of a tiny pillbox with an immense veil. She looked marvelous, darling.

"And, then," Nicky said, "I suppose I should recognize the notorious among us."

Macho Mario and the Fontana brothers stirred like a flock of starlings pointed out by the city fathers.

"I refer," Nicky went on, "to our esteemed but vindicated murder suspects, Miss Electra Lark of the Circle Ritz and Lovers' Knot Wedding Chapel—"

Electra had remained standing, circling her right hand gracefully in the royal wave affected by Queen Elizabeth II.

After the applause and cheers from the Circle Ritz tables faded, Nicky went on.

"And, all too briefly to cause the proper stir, Mr. Matt Devine of the Circle Ritz and radio station WCOO-AM. Even before his brief moment in the lineup, he had a gangster nickname befitting a murder suspect, 'Mr. Midnight of the Midnight Hour,' where he purports to advise solid citizens on troubles far less felonious than his."

Amid laughter, the whole room stood up and applauded.

Matt stood up to acknowledge their affection, swinging

Temple's and his linked hands high between them in a victory gesture.

"And then I must acknowledge," Nicky said, "the sleuths who saved the good name of the Crystal Phoenix. We have with us tonight Detectives Morrie Alch and Merry Su of the Las Vegas Metropolitan Police Department."

To applause and whistles, they stood and took a bow. Morrie wore the usual black dinner jacket and tie, but the tie was Columbo-askew. Su was a revelation in a black sequin-trimmed riding jacket and long, thigh-high slit skirt. All she needed was the whip.

The whistles from the Fontana brothers table grew piercing.

"And, of course, last but never least," Nicky said, "our own public relations wizard, erstwhile redhead, and resident gumshoe in designer spikes, Miss Temple Barr."

Temple stood and waved her tiny emerald-rhinestone vintage evening purse at the diners. They laughed when the elderly clasp gave and spilled cough drops she was carrying for Kit onto the tablecloth.

Something small in formal shiny black materialized at Nicky's elbow.

Midnight Louie sniffed at the contents of his wineglass.

"Ah, that reminds me. A final toast to our littlest but hardly least resident sleuths, whose stout resort to tooth and nail saved our friends and associates from arrest and murder.

"On my left is Mr. Midnight Louie, formerly of the Crystal Phoenix but relocated to the Circle Ritz."

Louie lifted his head and gazed on the assembly.

Another black form lofted onto the table at Nicky's left, to laughter and applause.

"And, oh yes, Miss Midnight Louise, currently engaged here in Mr. Louie's stead and doing a heck of job, Blackie."

The laughter resonated up to the mirrored ceiling.

Louie patted Nicky's sleeve, then looked out over the room.

Nicky make a slight face, but plowed ahead. "And I must thank our guest security force, the beautiful and deadly feline fatales, Miss Yvette and Solange Ashleigh, protégés of our esteemed Red Hat Sisterhood celebrity guest, Miss Savannah Ashleigh."

Savannah leaped to her feet to reveal that she was clad in a formfitting strapless tube of ivory sequins. The gown must have cost a fortune, but unfortunately it only made her look like a very long, pallid, glittery noodle surmounted by a pair of pearl onions.

Fortunately, Solange and Yvette were trained to recognize a curtain call. The long-haired Persians leaped atop the table and began licking daintily at their mistress's vanilla-caramel ice cream parfait.

Everyone laughed and began sitting again.

Matt's hand tightened on Temple's. Their momentous announcement would be the last item on the program.

A heavy silver spoon tapped on a glass, drawing attention.

Someone was quieting down the guests for a final announcement.

Temple craned her neck along the head table to see who. Not Nicky, but Aldo.

How did he know?

"Ladies and gentlemen, it is time for a surprise announcement among friends. One regarding not murder, but endeavors of the marital sort."

The crowd oohed and began looking around.

"I am here to announce an engagement."

Temple tightened her hand on Matt's. This wasn't in their personal script, but—

"I am pleased and happy to announce that a beautiful and clever redhead—"

Well, it wasn't back to red yet, and "beautiful" was a little excessive . . .

"—is engaged to be my wife. Miss Kit Carlson."

He held out his hand and Kit stood, shakily, next to him. She outshone Savannah with her midnight-blue column of sequins with the batwing sleeves and off-the-shoulder white rhinestone neckline.

A pear-shaped diamond solitaire winked on the left hand she held up before her face so everyone could see.

Everyone at the head table and in the room stood to applaud. Temple's bare hands clapped together as she and Matt were surrounded by standing people, their own formal stance lost in the celebration.

They sat with the rest, finally.

Kit spoke, the slight vocal rasp she shared with Temple much rougher still, but understandable.

"I came to Las Vegas simply to visit my beloved niece." She flashed a tearful smile Temple's way. "But I found a beloved. And almost lost him." Her voice and head had lowered, then lifted as the actress rose to her own most special occasion. "I imagine I'll be seeing a lot more of Las Vegas from now on, and all of you dear, delightful people."

Few would have believed this group capable of more applause, whistles, and hoots, but led by the Fontana brothers, the chaos clamored on for another three minutes. Everybody loves a wedding, or the promise of one.

Matt whispered to Temple during the mania, "We could still add our news to the evening."

She shook her head. "It's Kit's moment. After what she's been through, she doesn't need me making an anticlimax."

"But everyone we know is here, we're all dressed up to celebrate, and I know you—"

"I can wait," she told him. "We have decades and decades to go. Kit doesn't. Can you figure it? Another married Fontana brother at long last. And my very own aunt brought the eldest of the clan to his knees. Go, Kit!! Here's to the Carlsons," she said gamely, lifting her glass. "I guess I shouldn't say 'Skoal,' under the circumstances."

Matt sighed, despite his grin of surrender, and lifted her bare hand to his lips for a kiss. Right where his engagement ring would have gone public.

Chapter 63

Future Perfect

Temple and Matt stood on his balcony in the dark, gazing down on the shadowy forms of feral cats eating from the dishes they'd all set out for them under Electra's direction.

Electra was in a mood to embrace everything. Freedom, her small kingdom of residents, even the clan of feral cats who had followed Midnight Louie to the Promised Land.

If Electra Lark had anything to do with it, the Circle Ritz would deliver.

The round Circle Ritz building now had an outer, separate ring like Saturn's, but this was composed of fur and claw: wild guardian cats.

If Matt and Temple had looked up, they could have seen Electra's penthouse balcony three floors above. She was back in her aerie with her mystical Birman, Karma. All was right with the Circle Ritz world.

Except for the one topic that they didn't bring up right now. Where was Max, and in what condition? That was something for Molina to figure out, and she was obsessed enough with Max to do it.

Temple sighed and inhaled the scent of jasmine on the dry desert air. The long, hot summer was here.

Her hands rested on the balcony railing. In the combined glow of the moonlight and grapefruit-pink sodium iodide parking-lot lights, her engagement ring gleamed galaxy-bright, just for the two of them.

"I suppose," she said, "it's just as well that announcing this didn't work out tonight. We probably have more groundwork to do before our distant friends and family are ready to accept a new reality."

"You're saying—?"

"That we should let Kit and Aldo have the stage for now. She wants me to be her 'maid of honor,' which I can't do married."

"You could be her matron of honor."

"Matt, I wanted to celebrate Electra's exoneration by having her marry us in the Lovers' Knot."

"A civil ceremony? You're sure?"

She could hear his voice weighing what her decision really meant. Was it a stopgap, an easy out, as he had proposed? With divorce always an option. Or was it a first step?

"But now I've changed my mind. Let's not distract anyone from Kit and Aldo. They've never been married."

"Neither have we," he pointed out.

"Yes, but we're young. Anyway, the reaction to Kit and Aldo tonight had me rethinking things. We should visit Chicago and Minneapolis and meet the folks, so they don't feel hurt by a sudden announcement from far away."

"Whew," Matt said. "My mom would freak at the idea of a civil ceremony."

"My mom wouldn't. I could get married in a Quonset hut beside a swamp by a swami. Unitarians are highly inclusive. She won't even mind my marrying a Catholic. She *will* freak at the idea of my marrying someone she doesn't know. Or hasn't met."

"And my cousin Krys—"

"Yes? Boy or girl?"

"Girl. First year of college."

"Ah. First crush too, huh?"

"You sure you want to involve families? They'll try to tell us what to do. And anything we do won't appeal to someone on one side or the other."

"Weddings are always like that, from what I've seen. That's why we scout the territory first. To figure out if they'll make a later ecumenical church wedding too divisive to handle."

"If we're making a pilgrimage to the old folks at home, why even come back and get a civil marriage here?"

"To show them we're serious. Otherwise, they might raise holy hell. Ask us to wait forever. Decide to hamstring us by insisting on a religious ceremony they know the 'other side' can't stomach."

Matt eyed her with mock suspicion. "You know a lot about tribal behavior in the matter of weddings. I've officiated at many, and your low opinion of relations between families at such times is terrifyingly accurate. Like the unlamented but still-not-late Elmore Lark, do you have a few weddings of your own under your belt?"

"Always a bridesmaid, never a bride," she said lightly. "But I took notes."

He tightened his arms around her. "I want to have a church wedding, I want you to be a bride, to watch you coming down an aisle toward me looking like an angel, to take you to a hotel room after and seal the ceremony and the sacrament in bed all night."

He made a honeymoon sound so sexy, so seriously sexy, that Temple felt her knees get watery. He made being married sound like living in officially sanctioned sin. She could hardly wait. This boded well for them not wearing out their passion.

Their kisses grew so warm that Temple couldn't take the heat. Max had been sexually superb from a skill standpoint, but Matt's innocent intensity pushed her emotions as well as her body to a climactic peak. Sometimes it scared her, feeling these new depths in herself.

She kissed him lightly and pulled away to speak again. Lightly. "It all sounds so old-fashioned. Will your church expect me to wear off-white?"

His grip tightened. "Hardly. We've been winking for years at couples who rent separate apartments a few months before the wedding, as I was reminded recently."

"But you'd still be living in sin after a Lovers' Knot ceremony?"

"Semi-sin," he told her, smiling. He had a hard time discussing sin with her. "Some devout Catholics cleave to all the traditional rules, and some devout ones veer far from them, all in the name of God and the good of humankind. I went to seminary to learn how to be a priest. Maybe I needed to go to bed to learn how to be a husband."

Temple laughed. "I know a Unitarian minister who would say you were self-justifying."

"Really, though? Are you sure about these two-tiered wedding plans?"

"Why wouldn't I be sure?"

Matt was silent for a bit. "You haven't had a chance to—"

"To say good-bye to Max? I can't say I won't always wonder what happened to him, but I don't need to close one book to start reading another. Life is like that. No neat answers. We just go on. Besides, if Max is out there to be found, Molina will find him. Some way, someday."

Matt laughed in his turn. "There's a match made in hell."

He turned Temple to face him, pulled her close again. "So if we make a couple trips north first, then have a pre-wedding at the Lovers' Knot at some point, when do we schedule the formal wedding?"

"When my miserable, messed-up hair has all grown out in its natural color again. I am not going to walk down any church aisle with a dye job on my hair instead of my shoes."

Matt was laughing when he kissed her, and then they were too busy again to laugh.

One of the cats outside wailed like a banshee in the dark. Temple hoped it wasn't Irish. Or Midnight Louie, registering his opinion of their plans. He was sure to have them, and make them very well known. In his own good time.

Chapter 64

You'll Take Me Home Again, Kathleen

The man was portly and in his fading sixties, with still a certain flair to his expression and his voice, but moving deliberately, and perhaps heavily, as though burdened.

He lowered himself onto the leather-upholstered chair before the desk and sighed unconsciously at taking the load of himself off his burdened feet.

All in all, he was the kind of man easily overlooked in a crowd: travel-wrinkled suit, more bags under his eyes than he probably had brought across the Atlantic with him.

He offered his passport over the desk to the younger, nattier man who sat behind it. Draped windows framed a misty day and the smoke-blackened walls of stately buildings from the last two centuries.

A teapot whistled faintly from an office kitchen a decent distance away. The sound was both shrill and alarming, and somehow comforting.

In the British Isles, tea was the soothing social drug of choice.

John Kelly took the passport. He was an assistant to the undersecretary to the U.S. Consul-General in Northern Ireland, and the stately buildings outside the windows of Danesfort House were in Belfast.

"You look as if you could use a spot of tea, sir," he suggested to the visitor.

"I've just hopped the Atlantic. A bit confining for a lot of time for a man of my age and heft."

"You should have decompressed in a hotel room."

"Despite my condition, I'm eager to get on with this . . . task."

"Your phone call said something about wanting to track the trackless. Rather intriguing."

"I'd hoped it seemed so. I'm after an IRA agent from, oh, fifteen or more years ago."

"Ah."

A fiftyish female assistant, with hair as gray as her severe tweed suit, had arrived with a silver tea service. For a few moments liquids poured while utensils and china clinked.

When she left, the two men eyed each other through expression-concealing curtains of steaming tea. They sipped as cautiously as they talked.

Kelly spoke first. "Your name is apparently still potent in State Department circles, although no one would say why."

"That is how it should be, in an ideal world."

"*Hmmm,*" Kelly said. "This world is seldom ideal, but the Irish 'troubles' are now a cautiously optimistic mark on the global hot-spot map."

"Is it true? Have 9/11 and the Mideastern terrorists so upped the ante on mass terrorist destruction that the Irish rebels have lost heart?"

Kelly templed his fingers. "In a post-falling-twin-towers world, yes; mere political-religious Western anarchy pales by comparison to Mideastern political-religious violence. Of course, unrepentant IRA holdouts still wreak some havoc, but the mainstream IRA has no stomach for pub and bus bombings now. I give them credit for that. They've seen the true and vicious face of modern terrorism, and they don't want to be on that Most Wanted list."

"The civil and religious wrongs that created this rebellion over five hundred years ago still persist." The elderly gentleman set his teacup down on its saucer with almost supernatural quiet.

"Yes. But they modify. As do we. As for this former IRA agent you seek . . . I've heard of Kathleen O'Connor. Everyone has. She left very little trail. I take it, from your sparse hints, that you have evidence that she died in the U.S., unnoted. I'm not surprised. She was a legend here. Legends should die somewhere quiet and far away, like Butch Cassidy and the Sundance Kid in South America. From what I've heard, she was an angry, beautiful woman, an effective agent, and a terrorist who would never give up the fight even when it moderated."

"Yeats and Maude Gonne."

"What?"

"The great Irish poet, William Butler Yeats, loved a beautiful Irishwoman, Maude Gonne. But Maude was fiery, totally committed to revolution. She *became* the Cause. She had no time for beauty or love. Or poetry or Yeats. He mourned her before she was dead, because she was dead to any man in her passion for the motherland."

"Your Kathleen O'Connor could be such a one." Kelly handed over the copy of a disappointingly slim dossier. "Where is she now?"

"In a grave in Las Vegas under a simple headstone with her name and date of death. No one knew her birth date."

"Why track a dead woman?"

"A dear friend of mine suffered much because of her for many years. It's an obligation."

"And he? Dead too?"

He hesitated. "You might say that I'm on a mortuary mission, Mr. Kelly. I want to dig up this Kathleen O'Connor's history. I know her future and her fate. I want to know her past and the making of her. For my . . . lost friend's sake."

" 'You are old, Father William.' "

"Ah, the Irish. Always with the poetry. Lewis Carroll was old and still photographed lovely girl-children like Alice Liddell who'd inspired *Alice in Wonderland* decades earlier. Was this eccentric bachelor genius, or a repressed pedophile? Today's world allows for many divergent interpretations. I seek my own Alice who went down the rabbit hole: Kathleen O'Connor, before she was IRA, when she was the child of an Ireland that had never been for centuries."

"You have a touch of poet yourself, Mr.—" Kelly checked the name on the passport. "Mr. Garry Randolph. As you said, times have changed. What was vile, violent, and secret is now . . . just history, God willing. Do you have any idea how many Kathleen O'Connors there are, or were, in Ireland or Northern Ireland on any given day in any given year in any given century?"

"As many as shamrocks carpet the Irish ground and freckles dot the Irish face."

Kelly chuckled at the puckish, poetic lines his guest had produced with a grin. "I now have 'contacts' among the new IRA. I'll check with them. Kathleen O'Connor cut a wide swath for such a slip of a thing, I hear. Someone from her era may be willing to talk with you."

He rose to see his visitor out.

The phone rang that evening in a suite at the Malmaison Hotel. He'd avoided the Europa Hotel, which before the IRA truce had the unenviable reputation of being "the most bombed hotel in Europe." It was safe now, but he preferred the trendy comforts of a boutique hotel and the company of trendy young things with odd hair and arty tattoos sipping white wine and watching Fashion Channel runway shows on a huge, ceiling-hung television screen.

He had the money to indulge himself while following this cold trail on this haunting quest. Max'd had even more. He'd always made plain how he wanted Garry to spend it if, God forbid, he survived him.

From the black, red, and cream modernity of the rock and

roll suite he gazed at the misty towers of murderous Belfast. The city was doffing its violent past like a London Fog coat, showing off a thriving young figure under it.

The voice on the phone apologized for calling during the dinner hour.

"I have an old fellow," Kelly said, "maybe full of blarney, who remembers the girl in question. Something he said already made me think you should check the orphanages. Probably in County Clare. Do you know how many orphanages—?"

"Thank you. I've written down your information and will follow up."

"And let me know, of course, what you learn. People in our line of work are always curious."

Garry Randolph, once known as a magician named Gandolph the Great, nodded his head, although the man on the phone's other end couldn't see the gesture.

"Of course I'll let you know, Mr. Kelly, but it may be a while."

He hung up, biting his pale lower lip.

An orphanage. Talk about needles in haystacks. Not good, but he was used to dealing with orphans. And spies. And magicians.

He sighed again, and put a call through to Switzerland. Then he would call the contact in Las Vegas. While he waited to be connected, Garry brooded.

This was the most difficult assignment of his life, and perhaps would be the death of him, as Kathleen O'Connor had always been the death of so many, including herself, ultimately.

He remembered what that feisty, non-Irish redheaded love of Max Kinsella's life had so appropriately nicknamed her, in a place and time that now seemed long ago and far away to an old man full of duty, and doubt.

Kitty the Cutter.

Tailpiece

Midnight Louie's Deep Purple Mood

I certainly have developed an appreciation for vivid color combinations after seeing the Ashleigh girls decked out in imperial purple and royal red.

To these traditional colors of empire are not only Red Hat Sisterhood members entitled, but all those of the feline persuasion born.

Humans, unfortunately, are a pallid lot compared to the coats of many colors, and patterns, that felines sport. Unfortunately, our human companions are also up to their hairless ears in family matters tinged with large doses of dysfunction. (Not that we of the superior species do not have a few dysfunctions of our own. But they are minor matters involving litter boxes and finicky palates.)

Too many dysfunctions, however, make for crime and punishment, and I am always all too happy to lend a mitt to the crime-detecting part of the formula.

I must admit that I am most relieved that the aging females of my species do not feel obliged to make a habit out of raiding the plumage of other creatures. I imagine Ma Barker in such a getup, and shudder. She is formidable enough in her natural state. With her coat and temperament, Black is the New Blue.

While it is satisfying to have cleared Miss Electra Lark of murder charges, I am not sure I like the direction in which my domestic life is headed. I preferred the uncertain days of yesteryear, when I always had to come home wondering, *Who has been sleeping in my bed?*

Now I have Goldilocks, all right, but she seems to be set on eliminating all the creative tension from my existence by installing domestic bliss in the form of Mr. Matt. I confess that I no longer know who's who and what's what, and I think that this is a distressing state for an author to leave her collaborator in! Not to mention our loyal readers!

On the other hand, something very intriguing seems to be cooking on the international front. Could a jaunt to Ireland be in my future? I do have Irish eyes, you know. Not that they smile.

Midnight Louie, Esq.

If you'd like information about Midnight Louie's free Scratching Post-Intelligencer newsletter and/or T-shirt and other cool things, contact him at P.O. Box 331555, Fort Worth, TX 76163-1555 or www.carolenelsondouglas.com.

Tailpiece

Carole Nelson Douglas
Foresees a Rosy Future

Louie is such a sensitive soul.

He's deeply affected by his environment, so his human companion's change of partners is bound to affect his mood, if not his appetite. But people are far more inconstant than cats, so he will just have to display his inborn superiority and adjust.

I would respectfully suggest that humans must resort to celebrating their age instead of ignoring it because it shows so much. Those of Louie's persuasion don't show their age as easily as humans. That's the benefit of an all-over fur coat: no wrinkles. Plus, any sags and bags are always camouflaged.

As for trips abroad, Louie, I would not practice your version of "Danny Boy" on the back fence just yet.

There are plenty of hot times coming in Las Vegas, even with Max Kinsella apparently MIA or DOA and Gandolph off with the IRA. But what's new, after all?